William Berry Lapham

Bradbury Memorial

Records of some of the descendants of Thomas Bradbury, of Agamenticus (York) in

1634, and of Salisbury, Mass. in 1638

William Berry Lapham

Bradbury Memorial
Records of some of the descendants of Thomas Bradbury, of Agamenticus (York) in 1634, and of Salisbury, Mass. in 1638

ISBN/EAN: 9783337424732

Printed in Europe, USA, Canada, Australia, Japan

Cover: Foto ©Raphael Reischuk / pixelio.de

More available books at **www.hansebooks.com**

BRADBURY MEMORIAL

RECORDS OF SOME OF THE DESCENDANTS OF THOMAS BRADBURY

OF

AGAMENTICUS (YORK) in 1634

AND OF

SALISBURY, MASS., in 1638

WITH

A BRIEF SKETCH OF THE BRADBURYS OF ENGLAND

COMPILED CHIEFLY FROM THE COLLECTIONS
OF THE LATE

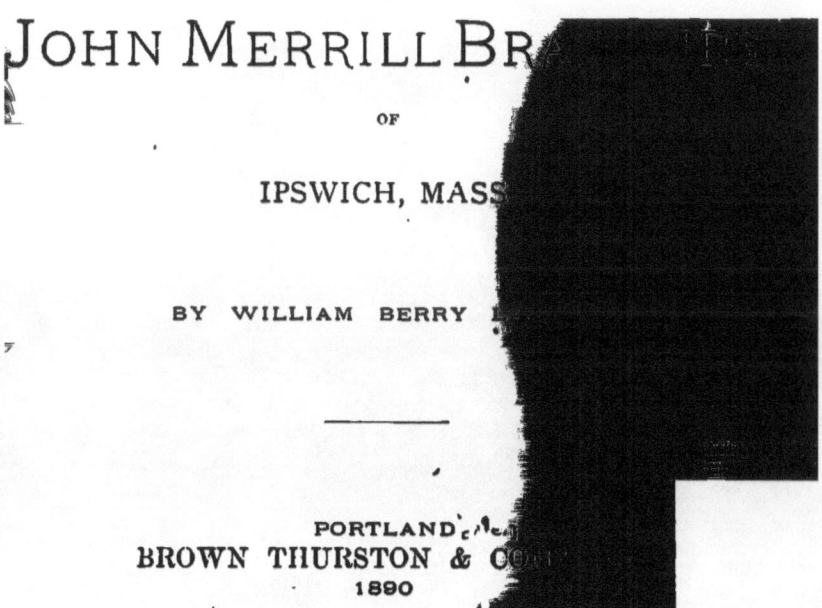

JOHN MERRILL BRADBURY

OF

IPSWICH, MASS.

BY WILLIAM BERRY LAPHAM

PORTLAND
BROWN THURSTON & CO.
1890

PREFACE.

It was nearly forty years ago that the late JOHN MERRILL BRADBURY, of Ipswich, Mass., began to collect materials for a Genealogy of the Bradbury Family. That his purpose was to make it one of the most complete and exhaustive family histories ever published, is abundantly shown by his correspondence, and had he lived there is little doubt that his intentions would have been fully carried into effect. But his health failed and death supervened before his self-imposed task was half accomplished. He died nearly fifteen years ago, and since that time until quite recently, his collections have remained undisturbed in the hands of his executor.

The venerable Hon. James W. Bradbury, of Augusta, had been for sometime intending to have compiled a limited sketch of his family, embracing only his own line, but after more mature deliberation and a correspondence with the executor of the late John M. Bradbury's will, who cheerfully offered to place the collections of his brother at his disposal, Mr. Bradbury concluded to modify his first intention so far as to utilize all the material attainable, with certain limitations as to the time of publishing the work. The expense of compiling and making additions within reasonable limits, is borne entirely by Mr. Bradbury, while it is hoped that the sale of books will be sufficient to meet the cost of publication.

The late Captain William F. Goodwin, of the United States army, who was connected with the Bradbury family, on the maternal side, was also interested in the history of his ancestors, and had collected more or less material bearing upon the subject, a portion of which—that relating to the York County families of this name—had been printed in Dawson's Historical Magazine. The extent of Capt. Goodwin's collections, and what disposition he intended to make of them had he lived, are entirely unknown to the compiler. The printed portion is all that has been accessible to him.

After the death of Capt. Goodwin, there was some correspondence between his family and the late John M. Bradbury, looking to a union of the two collections, and the only obstacle in the way appeared to be the unsettled condition of Mr. Goodwin's estate, but nothing was accomplished before Mr. Bradbury's death. In all probability the larger portion of the Goodwin material is duplicated in the collections of Mr. Bradbury, since the sources of information were equally open to each, while both were able and industrious investigators, and enthusiastic in the work they had taken in hand.

The compiler has been able to fill up many important omissions in the way of names and dates, and has added a considerable number of families, though none prior to the sixth generation. The personal sketches and notes on allied families, are all the work of the compiler, and also the arrangement of the entire materials. In its incomplete state, the collections of Mr. Bradbury are meager in personal history, being confined mostly to names and dates, while that portion of his correspondence which has come into the compiler's hands, throws but little additional light upon the personnel of the family. This defect has been remedied so far as has been possible in the brief time allowed; but very many of Mr. Bradbury's correspondents have gone to join him, while their families have grown up, are scattered abroad and are not easily accessible.

As a whole, the work as published is unfinished, and in some directions only fragmentary, but it contains valuable material representing no little labor and expense, and some future representative of the family may be induced to utilize it for the production of a more complete and comprehensive work. It is not claimed by the compiler that the work is free from errors. Accuracy in a work of this kind would be a novelty indeed, but it is hoped that not more than the usual number of mistakes will be found herein. Such as it is, the work is respectfully submitted to the charitable and discriminating consideration of those who are interested in its contents.

WM. B. LAPHAM.

Augusta, January, 1890.

BRADBURY MEMORIAL.

THE BRADBURY FAMILY IN ENGLAND.

THE name BRADBURY is of Saxon origin, and of the class styled "local." Its components are *Brad,* meaning broad, and *Bury,* which is variously defined, as a house, a hill, a domain, and a town. It is found variously spelled in English records, as *Bradberrie, Bradberrye, Bradberry* and *Bradbury.* The latter is the orthography adopted by the emigrant Thomas, and followed by his descendants generally. Unlike most local names, it never had a wide diffusion in England, and tracing it back through two centuries previous to the settlement of this country, it seems to have narrowed its limits and finally to have confined itself to a single parish in Derbyshire. The radiating point seems to have been Ollerset in the parish of Glossop, in the northerly part of the county of Derby. No mention of the name has been found prior to 1433, when there were living among the gentry at Ollerset, Roger de Bradbury and Rodolphus de Bradbury. The connection between these two persons is not known, nor the length of the time they had resided at Ollerset. But the interest of the American Bradburys centers in the line of which Robert is the head, and of whom but little is known. We know that he must have been born as early as 1400, that he lived at Ollerset, and that he married a daughter of Robert Davenport (written also Damporte), and that he had a son William, who settled at Braughing, county of Hertfordshire, and married Margaret, daughter of Geoffry Rokell, spelled also Rockhill. From him are said and believed to have sprung the Bradburys of Littlebury and Wickham Bonhunt, generally written at the present day, Wicken Bonant. They were a landed family, and from the Herald's Visitations and Inquisitions post mortem, quite easily traced, though the pedigrees that have been constructed and in some cases printed, are strangely unlike. In the report of the Visitation in Essex in 1558, William Bradbury, said to have married Jane or Joan, daughter of Sir John Fitzwilliam and widow of Thomas Bendish or Bendyshe, is placed at the head of the line; while in that of 1612, and also the pedigree published in the East Anglian in 1862, the head of the family is given to Sir Thomas Bradbury who was Lord-Mayor of London in 1509, and died while in office. The fallacy of both these pedigrees is shown in the fact that William Bradbury of Braughing was only ten years of age when Joan, widow of Thomas Bendish died, while Sir Thomas Bradbury died without issue, and William Bradbury, son of his brother Robert, was his heir. It also states what is probably correct, that William Bradbury was afterward of Littlebury, and "descended from ye Bradburys of Ollerset in ye West Country," etc.

In the Visitation of Hertfordshire in 1634, Robert Bradbury of Ollerset, county of Derby, is made the head of the family and the father of Sir Thomas. Now while absolute reliance cannot be placed upon pedigrees based upon the reports of these Visitations, yet it is the best and only evidence that can be obtained without original research, and is probably in the main correct. Robert Bradbury must have flourished in the time of King Henry the Sixth, and is the earliest ancestor of the family that can be relied upon with any degree of certainty. The pedigree here given is based upon the reports of the several Herald's Visitations, upon probate records and other public documents, and must be taken for what it is worth. The late Captain William F. Goodwin, whose mother was a Bradbury, employed Miss Harriet Bainbridge, then considered a reliable English genealogist, to inquire into the Bradbury pedigree, and she furnished him with one which she claimed was the result of her own original investigation, but which is now known to be incorrect in several essential points. There are professional genealogists in England who will write up a pedigree and furnish a coat of arms for any one who is able and willing to pay for them, and their customers are, for the most part, Americans. There are doubtless those who do honest work, but a majority of them are cheats, and fill their orders without regard to facts.

The branch of the Bradbury family from which the New England family claim their descent, settled at Wicken Bonant in the county of Essex, about the year 1560, and a brief sketch of this parish is compiled

WICKEN BONANT, COUNTY ESSEX. VILLAGE INN, SCHOOLHOUSE AND CHURCH.

largely from the number of the East Anglian, already referred to, and published in London in July, 1862. This number not only gives an account of the parish, but gives pedigrees of the Barlee and Bradbury families, the latter of which, so far as it appears to be correct, is made the basis of the pedigrees here given of the English families of Bradbury. The parish of Wicken Bonant is small, containing only eight hundred and forty-one acres, and less than two hundred persons. It lies in one of those long, winding valleys leading up to the backbone of the high ground which parts the tributaries of the Lea and the Cam. The subsoil is of chalk which, with occasional heads of gravel, crops up to the surface in the lower grounds. The uplands of this and the surrounding parishes are overlaid with a strong clay of considerable depth, which renders the air cold and damp, and considerably retards agricultural operations. A winter brook, which rapidly floods after rain, rises in the adjoining parish of Arkesden, to which it gives a name, and passing through the whole length of the parish it meets with some copious springs in the meadows adjoining Newport, and becomes a tributary of the Cam.

In ancient times the parish of Wicken was equally divided between wood and arable land. From Doomsday-book it appears that it then contained four *carucatæ*, and as much arable land as four ploughs would till in a year, beside wood for one hundred hogs. At the present time there is hardly any wood remaining, and but little pasture. The name has had various spellings. In Doomsday-book it is called Wica. In the court rolls of the Hall in the time of Edward the Second, it is called Wykes, and half a century after it was called Wyken. These are doubtless variations of Wickham which are still retained in official documents. The addition of Bonhunt, from one of the manors of the parish, is to distinguish it from Wickham St. Paul and Wickham Bishops, both of which are in the same county of Essex. From the earliest times there appear to have been two manors, that of Wicken or Wickham, and that of Bonhunt or Bonant. Both of these are mentioned in Doomsday-book. They were united in the sixteenth century, and since then have been reckoned as one. In Doomsday-book, the Hall is given as in the possession of Gilbert, son of Thorold, and after him in that of Sexius, a freeman. In 1446, it was in the Barlee family and was sold by William Barlee to Robert Chatterton, Esq., who in turn sold it to the Bradbury family. Precisely when this transfer was made is not known, but Matthew Bradbury was Lord of Wicken at the time of his death in 1587, and probably bought it in 1557. It continued in the hands of the Bradburys through several generations and until the early part of the eighteenth century, when, in default of male issue, Dorinda, daughter of Matthew Bradbury, Esq., carried it in marriage to Joseph Sharpe, Esq. He sold, with the exception of what is now called the Brick House, with about a hundred acres of land to John Hetherington, Esq., who sold it to Thomas Coventry, Esq., who in the beginning of this century sold to Joseph Smith, Esq., of Shortgrove in Newport, and in 1862 it was in possession of his son William Charles Smith, Esq., of Shortgrove.

The Brick House, as it has always been called, was built by William Bradbury, who died in 1622, for his son Wymond Bradbury, and continued in occupation of the second-branch family till, at their extinction, it reverted with the Hall to Mr. Sharpe. When he sold the Hall, it was his intention to have kept and resided in the Brick House, but the mortgages upon the Hall proving to be beyond its value, Brick House together with its one hundred acres was mortgaged for twelve hundred pounds in order to carry out the sale of the remainder. In consequence of this arrangement Brick House was held under mortgage by John Martin, Esq., banker of Lombard street, and it continued to be so held by his son and grandson till Joseph Martin came into possession of it in the early part of the present century. Brick House is of a picturesque structure with ornamental gables, and was formerly adorned with statues of which some remain in a mutilated state. The arms of Bradbury are still over the door. The Hall, now a farm-house, adjoins the church. It is a timber structure of the early part of the sixteenth century, with picturesque chimneys. With the Hall was once another farm called the Wood, but now it is known as Howland's farm, from a tenant who occupied it.

The manor house of Bonhunt is situated half a mile eastward of the church. We first hear of it in Doomsday-book, when it was in possession of a freeman named Aluric, and afterward in the hands of a man named Saisseline. No farther mention is made of it until 1341, when John Flambard of Bonhunt had a license to endow St. Leonard's Hospital at Newport, that the brethren might find him a chaplain to say mass for his soul within his manor of Bonhunt, in the chapel of St. Helen. After John Flambard, the manor of Bonhunt came to the Greene family, and continued with them from 1437 till 1580, when it was purchased by the Bradburys. They soon after sold it to the Nightingales of Newport, from whom it passed to the Turners of Quendon. In 1717, John Turner, Esq., sold it with Quendon Hall, to John Maurice, Esq., of Walthamstow, whose widow sold it to Joseph Cranmer, Esq. From Cranmer it passed to his son Henry, and subsequently it came to Henry Webb, Esq., at whose death it reverted to the representative of the Cranmers.

The church at Wicken Bonant, called St. Margaret, originally dated from the middle of the eleventh century, but the only relic of this date now remaining is a plain and square, massive Norman font, standing on a central and four corner pillars, also square. Toward the close of the twelfth century, the church was in great part rebuilt. With the exception of a porch, partly rubble and partly wood of the sixteenth century, nothing more appears to have been done to the church till early in the eighteenth century, when the tower was removed, and a small wooden cot placed over the

WICKEN BONANT. CHURCH OF ST. MARGARET.

west gable of the nave to hold the bells. The church
was restored and in part rebuilt in 1858-59, at the cost
of John Sperling, Esq., of Kensington, the patron of
the living. At present the church consists of the original English chancel restored, to which a new nave,
south porch and tower have been added in the decora-
tive style. The whole of the windows are of painted
glass, and represent mostly Bible characters. The
nave, which is filled with open seats, has a stone pul-
pit, while the Norman font occupies its ancient place,
and has been raised two steps and supplied with a
cover. Externally, the belfry stage of the tower is
very beautiful, having eight large traceried windows.
The whole is capped by a stone broach spire, rising to
a height of over ninety feet. In the church are no
monuments earlier than those of the Bradburys, which
are as follows :—

I. A monument against the north wall of the chancel, sur-
mounted by the arms of Bradbury, inscribed :—

"Beneath this stone lies interred the body of John Bradbury,
of the Inner Temple, Gent, eldest son of Francis Bradbury, Esq.,
Gent, and Anne his wife, who departed this life June 11–1693,
aged 25 years."

"Beneath this stone lies interred the body of Francis Bradbury
of Clifford's Inn, Gent, second son of Francis Bradbury, Gent,
and Anne his wife, who departed this life June 15, A. D. 1695,
aged 24 years."

"Beneath this stone lies interred the body of Anne Barrell,
wife of John Barrell of Clifford's Inn, Gent, and daughter of
Francis Bradbury and Anne his wife, who departed this life January 21–1677, aged 26 years."

II. On an elaborately sculptured monument by Scheemakers, against the south wall of the chancel, also with the arms of Bradbury:—

" Near this place lies buried the body of that hopeful youth, John James Bradbury, Gent, the son and heir apparent of Matthew Bradbury of this parish, Esquire, and Mary his wife, who departed this life Nov. 27, 1731, aged 10 years."

III. On a monument within the tower, is the following:—

" Wentworthius Bradbury, Suffolciencis, Hujus Ecclesiæ Rector Necnon vicarius de Arkesden, et Anna uxor ejus precharissima obit,

$$\begin{matrix} \text{ille } 1764 \\ \text{illa } 1795 \end{matrix} \Big\} \; \text{æt.} \; \begin{matrix} 82 \\ 95. \end{matrix}$$

Utrosque ultimus de puluere suo dies in gloriam simul evehet."

IV. On a flat stone may be seen the following inscription:—
" Sub hoc lapide sepulchrum jacet corpus Johannis Bradbury filii natu secundi Wentworthi Bradbury hujus ecclesiæ Rectoris, qui cum morbo insanbili viz, epilepsia diu laborasset morti tandem quiete se resignavit obiit Sept. 7 anno salutis 1758, ætatis 31, mortis ab hasta nec juvenes tuti."

V. The following inscription in Latin is found on another flat stone:—

" Quod mortale fuit Annæ filiæ charissime Wentworthi Bradbury hujus ecclesiæ Rectoris et Annæ uxoris ejus sub hoc lapide depositum est anno ætatis 23 anima pia voluntati dei libenter submisa corpus reliquit vicessimo die Septembris, anno domini, 1749. Multis illa bonis flebilis occidit, nullis flebilia quam parentibus."

2

There are other monuments within the church, all of more recent date than the above, and represent the families that succeeded the Bradburys at Wicken Bonant. A monument to James Pollitt, Esq., and Hannah his wife, who was a sister of Mrs. Joseph Martin, are among others.

The Registers of the church begin in 1598, and with the exception of a few years at the beginning of the present century, have been well kept. They contain nothing remarkable except the dates of the Bradbury family, which afford material aid in arranging their pedigree. Among other entries the following is of interest :—

Mr. William Bradbury, Lord of Wicken, died upon St. Addrews daie at night, about xij of the clock, November ye last, and was buried uppon ye seconde of December, 1622, and was laid under the high altar in ye chancel on ye southe side whose funerals was kept after uppon Thursdaie after the twelfthe, with the manie mourners to ye number of thirtie. Tho. Wadeson, Rector, preached.

The Rectory was originally on the north side of the churchyard, but having been burned down in 1590, it was not rebuilt on that side, but a house and two acres of freehold ground belonging to the Bradbury family, were granted to the Rectory by way of exchange. This parish was within the diocese of London, and distant therefrom about forty-five miles.

The following list embraces the Rectors and Patrons of Wicken Bonant parish from A. D. 1400 to the time of Wentworth Bradbury's Rectorship in 1720 :—

DATE.	NAME.	PATRON.
1410	Abraham Veel,	Henry Barlee.
1458	John Berwick,	" "
1460	Thomas Bures,	" "
1472	John Marchant,	" "
1482	John White,	William Barlee.
1501	William Wilton,	" "
1510	William Barlee, LL. B.	" "
1521	William Barlee, Jr.,	" "
1523	William Barlee,	John Byrde.
1528	Thomas Horsley,	" "
1540	John Clerke,	William Barlee.
1558	John Gryffyth,	" "
1566	William Swinnowe,	Matthew Bradbury.
1586	Richard Clayton, D.D.,	" "
1598	Thomas Wadeson,	Robert Wadeson.
1627	Theophilus Aylmer,	King Charles I.
1669	Lawrence Fogg,	Elizabeth Aylmer.
1671	John Bennet,	John Turner.
1692	Thomas Carter,	Francis Bradbury.
1712	James Bradbury,	" "
1720	Wentworth Bradbury,	" "
1765	Charles Gretten,	John Griffith.

In 1868, Mr. John Merrill Bradbury of Ipswich, who with his wife was making the tour of Europe, visited Wicken Bonant where his emigrant ancestor is supposed to have been born. Concerning this visit Mr. Bradbury wrote to a friend: " My visit to Wicken Bonant was the pleasantest experience I have had in

England. The rector was away on a vacation, and I did not therefore see the registers, which would have been a gratification, and I was indebted to the church-warden's wife for admission to the church. It is a small church and the addition made to it by Mr. Sperling, the late rector, has not improved its proportions. Of course the surfaces, internal and external, are new, and there is nothing to remind the visitor of its age, except a mural tablet in the chancel, date of 1697, and the square font standing on five square supports which is a veritable piece of antiquity. Undoubtedly Thomas Bradbury, supposed to be the emigrant, was baptized at this font.

"From the church our conductress guided us to the Brick House, where we were most cordially received by its proprietor, Mr. John Pollitt. He took us through the old mansion, pointing out the alterations and additions which have been made, giving us its traditions and history. He also showed us over the grounds which are well laid out and nicely kept, and took us to points where we could get the best views of the house and its surroundings, as well as the village generally."

A letter written in London in 1870, says: "The Bradbury Brick House at Wicken Bonant is forty-five miles from London. It was built by William Bradbury who died in 1622, for his second son Wymond Bradbury, and it continued in that branch until it became extinct. Mr. Joseph Martin then owned it until the

WICKEN BONANT.

Two views of the " Brick House " erected by William Bradbury, who died in 1622, for his
second son, Wymond.

last two years. At his demise it went to his son-in-law, Mr. John Pollitt, who now resides there."

Mrs. C. W. Bradbury of Winchester, Mass., has visited the ancestral home of the Bradburys at Wicken Bonant and writes: "By the kind hospitality of the occupant of the mansion called the Brick House, I made my headquarters there for the day, while taking excursions to the parish church and to the church at Clavering. But my stay was limited to one day, and that day was in the month of November, 1877. Darkness filled every corner, and I had to trust to hearsay as to what was inscribed on the monumental slabs. I was able to obtain copies of the publication called the East Anglian, devoted to antiquities, folk-lore, etc., in which is an article written by the sometime rector, describing the church, and giving some account of the Bradbury family."

The parish of Wicken Bonant just briefly described, is supposed to have been the birth-place of that Thomas Bradbury who, while a young man, came to the District of Maine as early as 1634, as the agent of Sir Ferdinando Gorges, and is the common ancestor of the Bradburys of New England. It would be highly gratifying to be able to state positively that Thomas Bradbury who came to New England was the identical Thomas who was baptized in the ancient Norman font, in the church of St. Margaret, in the parish of Wicken Bonant, February 28, 1610-11. It is true, the evidence is such as to remove all reasonable doubt, and such as to give great interest in the little parish of Wicken in

Essex, to the Bradbury families of the United States. The evidence in favor of the generally accepted theory may be briefly summarized as follows: The parish register of Wicken Bonant shows that a Thomas Bradbury was baptized there on the last day of February, 1610-11; and as his family had landed property, it is easy to trace his pedigree by the Herald's Visitations. This Thomas Bradbury is not mentioned in English records after his baptism. So far as is known, Thomas Bradbury of York and Salisbury, was the only one of the name that ever came to New England, and as none of his family came with him, it is presumed that he was of age; and on the score of age, there is nothing incompatible with the idea that Thomas of Wicken and Thomas of York were the same. That the latter was a young man of ability and well educated, the records abundantly prove. He was married in 1636, which was at a proper age, provided he was the young man from Wicken, and died in 1695, at a good old age. Unfortunately his age at death is nowhere stated, a circumstance that deprives us of important corroborative evidence. It was usual in the period in which he lived for persons making affidavits to be recorded to state their ages, but in the several sworn statements given by Mr. Bradbury, on file in Essex County records, no one has been found in which his age is stated.

Another strong point in the chain of evidence is found in the family names. Every genealogist knows that this is a pointer that rarely deceives. The father of Thomas of Wicken was named Wymond, a very unusual name. and the only person found so named in the Bradbury pedigrees that have been collected. Now it is a fact that Thomas of York and Salisbury named his first-born son Wymond. and it is also a fact that it was the usual practice in those days to name the oldest son either for his father or grandfather. If he did not name the child for his father, for whom did he name him? Not for any of the mother's relatives, and so far as the compiler is aware this name at that time had been borne by no other person in New England. The mother of Thomas of Wicken was named Elisabeth, and she had children William, Thomas, Jane and Ann, names all of which reappear in the family of Thomas Bradbury of Agamenticus and Salisbury. While all this does not furnish positive evidence of the identity of the two persons, it approaches so nearly to it that the compiler fully believes it, and feels himself justified in assuming it to be so.

It has already been stated that in the pedigrees published in England. based upon the Herald's Visitations, there are several discrepancies, and of course some mistakes. The pedigree is certainly wrong which makes Sir Thomas Bradbury of London the head of the family, for in his will, a copy of which is herewith printed. no mention is made of any children, and the only relatives bearing his name in the entire document are Henry and William Bradbury, the latter of whom he calls "cosen," and who inherited a large portion of his estate. It is known that this Henry and William were the sons of his brother Robert. He also mentions his sister, Mrs. Jocelyn.

From the Herald's Visitations in Derbyshire in 1569, 1611 and 1631, the following Bradbury pedigree is drawn :—

EDWARD[1] BRADBURY, of Ollersett in the county of Derby, married Eleanor, daughter of Thomas Shakerly of Longson.

Children:

i   Ottiwell[2], of Ollersett, m. Agnes Beard.
ii Robert[2], second son. = Robert[1] p. 27

OTTIWELL[2] BRADBURY, son and heir of the preceding, married Agnes, daughter of Nicholas Beard of Beard.

Children:

i   Ralph[3], d. without issue.
ii   Nicholas[3], m. Katherine Warren.
iii John[3], d. without issue.
iv   Anne[3], m. Robert Downes.

NICHOLAS[3] BRADBURY, son and heir of the preceding, married Katherine, daughter of Lawrence Warren of Poynton, in Cheshire.

Children:

i   Robert[4], m. Elizabeth Bradbury.
ii   John[4].
iii Ottiwell[4].
iv   Lawrence[4], m. daughter of Reynold Braye.
v   Nicholas[4].
vi   Edmund[4].
vii Alice[4].
viii Anne[4].

ROBERT[4] BRADBURY, of Ollersett, son and heir of the preceding, married Elizabeth, daughter of Ralph Bradbury of Bankhead.

Children :

i Nicholas[5], m. Mary Tettowe.
ii Francis[5].
iii Alice[5].
iv Katherine[5].

NICHOLAS[5] BRADBURY, of Ollersett, son and heir of the preceding, living in 1611, married Mary, daughter of Lawrence Tettowe in Lancashire.

Children :

i Edmund[6], m. Mary West.
ii Katherine[6], m. Robert Ridge of Highgate.
iii Jane[6].
iv Anne[6].
v Elizabeth[6].
vi Mary[6].
vii Margaret[6].

EDMUND[6] BRADBURY, son and heir of the preceding, married Mary, daughter of William West of Firbeck in Yorkshire.

Children :

i Edmund[7], b. 1586, m. Dorothy Bowdon.
ii John[7].
iii Mary[7].
iv Elizabeth[7].

EDMUND[7] BRADBURY, son and heir of the preceding, married Dorothy, widow of Thomas Bowdon of Derbyshire.

Children :

i Edmund[8], b. 1612.
ii Nicholas[8], b. 1614.
iii William[8], b. 1618.
iv John[8], b. 1624.
v Jordaine[8], b. 1630.

No dates are given in the foregoing, except in one instance in the seventh generation, and in case of the

eighth, but eight generations must represent a period
of about two hundred years, which would take us back
to the last of the thirteenth century, or the first of the
fourteenth, as the date of the birth of the first Edward. ~~It is quite possible that~~ Robert[2] Bradbury,
named as the second son of Edward, ~~may be taken as~~ the
one placed at the head of the family in the pedigree
which follows and which has been carefully compiled
from Heralds' Visitations, Inquisitions post mortem,
wills, parish registers, and every other available original document.

Absolute perfection is by no means claimed for it,
but the compiler believes it to be as nearly so as it
is possible to have it. It is made up from the minutes of the late John Merrill Bradbury of Ipswich,
and is the result of personal research in the archives
of various parts of England, covering a period of several years. He was a painstaking searcher and took
nothing for granted until proved.

ROBERT[1] BRADBURY, of Ollersett in Derbyshire, married a daughter of Robert Davenport (copied also
Damport), of Bramhall, county of Chester. She was
buried at Stansted, Mount Fitchet, county of Essex.

Children :

1   i   William[2], of Braughing, m. Margaret Rockhill.
2   ii   Thomas[2], inducted Rector of Meesden*, county Essex, Feb.
       6, 1486, d. 1513.

*The orthography of this word is somewhat in doubt. It is hardly
ever found spelled twice alike, but generally so nearly so that it is easily
recognized.

1

WILLIAM² BRADBURY (Robert¹), of Braughing, in Hertfordshire, Patron of the church of Westmill in Hertfordshire in 1462, married Margaret, daughter and co-heir of Geoffry Rockhill of Wormingford, county Essex.

Children :

3   i   Robert³, m. Anne Wyant. (?)

4   ii   Thomas³, Sir Thomas, Kt., Sheriff of London, 1498, Lord Mayor, 1509, Lord of several manors in Hertfordshire, Essex, and Kent, married Joan, daughter of Denis and Elisabeth Leach, whose first husband by whom she had issue, was Thomas Bodley of Devonshire. She died in 1530. Sir Thomas made his will Jan. 9, 1509-10, while Lord Mayor, and the same was proved Feb. 27 following. He and also his wife were buried in St. Stephen's church, Coleman street, London. He held the manor Stansted Mount Fitchet and mentions that his grandmother was there buried. He had no children, and his nephew William, son of his brother Robert Bradbury, whom he calls " cosen," succeeded to a portion of his estate.

5   iii   George³, was a London merchant. His will is dated June 6, 1506, and proved June 28 following, by his brother Henry. Wills lands and tenements in London, in Ware, county Herts, and Lamborne, county Essex. His sister, Phillippa Jocelyn, is made heir and after her, her daughter Johane Hannys (perhaps daughter by her former husband).

6   iv   Henry³, executor of his brother George's will, and named in the will of his brother Sir Thomas. Will dated Feb. 13, 1532-33, and proved Jan. 23, 1533-34. His consin Mary Woddam, wife of William Woddam, citizen and merchant tailor of London, is made executrix and residuary legatee.

7 v Phillippa², named in the wills of her brothers Thomas and George, married and was the second wife of John Jocelyn of High Roding, county Essex. He died July 14, 1525. His will states that William Bradbury, cousin and heir of Sir Thomas, was the son of Robert Bradbury.

3

ROBERT³ BRADBURY (William², Robert¹), named in the inquisition of his brother, Sir Thomas, then dead (supposed Justice of the Assize, Isle of Ely, Feb. 4, 1486, witness to will of George Nicholl of Littlebury, Dec. 2, 1484, died 1489, and buried in church of Grey Friars, London), is said to have married Anne, daughter of Infans Wyant. (See note.)

Children :

8 i William⁴, b. 1480, m. Joan (Fitzwilliams) Bendish.*

*We have followed the Herald's Visitation here, but there is evidently a serious mistake in their reckoning. Thomas Bendish died about 1477, and his wife Joan or Jane had deceased prior to May 4, 1490, at which date her inquisition post mortem was held, when it was found that Richard Bendish, grandson of Thomas, aged five years, was heir to her estate. She evidently belonged to a generation back of William Bradbury, and if she married a Bradbury, as she is reported, it must have been his father, Robert. When Symonds made his collection of epitaphs in Essex in 1639, there was in the church at Clavering a stone bearing the inscription in Latin: " Pray for the souls of William Bradbury, Esq., and wife Elisabeth," which Elisabeth died August 13, 1536. William Bradbury died later, after his removal to Littlebury, and was buried there. This would show that his wife's name was Elisabeth. The Herald's Visitations do not give the name of the wife of Robert Bradbury, and unfortunately he left no will, and there was no inquisition post mortem to solve the mystery. In some of the pedigrees he is said to have married Anne Wyant, and we have followed it, but with this explanation. His son having been assigned a wife that belonged to the generation of the father, it is quite probable that the Visitation has made a mistake of one generation, and that Jane (Fitzwilliam) Bendish was the mother and not the wife of William Bradbury⁴.

8

WILLIAM[4] BRADBURY (Robert[3], William[2], Robert[1]),
named in the inquisition post mortem on the estate of
his uncle, Sir Thomas, in 1510, then aged thirty years;
named in the will of his uncle Sir Thomas, to whose
estate he succeeded, Lord of the manor Mancenden,
acquired the manor of Catmere Hall in Littlebury,
county Essex, in 1443, and was buried at Littlebury,
June 15, 1546. He is incorrectly said to have married
Joan, daughter of Sir John Fitzwilliams. Lord of Elmyn
and Spotsbury, and widow of Thomas Bendish of Bowre
Hall, in Steeple Bumstead, Esq., who died in 1477,
leaving issue Richard Bendish, Esq.

Children :

9 i   William[5], m. Helen or Eleanor Fuller.
10 ii Phillippa[5], m. first to Michael Welbore of Pondes in
       Clavering, county Essex; second to John Barlee of
       Stapleford Abbots, county Essex.
11 iii Matthew[5], m. Margaret, daughter of —— Rowse, of the
       city of Cambridge.

9

WILLIAM[5] BRADBURY (William[4], Robert[3], William[2],
Robert[1]), of Littlebury, county Essex, Lord of the
manor of Catmere Hall; also of Meesden; acquired
the manor of Gifford's in Great Tampford, county
Essex, about 1548; also acquired the manor of Langley Hall in Clavering, county Essex, in 1550, alluded
to as son and heir of William Bradbury in the will of
Joan Bradbury. His will is dated August 11, and
proved Nov. 9, 1550; inquisition post mortem held

Oct. 4, 1550, buried at Littlebury. He married Helen
or Eleanor, daughter of Andrew and Barbara Fuller.
She was appointed executrix of her first husband's
will, but having died her son Robert was appointed
executor in 1561. She married for second husband
Giles Poulton, Esq., of Desborough in Northamton-
shire, Jan. 15, 1551-52.

Children :

12   i   Robert[6], b. 1537, m. Margaret, daughter of Edmund
         Tyrell.

13   ii   Henry[6], b. ——, m. Joan, daughter of Giles Poulton, and
         second Marian, daughter of George Nichols.

14   iii   Thomas[6], named in the wills of his father and brother
         Robert, of Milton, county Kent, married and had issue
         Thomas, Godfrey and Phillippa.

15   iv   Samuel[6], bap. January 27, 1548-49, buried at Wicken,
         March 4, 1551-52.

16   v   Anne[6], m. Christopher Fulnatby of Chelmsford, county
         Suffolk, Feb. 5, 1578.

17   vi   Elizabeth[6], b. ——, m. Feb. 2, 1562-63, Richard Trymell
         of Wybolston, county Bedford.

18   vii   Mary[6], bap. Jan. 19, 1549-50, m. Thomas Webb.

19   viii   Barbara[6], bap. March 5, 1550-51, m. Thomas Padget of
         the Middle Temple.

11

MATTHEW[5] BRADBURY (William[4], Robert[3], William[2],
Robert[1]), Lord of the manor of Wicken Hall, in the
parish of Wicken Bonhunt, which manor he acquired
by purchase in 1557. He purchased the manor of
Grange in Thaxted, county Essex, in 1551, and sold it
the next year. He is mentioned in the wills of his

brother William and his nephew Robert. He died
June 19, 1585, and an inquisition post mortem was
held Oct. 26. 1587. His son William was appointed
administrator of his estate June 30, 1585. He married
Margaret, daughter of —— Rowse of the city of Cambridge.

Children :

20   i   William[6], m. Anne, daughter and heir of Richard Eden.
21   ii   Thomas[6], m. Dorothy, daughter of Sir —— Southwell.
       He had issue Cordell[7], Wentworth[7], Elisabeth[7], and
       another daughter, wife of Matthew Martin.
22   iii   Barbara[6], m. first Sir Henry Cutts; second Sir Thomas
       Fludd; third Edward Gill, Esq., and fourth Walter
       Covert of Boxley, county Kent. She is mentioned
       in the will of her brother Thomas.

20

WILLIAM[6] BRADBURY (Matthew[5], William[4], Robert[3],
William[2], Robert[1]), of Wicken Bonhunt, Esq., aged 41
in 1585, named in the wills of his cousin Robert and
brother Thomas. His own will is dated April 19, 1622,
and was proved May 6, 1623. He died Nov. 30, 1622
and was buried at Wicken. He married Anne, daughter and heir of Richard Eden, Esq., LL. D., of Bury
St. Edmunds, county Suffolk, who died and was
buried at Wicken, Feb. 8, 1611-12.

Children :

23   i   Matthew[7], m. Jane, daughter of William Whitgift.
24   ii   Wymond[7], m. Elizabeth, daughter of William Whitgift,
       who had been twice married before.
25   iii   Henry[7], d. young ; buried at Wicken, Aug. 20, 1616.

26 iv Thomas[7], d. young.
27 v Thomas[7], d. young.
28 vi Bridget[7], m. Francis Bridgewater.
29 vii Anne[7], m. Thomas Kinethorpe of Louth, county Lincoln.
30 viii Alice[7], bap. at Newport Pond, February 23, 1572-73 ; m.
          first George Yardley of Weston, county Herts ; second
          Thomas Wadeson.

23

MATTHEW[7] BRADBURY (William[6], Matthew[5], William[4], Robert[3], William[2], Robert[1]), of Wicken Bonant, died Sept. 22, 1616. His marriage settlement is dated June 6, 1594. He married Jane, daughter of William Whitgift of Clavering, county Essex. For second husband she married Henry Bradbury, supposed son of Henry Bradbury of Littlebury.

Children :

31 i John[8], of Wicken, m. Mary, daughter and heir of Michael
       Morsetrod of Croyden, county Sussex. He d. Aug.
       1, 1624, and his widow m. Charles Millicent, and d.
       in November, 1628.

32 ii Francis[8], bap. Jan. 12, 1600-1, d. Jan., 1644-45, admin-
        istration granted to wife Bridget, Jan. 28, 1644-45.
        They had issue John[9], and Francis[9], b. December 29,
        1642, who m. Ann, daughter of George James, and had
        John[10], Francis[10], William[10], Matthew[10], George[10],
        James[10] and Anne[10]. All these save Matthew d. with-
        out issue, and he had an only child, Dorinda[11], who
        carried the estate at Wicken to her husband Joseph
        Sharpe.
        3

33 iii Matthew[6], named in the will of his grandfather, William
          Whitgift, dated June 13, 1615. Administrator of the
          estate of his father, Oct. 19, 1624. He filed a bill in
          chancery against the execution of the will of George
          Whitgift, May 27, 1625.
34 iv   Edward[6], not named by his brother Matthew as an heir
          of Archbishop Whitgift in the suit against the execu-
          tors of the will of George Whitgift.
35 v   Phillippa[6], m. Ferdinando Clark. She is named in the
          will of her grandfather, William Whitgift, dated June
          13, 1615, and was then married.
36 vi   Barbara[6].
37 vii Margaret[6], m. William Hyde.
38 viii Elizabeth[6], m. Thomas Wells, a minister.
39 ix   Martha[6], bap. April 14, 1606.

24

WYMOND[7] BRADBURY (William[6], Matthew[5]. William[4].
Robert[3], William[2], Robert[1]), of Wicken Bonant, afterward of the parish of Whitechapel, county Middlesex.
died in 1650, and his daughter Anne Stubbles was appointed administratrix. Nov. 20, 1650. He was baptized at Newport Pond. May 16. 1574. and was of
London, Oct 17, 1628. He married Elizabeth. daughter of William Whitgift, and sister of the wife of his
brother Matthew. She died June 26. 1612. aged 38
years and 3 months, and was buried at Croyden. county
Surrey. Her first husband was Richard Coles of Leigh.
Worcestershire, who died Nov., 1600. She married.
second, Francis Gill of London. who died in 1605.
and third, Wymond Bradbury.

Children :

40 i   William⁸, bap. at Newport Pond,* Sept. 28, 1607, b. Sept. 13, 1607, and was living Oct. 23, 1628.

41 ii Thomas⁸, bap. at Wicken Bonant, Feb. 28, 1610-11, supposed to have come to New England prior to 1634, and settled at Salisbury, Mass., in 1638.

42 iii Jane⁸, bap. at Wicken Bonant, June 2, 1606.

43 iv Anne⁸, m. first, —— Troughton, and second, —— Stubbles, administratrix of her father's estate, 1650, bap. at Newport Pond, Feb. 20, 1608-9.

ARMS AND QUARTERINGS OF BRADBURY.

1   Bradbury sab. a chev. erm. between 3 buckles arg.
2   Rockhill arg. a chev. between 3 chess rooks sab.
3   Bendy of 10 or az.
4   arg. a lion ramp. az.
5   Langham arg. 3 bear's heads erased sab. muzzled or.
6   Ashwell arg. on fess indented sab. 3 cross corselets arg.
7   erm. a lion ramp. gu.
8   Filmer   gu. 3 bars arg. a canton of last.

            Crest—a falcon rising, or.

ii Bradbury impaling Fitzwilliams lozengy arg. gu. a border. az. charged with fleur de lis and besants alternately.

iii Bradbury imp. Rowse per pale or. and az. 3 lions ramp. counter-charged.

iv Bradbury imp. Eden arg. on fess. gu. between 2 chess. az. each charged with 3 escallops of the field, 3 garbs or.

v   Bradbury imp. Whitgift arg. on a cross flore sab. 5 besants.

vi Bradbury imp. James quarterly 1-4 arg. a chev. between 3 fer de moulins barwise sab. 2-3. arg. 2 bars counter embattled gu.

*Newport Pond, where Mr. Wymond Bradbury appears to have been living at this time, is a small hamlet situated little more than a mile from Wicken.

vii   Bradbury impaled by Barlee erm. 2 bars wavy sab.
viii   Bradbury by Cutts arg. on bend. eng. sab. 3 plates.
 ix   Bradbury by Flude erm. a chev. between 3 cresents gu.
  x   Bradbury by Gill lozengy or. and arg. lion ramp. gu.
 xi   Bradbury by Covert gu. a fess erm. between 3 martletts az.

WILL OF SIR THOMAS BRADBURY,

MAYOR OF LONDON.

In the name of god amen the ix[th] day of the moneth of January the yere of our lord god m[l] v[e] and ix and the first yere of the Reign of Kyng Henry the viii[th]. I Thomas Bradbury mayre of the citie of London beying in hole mynde and of goode memory thanked be our lord god make ordeyne and declare this my present testament conteynyng my last will as to the disposition of all my goods cattells lands and tents in manner and forme folowing that is to say

First I bequeath and Recomend my soule to almighty god our lady seynt Mary and all the seynts in heaven.

Item. My body to be buried in the pisshe churche, of seynt stephen in Colman strete. Where I am pisshen, that is to say in the chapell of oure laydy in the said churche. if I happen there to dye orells in the pisshe churche where it shall fortune me to decesse and passe oute of this world bifore thymage of our lady in the same churche etc.

Item. I will that mye executors hereunder named Immediately after my decesse cawse i j trentalls of masses to be songen and said by the freers (blank). praying for my soule and all cristen soules and I will and bequeath to the same freers for their labor aboute the same xx[s].

Item. I will and bequeath to evry of the iiij orders of freers in the citie of London to bring my body to erthe and to be present at my burying praying for my soule xx[s].

Item. I bequeath to the said churche of seynt Stephen toward the reparacens of the same x[li] or more after the discretion of mye executors.

Item. I bequeath to the vicar of the said churche xx' to pray for my soule.

Item. I will that evry off my lovenut sirvants being with me att the time of my decesse have a blake gowne after the discrecion of myn executors.

Item. I will that Robert Blag of therche quier have a blake gowne and a ryng of the value of v mro, in money.

Item. I will that my broder-in-law John Josselyn and my sister his wife and either of theym, haue a blake gowne and either of theym a ryng of the value of ıı ⁱ ᴵᴵ or ıı ⁱ ᴴ in money aft. the discretion of myn executors.

Item. I will that Thomas Stoks, gent, haue a blake gowne and a ryng of the value of xl' or xl' in money after the discrecion of myn executors

Item. I will that either of my brethren Henry & Thomas Leech haue a blake gowne.

Item. I will that myn executors giue unto as many of my kynsmen and frends as they shall think conveyent after their discretion, blake gouns.

Item. I will that my said executors provide all things for and about my funerall burying and moneths mynde as by their discrecion shall seme behoveful, nedeful and conveyent.

Item. I bequeath to the pisshe of brawing where I was borne a sute of vestments of the value of xx ᴴ or more after the discrecion of myn exec.

Item. I bequeath to the pisshe church of Manceden in Essex, a single sute of vestments of the value of xx ᴴ after the discrecion of my exec.

Item. I bequeath to the pisshe church of Stanstede Monfichet in Essex where my grandmother ys buried a syngle sute of vestments of the value of xx ᴴ or more at the discretion of myn exec.

Item. I bequeath to the poore people of the pisshe of Braughyng aforesaid xl' to be distributed by the discrecion of myn exec.

Item. To the poore folks of the pisshe of Mancenden aforesaid xx' to be distributed by the discrecion of myn exec.

Item.   I bequeath to the pisshe of Mountfichett aforesaid xx[s]
to be distributed in likewise aft. the discrecion of myn exec.

Item.   I bequeath to my brother Henry xx[li].

Item.   I bequeath to my sisters Illesleys daughters toward hir
mariage xl[li], evenly to be divided amongs theym, to be delivered
to them by myn executors at the mariage of eny of theym, and
if any of theym decease bifore mariage then the part or portion
of hir so deccesed to the other enlyving equally to be devided
betweene theym etc.

Item.   I bequeath to my sister Yllsley vii[li] or more after the
discrecion of Johane my wif.

Item.   The Residue of my goods and cattalls after my debts
paid my funeralls doon and this my present testament in everything fulfilled and executed I holly gine and bequeath unto the
said Johane my wife therewith to doo and dispose her free will.

And of this my present testament and last will, I ordeyne and
constitute the said Johane my wif, Richard Bishope of Norwich
and Richard Broke myn executors, and either the said Richard
Bishop and Richard Broke to haue xx[li].

Item.   This is the last will of me the said Thomas Bradbury
made the day and year aforesaid as to the disposicion of all my
lands and tents in the counties of Essex, Hertfordshire, Kent and
the citie of London and eleswhere within the Realme of England.

First I will that my said wif have all my manors lands and tents
rents and services which I or any psons to myn use been seasid
of wt. in the said counties and citie or eleswhere to have to hir
term of life without empeschment of wast except the manor of
Bawdes and my mylne in the countie of Essex which I will John
Leeche have for term of his life.

Item.   I will that Immediately after his death Humfrey Tyrell
son of William Tyrell and Elisabeth his wife my wife's daughter,
haue all that my moytie of that manor or lordship of Bekenham
in the countie of Kent a[t] theappurtences to haue to him and the
heyres of his body, and for defaulte of suche yssue to the sisters
of the said Humfrey begotten betweene the said William and my

said wif's sayd daughter and to theyres of their bodyes. And for
defaulte of yssue of any of their bodyes, hir part so decessing to
remayn to the other surviving and the heyres of his body. And
for defaulte of suche issue, the remaynder to the said William
the fader and to his heirs forev.

Item. I will that the said Humfrey & Johane the daughter of
my said brother and sister Josselyn his wife if the said Humfrey
and Johane be content and doo mary theym self togider, then immediately after the decease of my said wif and John Leech the
said Humfrey and Johane haue the manor of bawdes and my
mylees in the countie of Essex to theym and to the heyres off
their two bodys lawfully begoten. And for defaulte of such yssue
to my cosyn William Bradbury and his heyres forever. And if
the said Humfrey and Johane will not mary togider when they
bothe come to their lawfull age of consent of marriage but refuse
to be married togider when they be required by my said executors
or their assignes. Then I will the said my cosyn William haue
the said lands to him and to his heirs after the decees of the said
Johane myn wif and the said John Leeche. Forseen that my wif
have the saide manor and mylees after the death of the said
Leeche for time of his life etc.

Item. I will that Denys Bodely my wif's daught. Immediately
after my said wif's decees haue the manor lands and tents called
Westcot in the countie of Kent with theappurtences to hir and
to hir heirs of hir body and toward hir mariage. And for default of suche yssue I will the said manor be sold by my executors and the money thereof comyng to be disposed by my said
wif for my soule and the soules of my said wif and all lxpen
soules as shall think best.

I will that my said wif shal haue my house whereyn I now
dwell and all other houses and edeficious djoyning or beying aper-
ment or pcell of the same for terme of hir life and the Reversion
thereof to be sold by my said executor and the money thereof
coming to be disposed by my said wif for the welth of my soule
and hirs as she shall think best.

Item. I will that after the decesse of my said wif, Thomas Josselyn son of my said brother and sister Josselyn haue the manor of Mancenden and all those lands & tents that I late bought of Henry Woodcocks in the county of Essex. To haue to the said Thomas and to the heyres of his body. And for defaulte of such yssue the remainder thereof to the said William Bradbury and his heyres.

Item. Where certeyn lands and tents were lately recovered by certeyn p'cesses agaynst Thomas Nevell to thuse and entent that if an annytie or annell rent of x^li were truly content and paied owte of the manor of Hanyngfield to me and my said wif covenanted and guarantied to be paid for term of our lives by the Lord of Burgeneny according to endentures of covenants thereof made that then the said Record of the said lands against said Thomas Nevell shuld be to them made of the said Thomas Nevell and his heyres males of his body. And for defaulte of such yssue the remaynder unto the said Lord of Burgeneny. And if defaulte were made contrary to the forme of the said indentures, that then the said lands shuld be to me and to myn said wife and myn heyres. I will that if defaulte of payment be made of the said annual rent contrary to the forme aforesaid that the said lands to be to my said wife for term of hir life and the reversion thereof to be sold by my said executors & the money thereof coming to be disposed by my said wif for our souls as shall think best.

ABSTRACTS OF BRADBURY WILLS.

March 30, 1529. Dame Joan Bradbury of London, widow of Thomas Bradbury, late Mayor of London, Bequeaths her soule to God, the Virgin Mary and all the saints in heaven, and desires to be buried by the side of her husband. Legacies to ―――― Bradbury, son and heir of William Bradbury, and others. Proved April 29, 1530.

August 13, 1559. William Bradbury of Littlebury, county Essex, Esq., desires to be buried without pomp. Bequeaths to the poor men's box at Littlebury £4, at Clavering £20, at Mysoden £5, at Langley £3, at Sampford £5, and at Walden 40s. To the poor people every year during lent, for fiue years, a barrel of herrings or 16ˢ in money. To his wife, the capital messuage lands and tenements where he dwells at Littlebury, his manor at Catmerchall and other lands, and his manor of Langley in Essex and Hertfordshire, during her life. Sons Robert, Henry not 21, and Samuel not 20. Daughters Anne, Elisabeth, and Mary not 21. To his mother-in-law, Barbara Fuller, an annuity out of his manor of Giffords in Sampford. Speaks of his manor at Messoden. To his son Robert, the great gold ring that was his father's. Mentions his brother Matthew. His wife Helen appointed executrix. Proved November 11, 1550.

January 7, 1576-77. Robert Bradbury of Littlebury, county Essex, desires to be buried in the chancel of the church without pomp, and requests a stone laid over his grave and the grave of his father. Mentions the will of his late father, his brothers Henry and Thomas, wife's late father Edmund Tyrell, deceased, sister Mary Bradbury, Samuel Donne, cousin William Bradbury, cousin Thomas Bradbury, uncle Mr. Matthew Bradbury, aunt Rutter, Thomas Welbore, godson Thomas Fulnatby, cousin Catherine Keble, sister Susan and cousin John Olyff. To Lady Anne Peter, a gold ring as a token. His wife Margaret appointed executrix. Will proved May 4, 1577.

October 27, 1592. William Bradbury of the parish of St. Clement Danes, without the bars of the new Temple, county Middlesex, yeoman. Mentions his cousin William Matterman of St. Clement Danes, and his sister Isabel Humstone and children. Will proved Nov. 4, 1592.

June 12, 1594. Thomas Bradbury the younger, desires to be buried in the church of Milton, county Kent. Bequeathes his mother £40, to his wife Susan £20, to his brother Godfrey Bradbury £40. Legacies to his brother Richard Askew, to the poor of Milton, to Thomas Boothe, Elisabeth Crockett, and her son Robert,

and Grace, daughter of Henry Botham. Appoints his father
Thomas Bradbury, executor. Proved Oct. 15, 1594.

February 26, 1596-97. Henry Bradbury of Littlebury, county
Essex, Gentleman, being very sick of body, but of good and perfect remembrance, etc., Desires to be buried in the chancel of the
church at Littlebury, as near as conveniently may be to the body
of Jane Bradbury, his late wife. Bequeaths to the reparation of
the church yard £6 8s., to the poor of Littlebury £40, to the poor
of Mesden £6 8s., to the poor of Sampford £5, to the poor of
Langley £5. To his wife Marian during her life, the manor of
Langley Hall in Langley and Missenden, counties of Essex and
Herts ; his manor at Giffords alias Stanleys, in Sampford, Essex.
Mentions father-in-law, Mr. George Niccolls, brother, Mr. John
Michell ; son and heir William Bradbury, sons Henry, Robert and
George. To daughter Mary, wife of John Muffett, daughter
Barbara not 21, daughter Ellen not 21, and to his sister-in-law,
Mrs. Margaret Daniell, sometime wife of his oldest brother Robert
Bradbury, deceased. Son William executor. Will proved April
19, 1597.

April 10, 1604. Thomas Bradbury, merchant of London, gives
to the poor of St. Paul's in Exeter, £20, speaks of the expected
arrival of the good ship called the Delight of Topisham. Appoints
Mr. Valentine Tedbury, executor and residuary legatee. Proved
May 4, 1604.

Henry Bradbury, haberdasher of London (no date), to his
brother Justinian, the lease of his house; to brothers Robert and
John each £5 ; to each of John's children £40 ; to his sister £3,
and to his father £5. Proved August 31, 1606.

September 10, 1610. Robert Bradbury of Poplar, county Middlesex, Gentleman. Bequeaths to his minor daughter Martha,
his manor at Cheswick, called Cheswick Hall, in county Essex,
which he lately purchased of George Nicholas, Esq., she paying
to wife Ann £50 per annum during her life. To his wife, house-

hold furniture and silver plate, also £100, on the condition that she sees him brought to the ground and pays all funeral expenses. To his four brothers John, Leonard, George and Nicholas Bradbury, each £20. To his three sisters dwelling in Derbyshire, each £20. Makes bequests to the poor of several places, and appoints Mr. Anthony Luther and Mr. Robert Fulnathbee of the Middle Temple, executors. Proved Nov. 15, 1611.

September 8, 1610. Thomas Bradbury of South Pickenham, county Norfolk, Esq., desires to be buried in the chancel of the church. Legacies to the poor of several parishes. To his wife Dorothy his lands in Burningham, county Suffolk, during her life, then to son Cordell Bradbury. To his son Wentworth Bradbury his manor of Woottons in West Broddenham, which he purchased of John Grundye. His house in South Peckenham is called Starkey Hall. He makes bequests to grandchild Anthony Bradbury, to his grandchild Thomas Bradbury not 18, to his brother Anthony Bradbury, and others.

May 14, 1695. Francis Bradbury the younger of Saffron Walden, county Essex, Gent. To his mother Anne Bradbury and to his sister Anne, each £10 for mourning; also his sister Anne £100, to brothers William, Matthew and James, each £100; to brother George £150. To his father, Francis Bradbury; Gent, all his lands and tenements in Newport Pond and Langley, and elsewhere in county Essex. To his father all those his chambers at Clifford's Inn, No. 6, up two flights of stairs, over the chambers of John Oliver, Gent, and two parts of cellars underneath. His father executor. Proved April 3, 1696.

WILL OF WILLIAM WHITGIFT.

In the name of God, amen: the thirteene daye of June in the yere of oure lord god one thousand sixe hundred and fifteene. I William Whitguifte of Clavering in the Countie of Essex, gent. beying weake in bodye but of good memorye (praised be Almightie god) doe hereby annihillate revoke and make voyde all former willes by me at any tyme heretofore made and nowe do make and ordayne this my last Will and Testament in manner and forme following. First I Commend my soule into the handes of Almightie god my heavenlie father and of Jesus xpiste my only Savyoure and of the holie ghost the blessed Sanctifier of me and all the Elect of god trusting assuredlie to have remission of all my synnes and to dwell in the most sweete presence of that heavenlie Maiestie of god forever thoroughe the greate mercye meritts and passion of my gracious Sayvoure and Redemer Jesus Christe in whom all Nations are blessed. Next I will that my bodye according to the order of xpistian Buryall be honestlie and decentlie conveyed into the bosome of the Earthe there to be layed within the parishe Churche of Clavering aforesayd as neere unto the grave of my welbeloved wife latelye deceased as convenientlie may be. And as for the disposition of all my worldlie goodes Chattells plate money houshold stuffe Bondes and Debts of what kynd nature and qualitie soever they be which god of his goodness hathe lent me here in this life, First I will and bequeathe to Wymond Bradburye of Wicken Bonnant gent. twoe hundred and fifteene poundes of good englishe money in lieu satisfaction and full compensacōn of one Bond of twoe hundred poundes of good english money nowe in the handes of the saied Wymond Bradburye in which bond I William Whitgift stood bound to Fraunces Gill my kynd and loving sonne in lawe late deceased for the payment of one hundred and tenne poundes of good englishe money to the sayd Fraunces Gill the Eleaventh daye of Januarye which was in the yere of oure lord god one thousand six hundred and fower the which bond remaynes as yet unpayed and resteth in the hands of Wymond Bradburye aforesayed gent. by occasion of his marriage with my daughter Elizabeth the late wife and widow of the saied Fraunces Gill deceased. The which somme of twoe hundred and fifteene poundes of good englishe money I will to be payed to the sayed Wymond in manner and forme following that is to saye one hundred pounds of good englishe money within three monthes next after my decease out of this my naturall life. And fiftie poundes of good english money (another part of the sayed twoe hundred and fifteene poundes) to be payed within one whole yere next after the day of my naturall deathe. And sixtie fyve poundes (the last parte of the twoe hundred and fifteene poundes) to be payed within twoe whole yeres after my naturall deathe to the saied Wymond Bradburye or his Assignes uppon satisfaction as aforesayed. Item I give and bequeathe to the poore people of Clavering the somme of six poundes of good English money to be distributed amongst them on ye daye of my Buryall or within one monethe next after by the oversighte and discrecon of my executor herein named. Item I give and bequeathe to John Mason a poore childe whome I broughte up twentie shillinges to be payed when he shalbe one and twentye yeres ould. Item I give and bequeathe to Jane Bradburye my daughter the wife of Matthew Bradburye gent. the somme of twentie poundes of good english money to be payed her within one whole yere next after my decease out of this life. Item I give and bequeathe to Philipp Clarke the daughter of Jane Bradbury my daughter the somme of twentie poundes of good englishe money to be payed her within the terme of twoe yeres next after my deathe. Item I give and bequeathe to Mathew Bradburye one of the sonnes of my daughter Jane the somme of twentie poundes of good englishe money to be payd hym at his age of one and twentie yerea. Item I give and bequeath to Mathewe Bradburye gent. my kynde sonne in Lawe a Ring of gould of fortie shillinges to be graven with my Arms uppon y^t signet wise. Item I give and bequeath to Anne Whitgifte the wife of my sonne John Whitgifte one Ryng of gould of the like value to be graven in the manner aforesayed. I give and bequeathe to George Anthony Clerk one Ryng of goulde of twentie shillings. Item I give and bequeathe to John Whitgifte the youngest the sonne and heire of John Whitgifte my sonne one yron Chest standing in the great chamber over the parlor with one Bason and Ewer of silver duble guilt seaven silver Bolles guilt with silver Covers guilt belonging to each of them twoe Belsalts of silver guilt twoe white silver bolles one dozen of silver spoones guilt one dozen silver spoones unguilt. All which parcells or peaces of plate before mentioned are usuallie remayning fast locked in the sayed yron chest. Item I give and bequeathe to Mary Whitgifte the daughter of my sonne John Whitgifte the summe of twoe hundred markes of good englishe money to be payed her at her age of Fifteene yeres or at the daye of her marriage which soever of them shall first happen. Item I give and bequeathe to Alexander Woodcocke my man the somme of Eight poundes of good englishe money to be payed hym within one yere next after the daye of my death. The Residew of all my goods and chattells aswell moveable as unmoveable stocke store sommes of money Jewells plate and thinges of what kynde nature or qualitie soev. they are or be before by this my last will not bequeathed nor given my Debts Legaeseys funerall chardges and expences payed and dischardged I whollie give and bequeathe to John Whitgifte my sonne whom I ordayne and make the sole executor of this my last will and testament. And I do appoynte and make Thoms Tompson the elder of Berelen in the Countie of Essex gent. Supervisor of this my last will authorising and requesting hym to cause entreat or compell my sayed executor iuslie and trulie to accomplishe and performe this my last will and testament. And in consideracon of his freindshipp and paynes to be ymployed therein I do give and bequeathe to the saied Thomas Tompson a Ryng of gould of fortie shillinges to be graven with my Armes uppon yᵗ signet wise desyring hym according to my truste to call uppon my sayed executor for the true accomplishment and performance of his dutie and fidelitie in the premises.

In witness whereof I the said William Whitgifte to this my last will have putto my hand to every leafe thereof and sealed the whole on the fylinge thereof togeather with my Seale of Arms in the presence of those whose names are hereunto subscribed.

WILLIAM WHITGIFT, his mark.

Sealed signed and delivered in the presence of Thomas Tompson, Ro. Younge, George Anthonye.

Proved in the Prerogative Court, at London, Nov. 8, 1615. Book Rudd, folio 108.

ABSTRACT OF WILL OF GEORGE WHITGIFT.

George Whitgift of the town and county of Hertford, Esq. Will dated May 1, 1610; proved at London, April 30, 1611. Bequeaths to his niece Elizabeth, wife of Wymond Bradbury, Gent, and to her children, all his lease and term of years unexpired at the time of his death of and in Whaddon Myllne, in the county of Surry, granted to him by his brother, the most Reverend Father, the late Archbishop of Canterbury. To his niece Jane, wife of Matthew Bradbury, Gent, all his lease and term of unexpired years in the meadows called Shoulford Meadows, in the county of Kent, near Canterbury. To his niece Bridget, wife of Robert Collingwood, Gent, and to her children, his lease and term of years in the farm of Shelvingford in the county of Kent. To his brother William Whitgift £20; to his god-daughter, daughter of his nephew John Whitgift, £50; to John Whitgift, the younger son of said nephew John, his lands in Tony, county of Kent; to Matthew Bradbury, John Whitgift the elder, Robert Collingwood, and Anne the wife of said John Whitgift, each a gold ring of the value of 40s, for a remembrance. The residue of his goods to Robert Collingwood and Wymond Bradbury, whom he appoints executors.

ABSTRACT OF WILL OF JOHN WHITGIFT,

ARCHBISHOP OF CANTERBURY.

Dated October 27, 1602, proved March 31, 1604. He desires to be buried where it is thought most convenient by his executors, but if he dies in Surry (?) to be buried at Croyden, in the chapel there within the parish church, which he has appointed for the poor scholars to sit. If he dies in Kent to be buried in the Cathedral church in Canterbury. He bequeaths to his successor in the office, various musical instruments and other articles described in detail. To the Wardens of the Hospital of the Holy Trinity in Croydon, all the buildings, appurtenances, furniture, utensils, etc. To his nephew John Whitgift his house at

Sporm, (?) county Kent, and other property there. Also he leaves legacies to his niece Elizabeth Coles and Jane Bradbury. Among the legacies are articles of plate and also money. He appoints Richard Bancroft, Bishop of London, and his brother George Whitgift, executors. The will was proved by George Whitgift, and December 2, 1618, a further proof was made by Wymond Bradbury, as executor of the will of George Whitgift.

ITEMS FROM HISTORY OF ESSEX, ENGLAND.

William Bradbury, Esq., of Littlebury, bought estate of "Gifford's" in 1547 and died in 1550. He left a son Robert, his heir, whose younger brother Henry was his successor in 1576, and died in 1596, leaving William his son and heir.

Gifford's was in the parish of Great Samford. Dame Johane Bradbury of London, widow, sister of Rev. John Leeche, endowed a grammar school at Saffron, Walden, May 18, 1525.

Henry Mordaunt, living at Thundersley in 1620, married Barbara, daughter of Henry Bradbury, Esq., of Littlebury.

Wickham Hall purchased after 1557 by Matthew Bradbury, second son of Robert and nephew of Thomas, Lord Mayor. He was succeeded by his eldest son, William, followed by Matthew, he by his son Francis, who was succeeded by his brother Matthew, whose daughter Dorinda conveyed it to her husband, Joseph Sharpe.

Jane, wife of Henry Bradbury, daughter of Gyles Poulton, county of Northampton, died August, 1578. Tablet in Littlebury church.

Langley Hall Grove, conveyed in 1550, to William Bradbury who died in possession the same year, leaving his son Robert his heir, who dying in 1576, was succeeded by his brother Henry whose son William died in 1607, leaving his son Henry under age.

In 1509, Thomas Bradbury died holding Manceden and other estates in which he was succeeded by his nephew William Bradbury, son of Robert.

In 1518, Robert Newport died in possession of the manor of Packenham Hall, which he held of Lady Bradbury.

Matthew Bradbury bought the manor of Vernors in 1551, and sold in 1552.

Spain's Hall, parish of Willingale, Spain, was once in possession of the Bradbury family.

Johane Bradbury, widow of Thomas Bradbury, died May 11, 1530.

Thomas Bradbury died Jan. 9, 1509-10. William Bradbury, son of brother Robert, became heir to Bawdys and Manceden.

ITEMS FROM HISTORY OF HERTFORDSHIRE, ENG.

Anne Vernon, 1430, married Sir John Bradbury of Hough Derbyshire.

William Bradbury was rector of Stapleford, July 5, 1664, and his successor was appointed Feb. 15, 1677.

John Jocelyn died July 14, 1525. He married Philippa, daughter of William Bradbury of Braughing, Hertz.

William Bradbury was the patron of Westmill Rectory, March 31, 1462.

Robert Bradbury, Esq., patron of Mesdon Rectory, December 28, 1566.

William Bradbury, Gent, patron of same December 7, 1575.

Thomas Bradbury was rector of Mesden, and died before March 15, 1513.

BAPTISMS.

1572-3, Feb. 23. Alice filia Willi Bradbury.

1574, May 16. Wimondus filius Willi Bradbury, etc.

" " 23. Cordel filius Thome Bradbury.

1607, Sept. 28. William filius Wymanni Bradbury, gen. William Bradbury ar. et William Whitgift et Dūa Barbara fflud filii Qui William filius natus est 13 die Septembris.

1608-9, Feb. 20. Anna filia Wymanni Bradbury.

4

INQUISITIONS POST MORTEM.

Inquisition held in Kent, January 20, 1510, first year of Henry VIII, after the death of Thomas Bradbury, citizen and merchant of London, who died January 9, 1510, and William Bradbury aged thirty years and more was his heir. Speaks of and describes his lands in Chatham and his manors in West coats and Gillingham, in Kent. Also lands in Essex and Hertfordshire. Mentions his brother George Bradbury of London, merchant.

Inquisition held in Hertfordshire, Nov. 11, 1510, second year of Henry VIII, after the death of Thomas Bradbury, who died Jan. 9, 1510 preceding, and his nephew William Bradbury, son of his brother Robert, deceased, was his heir. Manor of Horbury and lands in Cherfield, London and Kelshall, in Herts.

Inquisition held in Bentwood, county Essex, after the death of Thomas Bradbury, nephew and heir, William, son of brother Robert Bradbury. Mentions Thomas and Joan, children of John and Philippa Joselyn, Humphrey, son of William, and Elizabeth Tyrell and George Bowman.

Inquisition held in Chelmsford, county Essex, June 10, 1530, after the death of Joan Bradbury, relict of Thomas Bradbury, late of the city of London, merchant. She died May 11, 1529, at Coleman street, London. Mentions her daughter, wife of Thomas Crofford, and their daughter Joan; daughter of Elizabeth, wife of William Tyrell, and their son Humphrey. No Bradburys are named in the inquisition.

Inquisition in Ware, county Herts, Oct. 25, 1550, the fourth year of Edward VI, after the death of William Bradbury, Esq., who died August 26, previous, and his son Robert, aged twelve years, was his heir.

Inquisition in Stratford Langthorne, county Essex, April 30, 1577, the nineteenth year of Elizabeth, after the death of Robert Bradbury, who lived at Ramesden and died on the eleventh of the preceding January. Mentions his wife, brothers Thomas and

Henry, James Tremill, his sister's son, and godson Robert Fulnetby.

Inquisition at same place as last, Oct. 29, 1587, twenty-ninth year of the reign of Elizabeth, after the death of Matthew Bradbury, who died at Wicken, June 19, 1585, and William Bradbury, aged forty-one at the time of his father's death, was his son and heir. Ann, wife of said William, is mentioned. Manor of Wicken Hall alias Wicken Bonant.

Inquisition held at Stratford Langthorne, April 29, 1597, thirty-ninth year of Elizabeth, after the death of Henry Bradbury of Littlebury, county Essex, whose son and heir was William Bradbury, aged twenty-one years and six months. Wife Marian and eldest brother Robert mentioned; also John Daniell and his wife Margaret. Manors of Missenden, Catmerehall, Langley Hall and Wimblshe.

Inquisition at Chelmsford, county Essex, April 21, 1615, thirteenth year of James I, after the death of William Bradbury, whose son Henry, aged seventeen, was his heir. Wife Marian. Extract from the will of his father Henry; mentions Langley Hall.

Inquisition at Stratford Langthorne, Oct. 30, 1611, ninth of James I, after the death of Robert Bradbury, Gent, who died Sept. 30, preceding, and Martha Bradbury, one of his daughters, was at that time five years, eight months and thirty days old. He was seized before and at the time of his death of the lordship of Cheswick Hall, and had lands in Chresthall, Elmden and Loftes in Essex.

Inquisition held Nov. 9, 1624, twenty-second of James I, after the death of John Bradbury, who died August 1, preceding, and his posthumous son and heir, Matthew, was born Aug. 7, 1624. Wife Mary, brother Francis Bradbury, and mother Jane Bradbury.

Inquisition at Barking, county Essex, Dec. 14, 1624, twenty-second of James I, after the death of Matthew Bradbury of Wicken, county Essex, Gent, who was the son and heir apparent of William Bradbury, lord of the manor of Wicken, alias Wicken Hall, alias Wicken Bonhunte.   John Bradbury, aged twenty-four, son and heir of Matthew; Jane, wife of Matthew, and Anne, wife of said William.   Mentions Henry Bradbury of Littlebury, and William Whitgift.

Inquisition at Stratford Langthorne, Oct. 31, 1645, twenty-first of Charles I, after the death of Matthew Bradbury, who died Sept. 23, preceding, without issue.   He was the son and heir of John Bradbury, Esq., whose inquisition is dated Nov. 9, 1624. Mary, wife of said John Bradbury, married, secondly, Charles Millicent, Esq., and died in November, 1628.   Francis Bradbury, brother of said John, by wife Bridget, had a son Francis who, his father having deceased, became heir to his cousin Matthew, aforesaid, and at this time was eight months, three weeks and four days old.   Mentions the manor of Wicken.

Inquisition at Deptford, county Kent, June 8, 1603, after the death of Thomas Bradbury, Gent.   Lands in Shoppy, etc.   Manor house in Milton.

Inquisition at Bakewell, county Derby, May 27, 1616, eighth of James I, after the death of Nicholas Bradbury of Ollersett, Gent, who died at Ollersett, April 12, 1614, and Edmond Bradbury, his son and heir, was then thirty-four years old.

Inquisition held at Cannock, county Strafford, April 3, 1637, after the death of Ralph Bradbury, son of John and Anne Bradbury.   He died September 3, 1636, twelfth of Charles I, and his daughter Elizabeth, aged eight years and six months, was his heir. He had lands in East Greenwich, county Kent, and in Cheadleton, county Stafford.

Inquisition held at Stratford Hawthorne, county Essex, after the death of Matthew Bradbury, Oct. 26, 1587, twenty-ninth of

Elizabeth. He died at Wicken Bonant, June 19, 1585. William Bradbury is his son and heir, aged forty-one at the time of his father's death. Anne was wife of William. Speaks of the manor Wicken, alias Wicken Hall, alias Wycken Bonant. The document was written in Latin, as all such were.

WILL OF WILLIAM BRADBURY,

OF WICKEN BONANT.

In the name of God amen, the nyenth daye of Aprill in the yeres of the Raigne of our Soveraigne Lord Jeames by the grace of god of Ingland Scotland Fraunce and Ireland Kinge, defender of the fayth etc. That ys to saye of Ingland Fraynce and Ireland the twentieth & of Scotland the fyve and fyftieth. I Wm Bradburie of Wicken Bonant in the countie of Essex Esquire beinge of good and pfect Remembrance lawd and prayse be gyven to allmyghtie god do ordeyne & make this my last will and testament in wryting as followeth. Fyrst I bequeath my soule into the hands of allmighty god my creator and maker hopinge of salvation by the death & passion of his sonne my lord & savior Jesus Christ & my bodie I will to be in Christien buriall according to the descretion of my executor hereafter named & appointed. And as towiching the disposition of all & singular my goods and chattells as well moveable as immoveable whatsoever I gyve and dispose to my well beloved sonne Wimond Bradburie whome I make ordeyne constitute and appoint executor of this my last will & testament.

In testimony whereof I have hereunto sett my hand seale the day and yeare abovesaid.

WILLIAM BRADBURY.

Sealed and delyvered
  in the p'sens of us
   John Barlee
   Thomas Chesshiere.

Proved May 6, 1623.

This closes our brief and somewhat fragmentary account of the Bradbury family of England. Much of it is irrelevant to the line of Thomas, the emigrant, but it is not without interest as showing the standing of the family in England several centuries ago. The Bradburys, or many of them, were large land owners, and consequently men of influence and standing in both church and state. The lord mayor, who had been a distinguished London merchant and was possessed of great wealth, was a devoted Catholic, as were all the chief men and women of England at that date. Some of the provisions of his will, which appear ridiculous in the light of the nineteenth century, were in perfect keeping with the superstitions of the age in which he lived. The wording and provisions of the will of William Bradbury, father of Wymond, executed little more than a century later, are in strong contrast with those expressed in the will of Sir Thomas, and go to emphasize the great changes in religious sentiment which a hundred years had wrought. The wording in William Bradbury's will is quite similar to that in the will of his grandson Thomas, which was probated in Salem, Essex County, Mass., near the close of the same century.

The compiler desires not to be held responsible for errors in dates or for other discrepancies which may be found in the foregoing extracts from English archives. Doubtless there are errors in the original records, and others may have been made in copying. In the will of Sir Thomas Bradbury, and in other an-

cient documents, care has been taken to follow the
original orthography, which somewhat obscures the
meaning to the modern reader, unacquainted with ancient forms of expression and ancient modes of spelling.
The compiler will only add that these documents are
printed in the manner and form in which they came
into his hands.

We are now ready to take up the lines of which
Thomas Bradbury, the early settler in Salisbury, Mass.,
is the head, and in order that his English descent
may be clearly understood, it is epitomized below as
follows :—

ROBERT[1],   of Ollersett, county of Derby.
WILLIAM[2],   of Braughing, county of Hertfordshire.
ROBERT[3],   of Littlebury, county of Essex.
WILLIAM[4],   of Littlebury, county of Essex.
MATTHEW[5], of Wicken Bonant, county of Essex.
WILLIAM[6],   of Wicken Bonant, county of Essex.
WYMOND[7],   of the "Brick House," Wicken Bonant.
THOMAS[8],   of Salisbury, Mass.

BRADBURY MEMORIAL

THOMAS BRADBURY OF SALISBURY, MASS.

AND

SOME OF HIS DESCENDANTS

DECENDANTS OF THOMAS BRADBURY.

FIRST GENERATION.

THOMAS[1] BRADBURY, (THOMAS[8] in the English pedigree), second son of Wymond and Elizabeth (Gill *nee* Whitgift) Bradbury, was baptized at Wicken-Bonant, Essex County, England, on the last day of February, 1610-11, as appears by the parish register. Early in 1634 he appeared at Agamenticus, now York, Me., as the agent or steward of Sir Ferdinando Gorges, the proprietor of the Province of Maine. He was one of the original proprietors of the ancient town of Salisbury, Mass., one of the earliest settlers there, and was one of the foremost citizens there for a period of more than half a century. He was made a freeman in 1640, held at various times the offices of schoolmaster of the town, town clerk, justice of the peace, deputy to the general court, county recorder, associate judge and captain of the military company, and always filled these important positions with credit to himself and satisfaction to the public. For a recording officer he was peculiarly fitted by his tastes and acquirements. He wrote an easy, graceful and legible hand, and had a clear and concise style of expression. His chirography may still be seen in numerous official documents on file in the archives of Essex County, Mass., and also at Exeter, N. H. In 1636. Mr. Bradbury became a grantee of Salisbury, and that year married Mary, daughter of John and Judith Perkins. of Ipswich.* In the days of the witchcraft delusion. she was tried as a witch and convicted. but escaped punishment. Mr. Bradbury died March 16. 1695. and his widow died Dec. 20. 1700.

THOMAS BRADBURY'S WILL.

In the name of God, amen. The fourteenth day of February, in the year of our Lord one thousand six hundred and ninety-four. I Thomas Bradbury of the town of Salisbury in the Province of the Massachusetts Bay in New England, aged, weak in body, but of good and perfect memory, thanks be to God Almighty for the same, do make, ordain, constitute and declare this my last will and testament in manner and form following: revoking and annulling by these presents, all and every testament or testaments, will or wills heretofore by me made and declared either by word or by writing, and this to be taken only for my last will and testament and none other: And being penitent for my sins, I

---

*Mary Perkins was the daughter of John Perkins, the elder, of Ipswich, who was born in Gloucestershire, England, in 1590, embarked with his family at Bristol, England. in the ship Lyon, Capt. Wm. Pearce, master, and after a very tempestuous voyage arrived in Boston, Feb. 5, 1631. Roger Williams was a fellow-passenger. Mr. Perkins was admitted freeman, May 18, 1631, remained in Boston two years, and then removed to Ipswich. He was representative to the General Court in 1636, held various town offices, and was a man of respectability. He owned a large island at the mouth of Ipswich river, which was known as Perkins' Island. He died previous to 1655, at the age of 64 years. By wife Judith he had six children, viz.: John[2] m. Elizabeth ——, Thomas[2] m. Phebe Gould, Elizabeth[2] m. William Sargent, Mary[2] m. Thomas Bradbury, Lydia[2] m. —— Bennet, and Jacob, b. 1624. m. Elizabeth, who died in Ipswich, Feb. 12, 1685. John Perkins has a numerous posterity.

give and commit my soul unto Almighty God my Saviour and my
redeemer in whom by the merits of Jesus Christ I trust and
believe it assuredly to be saved; and my body to be buried in
such place where it shall please my executors to appoint: And
for the settling of my temporal estate, such goods, chattels and
debts as it hath pleased God far above my deserts to bestow upon
me, I do order, give and dispose the same in manner and form
following, that is to say: first, I will that all those debts and
duties that I owe in right and conscience to any manner of person or persons in favor, shall be well and truly contented and
paid or ordained to be paid within convenient time after my
decease. So by my executor or executrixes hereafter named,

Item. I give and bequeath unto my grandchildren, Thomas
Bradbury and Jacob Bradbury, all my housing and lands which I
have now situate, lying and being within the bounds of Salisbury
aforenamed and which arable lands and meadow marsh, pasture
and swamp lands, or of what sort soever they be, with all rights
privileges and commonages thereunto belonging or any ways
appertaining; unto them my said grandchildren and the heirs of
their body lawfully begotten; the given and bequeathed and
demised to be equally divided between my said grandchildren
Thomas and Jacob, and not to be disposed by selling, letting or
any other ways improved, but each to other, and my said grandchildren shall pay unto their Aunt True fourteen pounds, each of
them in good pay within one year after they come to the age of
one and twenty years. As also my said grandchildren shall acquit
and discharge their brother, William Bradbury from all orders of
court concerning the division of their father's estate; also my
will is that my said grandchildren Thomas and Jacob shall pay
unto their grandmother, twenty bushels of corn yearly, such as
she shall have need of during her natural life and to find her
sufficient wood, winter and summer cut and fit; as also winter
and summer meat for two cows, all during her natural life or
widowhood: and my will is that my wife what part of my house
she thinks meet to require unto the half of it, shall have during
her widowhood or natural life, unto her own particular use if she

thinks good to require the same. *Item.* I give and bequeath unto my grandchild Thomas Bradbury all my implements of husbandry and also my young colt. *Item.* I give and bequeath unto my daughter Mary Stanyan twenty shillings she having had her portion upon her marriage. *Item.* I give and bequeath unto my daughter Jane True ten pounds to be made in good pay within one year after my decease. *Item.* I give to my grandchild Elizabeth Buss five pounds in good pay. Also my will is that five pounds be delivered to the selectmen in good pay, then in being of said town of Salisbury by them to be disposed to such of the poor as they judge to have most need of it. And lastly, I do ordain and appoint my dearly and well beloved wife, Mary Bradbury and my dearly and well beloved daughter Judith Moody my executors or executrixes to this my last will and testament.

In witness whereof I have hereunto set my hand and seal the day and year above named.

Tho: Bradbury   Seal.

Signed sealed and declared to be the last
  will and testament of Mr. Thomas
  Bradbury in ye presence of
    WILLIAM BUSWELL,
    ISAAC BUSWELL,
    WILLIAM BUSWELL, JR.

Mr. Bradbury was appointed first clerk of the writs in Salisbury in 1641. In 1651, he was chosen a deputy to the General Court, and again successively in 1652, 1656, 1657, 1660, 1661 and 1666. In 1654, 1656 and 1658, and 1659, he was appointed on various committees to settle differences concerning lands, to fix boundaries and locate grants. As agent for Gorges, he executed some of the earliest deeds recorded in the York County records. An indenture made the 5th day of

May, 1636, reads as follows: "Thomas Bradbury, Gent., now agent of Sir Ferdinando Gorges, Knight, confirmed unto Edward Johnson for the proper use of John Treworgy of Dartmouth, merchant, the use of five hundred acres of land, conditioned to pay annually one hundred of merchantable cod dried and well conditioned, as an acknowledgement of the royalty of Sir Ferdinando Gorges, Knight, to Sir Ferdinando Gorges or his assigns, at or upon the Feast of Saint Michaels, the Arch High Angel." This sufficiently establishes the fact that Mr. Bradbury was the recognized agent of the proprietor of the Province of Maine, granted together with New Hampshire, by royal patent in 1622, to Gorges and Mason, and taken as his portion by Gorges, in 1629.

During the trial of Mrs. Bradbury, July 28, 1692, upon the charge of being a witch, her aged and devoted husband bore testimony to her high character and the purity of her life in the following terms : "Concerning my beloved wife, Mary Bradbury, this is what I have to say : We have been married fifty-five years, and she hath been a loving and faithful wife unto me unto this day. She hath been wonderful laborious, diligent and industrious in her place and employment about the bringing up of our family which have been eleven children of our own, and four grandchildren. She was both prudent and provident, of a cheerful spirit, liberal and charitable. She being now very aged and weak, and grieved under afflictions, may not be able to speak much for herself, not being so free of speech as some others might be. I hope her life and conversation among her neighbors has been such as gives a better or more real testimony than can be expressed by words."

One hundred and eighteen of Mrs. Bradbury's acquaintances, consisting of both men and women, gave evidence as follows: "We the subscribers do testify that it (her life) was such as becomes the gospel. She was a lover of the ministry in all appearance, and a diligent attender upon God's holy ordinances, being of a courteous and peaceable disposition and carriage, neither did any of us (some of whom have lived in the town with her above fifty years), ever hear or know that she had any difference or falling out with any of her neighbors, man, woman or child, but was always ready and willing to do for them what lay in her power, night and day, though with hazard of her health and other danger. More might be spoken in her commendation, but this for the present."

To the charge of witchcraft, Mrs. Bradbury pleaded not guilty, and this is what she said in her own behalf: "I am wholly innocent of any such wickedness through the goodness of God who has kept me hitherto. I am the servant of Jesus Christ and have given myself up to him as my only Lord and Saviour, and to the dilligent attendance upon him in all his holy ordinances, in utter contempt and defiance of the devil and all his works as horrid and detestable, and have accordingly endeavored to frame my life and conversation according to the rules of His holy word, and in that faith and practice, resolve by the help and assistance of God to continue to my life's end. For the truth of what I say, I humbly refer myself to my brethren and neighbors that know me, and unto the searcher of all hearts for the truth and uprightness of my heart therein (human frailties and unavoidable excepted), of which I bitterly complain every day."

Rev. James Allen testified as follows: "I, having lived nine years at Salisbury in the work of the ministry, and now four years in the office of pastor, to my best notice and observation of Mrs. Bradbury, she hath lived according to the rules of the gospel amongst us; was a constant attender upon the ministry of the word, and all the ordinances of the gospel; full of works of charity and mercy to the sick and poor; neither have I seen or heard anything of her unbecoming the profession of the gospel."

Upham, the historian of the Salem witchcraft, says of Mrs. Bradbury: "The position as well as character and age of Mary (Perkins) Bradbury, entitled her to the highest consideration in the structure of society at the time. This is recognized in the title 'Mrs.' uniformly given her. She had been noted through life for energy, business capacity, and influence; her husband Thomas Bradbury had been a prominent character in the colony for more than fifty years."

The character of the evidence used against Mrs. Bradbury may be judged by the following: "The deposition of William Carr, who testifieth and saith that, about thirteen years ago, presently after some

5

difference that happened to be between my honored
father, Mr. George Carr, and Mrs. Bradbury, the prisoner at the bar, upon a Sabbath at noon, as we were
riding home by the house of Capt. Thomas Bradbury,
I saw Mrs. Bradbury go into her gate, turn the corner
of, and immediately there darted out of her gate a
blue boar, and darted at my father's horse's legs which
made him stumble; but I saw it no more. And my
father said, 'Boys, what did you see?' And we both
said, 'A blue boar.'"

This venerable woman was about eighty years of
age when she was arrested for the crime of bewitching
John Carr so that he became crazed and prematurely
died. The testimony of William Carr at the trial,
went to show that his brother fell in love with Jemima
True, but the proposed match being opposed and
broken off by the father of young Carr, on account of
his youth, he became melancholy and at times insane.
He further stated that he was with his brother and
cared for him in his last sickness, and that his brother
died peaceably and quietly, and never spoke anything
to the harm of Mrs. Bradbury or anybody else. Mrs.
Bradbury was defended by Major Robert Pike. She
was convicted with four others who were executed
September, 1692. Mrs. Bradbury escaped punishment,
but by what means, does not appear.*

*The Salem witchcraft craze was one of the most remarkable delusions
on record. It affected all classes of the community, and was a sad com-
mentary on the intelligence of the period as well as a plague spot upon
the ermine of the judiciary. It broke out in the year 1692, and within
the space of about three months nineteen persons, including **Rev. George**

SECOND GENERATION.

The children of Thomas[1] and Mary Bradbury, all except the eldest born in Salisbury, were as follows:—

2   i   Wymond[2], b. Apr. 1, 1637, m. May 7, 1661, Sarah Pike.

3   ii   Judith[2], b. October 2, 1638, m. Oct. 9, 1665, Caleb Moody* of Newbury.

4   iii   Thomas[2], b. Jan. 28, 1641; he was living in 1662, but probably died unmarried.

5   iv   Mary[2], b. March 17, 1643, m. Dec. 17, 1663, John Stanyan of Hampton, N. H.

6   v   Jane[2], b. May 11, 1645, m. March 15, 1668, Henry True.

7   vi   Jacob[2], b. June 17, 1647, d. at Barbadoes, unmarried.

8   vii   William[2], b. Sept. 15, 1649, m. March 12, 1672, Rebecca Maverick *nee* Wheelwright.

Burroughs, formerly minister at Casco Bay, and later of Salem Village, were tried, convicted on the most ridiculous testimony, and executed on "Gallows Hill," in Salem. The principal charge against Mr. Burroughs was his great physical strength. The great Cotton Mather was present on horseback and consented to his death, and while he was suspended in mid-air, the great divine harrangued the people and congratulated them on the good work accomplished. It was pre-eminently a reign of terror. No one felt safe. The most eminent citizens of Essex County, noted for intelligence and lifelong piety, were arrested and dragged to prison, tried and condemned on the most unreliable evidence, and executed in the most brutal manner. Finally the imprisonments, torturings and executions rose to such a height as to be no longer endurable, and a sudden revulsion of feeling put a stop to the whole infamous business. There was no execution after September 22, and a general jail delivery of all the accused took place the May following. It seems strange that Gov. Phips should permit the persecution to proceed as far as it did. He alone had the power to nip the miserable business in the bud, but he showed no disposition to interfere to stay the judicial slaughter of innocents, until the bubble burst by its own tension.

*Caleb Moody, son of William, the emigrant who settled at Newbury, married first, Sara Pierce, and had issue. She died August 25, 1665, and he married Judith Bradbury, Nov. 9, 1665. The children by this marriage were Caleb, b. Sept. 9, 1666; Thomas, b. Oct. 20, 1668; Judith, b. Sept 23, 1669, and died at Salisbury, January 28, 1679; Joshua, b. Nov. 3,

9   viii   Elizabeth[2], b. Nov. 7, 1651, m. May 12, 1673, **John Buss*** of Durham, N. H.

10   ix   John[2], b. April 20, 1654, d. unmarried, Nov. 24, 1678.

11   x   Ann[2], b. April 16, 1656, d. 1659.

12   xi   Jabez[2],b. June 27, 1658, d. April 28, 1677.

THIRD GENERATION.

WYMOND[2] BRADBURY (THOMAS[1]) married Sarah, daughter of Robert and Sarah (Sanders) Pike†, May 7, 1661. He died April 7. 1669, on the Island of Nevis, in the West Indies. This is stated in a record made

1671; William, b. Dec. 15, 1673; Samuel, b. Jan. 4, 1676; he graduated at Harvard College, 1697, was ordained at York. Dec. 20, 1700, and died there Nov. 13, 1747; Mary, b. Oct. 23, 1678, and Judith, b. Feb. 12, 1683. Caleb Moody, senior, died Aug. 25, 1698, and his widow died January 24, 1700. Caleb Moody, junior, married Ruth Morse by whom he had eight children. His fifth child, Eleanor, b. October 17, 1700, married James Bridges of Andover, whose son Moody Bridges, married Naamah Frye, and was the father of Sarah Bridges, who married John Dean who was the father of Charles Dean who married Patience Tappan Kingsbury, and who was the father of John Ward Dean, A. M., the eminent historian and editor of the New England Geneological Register. Moody Bridges also had a daughter Sarah Naamah Bridges, born Sept. 7, 1748, who married Jedediah Jewett of Exeter, N. H., and Pittston, Me., whose daughter, Martha Jewett, married James North, and was the mother of James William North, author of the History of Augusta.

*Rev. John Buss was the minister at Oyster River, now Durham, N. H. In 1694, his house was burned by the Indians and many valuable records destroyed. John Buss died in 1737 at a very advanced age. Elizabeth Buss, daughter of Rev. John and Elizabeth (Bradbury) Buss, married James Smith, who was the ancestor of Col. Thomas Westbrook Smith of Augusta, Me., whose daughter, Eliza Ann, became the wife of Hon. James W. Bradbury.

†Robert Pike was one of the most remarkable men of the period in which he lived. Born in England in 1616, he came to Salem, Mass., with his father's family when nineteen years of age. He was one of the founders of Salisbury, Mass., and resided there from 1639 to the time of

by his father and now in Essex County archives, in Salem, Mass. Sarah, widow of Wymond Bradbury, married, second, John Stockman, who died December 10, 1686, and by him she had five children. The children of Wymond and Sarah Bradbury were :—

13 i Sarah³, b. Feb. 26, 1662, m. Abraham Merrill.
14 ii Ann³, b. Nov. 22, 1666, m. Jeremy Allen.
15 iii Wymond³, b. May 13, 1669, m. Mariah Cotton.

his death in 1707, aged 91 years. He married Sarah Sanders and had a family of eight children, one of whom was Rev. John Pike, minister in Dover. His biographer says of Robert Pike that he was engaged in three conspicuous controversies during his life. The first was his arraignment by the General Court in 1653, for his hostility to the persecution of the Quakers. The second was his resistance to the dogmatic authority of the clergy, in the person of his pastor, Rev. John Wheelwright. The third was his bitter opposition to the witchcraft prosecutions in 1692. In all of these controversies, Mr. Pike stood practically alone. He was a century in advance of his time, and a century more than vindicated his advanced positions. The historian of the Salem witchcraft delusion says that "not a voice comes down to us of deliberate and effective hostility to the movement, except that of Robert Pike in his cool, close and powerful argumentative appeal to the judges who were trying the witchcraft cases. It stands out against the deep blackness of those proceedings like a pillar of light upon a starless midnight sky." Confronting the judges stood this sturdy old man, his head whitened with the frosts of seventy-six winters, and demonstrated that there was no legal way of convicting a witch, even according to the laws and beliefs of those times. It required no small amount of courage for him to take the stand he did against the opinions of the highest judicial tribunal in the province, when no one was considered safe from the charge of having dealings with the evil one, and he himself might be the next one arraigned. But having the courage of his convictions he rose to the demands of the situation and proclaimed his opposition by a formal and thorough exposition. The great merit of this position, so far as it has come down to us, belongs solely to him, and no man of his century is entitled to greater honor. He was a leading man in Salisbury, often associated with Thomas Bradbury on committees and commissions for the transaction of public business. At the age of thirty-two he was chosen a

8

WILLIAM[2] BRADBURY (Thomas[1]), married Rebecca, widow of Samuel Maverick, jr., and daughter of Rev. John Wheelwright. Her first husband died at Boston, March 10, 1664. Samuel Maverick, jr., was the son of the king's commissioner; Rev. John Wheelwright was the founder of Exeter. N. H., and his wife Mary was daughter of Edward Hutchinson, and grand- daughter of John Hutchinson, mayor of ~~London,~~ Lincoln England. William Bradbury died Dec. 4, 1678, and his widow died Dec. 20, 1678. Their children were brought up by their grandparents, and two of them are mentioned in his will.

Children :

16   i   William[3], b. Oct. 16, 1672 ; m. Sarah Cotton.
17   ii   Thomas[3], b. Dec. 24, 1674 ; m. Jemima True.*
18 iii   Jacob[3], b. Sept. 1, 1677 ; m. Elizabeth Stockman.

member of the General Court, and had a much longer service in that capacity and as councilor and assistant, than any of his contemporaries. He was well educated, wrote a fine, flowing hand, apparently with great facility, and was an eloquent and forcible speaker. He defended Mrs. Mary Bradbury on her trial for witchcraft, but all eloquence and argument were lost upon the infatuated judges and jury. It is a marvel how Mr. Pike breasted the storm, when any resistence to the popular demand was deemed evidence of complicity with witches, imps and all the powers of darkness, to overthrow the true church on earth. He also plead the cause of Susanna Martin, whose memory is perpetuated by the poet Whittier, and of several others of the accused, and his opposition to the infamous proceedings and rulings of the court, and the insane demands of the people, appear to have caused no charge to be made against him.

*She was the daughter of Henry[2], jr., and Jane (Bradbury) True, and cousin to her husband. Henry True[1], the ancestor of the New England family of this name, was of Salem, Mass., in 1644, and according to the record (though the name is an unusual one for a female), he married

FOURTH GENERATION.

15

Wymond[3] Bradbury (Wymond[2], Thomas[1]), married Mariah, daughter of Rev. John, jr., and Joanna (Rosseter) Cotton.* who was born January 14, 1672. Her father was the son of Rev. John and Sarah (Story) Cotton, and her mother the daughter of Dr. Bryan Rosseter† of Guilford, Conn. Wymond Bradbury died

Israel, daughter of John Pike. He removed to Salisbury and was there made a freeman in 1673. Henry[2] True, jr., married Jane, daughter of Thomas Bradbury. He lived at Salisbury and had the following children: i Mary[3], b. May 30, 1668 ; ii William[3], b. June, 1670 ; iii Henry[3], b. Jan. 6, 1674 ; iv Jane[3], b. Dec. 5, 1676 ; v John[3], b. Feb. 23, 1679 ; vi Jemima[3], b. March 16, 1681, m. Thomas[3] Bradbury (17); vii Jabez[3], b. Feb. 19, 1683.

*John Cotton, jr., and Joanna Rosseter were married November 7, 1660. Mrs. Cotton was born in July, 1642. She was a very amiable woman and had uncommon intellectual endowments. Great pains were taken with her education. She had poetic talent, was well versed in the Latin and other languages, and had a "good insight into the medical arts." They had eleven children, as follows: John, b. August 3, 1661 ; Elizabeth, b. August 5, 1663; Sarah, b. June 17, 1665, d. Sept. 8, 1669; Roland, b. at Plymouth. Dec. 27, 1667; Sarah, b. Apr. 5, 1670, m. William Bradbury; Mariah, b. Jan. 14, 1671-72, m. Wymond Bradbury: Josiah, b. Sept. 10, 1675, d. Jan. 9, 1676-77; Samuel, b. Feb. 10, 1677-78, d. Dec 23, 1682; Josiah, b. Jan. 8, 1679-80; Theophilus, b. May 5, 1682.

†Dr. Bryan Rosseter, son of Mr. Edward Rosseter, was a gentleman of liberal education, and early chose the medical profession as his life pursuit. He settled first at Windsor, Conn., but afterward moved to Guilford, when that township was under the government of the New Haven Colony. A letter written by him Sept. 24, 1669, mentions the death of his daughter Sarah, August 9, and her mother, overcome with grief, took no sustenance for ten days, and died August 29. Then the second day of the following week the grand-daughter Sarah died. Dr. Bryan Rosseter died Sept. 30, 1672. "He was a good man, and one that feared God, with his household." Beside Mrs. Cotton, his children were John, Josiah, Sarah, and Susanna who married Zachariah Walker.

in York. Me.. April 17, 1734. His widow married
John Heard of Kittery, and died in that town January
30. 1736.

Children :

19 i   Jabez⁴*, b. Jan. 26, 1693 ; d. Jan. 13, 1781.   He resided
        in Boston and was never married.
20 ii Wymond⁴, b. Aug. 18, 1695 ; m. Phebe Young.
21 iii John⁴, b. Sept. 9, 1697 ; m. Abigail Young³, s. York, Me.
22 iv Rowland⁴, b. Dec. 15, 1699 ; m. Mary Greenleaf.
23 v   Ann⁴, b. March 9, 1702 ; m. 1743, Jabez Fox of Falmouth.
24 vi Josiah⁴, b. July 25, 1704 ; m. Anna Stevens.
25 vii Theophilus⁴, b. July 8, 1706 ; m. Ann Woodman.
26 viii Maria⁴, b. ——, 1708 ; m. Samuel Service of Boston.
27 ix Jerusha⁴, b. July 5, 1711 ; m. John† Pulling of Salem.

*Jabez Bradbury was long in the military service of the Colony, and
was an officer of ability and conspicuous bravery. He was appointed to
command Fort Richmond, situated on the right bank of the Kennebec
river at the head of Swan island, June 13, 1734, and in Sept., 1747, he was
in command of George's Fort near Penobscot. "A party of the enemy
(Indians) appeared at George's Fort in the eastward. Lieut. Kilpatrick,
with twenty-five men, went from the blockhouse to scour the woods and
haul wood to the landing-place. They were soon fired upon by the
Indians. Captain Bradbury hearing the report of the guns, issued from
the fort with a party of his men and engaged them; fought them about
two hours, in which time four men were killed."—(Nile's Indian Wars.)
"In September, 1749, Lieut.-Governor Phips communicated to the Council
a letter from Captain Bradbury who commanded the fort near Penobscot,
informing them that the Indians there were desirous to treat with the
government and be at peace with it."—(Mass. Hist. Soc. Coll., vol. 9, p.
219.)

†John Pulling of Salem, who married Jerusha⁴ Bradbury for his second
wife, had by this marriage one son, Edward Pulling, who graduated from
Harvard College in 1775, and became a distinguished lawyer in Salem.
Edward Pulling had daughter Mary Robinson Pulling, who became the
wife of Dr. Daniel Oliver, and had Fitch Edward Oliver, M.D., of Boston,
and Rev. Andrew Oliver, who graduated from Harvard College in 1842,
and is a Protestant Episcopal clergyman in New York City, and a pro-

16

WILLIAM[3] BRADBURY (William[2], Thomas[1]), married March 16, 1697, Sarah, daughter of Rev. John Cotton, jr., and sister of Mariah Cotton *ante.* She was born April 5, 1670, and died Feb. 21, 1733. He died April 20, 1756. He resided at Salisbury.

Children :

28   i   Samuel[4], } twins, b. March 23, 1698; d. young.
29   ii   Infant[4], }
30   iii   William[4], b. June 30, 1699 ; d. young.
31   iv   John[4], b. June 30, 1699; m. Hannah Greely.
32   v   James[4], b. May 9, 1701 ; m. Elizabeth Sanders.
33   vi   Rebecca[4], b. Jan. 17, 1703.
34   vii   Jacob[4], b. Aug. 21, 1704.
35   viii   Joanna[4], b. June 7, 1706.
36   ix   Mary[4], b. March 18, 1708.
37   x   Sarah[4], b. Jan. 10, 1710.
38   xi   Crisp[4], b. April 21, 1712; m. Mary Paine.
39   xii   Benjamin[4], b. Jan. 24, 1714; m. Jemima True.
40   xiii   Barnabas[4], b. April 14, 1716; m. Miriam Morse.

17

THOMAS[3] BRADBURY (William[2], Thomas[1]), married for his first wife, October 30, 1700, Jemima True, his cousin, who was born March 16, 1681, and died Dec. 5, 1700. For second wife Thomas Bradbury married, October 14, 1702, Mary Hilton, who died June 15, 1723.

fessor in the General Theological Seminary. Among the relics preserved in the family are the mourning ring of Jerusha (Bradbury) Pulling, and a piece of silver ware which belonged to her mother, Mariah (Cotton) Bradbury.

Children :

41   i   Jemima[4], b. January 25, 1704; m. May 22, 1725, William Chandler* of Woodstock, Conn.

42   ii   Child, b. June 11, 1707. There may have been other children not on record.

18

Jacob[3] Bradbury (William[2], Thomas[1]), married Elizabeth Stockman, July 26, 1698, and died May 4, 1718. She was the daughter of Rev. John Stockman and his wife Sarah, daughter of Major Robert Pike and widow of Wymond[2] Bradbury.

Children :

43   i   Thomas[4], b. Aug. 16, 1699; m. 1724, Sarah Merrill.

44   ii   Ann[4], b. Sept. 23, 1701 ; d. Oct. 16, following.

45   iii   Anna[4], b. Sept. 3, 1702; m. 1721, Capt. William True.†

46   iv   Elizabeth[4], b. Feb. 25, 1706 ; d. at Ipswich, Oct. 14, 1723.

47   v   Dorothy[4], b. May 27, 1708 ; m. Rev. Ammi Ruhamah Cutter, first pastor of the church in North Yarmouth.

*It is said that a likeness of the above Thomas[3] Bradbury is in the family of John J. Chetwood of Elizabeth, New Jersey. William Chandler was son of the first Judge John of Worcester, Mass., and was born in 1698, died 1754. Their first child was Rev. Thomas Bradbury Chandler who was rector of St. John's Church, Elizabeth, N. J. He married Jane Emott and had William, who was a captain in the British army; Mary Ricketts; Elizabeth C., m. Gen. Elias B. Dayton; Jane, m. Major Wm. Dayton, one of whose daughters, Margaret, m. John Joseph Chetwood.

† William[4] True, who married Anna[4] Bradbury, was the father of Jonathan[5] True who by wife Anne Stevens had Eleanor[6] True, who married John Sargent, whose son William True[7] Sargent married Hannah B. Mitchell, and had William Mitchell[8] Sargent of Portland, the well-known historical writer. William True[4] who married Anna[4] Bradbury, was a grandson of Henry[2] True who married Jane[2], daughter of Thomas[1] Bradbury. Nathaniel Tuckerman[8] True, A.M., M.D., late of Bethel, the veteran teacher, scientist and historical writer, was the son of John[7] and Mary (Hatch) True, grandson of Jonathan[6] and Mehitable (Worthley) True, great-grandson of Jonathan[5] and Anne (Stevens) True, and great-great-grandson of Capt. William[4] True who married Anna Bradbury. Like Mr. Sargent he was doubly connected with the Bradbury family.

48 vi Jacob⁴, b. Oct. 6, 1710; m. 1733, Abigail Eaton.
49 vii Sarah⁴, b. April 15, 1713; m. June 4, 1730, Elisha Allen.
50 viii Moses⁴, b. Nov. 3, 1715; m. Abigail Fogg, r. North Yarmouth.
51 ix Jane⁴, b. (posthumous), 1718; m. 1737, Barnabas Soule* of North Yarmouth.

FIFTH GENERATION.

20

WYMOND⁴ BRADBURY (Wymond³, Wymond², Thomas¹), married Phebe, daughter of Lieutenant Joseph and Abigail (Donnell) Young of York, who was born January 25, 1702. His wife died and he married second, Mary Donnell who died in Brunswick at the age of ninety-seven years. He moved from York to Brunswick Fort, and a part of his children were born there. He was a boat builder and his house stood near the fort.

*Barnabas⁴ Soule was the fourth in descent from George¹ Soule (Sole Soul, Soal, Sowl), who came to New England in the Mayflower, in the family of Edward Winslow. The descent is George¹, John², Moses³, Barnabas⁴. The latter, born in Duxbury in 1705, came to North Yarmouth about the year 1742. He had previously married Jane, daughter of Jacob and Elizabeth Bradbury. Barnabas Soule and wife were admitted to the church in North Yarmouth in 1742. He had a family of nine children. From his sons John, Cornelius and Barnabas, jr., sprang the famous ship-builders and ship-masters of Freeport, Enos, Henchman, Clement Soule and others. His daughter Mercy Soule was the maternal ancestor of Philip H. and General John Marshall Brown of Portland, and from this branch of the Soule family was Rev. Charles Soule the maternal grandfather of Dr. Charles E. Banks of the United States Navy, a prominent historical writer. Barnabas Soule died April 8, 1780, and his remains were buried in the old North Yarmouth burying-ground.

Children :

By his first marriage :

52   i   Susannah⁵, b. January 26, 1729.
53   ii   Samuel⁵, b. March 26, 1731 ; m. Abigail Sawyer.

By second marriage :

54   iii   Mary⁵, b. Apr. 30, 1734; m. Feb. 15, 1751, Isaac Ilsley, jr.
55   iv   Jacob⁵, b. May 8, 1736; m. Lydia Mitchell.
56   v   Thomas⁵, b. May 8, 1736; m. Hannah Freeman.
57   vi   Elizabeth⁵, b. July 6, 1738.
58   vii   Rebecca⁵, b. ———; m. John Lowther.
59 viii Jemima⁵, b. ———; m. May 26, 1764, John Minot.

21

John⁴ Bradbury (Wymond³, Wymond², Thomas¹), known as the "Elder," married Abigail, daughter of Lieutenant Joseph and Abigail (Donnell) Young of York. He was the founder of the York family of Bradbury, a leading man in town affairs and in the Presbyterian church of which he was elder. At the breaking out of the revolutionary war he warmly espoused the cause of the colonies, and it is said that on one occasion he rebuked his minister in open meeting for disloyal sentiments expressed in his sermon. He died December 3, 1778, and his widow died Sept. 28, 1787. He was several terms a member of the provincial legislature, and of the executive council ten years. He was also judge of probate.

Children :

60   i   Cotton⁵, b. Oct. 8, 1722; m. Ruth Weare* of York.

---

*This name is variously written, Weare, Ware, Wier and Waier. On the records of the town of York it is Weare.

61   ii   Lucy⁵, b. Jan. 18, 1725.
62   iii   Bethulah⁵, b. March 20, 1727 ; m. James Sayward.
63   iv   Mariah⁵, b. April 5, 1729 ; m. —— Simpson.
64   v   Abigail⁵, b. August 12, 1731.
65   vi   Elizabeth⁵, b. January 5, 1734.
66   vii   John⁵, b. Sept. 18, 1736 ; m. Elizabeth Ingraham.
67   viii Joseph⁵, b. Oct. 23, 1740 ; m. Dorothy Clark.
68   ix   Anne⁵, b. June 2, 1743 ; m. —— Moulton.

22

ROWLAND⁴ BRADBURY (Wymond³, Wymond², Thomas¹), married November 15, 1723, Mary Greenleaf. For second wife he married Elizabeth Oliver and removed from York to Falmouth. He was by occupation a calker. He died April 5, 1781.

Children :

By first marriage :
69   i   Jabez⁵, b. Sept. 17, 1724; m. May 16, 1749, Mary Merrill.
By second wife :
70   ii   Oliver⁵, b. Falmouth, Oct. 25, 1732 ; d. 1754.
71   iii   Mary⁵, b. April 5, 1734 ; m. 1st, John Boggs, 2d Stephen
            Hussey.
72   iv   Ann⁵, b. Jan. 3, 1736 ; m. Nov. 3, 1758, John Kirk-
            patrick.*
73   v   Abigail⁵, b. April 9, 1738 ; m. Watson Crosby.
74   vi   Maria⁵, b. —— ; m. July 2, 1764, William Pearson.
75   vii   Elizabeth⁵, b. —— ; m. —— Baker.
76   viii Jerusha⁵, b. —— ; m. July 17, 1764, John Rand.
77   ix   Wymond⁵, b. —— ; m. Feb. 27, 1766, Mary Butman.
78   x   Rowland⁵, b. —— ; d. unmarried in England.

*John Kirkpatrick, born 1734, came with the Scottish colony in 1753 and settled in Warren. (Some of the family have changed the name to Kirk.) He married Ann Bradbury and had the following children: Elizabeth, b. 1759, d. April 13, 1812; Ann, b. 1761, m. Thomas Starrett, d. August 15,

24

JOSIAH[4] BRADBURY (Wymond[3], Wymond[2], Thomas[1]), married March 6, 1738, Anna Stevens who was born January 22, 1714. His children were born in Gloucester, Mass. He was living in 1773, and his wife ten years later.

Children :

79   i   Josiah[5], b. Feb. 16, 1739; m. Catherine Larkin.
80   ii   Anna[5], b. Feb. 21, 1742.
81   iii Maria[5], b. Aug. 29, 1744.

25

THEOPHILUS[4] BRADBURY (Wymond[3], Wymond[2], Thomas[1]), married August 4, 1730, Ann Woodman, who was born July 23, 1708. He died Feb. 3, 1764, and his first wife died July 12, 1743. For second wife, he married March 28, 1744, Judith Moody. There was no issue by this marriage. He resided in Newbury, Mass., and was a prominent man.

Children :

82   i   Ann[5], b. May 8, 1731 ; m. May 17, 1749, Samuel Greenleaf.
83   ii   Jonathan[5], b. Nov. 1, 1732; m. Abigail Smith.
84   iii Theophilus[5], b. Jan. 7, 1735; d. in infancy.

1832; William, b. ——, m. Elizabeth Libbey, d. Aug. 27, 1802; Capt. Rowland, b. 1764, lost at sea 1801; Thomas, b. March 3, 1767, m. Margaret Starrett, d. Nov. 13, 1858; Mary, b. 1769, d. Sept. 19, 1845; Daniel, b.——, m. a Prescott and moved to Ohio; Jabez, b. · ——, lost at sea; Abigail B., b. 1775, m. Parker Coburn, d. March 5, 1860; James, b. ——, m. a Williams, s. Long Island, Me. John Kirkpatrick died in June, 1785; his widow died January 19, 1817, aged eighty-two. They have a numerous posterity in Warren and the surrounding towns.

85 iv Wymond[5], b. April 5, 1737 ; m. Judith Moody.
86 v Theophilus[5], b. Nov. 13, 1739 ; m. Sarah Jones. He was
    Judge Bradbury of the Massachusetts Supreme Court.

31

JOHN[4] BRADBURY (William[3], William[2], Thomas[1]), married February 13, 1724, Hannah Greeley.

Children :

87 i   Rowland[5], b. Jan. 15, 1725 ; m. Mary Stevens.
88 ii   Martha[5], b. Feb. 3, 1727.
89 iii Sarah[5], b. June 21, 1730.
90 iv   Jemima[5], b. Feb. 4, 1735 ; m. Dec. 1, 1754, Nathan Sargent of Amesbury.

32

JAMES[4] BRADBURY (William[3], William[2], Thomas[1]), married June 16, 1726, Elizabeth Sanders.

Children :

91   i   James[5], b. Nov. 30, 1727 ; d. Dec. 31 following.
92   ii   Ruth[5], b. March 17, 1729.
93   iii Elizabeth[5], b. Aug. 14, 1731 ; d. Nov. 15, 1736.
94   iv   Samuel[5], b. Sept. 23, 1733 ; m. Judith Morse.
95   v   Sarah[5], b. Jan. 4, 1736 ; d. Nov. 25 following.
96   vi   Sanders[5], b. Nov. 29, 1737 ; m. Sarah Colby.
97   vii Elizabeth[5], b. Sept. 23, 1741.
98   viii Sarah[5], b. April 2, 1744.
99   ix   Ebenezer[5], b. Aug. 3, 1747 ; d. March 6, 1748.

33

CRISP[4] BRADBURY (William[3], William[2], Thomas[1]), married December 22, 1737, Mary Paine. He lived in York, then moved to Biddeford and thence to Newbury,

Mass. He was a carpenter. and dealt largely in real estate. He died in 1753.

Children :

100	i	John[5], b Oct. 11, 1738 ; m. Mary Riggs.
101	ii	Mary[5], b. Aug. 16, 1740 ; m. Nov. 17, 1757, Sam'l Noyes.
102	iii	Elizabeth[5], b. Jan. 5, 1742 ; m. Oct. 28, 1762, Samuel Nelson.
103	iv	Sarah[5], b. Feb. 10, 1744.
104	v	Ruth[5], b. ——, 1748 ; d. March 15, 1801.
105	vi	James[5], b. Sept. 9, 1749 ; m. Eunice Stone.
106	vii	Hannah[5], b. Oct. 22, 1750.

39

BENJAMIN[4] BRADBURY (William[3]. William[2], Thomas[1]), married February 10, 1749, Jemima True, who was born June 20, 1720.

Children :

107	i	Sarah[5], b. May 22, 1750; m. March 12, 1779, Nathaniel Osgood.
108	ii	Jabez[5], b. Oct. 29, 1752.
109	iii	Elizabeth[5], b. Feb. 20, 1755 ; m. Aug. 7, 1773, Anthony Kelley.
110	iv	William[5], b. June 3, 1757 : m. Hannah Tufts.
111	v	Rebecca[5], b. March 19, 1760 ; m. William Haskell.

40

BARNABAS[4] BRADBURY (William[3], William[2], Thomas[1]), married January 26, 1743, Miriam Morss. He lived in Amesbury. Mass., and his children were born there.

Children :

112 i William⁵, b. August 22, 1744.
113 ii Jacob⁵, b. March 17, 1750.
114 iii Miriam⁵, b. April 10, 1758.
115 iv Sarah⁵, b.
116 v Elizabeth⁵, b.
117 vi Mary⁵, b.

43

THOMAS⁴ BRADBURY (Jacob³, William², Thomas¹), married Sarah Merrill of Salisbury, April 16, 1724. He moved to Biddeford in 1744. He was known as Captain Bradbury, and had command of the blockhouse in 1748 and 1749. He was much in the military service during the Indian wars, and after they were over he moved to what is now Buxton, where he died about the year 1775.

Children :

118 i Samuel⁵, b. Oct. 16, 1724; d. Jan. 6, 1730.
119 ii Elizabeth⁵, b. April 13, 1727; m. Samuel Merrill.
120 iii Jacob⁵, b. ——, 1729; m. Abigail Cole.
121 iv Moses⁵, b. Feb. 14, 1731; m. Mary Page.
122 v Samuel⁵, b. Oct. 14, 1733; d. young.
123 vi Thomas⁵, b. Jan. 10, 1736; m. Ruth Page.
124 vii William⁵, b. May 5, 1738; m. Susannah Hopkinson.
125 viii Sarah⁵, b. Dec. 10, 1739; m. Joseph Leavitt.
126 ix Benjamin⁵, b. March 2, 1744; m. Mary Elden.
127 x Mary⁵, b. ——; m. Nov. 5, 1767, Samuel Sands.
128 xi Mercy⁵, b. Jan. 29, 1746; m. Sept. 12, 1771, John Appleton.
129 xii Jabez⁵, b. April 22, 1749; d. May 10 following.

6

48

JACOB[4] BRADBURY (Jacob[3], William[2], Thomas[1]), married December 18, 1733, Abigail Eaton. He moved from Biddeford to Buxton, where he died in 1797.

Children:

130   i   Joseph[5], b. March 2, 1735; d. Oct. 19, 1736.

131   ii   Moses[5], b. Sept. 22, 1736. Taken prisoner at Fort William Henry in August, 1757.

132   iii   Jacob[5], b. April 10, 1738; d. next day.

133   iv   Elizabeth[5], b. Mar. 18, 1739; m. Sept. 17, 1764, Stephen Palmer.

134   v   Abigail[5], b. July 15, 1741; m. May 5, 1762, Daniel Leavitt.

135   vi   Jacob[5], b. Oct. 30, 1743; m. Mary Goodwin.

136   vii   Hannah[5], bap. 1746; m. April, 1766, Joshua Head of Berwick.

137   viii   Sarah[5], bap. 1750; m. April 3, 1770, John Owen.

138   ix   Dorothy[5], bap. May 2, 1754; m. Samuel Beard of Scarboro.

139   x   Miriam[5], bap. 1758; m. Brice Boothby.

140   xi   Jabez[5], b. ——; m. Sarah Atkinson.

141   xii   Winthrop[5], bap. Oct. 9, 1763; m. Susan Haseltine.

142   xiii   Elijah[5], bap. 1737; m. Sarah Lane.

143   xiv   Joseph[5], bap. 1748; m. Patience Goodwin.

50

MOSES[4] BRADBURY (Jacob[3], William[2], Thomas[1]), removed from Salisbury to North Yarmouth, and there married, December 28, 1737, Abigail Fogg. In 1790 he moved to New Gloucester.

Children:

144   i   Mary[5], b. Sept. 11, 1738; m. Capt. William Harris.

145   ii   Jacob[5], b. Dec. 13, 1740,

146 iii Hannah⁵, b. April 11, 1742.

147 iv Benjamin⁵, b. June 30, 1745 ; m. Eleanor Fellows.

148 v Enos⁵, b. May 10, 1748. He went to England and was pressed into the service, but returned.

149 vi Sarah⁵, b. April 9, 1751 ; m. David Dinsmore of Minot.

150 vii Moses⁵, b. June 29, 1755 ; m. Eunice Millett.

151 viii Samuel⁵, b. ———; m. 1st Bethulah Haskell; 2d Hannah Noyes.

152 ix Naomi⁵, b. ———; m. Abner Brown of Greene.

153 x Abigail⁵, b. ———; m. Dea. Isaac Allen of Minot.

SIXTH GENERATION.

53

SAMUEL⁵ BRADBURY (Wymond⁴. Wymond³, Wymond², Thomas¹), married Nov. 2, 1754, Abigail Sawyer who died August 22, 1787. He died May 2, 1799.

Children :

154 i Wymond⁶, b. ———; m. April 12, 1787, Elizabeth R. French. No issue.

155 ii Jacob⁶, b. ———.

156 iii William⁶, b. ———; m. Lorana Blackmore of Bath ; went South.

157 iv David⁶, b. ———; m. Mary Henshaw. No issue.

158 v Phebe⁶, b. ———; m. 1791, Daniel Herrick.

159 vi Nancy⁶, b. ———; m. April 27, 1800, Jeremiah Mitchell.

160 vii Elizabeth⁶, b. ———; m. Joseph Shaw.

161 viii ———, b. ———; m. Samuel Collins.

55

JACOB⁵ BRADBURY (Wymond⁴, Wymond³, Wymond², Thomas¹), married Lydia Mitchell. He died August 30, 1816. He was of Salisbury.

Children:

162　i　Jacob⁶, b. ——; d. unmarried.
163　ii　John⁶, b. ——, 1777; m. Theodocia Small.
164　iii　Reuben⁶, b. July 26, 1780; m. Eunice Freeman.
165　iv　Jabez⁶, b. ——; d. at sea, unmarried.
166　v　Wymond⁶, b. June 2, 1783; m. Ruth Matthews.
167　vi　Andrew⁶, b. ——; m. Mary Muzzey.
168　vii　Rebecca⁶, b. ——; d. aged 12 years.

Two children died, one aged 1 year and the other 16 months.

56

THOMAS⁵ BRADBURY (Wymond⁴. Wymond³, Wymond², Thomas¹). married Sept. 18. 1764, Hannah Freeman, who died August, 1829.

Children:

169　i　Mary⁶, b. August 11, 1765; m. 1st —— Pettengill, 2d Joseph Plummer.
170　ii　Hannah⁶, b. March 21. 1767; m. William Moulton.
171　iii　Jabez⁶, b. Jan. 1, 1769; d. March, 1778.
172　iv　Daniel⁶, b. May 17. 1771; m. Rhoda Plummer.
173　v　Thomas⁶, b. March 4, 1775; m. Dorcas Mitchell.
174　vi　Charles⁶, b. Oct. 20, 1777; m. Jane Brackett. No issue.
175　vii　William⁶, b. April 18, 1781; m. Mary Hinckley.
176　viii　Almira⁶, b. Dec. 14, 1784; m. 1st Joseph Hale; 2d James P. Stetson.
177　ix　Henry⁶, b. Aug. 19, 1787; d. unmarried.

60

COTTON⁵ BRADBURY (John⁴. Wymond,³ Wymond², Thomas¹). married Ruth. daughter of Mr. Elias Weare of York. He resided in York. and his children were born there. He died June 14. 1806.

Children :

178   i   Lucy[6], b. June 20, 1754; m. Nathaniel Moulton.
179   ii   Edward[6], b. May 20, 1757; m. Eunice Berry; d. May, 1828.
180   iii   Daniel[6], b. April 7, 1759; m. Abigail Junkins; d. 1810
181   iv   Betsey[6], b. Dec. 10, 1760; m. Daniel Knight.
182   v   Abigail[6], b. Dec. 16, 1765; m. Elihu Bragdon.
183   vi   Olive[6], b. Jan. 3, 1768; m. Jan. 15, 1795, Nathaniel Dorman of Arundell.
184   vii   Joseph[6], b. May 1, 1770; m. Jerusha Harmon; d. Jan. 25, 1859.
185   viii   James[6], b. April 24, 1772; m. Ann Moulton; d. Feb. 7, 1844.
186   ix   Ruth[6], b. Oct. 19, 1774; m. Joseph Haley.

66

JOHN[5] BRADBURY (John[4], Wymond[3], Wymond[2], Thomas[1]), married January 26, 1764, Elizabeth, daughter of Edward and Lydia (Holt) Ingraham, who was born in York. August 6, 1743. He served as lieutenant in Captain Moulton's company of provincial troops near Lake George in 1760-61, and kept a journal which is still in existence. He continued this journal up to near the close of his life. He was deacon of Christ Church in York, and a useful citizen. He lived for a time in Newtown, but returned to York and died there July 11, 1821. Several of his family removed to what was then called Chester. now Chesterville. Maine.

Children :

187   i   John[6], b. Oct. 29, 1764; m. Priscilla Burbank, r. Chesterville.
188   ii   William[6], b. Jan. 18, 1766; m. Anna Mitchell.

189 iii Lydia⁶, b. Aug. 27, 1767; m. Jan. 27, 1791, Thomas
       Davenport of Hallowell.

190 iv Joanna⁶, b. Nov. 6. 1768; m. Feb. 9, 1801, Jonathan
       Davenport of Hallowell.

191 v Samuel⁶, b. Feb. 9, 1771: m. Dorcas Remick.

192 vi Elizabeth⁶, b. January 25, 1773; m. Samuel Linscott;
       moved to Utica, N. Y.

193 vii Mary⁶, b. Nov. 8, 1774; d. unmarried.

194 viii Joseph⁹, b. Nov. 9, 1776; d. Aug. 27, 1778.

195 ix Joseph⁶, b. March 24, 1779; m. Abigail Chaney.

196 x Dorcas⁶, b. May 8, 1781; m. Oct. 7, 1803, Rufus Simp-
       son of York.

197 xi Jotham⁶, b. July 8, 1783.

198 xii David⁶, b. June 5. 1785; m. Sophia Chase.

67

JOSEPH⁵ BRADBURY (John⁴. Wymond³, Wymond²,
Thomas¹), married Dorothy, daughter of Daniel Clark,
esq. He died in Saco, December 23, 1821. and his
widow, who was born in York in 1748, died June 7,
1831, aged eighty-one years. Mr. Bradbury was an
officer in the war for independence. and had been a
resident of Saco fifty-three years.

Children :

199 i Jeremiah⁶, b. at Saco, Oct. 22, 1780; m. Mary Langdon
      Storer.

200 ii Anna⁶, b. Dec. 4, 1777; m. Joshua Moody; d. Sept. 26,
      1817.

201 iii Dorothy⁶, b. Aug. 1, 1781; m. Oct. 12, 1809, David Bacon.

202 iv Narcissa⁶, b. April 17, 1785; m. Nov. 19, 1823, Joshua
      Moody.

79

JOSIAH[5] BRADBURY (Josiah[4]. Wymond[3]. Wymond[2], Thomas[1]), married Catherine Larkin of Boston. He lived at Wiscasset and sailed a schooner between that port and Boston. In 1772, his vessel was wrecked at Seguin island, off the mouth of Kennebec river, and he and his son Josiah both perished. His widow was subsequently twice married. His children were:

203   i   Josiah[6], b. ——; lost at sea in 1772.
204   ii   Catherine Frothingham[6], b. Oct. 29, 1771; m. Ebenezer Clough of Boston. They had eight children.
205   iii   John[6], after the death of his brother, changed to Joseph[6], b. Feb. 6, 1773; m. Anna Lander. He had four sons and seven daughters. He died Feb. 12, 1860. The family lived in Starks, Me., but many of them went westward.

83

JONATHAN[5] BRADBURY (Theophilus[4], Wymond[3], Wymond[2], Thomas[1]), married December 20, 1758, Abigail, daughter of John and Martha (Toppan) Smith of Newbury. Mass., who was born Nov. 29, 1732. He died March 6, 1812, and she died April 14, 1812. His children were born in Newburyport.

206   i   Ebenezer[6], b. Sept. 18, 1759; lost at sea Aug., 1777.
207   ii   John[6], b. March 15, 1762; lost at sea Aug., 1777.
208   iii   Theophilus[6], b. Nov. 22, 1763; m. Lois Pillsbury.
209   iv   Smith[6], b. Nov. 30, 1765; m. Mary Hovey.
210   v   Samuel[6], b. Jan. 13, 1768; d. Nov. 30, 1826, unmarried.
211   vi   Martha[6], b. Sept. 15, 1770; m. Obediah Horton.

85

WYMOND[5] BRADBURY (Theophilus[4], Wymond[3], Wymond[2], Thomas[1]), married Judith Moody.

Children :

212   i   Anne[6], b. October 28, 1765; m. Ebenezer Symonds of Lexington.
213   ii   Charles[6], b. Sept. 8, 1767; m. Sarah Blanchard.
214   iii   William[6], b. Sept. 30, 1769; m. Elizabeth Floyd.
215   iv   Judith[6], b. Aug. 31, 1771.
216   v   Abigail[6], b. Sept. 28, 1773.
217   vi   Polly[6], b. Nov. 22, 1775.
218   vii   Mary[6], b. April 25, 1780.
219   viii   Edward[6], b. July 17, 1782; m. Abigail Hill.
220   ix   Henry[6], b. May 29, 1785; d. young.

86

THEOPHILUS[5] BRADBURY (Theophilus[4], Wymond[3], Wymond[2], Thomas[1]), born in Newbury, Mass., November 13, 1739, graduated from Harvard College in 1757, studied law and removed to Falmouth, Me. He taught the school here one year and then commenced the practice of law. Mr. William Willis says he was the first educated lawyer that settled between York and Pownalborough. In 1762, he married Sarah, daughter of Ephraim Jones, and two years later he purchased of Moses Parsons a lot of land on the corner of Middle and Willow streets, where he built a house which is still standing. While in Portland he had for a law student, among others, Theophilus Parsons, who became one of the most distinguished jurists in the country. In 1766, Mr. Bradbury and wife, with sev-

eral other leading citizens of Falmouth, were indicted
for the crime of dancing at Joshua Freeman's tavern.
Mr. Bradbury brought himself and friends off by
pleading that the room in which they danced was not
to be regarded as a place of public resort, having been
hired by private parties, and that the persons there
assembled had a right to meet and dance in their own
room. The plea was sustained by the court. While
in Falmouth Mr. Bradbury was attorney for the state
two years. He returned to Newbury in 1779, and was
elected to congress from the Essex district. In 1797,
he was appointed a judge of the supreme court of the
commonwealth, and was regarded as an able jurist.
While holding this position, Sept. 6, 1803, he died aged
sixty-four years.

Children :

221   i   Theophilus⁶, b. —, 1763; m. Oct. 8, 1798, Harriet Har-
            ris; no issue.
222   ii   Francis⁶, b. —, 1766; m. Hannah Jones Spooner.
223   iii   William⁶, b. —, 1768; d. unmarried in San Domingo.
224   iv   Frances⁶, b. ——; d. in infancy.
225   v   George⁶, b. —, 1770; m. Mary Kent.
226   vi   Harriet⁶, b. —, 1773; m. Thomas W. Hooper.
227   vii   Charles⁶, b. —, 1775; m. Elenora Cumming.
228   viii   Francis⁶, b. —, 1777; d. Nov. 30, 1801, unmarried.

87

ROWLAND⁵ BRADBURY (John⁴, William³, William²,
Thomas¹), married May 9, 1746, Mary Stevens, who
died March 31, 1800, and he married second, Miriam
French. He died Feb. 10, 1812.

Children:

229   i   John[6], b. June 23, 1751; m. Susannah Hutchinson.
230   ii   Jenny[6], b. Sept. 18, 1753; d. young.
231   iii   Janne[6], b. Sept. 16, 1754; m. Benjamin Choate.
232   iv   Paul[6], b. March 27, 1758; m. Ruth Weare.
233   v   Molly[6], b. Aug. 9, 1760; m. Aug. 31, 1781, John Bur-
                bank.
234   vi   Ephraim[6], b. ——; m. Molly Wier.

94

SAMUEL[5] BRADBURY (James[4], William[3], William[2], Thomas[1]), married March 2, 1763, Judith Morse.

Children:

235   i   William[6], b. April 5, 1759; m. Polly Meacham.
236   ii   James[6], b. Sept. 12, 1760; m. Sarah Coffin.
237   iii   Ebenezer[6], b. March 12, 1762; d. at West Point.
238   iv   Battee[6], b. March 30, 1764; m. Feb. 13, 1788, Aaron
                Welch.
239   v   Samuel[6], b. March 14, 1766; m. Christiana Gates.
240   vi   Judith[6], b. May 24, 1769; m. Benj. Davis of Plaistow,
                New Hampshire.
241   vii   David[6], b. May 24, 1769; m. Abigail R. Simpson.
242   viii   Sarah[6], b. Aug. 30, 1771; m. Abner Bailey, jr. (?)
243   ix   Prudence[6], b. April 10, 1774.

96

SANDERS[5] BRADBURY (James[4], William[3], William[2], Thomas[1]), was of Nottingham, N. H. He served in the continental army in the war for independence, in the regiment of General Joseph Cilley. He married May 26, 1763, Sarah Colby of Sanbornton, N. H. He died at White Plains, Nov. 15, 1779, and his widow married Josiah Brown, and died in 1828.

Children :

244 i Daniel⁶, b. Oct. 16, 1763; m. Elizabeth Lunt.
245 ii Anna⁶, b. Nov. 29, 1764; m. John Ball of Woodstock, Vermont.
246 iii Sarah⁶, b. July 23, 1766; m. Austin George.
247 iv James⁶, b. April 20, 1768; m. Catherine Conant.
248 v Abner⁶, b. March 4, 1770.
249 vi Mary⁶, b. Jan. 30, 1771.
250 vii Betsey⁶, b. Feb. 25, 1773; m. Edwin Dimmick.
251 viii Jacob⁶, b. Jan. 9, 1775; m. Mary Hutchinson.
252 ix William⁶, b. Dec. 6, 1776; m. Sarah (Lunt) Mitchell.
253 x Joseph⁶, b. Dec., 1778; m. Hannah Putnam.

105

JAMES⁵ BRADBURY (Crisp⁴, William³, William², Thomas¹), married Eunice Stone. He died in Biddeford, February 24, 1830.

Children born in York:

254 i Eunice⁶, b. ——; m. 1st Andrew Tarbox; 2d George Tucker.
255 ii Martha⁶, b. ——; m. ——, settled in Biddeford.
256 iii Polly⁶, b. ——; d. in Biddeford, March 31, 1859.
257 iv James⁶, b. Nov. 11, 1781; m. Mary Scammon.
258 v Rufus⁶, b.——; d. at sea, aged 21.
259 vi Nancy⁶, b. ——; m. Rufus Bridges.
260 vii Crisp⁶, b. March 20, 1786; m. Mary Rummery of Biddeford.
261 viii Almira⁶, b. ——; d. 1857, aged 66.
262 ix Benjamin⁶, b. ——; d. at sea, aged 19.

110

WILLIAM⁵ BRADBURY (Benjamin⁴, William³, William², Thomas¹), settled in New Gloucester, where he married

Hannah Tufts. He was a leading and influential citizen of the town and among the earlier settlers. He died August 19, 1826, and his wife May 19, 1820, aged seventy years.

Children:

263 i   Hannah[6], b. 1781; m. Dr. William Bridgham,* s. Buckfield.

264 ii   William[6], b. Nov. 19, 1783; m. Sarah Merrill. He was a justice of the peace, and representative to the legislature in 1822. He had a son who died unmarried, and a daughter who married Mr. Spring and resides in Portland. He died Oct. 16, 1859.

265 iii John[6], b. 1785; m. Sarah Tufts. He died Aug. 20, 1855.

266 iv   Benjamin[6], b. 1792; d. young.

267 v   Jabez[6], b. 1789. He m. Priscilla Joselyn and moved to Hodgdon, Me.

268 vi   Osgood[6], b. 1798. He was a lawyer and writer of fiction. He settled in Buckfield but was not there long. He represented New Gloucester in the legislature in 1838 and 1839. He married Mary M. Dinsmore of Burlington, Vt., and had no issue. He died at Sebago Lake, aged nearly 90.

*William Bridgham, M. D., was the son of Dr. William and Lydia Bridgham, who was early in New Gloucester, and was born in Plympton, Mass., Dec. 13, 1781. He settled in Buckfield where he spent a long and useful life, highly respected, not only as a physician, but as a man and citizen. His wife Hannah died in Buckfield, Nov. 27, 1859, and he died Nov. 13, 1864. His children, all born in Buckfield, were: i Hannah, b. Jan. 13, 1805, m. Isaac Chase, and died Oct. 29, 1874; ii Caroline, b. Sept. 13, 1806, m. Luther Crocker; iii Sydenham, b. Sept. 15, 1808, m. Lucretia Sheppard, d. May 10, 1882; iv Orville, b. April 3, 1811, m. Mary Atwood, d. Dec. 25, 1875; v William Pinckney, b. Sept. 3, 1816, m. 1st Delphina Hayford, and 2d widow Lucy L. Farrar; he graduated at the Maine Medical school in 1844, and resides at Buckfield village, where he has long been in practice. vi Mary Ann, b. June 13, 1825, d. Nov. 14, 1863.

120

JACOB⁵ BRADBURY (Thomas⁴, Jacob³. William². Thomas¹). married Abigail Cole. He lived in Biddeford, but moved to Limerick and was deacon of the church there. He died in 1801.

Children :

269　i　Anna⁶, bap. 1752; m. Thomas Gilpatrick, jr.
270　ii　John⁶. bap. 1753; m. —— Page of Conway.
271　iii　Ammi⁶ R., bap. 1754.
272　iv　Betty⁶, bap. 1756; m. Gile Follett, 1787.
273　v　Lucy⁶, bap. 1758; m. Thomas Parsons of Parsonsfield.
274　vi　Abigail⁶, bap. May 13, 1759; m. Jere Page of Fryeburg.
275　vii　Eunice⁶, bap. 1760; m. Reuben Hill, d. in Limerick.
276　viii　Ammi⁶ R., bap. 1762.
277　ix　Esther⁶, bap. 1764; m. Thomas Lord of Freedom, N.H.
278　x　Sarah⁶, bap. 1765; m. Robert Page of Fryeburg.
279　xi　Rebecca⁶, bap. 1766; m. Phineas Colcord.
280　xii　Jacob, bap. 1769; m. Jane Piper, d. in Parsonsfield, 1837.
281　xiii　Molly⁶, bap. 1772; m. Joshua Hutchinson of Buxton.
282　xiv　Thomas⁶, bap. 1775; m. Sally Webster.
283　xv　Joseph⁶, b. ——; m. Betsey Stevens, s. Exeter, Me.; went to Ohio.
284　xvi　Charles⁶, b. ——.
285　xvii　Susan⁶, b. ——; m. —— Harvey of Buxton.
286　xviii　Olive⁶, b. ——.
287　xix　name not known.
288　xx　name not known.

The last six were born in Limerick.

121

MOSES⁵ BRADBURY (Thomas⁴, Jacob³, William², Thomas¹), married Mary Page. He lived in Biddeford.

Children :

289   i   Samuel⁶, b. ——: m. Abigail Cleaves.

290   ii   Moses⁶, b.——; m.—— : s. Spring Island.

291   iii   Nehemiah⁶, b. ——.

292   iv   Ruth⁶, b. Nov., 1759; m. Ezekiel Foster; 2d Stephen Woodman.

293   v   Abigail⁶, b. ——.

294   vi   Molly⁶, b. March 22, 1768; m. Obed Foss.

295   vii   Sally⁶, b. ——; m. Samuel Merrill.

123

THOMAS⁵ BRADBURY (Thomas⁴, Jacob³, William², Thomas¹), married at Biddeford, June 5, 1762, Ruth Page of Salisbury, Mass. He died in Buxton, Nov. 9, 1803, and she died January 9, 1822. He settled in Buxton, and was deacon of the church there. He was a lieutenant in the expedition to Crown Point and Ticonderoga, and kept a diary.

Children :

296   i   Jabez Page⁶, b. Jan. 14, 1763; m. Sarah Hilton Whitney.

297   ii   Daniel⁶, b. Dec. 20, 1764; m. Mary Wingate.

298   iii   Elizabeth⁶, b. June 29, 1772; m. July 16, 1804, Toppan Wentworth.

299   iv   Thomas⁶, b. Oct. 7, 1778; m. Abigail Boothby.

300   v   Anna⁶, b. Aug. 14, 1785; m. 1st June 8, 1815, James Folsom; 2d Robert Wentworth, Jan. 31, 1850.

124

WILLIAM⁵ BRADBURY (Thomas⁴, Jacob³, William², Thomas¹), married May 19, 1765, Susannah Hopkinson. He lived in Buxton on his father's farm.

Children :

301	i	Sarah⁶, bap. 1769; m. Thomas Lord, jr., of Limerick.
302	ii	Samuel⁶, bap. 1769; m. Sarah Hutton, r. Hollis.
303	iii	Susannah⁶, bap. 1771; m. Benjamin Leavitt.
304	iv	Hannah⁶, bap. 1773; m. Rev. John Seavy.
305	v	William⁶, bap. 1775; m. Susannah Dunnell, r. Hollis.
306	vi	Lucy⁶, bap. 1784.
307	vii	Molly⁶, bap. 1784; m. Elias Dearborn.
308	viii	Dorcas⁶, bap. 1784; m. Samuel W. Varnum.
309	ix	John⁶, ——; m. Hannah Hanscom.
310	x	Betsey⁶, bap. 1778; m. —— Small.

126

BENJAMIN⁵ BRADBURY (Thomas⁴. Jacob³, William², Thomas¹), married July 9, 1767, Mary Elden, who was born May 17, 1750, and who died April 4, 1833. He died September, 1834. In August, 1800, he emigrated from Buxton, Me., to Brown County, Ohio.

Children :

310½	i	Mary⁶, b. June 11, 1768; m. Nov. 25, 1793, William Boulter
311	ii	Benjamin⁶, b. Dec. 24, 1769; m. Betsey Eaton.
312	iii	John⁶, b. April 6, 1772; d. June 26, 1826.
313	iv	Ruth⁶, b. July 10, 1774; d. 1777.
314	v	Sarah⁶, b. Oct. 31, 1776; m. Jotham Bragdon, s. Ohio.
315	vi	Gibeon⁶, b. June 13, 1779.
316	vii	Moses⁶, b. July 23, 1781; m. Agnes Hunt.
317	viii	Jacob⁶, b. Nov. 8, 1783; m. Patience (Rounds) Quinby.
318	ix	Thomas⁶, b. Sept. 29, 1785; m. Katherine Hunt.
319	x	Nathan⁶, b. Feb. 1, 1788; m. Mehitable Warren.
320	xi	Samuel⁶, b. April 12, 1790; m. Mary Hanley.

135

JACOB[5] BRADBURY (Jacob[4], Jacob[3]. William[2], Thomas[1]), married May 8, 1766, Mary Goodwin, who died in 1786. He lived in Buxton. on the Beach Plain road, and was known as "Esquire Bradbury." Majestic and dignified in appearance, he was a noble specimen of manhood. For thirty years from the time he became of age, he was constantly in public employment. He was the first representative from Buxton to the general court, which position he held for a number of years. He died in 1811. His second wife was Catherine (Flint) Simonton.

Children :

321   i   Moses[6], b. April 12, 1767 ; m. Mercy Garland.
322   ii   Martha[6], b. March 8, 1769; m. Sept. 2, 1790, Thomas Leavitt.
323   iii   Jacob[6], b. Jan. 6, 1771 ; d. about 1795, unmarried.
324   iv   Edmund[6], b. Jan. 31, 1773 ; m. Martha Whitney.
325   v   Andrew[6], b. Dec. 8, 1778; m. Deborah Cressey.
326   vi   Simeon Goodwin[6], Aug. 21, 1781 ; m. 1st Ruth Sands.
327   vii   Mary[6], b. July 27, 1782.

By second marriage :
328 viii   William Flint[6], b. Jan. 3, 1791 ; m. Mary ——.

140

JABEZ[5] BRADBURY (Jacob[4], Jacob[3]. William[2], Thomas[1]), married May 19, 1774, Sarah Atkinson, who died July 2. 1807. He married second, December 27, 1807, Mary (Cutts) Billings. He resided in Buxton, and was an enterprising business man.

Children :

329   i   Joseph⁶, b. Nov. 12, 1775; m. Susan Crockett of Gorham.

330   ii   Abigail⁶, b. Nov. 10, 1780; m. Dec. 8, 1806, Rev. Abner Flanders.

331   iii   Eunice⁶, b. March 27, 1783; m. Nov. 28, 1810, Samuel Sawyer; d. Feb. 6, 1843.

332   iv   Jabez⁶, b. Nov. 14, 1784; m. Elizabeth Page.

333   v   Mary⁶, b. March 27, 1787; m. Nov. 28, 1813, Joseph Crockett.

334   vi   Sally⁶, b. Dec. 17, 1791; m. Jan. 11, 1819, Jacob Bradbury.

335   vii   Betsey⁶, b. Nov. 13, 1794; m. James Fogg.

336   viii   Nancy⁶, b. March 5, 1800; m. James Palmer.

By second marriage :

337   ix   Enoch Billings⁶, b. Nov. 16, 1800; m. Mary Chase Huse.

338   x   Caroline⁶, b. Nov. 20, 1811; m. Hartley Cutts of Pittston.

141

WINTHROP⁵ BRADBURY (Jacob⁴, Jacob³, William², Thomas¹), married September 8, 1785, Susan, daughter of Deacon Timothy and Ruth (Wilson) Haseltine of Buxton. He resided in Buxton and Hollis. In 1788, he went to Saco Pool with a load of wood and never returned. His fate was ever a mystery.

Children :

338¼   i   Ruth⁶, b. Dec. 24, 1786. She married Hudson Bailey of Portland, who was born in Portland, September 17, 1786, by occupation a cooper, and spent many years at sea and in the West Indies. About the year 1839, he moved to a farm on Hamlin's Gore in the county of Oxford, and built the brick house above

7

North Woodstock on the Rumford road. He sold
out and went West, but returned, and he and his wife
died at the residence of their daughter, Mrs. Elizabeth Webster, at Cape Elizabeth. Their children
were Susan, Samuel, Elizabeth, Louisa, George, Hollis
and Hiram Hudson.

338½ ii Abigail[6], b. ——, 1789. She married 1st Stephen Mitchell
of Portland, and had Stephen Mitchell, jr. She married second, Jonas Hamilton who long resided at
South Paris, and hauled goods from Portland before
the days of railroads, and had Rachel L., William,
Phebe Ann, Ruth Bailey, Jonas, jr., the well-known
superintendent of the Portland and Ogdensburg railroad, and Nancy.

142

ELIJAH[5] BRADBURY (Jacob[4], Jacob[3], William[2], Thom-
as[1]), married December 16, 1779. Sarah, daughter of
Capt. John and Sarah (Hancock) Lane, who was born
November 28, 1756. He enlisted and served under
General Washington on the Hudson. He was also in
the battle of King's mountain, at Guilford Court
House, and in several other engagements. He return-
ed, settled in Buxton and was a farmer.

Children:

339   i   Elizabeth[6], b. Sept. 14, 1780; m. July 25, 1802, James
           Palmer; d. 1837.

340   ii Sarah[6], b. April 5, 1782; m. July 5, 1807, Timothy
           Ricker, s. New Portland.

341   iii Elijah[6], b. March 28, 1784; m. 1st Sallie Gleason How-
           ard of Brownfield, and 2d Ann Pray Hunt.

342   iv Abigail[6], b. July 31, 1785; d. Jan. 8, 1804.

343 v Isaac⁶, b. June 11, 1787; m. Abigail S. Lane, s. Haynesville.
344 vi Anna⁶, b. Jan. 2, 1789; d. Sept. 18, 1807.
345 vii Jabez⁶, b. Sept. 22, 1790: m. Ann Maria Knight of Calais.
346 viii Joanna Lane⁶, b. Aug. 28, 1792; m. July 19, 1821, Charles Smith; d. 1845.

143

Joseph⁵ Bradbury (Jacob⁴, Jacob³, William², Thomas¹), married November 17, 1774, Patience, daughter of John Goodwin of Kennebunk. He died September 7, 1819, aged seventy-two years. She died November 13, 1840, aged eighty-two. He was born in Buxton and resided there.

Children :

347 i John⁶, b. July 5, 1776; m. Alice Tyler, s. Hollis.
348 ii Joseph⁶, b. Dec. 22, 1777 ; m. Ruth Libby.
349 iii Winthrop⁶, b. Feb. 22, 1780; m. Lucy McKenney.
350 iv Jacob⁶, b. March 18, 1783 ; m. Mehitable Marston.
351 v Martha⁶, b. Dec. 21, 1786; m. May 30, 1810, Elias Libby.
352 vi Mary⁶, b. June 24, 1788 ; m. Nov. 28, 1810, Amos Woodman.
353 vii Benjamin⁶, b. Aug. 1, 1791; m. Jane Plaisted.
354 viii Betsey⁶, b. Jan. 16, 1796; m. Nov. 27, 1826, Simeon Andrews.
355 ix Miriam⁶, b. Sept. 26, 1798; m. Sept. 25, 1822, Edmund Dresser.
356 x Brice⁶, b. Jan. 29, 1800.

147

Benjamin⁵ Bradbury (Moses⁴, Jacob³, William², Thomas¹), married April 23, 1766, Eleanor, daughter of Joseph and Mary (Mitchell) Fellows of North Yarmouth, who was born Oct. 25, 1746. She was of the Bridgewater family of Mitchell. Benjamin with his family moved to Bradbury Hill in Minot in 1777, and has descendants in Androscoggin, Oxford and Franklin counties.

Children :

357   i   Hannah[6], b. July, 1766; m. Oct. 10, 1784, Samuel Freeman. She died Nov. 7, 1851.

358   ii   Joseph[6], b. May 10, 1768; m. Tabitha Cotton, s. Norway.

359   iii   Abigail[6], b. Aug. 20, 1771; m. May 19, 1797, Wiswell Seabury; d. Nov. 6, 1849.

360   iv   Benjamin[6], b. April 10, 1775; m. 1st Anna Hersey; 2d Asenath Wheeler.

361   v   Samuel[6], b. Dec. 4, 1777; m. Jane Gurney.

362   vi   Mary[6], b. Dec. 24, 1780; m. June 20, 1801, Josiah Berry; d. Sept. 6, 1820.

363   vii   Eleanor[6], b. July 15, 1782; m. Wilber Caswell, July 7, 1803; d. 1868.

364   viii   David[6], b. May 3, 1785; m. 1st Mary Robertson; 2d Sarah Vickery.

365   ix   Bethula[6], b. July 10, 1787; m. April 21, 1805, William Tuck.

366   x   Jacob[6], b. May 10, 1789; m. 1st Sarah Chamberlain; 2d Mary Chamberlain.

150

Moses[5] Bradbury (Moses[4], Jacob[3], William[2], Thomas[1]), married Eunice Millett. He lived in Minot. Me., and his large family of children were born there.

Children :

367   i   Deborah[6], b. Jan. 6, 1782 ; m. Dea. Benj. Herring.
368   ii   Charles[6], b. May 4, 1783; m. Polly Chase ; d. in Anson.
369   iii   Moses[6], b. Oct. 28, 1784; d. in Foxcroft, Apr. 13, 1813.
370   iv   John[6], b. Aug. 15, 1786; m. Alethea Hersey, r. Bangor.
371   v   Eunice[6], b. June 9, 1788 ; m. Samuel Hersey; d. Sumner, May 5, 1830.
372   vi   Sarah[6], b. Oct., 1790; m. Benj. Hersey; d. Foxcroft.
373   vii   Mary[6], b. July 5, 1792; m. Samuel Hersey; d. Sumner.
374   viii   Hannah[6], b. May 18, 1794; d. Norway, May 30, 1815.
375   ix   Enos[6], b. April 9, 1796; m. 1st Lucy Atkinson ; 2d Mary Howard; he died in Minot, Dec. 3, 1842.
376   x   Nathaniel[6], b. March 10, 1798; m. Nancy P. Mitchell ; d. Foxcroft, March 16, 1827.
377   xi   Joanna[6], b. March 27, 1800.
378   xii   Hiram[6], b. April 24, 1804; m. Nancy Washburn.

151

SAMUEL[5] BRADBURY (Moses[4], Jacob[3], William[2], Thomas[1]), married first, in 1780, Bethulah Haskell, and second, September 25, 1788, Hannah Noyes.

Children :

379   i   Betsey[6], b. —— ; m. —— Loomis.
380   ii   Naomi[6], b. —— ; d. young.
381   iii   Bethulah[6], b. —— ; m. Ezekiel Warren.

By second wife :
382   iv   Abigail[6], b. June 13, 1789; m. Isaiah Hutchins.
383   v   Naomi[6], b. April 20, 1791; m. Jonathan Hutchins.
384   vi   Samuel[6], b. July 26, 1793; m. Frances M. Rochead.
385   vii   Sarah[6],   ) m. Rufus Chandler.   (b. June 28, 1795.
386   viii   Hannah N.[6],   ) m. William Hackett.   (

SEVENTH GENERATION.

163

JOHN[6] BRADBURY (Jacob[5], Wymond[4], Wymond[3] Wymond[2], Thomas[1]), married Theodocia Small who was born in 1783, and died June 14, 1839.

Children :

387   i   Jacob[7], b. 1800; d.——.
388   ii   George Lowther[7], b. Sept. 10, 1802; m. Elizabeth Condon.
389   iii   Rebecca[7], b. March 10, 1804; d. Dec. 23, 1826.
390   iv   Jabez[7], b. Feb. 26, 1806; d. Sept. 14, 1807.
391   v   Jabez[7], b. Feb. 27, 1808; d. Oct. 18, 1826.
392   vi   Reuben[7], b. June 10, 1810, s. New Haven, Conn.; d. 1845.
393   vii   John[7], b. Aug. 12, 1812; d. Aug. 10, 1813.
394   viii   Sarah Small[7], b. July 11, 1814; m. Aug. 1. 1833, Chas. F. Bryant.
395   ix   William[7], b. Nov. 16, 1816; d. Aug. 4, 1818.
396   x   William[7], b. Nov. 7, 1819; d. July 15, 1821.
397   xi   Enos Small[7], b. Feb. 10, 1822; m. Ann Henley.

164

REUBEN[6] BRADBURY (Jacob[5], Wymond[4], Wymond[3], Wymond[2], Thomas[1]), married January 14, 1807, Eunice Freeman, who was born Feb. 18, 1782. He died Feb. 20, 1829.

Children :

398   i   Martha[7], b. April 12, 1808 ; m. Dec., 1830, Stephen Foster.
399   ii   Lydia[7], b. April 12, 1808; d. April 12, 1821.
400   iii   Wymond[7], b. April 24, 1810; d. July 4, 1811.

401 iv Edward[7], b. June 8, 1811; m. Mary Ann Crockett.

402 v Jane[7], b. Jan. 8, 1813.

403 vi Mary Ann[7], b. May 10, 1814; d. Aug. 11, 1832.

404 vii Louisa[7], b. Jan. 6, 1816; m. 1st William Ross; 2d J. P. Sawyer.

405 viii Angeline[7], b. April 27, 1817; m. Nov. 6, 1833, John Paine.

406 ix William[7], b. April 26, 1819.

407 x George Freeman[7], b. Oct. 29, 1825; d. Jan. 9, 1828.

166

WYMOND[6] BRADBURY (Jacob[5], Wymond[4], Wymond[3], Wymond[2], Thomas[1]), married September 11, 1810, Ruth Matthews, who was born June 2, 1790, and died September 26, 1861. He was a shoemaker and moved from Portland to South Thomaston, where he died July 6, 1837.

Children:

408 i Samuel Andrews[7], b. Sept. 28, 1811; m. Lucy R. Butler.

409 ii Archibald Matthews[7], b. April 19, 1814; a mariner.

410 iii Rebecca[7], b. Aug. 16, 1816; m. 1st Abiezer Coombs; 2d David Owens.

411 iv Charles[7] (captain), b. May 25, 1819; m. Nancy M. Butler.

412 v Almira S.[7], b. May 28, 1822; d. Oct. 12, 1825.

413 vi Henry Paine[7], b. May 20, 1825; m. Nancy C. Suckforth.

414 vii George[7], b. March 7, 1828, mariner; m. Irene Kalloch.

415 viii Caroline F.[7], b. Dec. 13, 1830; d. Feb. 22, 1860.

416 ix Sarah W.[7], b. Oct. 1, 1837; d. Dec. 18, 1846.

167

ANDREW[6] BRADBURY (Jacob[5], Wymond[4], Wymond[3], Wymond[2], Thomas[1]), married Mary Muzzey.

Children :

417   i   Caroline⁷, b. ——; m. Algernon Howe.
418   ii   Maria⁷, b. ——.
419   iii   Theodore Muzzey⁷, b. ——; m. Lucy Chadbourne.

172

DANIEL⁶ BRADBURY (Thomas⁵, Wymond⁴, Wymond³, Wymond², Thomas¹), married February 9, 1800, Rhoda Plummer, who was born April 24. 1775, and died November 13, 1844. He died July 9, 1845.

Children :

420   i   Abigail⁷, b. Nov. 3, 1800; d. Sept. 23, 1801.
421   ii   Mary⁷, b. Dec. 1, 1801; d. Sept. 23, 1802.
422   iii   Edward⁷, b. Oct. 26, 1803 ; d. July 30, 1804.
423   iv   Sophia⁷, b. Oct. 26, 1803; m. May 20, 1847, George Fickett.
424   v   Harriet⁷, b. March 21, 1805; d. July 11, 1832.
425   vi   Joseph⁷, b. Nov. 9, 1806; m. Mary Bryant.
426   vii   Henry⁷, b. Nov. 5, 1808.
427   viii   Francis⁷, b. Sept. 15, 1810; d. Nov. 10, 1846.
428   ix   Thomas⁷, b. Oct. 6, 1812; d. April 13, 1814.

173

THOMAS⁶ BRADBURY (Thomas⁵, Wymond⁴, Wymond³, Wymond², Thomas¹), married Sept. 25, 1801, Dorcas Mitchell, who was born April 8, 1779.

Children :

429   i   Infant⁷, d. unnamed.
430   ii   Infant⁷, d. unnamed.
431   iii   Charles⁷, b. Dec. 15, 1804; m. Martha McPherson.
432   iv   Almira⁷, b. Feb. 27, 1807; m. Joseph Carr, jr.

433   v   Eliza[7], b. March 18, 1809 ; d. Sept. 12, 1828.
434 vi Mary[7], b. June 24, 1811.
435 vii Caroline[7], b. Aug. 2, 1814; m. John C. Swan.
436 viii Harriet[7], b. April 17, 1821 ; m. Silas H. Buttrick.

175

WILLIAM[6] BRADBURY (Thomas[5], Wymond[4], Wymond[3], Wymond[2], Thomas[1]), married in 1815, Mary Hinckley. He resided in Eastport, and there he died in 1839. His wife died in 1838.

Children :

437   i   Almira Haile[7], b. Oct. 28, 1818.
438 ii John Hinckley[7], b. Feb. 3, 1821 ; m. June 27, 1852, Mary E. (Treat) Park.
439 iii Abigail Hinckley[7], b. Oct. 28, d. Aug. 23, 1834.
440 iv Mary[7], b. March 20, 1825 ; d. Jan. 20, 1830.
441 v   William Henry[7], b. Oct. 31, 1827 ; m. Lydia Ann Tobey.
442 vi George Freeman[7], b. Dec. 15, 1831 ; m. Sarah Jane Griffin.

179

EDWARD[6] BRADBURY (Cotton[5], John[4], Wymond[3], Wymond[2], Thomas[1]), married Eunice Berry. He lived in Buxton where he died in May, 1828.

Child :

443 i Cotton[7], b. April 1, 1790 ; m. Mary Hobbs.

180

DANIEL[6] BRADBURY (Cotton[5], John[4], Wymond[3], Wymond[2], Thomas[1]), married Abigail Junkins, who was born August 6, 1761. He died in March, 1813, and she in 1817. He was of York.

Children :

444 i Harriet[7], b. March 15, 1786; m. Dec. 18, 1808, Enoch
         Emery.
445 ii George[7], b. July 23, 1788 ; m. Maria Norton.
446 iii Charles[7], b. April 28, 1790 ; d. at York, 1822.
447 iv William[7], b. Oct. 3, 1793 ; d. at Martha's Vineyard, 1823.

184

JOSEPH[6] BRADBURY (Cotton[5], John[4], Wymond[3], Wymond[2], Thomas[1]), married Jerusha, daughter of Nathaniel Harmon, who was born February 23, 1773.
He was of York.

Children :

448 i   Nathaniel Harmon[7], b. Sept. 16, 1795 ; m. Sophia
          Moulton.
449 ii   Paulina[7], b. Sept. 19, 1797 ; m. Washington Remick.
450 iii Ruth[7], b. April 5, 1799 ; m. William Tilden.
451 iv   Joseph[7], b. Jan. 23, 1801.
452 v   Andrew[7], b. Sept. 27, 1802 ; m. Mrs. — Bowers.
452½ vi   George[7], b. March 8, 1808.
453 vii Jerusha[7], b. July 26, 1810 ; m. Luther Junkins.
454 viii Sarah[7], b. Dec. 12, 1812.

185

JAMES[6] BRADBURY (Cotton[5], John[4], Wymond[3], Wymond[2], Thomas[1]), studied the medical profession, and
after graduation practiced a year in Ossipee, N. H.,
and then, in 1798, settled in Parsonsfield, Me. He had
obtained a good general education, and his medical
education was the best that could be obtained at that

day. He soon had an extensive practice in which he continued for nearly half a century. When old age came on he moved to Windham, that he might be near his only daughter, who had married and resided there. He died February 7, 1844. While in active practice at Parsonsfield he had a large number of medical students, among whom were Moses Sweat, Burleigh Smart, Eleazer Burbank, Jesse Mighil, Alvah Moulton, son of Mrs. Bradbury by her first marriage, Nathaniel Pease, Levi Hannaford, Gilman L. Bennett, Samuel M. Bradbury, Sumner Gilman, Tristram Redman, Charles G. Parsons, Levi Moore and Thomas Drown. Some of these became eminent physicians. Dr. Bradbury was a good physician, possessed excellent judgment, and had the respect and confidence of his large circuit of practice. He was upright and honest in his dealings with mankind, and courteous in his intercourse with members of his profession. He joined the Free Baptist church in 1816, and continued in communion with that body until the time of his death. Dr. Bradbury married in 1800, Mrs. Ann, daughter of Samuel Moulton. Mrs. Bradbury was born in Newbury, Mass., September 2, 1777, and for first husband married her cousin, Samuel, son of Cutting Moulton. By this marriage she had two children.* Her mother was Hannah

---

*Alvah Moulton[7], son of Samuel[6] and Ann (Moulton[6]) Moulton, whose father died in 1800, and whose mother married Dr. James Bradbury, born Oct. 11, 1798, married in 1821, Mary Dalton. He was the seventh in descent from William[1] Moulton, who came from Ormsby, England, in 1637, married Margaret, daughter of Robert Page, and settled in Hampton,

Noyes of Newbury. The children of Dr. James and Ann (Moulton) Bradbury were :

455 i   James Ware[7], b. June 10, 1802; m. Eliza Ann Smith.
456 ii Samuel Moulton[7], b. Aug. 22, 1804; m. 1st Susan Brackett; 2d Elizabeth Brackett; d. Sept. 22, 1888.
457 iii Clarissa Ann[7], b. June 19, 1807; m. Dr. Charles G. Parsons of Windham; she died Dec. 5, 1850.

   For second wife Dr. Bradbury married and had :
458 iv Cotton M.[7], b. —, 1837; m. 1st Susanna D. Hussey, and 2d Ella T. Harris.

187

John[6] Bradbury (John[5], John[4], Wymond[3], Wymond[2], Thomas[1]), married Priscilla Burbank, who was born August 2, 1764, and died April 8, 1831. He died July 24, 1851. He moved from York to Chesterville.

N. H., and was afterward of Newbury, Mass. The descent is as follows: William[1], William[2], Joseph[3], Samuel[4], Cutting[5], Samuel[6], Alvah[7].

   Children of Dr. Alvah and Mary (Dalton) Moulton, born in Ossipee, N. H.

  1 Anne B., b. April 21, 1822; m. John C. Dore.
  2 Louisa F., b. Aug. 7, 1823; m. Warren A. Nickerson.
  3 Ferdinand, b. Sept. 26, 1824.
  4 Maria A., b. Nov. 5, 1826; m. Henry C. Jackson.
  5 Clarissa B., b. June 22, 1828; m. Daniel O. Quinby.
  6 Alvah D., b. May 23, 1829.
  7 James B., b. June 20, 1830.
  8 George F., b. Dec. 1, 1831.
  9 Henry William, b. May 3, 1833.
 10 Sarah E., b. March 23, 1835; m. Charles H. Dow.
 11 Nellie E. M., b. May 4, 1839; m. Amos M. Towle.
 12 Charles E., b. Feb. 17, 1843.

Children :

459   i   Abigail Sewall[7], b. July 11, 1789; d. Jan. 31, 1797.

460   ii   Eliza Jane[7], b. Nov. 2, 1791; m. March 2, 1812, John Storer of Carthage, Me.

461   iii   Rachel Crosby[7], b. March 7, 1794; m. Jotham Sewall jr.*

462   iv   Maria[7], b. June 11, 1796; m. June 11, 1816, Elisha Bennett of Chesterville.

463   v   Sabrina Ann[7], b. May 13, 1798; m. March 8, 1821, Jonas M. Oakes.

464   vi   John Roger Williams[7], b. June 4, 1800; m. Phebe R. Mayhew.

465   vii   Benj. Burbank[7], b. Sept. 24, 1802; m. Betsey Lowell.

466   viii   Lois Palmer[7], b. May 26, 1806; m. Dec., 1823, Reuben Lowell of Chesterville.

188

WILLIAM[6] BRADBURY (John[5], John[4], Wymond[3], Wymond[2], Thomas[1]), married at Bath, February 24, 1788.

*Rev. Jotham Sewall, jr., son of Rev. Jotham and Jenny (Sewall) Sewall, born Dec. 6, 1791, was a Congregational clergyman, had a fifteen years' settlement at Newcastle, Me., and was also settled as pastor at other places. He died Dec. 18, 1884. His wife, Rachel Crosby (Bradbury) Sewall, died Nov. 10, 1837. Children: i Stephen Bayley, b. Nov. 22, 1815, m. Hannah W. Shepard of Hallowell and d. Dec. 23, 1864; ii David Brainerd, b. Jan. 18, 1817 (Bowdoin College, 1836), m. Mary Drummond of Bristol; he is a Congregational minister at South Berwick. iii Priscilla, b. March 8, 1819, d. July 26, 1822; iv Jane Stinson, b. April 11, 1821, m. William J. Thorne of Westbrook, and d. Dec. 6, 1853; v Abigail Titcomb, b. Sept. 4, 1823, d. Oct. 18, 1824; vi Jotham Bradbury, b. Oct. 3, 1825 (Bowdoin College, 1848), m. Frances Swett of Dedham, Mass. He is head master of Thayer Academy at Braintree, Mass. vii Mary Chapman, b. April 16, 1827, d. Aug. 15, 1848; viii John Smith, b. March 20, 1830 (Bowdoin College, 1850), m. Louisa Benson of Winthrop. He is professor in the Bangor Theological Seminary; ix Edward Payson, b. March 14, 1832, d. April 6, 1882; x Harvey Loomis, b. May 12, 1834, d. Aug. 13, 1837.

Anna Mitchell. He lived in Chester plantation, now Chesterville, and died November 22, 1846. His wife died November 13, 1827. He was deacon of the Baptist church in Chesterville, and a highly respected citizen. He was treasurer of the town from its incorporation to the time of his death. When no minister was present he took charge of religious meetings in the neighborhood, and led the singing.

Children:

467　i　Jenny[7], b. Dec. 26, 1788; m. March 18, 1810, Daniel Storer,* s. Carthage, Me.
468　ii　Jotham[7], b. Nov. 17, 1790; m. 1st Nancy Merrick; 2d Rachel (Hinckley) Merrick.
469　iii　Hannah[7], b. Aug. 22, 1793; d. July 13, 1822.
470　iv　William Otis[7], b. June 5, 1800; m. Lavina Pierce.

191

SAMUEL[6] BRADBURY (John[5], John[4], Wymond[3], Wymond[2], Thomas[1]), married July 10, 1802, Dorcas, daughter of Nathaniel Remick of Newcastle, N. H., who was born November, 1770, and died December 9, 1806. For second wife he married, March 14, 1815, Sally (Leighton) Harold, daughter of William Leighton of Eliot, who was born August, 1782, and died December 15, 1863. He died Nov. 10, 1849.

---

*A communication, from one well acquainted, says: "They (Mr. and Mrs. Storer), were two of the best people in the world. They had no children, and left a good property to distant relatives. Their fireside was the home of the destitute of many other families."

Children :

By first marriage :

471   i   Susan Preble[7], b. May 2, 1803.
472   ii   Theophilus Washington[7], b. Nov. 5, 1804.
473   iii   Nathaniel Remick[7], b. Dec. 2, 1806.

By second marriage :

474   iv   Charles Leighton[7], b. Dec. 20, 1815; m. Hannah P. Brasbridge of Alton, N. H.
475   v   Samuel Adams[7], b. April 15, 1817; m. Louisa Maria Welch of Monmouth, Me.
476   vi   Miriam S.[7], b. June 20, 1819; m. John Terry.
477   vii   Cotton Chase[7], b. Aug. 18, 1822, m. Rebecca Brewer of Providence, R. I.
478   viii   John William[7], b. Dec. 12, 1827; m. Ann Eliza Wells.

195

JOSEPH[6] BRADBURY (John[5], John[4], Wymond[3], Wymond[2], Thomas[1]), married January 28, 1806, Abigail, daughter of Captain John Chaney, who was born in Dunstable, Mass., April 26, 1786. She died in Wilton, Me., January 25, 1860, and he in Bangor, June 11 following. Their children were born in Chesterville.

Children :

479   i   Milton[7], b. Feb. 19, 1807; d. Nov. 6, 1822.
480   ii   Chaney Cortez[7], b. June 30, 1810; d. Dec. 14, 1822.
481   iii   David[7], b. Jan. 20, 1812; m. Julia A. Livingston.
482   iv   Amanda[7], b. Sept. 21, 1814; m. March 26, 1833, Daniel Butterfield.
483   v   Simon Pierce[7], b. April 18, 1816; m. Mary A. Gowen.
484   vi   Mary[7], b. June 4, 1819; m. Nov. 26, 1835, Reuben Lord of Wilton.

485 vii Matilda French⁷, b. Jan. 1, 1824; m. Dec. 5, 1844, Joseph
G. Hoyt of Wilton. Mr. Hoyt was a prominent man
in town and county. He served in the Maine Senate
and was long route agent on the Androscoggin branch
of the Maine Central railroad. He died in 1889.

198

DAVID⁶ BRADBURY (John⁵, John⁴, Wymond³, Wymond², Thomas¹), married Sophia, daughter of Josiah
Chase. He died in 1840. The births of his children
are recorded in York.

Children :

486 i   Elizabeth C.⁷, b. Jan. 28, 1813.
487 ii Cotton Chase⁷, b. Nov. 23, 1814.
488 iii William B.⁷,* b. Oct. 6, 1816; d. Jan. 7, 1868, in New
Jersey.
489 iv Jotham C.⁷, b. Jan. 3, 1819.
490 v   Edward Grow⁷, b. Dec. 4, 1820.

199

JEREMIAH⁶ BRADBURY (Joseph⁵, John⁴, Wymond³,
Wymond². Thomas¹), born in Saco, October 22, 1779,
studied law in the office of Cyrus King, Esq., of Saco,
and also in the office of Nicholas Emery of Parsonsfield. He was admitted to the York county bar in
1805, and opened an office in Saco. In 1810 he moved
to Biddeford, and in 1812 to South Berwick. In 1813

---

*William B. Bradbury was a distinguished musician, a popular teacher
of music and author of several singing-books, embracing a wide range
of song, both secular and sacred. His name will long be remembered by
lovers of good music.

he was appointed collector of customs for the district
of York, and in May, 1815, moved to York. In 1820
he was appointed by Governor King clerk of the judicial courts of York county, when he resigned his col-
lectorship and moved to Alfred. He held this position,
with the exception of a single year, until 1841, when
he moved to Calais where he continued the practice of
law, a portion of the time in company with George
Walker, Esq., until November, 1848, when he died.
He was married October 28, 1810, to Mary Langdon, daughter of Seth Storer of Wells and Saco, who
was born in Saco, December 5, 1789. Mrs Bradbury's
mother was Olive, daughter of Col. Tristram Jordan,
who died in Saco, August 4, 1842, aged eighty-four
years.

Children:

491 i Bion⁷, b. Biddeford, Dec. 6, 1811; m. Alice H. Williams.

492 ii Lucius⁷, b. South Berwick, Aug. 3, 1814. He graduated
from the military academy at West Point in 1835.
He went to Calais, and was connected with the press,
studied law, was deputy collector of the district of
Passamaquoddy until his death, which occurred June
27, 1850. He married, Nov. 26, 1846, Emily Hall
Goold, who died in 1848. He then married Lucy A.
Goold, Nov. 29, 1849. One daughter by the second
marriage, Marcia Gardner⁷, was born Sept. 25, 1850.

493 iii Mary Langdon⁷, b. April 2, 1817; m. April 5, 1841,
Rev. William T. Savage of Amherst, N. H. They
afterward moved to Houlton, Me., then to Franklin,
N. H., where she died Jan. 1, 1872. She was a writer
of decided merit; wrote a novel founded on incidents
connected with the great fire at Miramichi, a sketch

8

of her sister Marcia, and a small volume entitled "The Soldier's Child." She contributed more or less of poetry to the public press.

494   iv   Ann Eliza⁷, b. May 28, 1819. She married in 1852, Judge Anson G. Chandler and accompanied him abroad where he had been appointed consul. They returned in 1860, and after that spent much of their time in the middle and southern states. She survived her husband two years, and died in Providence, R. I., March 26, 1865. Their children died in infancy.

495   v   Emily⁷, b. Alfred, May 18, 1821; m. Francis K. Swan·

496   vi   Frederic Storer⁷, b. Aug. 28, 1823; d. Sept. 29, 1824.

497   vii   Marcia⁷, b. July 15, 1825; d. Feb. 28, 1840.

498   viii   Frederic Storer⁷, b March 13, 1829. He served during the early part of the war of the rebellion in the 90th regiment, Pennsylvania volunteers, and was afterward transferred to the 11th Pennsylvania volunteers. He was taken prisoner Aug. 19, 1864, at the attack on the Weldon railroad, and was carried to Richmond. He was transferred to the Salisbury, N. C. prison, where he died Dec. 14, 1864, as the result of the infamous treatment received by Union prisoners at that institution.

205

JOSIAH⁶* BRADBURY (Josiah⁵, Josiah⁴, Wymond³. Wymond², Thomas¹), born February 6, 1773; married Anna Lander, and died February 12, 1860. His wife died at Dead River settlement in September, 1836. His children, born in Starks, Maine, were:

499   i   Josiah⁷, b. ——; d. young.

500   ii   Catherine Frothingham⁷, b. ——; m. —— McKecknie.

---

*He was first named John, but after the death of his brother, his name was changed to Josiah, not Joseph, as stated on page 87.

501 iii Mary Ann[7], b. Feb. 15, 1805; m. Nov. 6, 1823, William Meader.
502 iv Tamar Lander[7], b. March 15, 1807; m. 1830, John D. Caster.
503 v Josiah[7], b. ——.
504 vi Abigail[7], b. ——; m. —— Withes.
505 vii Lydia[7], b. ——; m. —— Fairbanks.
506 viii Ebenezer Clough[7], b. ——; d. unmarried.
507 ix Sarah Jane[7], b. ——.
508 x Learned Greaton[7], b. ——; d. unmarried.

208

THEOPHILUS[6] BRADBURY (Jonathan[5], Theophilus[4], Wymond[3], Wymond[2], Thomas[1]), married October 3, 1792, Lois Pillsbury, who was born July 11, 1775. He resided at Newburyport, and died June 19, 1848; his wife died September 4, 1828.

Children:

509 i Ebenezer[7], b. July 31, 1793; m. Nancy Merrill; 2d Mary Tappan.
510 ii John[7], b. ——, 1795; d. same year.
511 iii daughter[7], b. ——, 1897; d. same year.
512 iv Rebecca[7], b. July 7, 1799; m. John Hughes.
513 v John[7], b. Aug. 18, 1801; m. Rebecca Moody Boardman.
514 vi Mary[7], b. ——, 1803; d. 1808.
515 vii Mary Louisa[7], b. Dec. 13, 1810; m. Moses Hale.

209

SMITH[6] BRADBURY (Jonathan[5], Theophilus[4], Wymond[3], Wymond[2], Thomas[1]), married April 9, 1793, Mary, daughter of Deacon John Hovey. He was a merchant, resided at Kennebunkport, and his children were born there.　He died June 28, 1823.　His widow born February 29, 1768, died May 13, 1838.

Children:

516　i　Harriet[7], b. Dec. 26, 1793; d. Feb. 28, 1814.
517　ii　Mary[7], b. May 22, 1795; m. Dec. 10, 1817, Stephen Towne.
518　iii　Amelia[7], b. May 4, 1797; d. Sept. 12, 1842, at Syracuse, New York.
519　iv　Charles[7], b. Oct. 7, 1798; m. Juliet Walker.
520　v　Caroline[7],* b. Jan. 15, 1803; m. Oliver Smith.

213

CHARLES[6] BRADBURY (Wymond[5], Theophilus[4], Wymond[3], Wymond[2], Thomas[1]), married May 14, 1794, Sarah Blanchard, who was born December 7, 1768. She died February 23, 1801, and he married, second, January 17, 1803, Hannah Oakes, who was born February 27, 1782, and died May 6, 1806. He married, third, April 26, 1807, Mary Oakes, who was born November 9, 1787, and died March 18, 1866.

[*Caroline Bradbury married Capt. Oliver Smith, master-mariner, Nov. 8, 1826, and died in Strafford, Conn., Aug. 17, 1853. Their children were as follows: Frederick, b. Sept. 2, 1827, d. Aug. 8, 1829; Ellen, b. Dec. 20, 1828, d. same day; Frederick Oliver, b. May 28, 1830, d. in New York city June 1, 1855;]Edwin Bradbury, b. Oct. 3, 1832. He graduated from Bowdoin College, in 1856, studied law in the office of Edward E. Bourne, was admitted to the bar of York county, and after practicing three years in Limerick, he opened an office in Saco. Here he was deputy collector of customs three years, represented Saco three years in the state legislature, the last term being elected speaker of the house, and in 1873, he was appointed by Governor Perham, reporter of decisions of the supreme judicial court. In 1875, he was appointed assistant attorney-general of the United States, and resided some years in Washington. He then removed to New York city and was connected with a law firm there. He was never married.

Children, the last eight born in Charlestown :

521 i Charles[7], b. July 10, 1795; d. Sept. 25 following.
522 ii Charles[7], b. Oct. 1, 1796; d. Aug. 31, 1843.
523 iii Sally[7], b. Dec. 26, 1798; d. March 3, 1826.
524 iv Judith[7], b. Feb. 4, 1801; d. Aug. 21, 1803.

By second wife :

525 v James Oakes[7], b. June 30, 1805; d. Sept. 4, 1806.

By third wife :

526 vi infant[7], b. Aug. 16, 1808; . d. aged two days.
527 vii George[7], b. Oct. 28, 1809; d. March 11, 1866.
528 viii Wyman[7], b. Oct. 19, 1812; m. Elizabeth Ann Starbuck.
528½ ix Jonathan Oakes[7], b. April 12, 1815; d. Feb. 14, 1816.
529 x Mary Elizabeth[7], b. Nov. 16, 1817; m. March 7, 1844, John Sanborn of Charlestown.
530 xi Jonathan Oakes[7], b. July 21, 1819; m. Rachel G. Brooks.
531 xii Jane Moody[7], b. March 16, 1822; d. July 9, 1825.
532 xiii Sarah Jane[7], b. July 4, 1826; m. Jan. 24, 1850, William F. Conant of Charlestown.

214

WILLIAM[6] BRADBURY (Wymond[5], Theophilus[4], Wymond[3], Wymond[2], Thomas[1]), married in 1794, Elizabeth Floyd, and died January 4, 1848.

Children :

533 i Eliza[7], b. Aug. 14, 1795; m. Thomas R. Peck of Medford.
534 ii Mary[7], b. Sept. 14, 1797; d. Aug. 15, 1848.
535 iii William Moody[7], b. July 21, 1800; d. Sept. 6, 1821.
536 iv Susan Newhall[7], b. July, 1802; d. May 29, 1867.
537 v Henry Wymond[7], b. March 5, 1804; d. Nov. 8, 1810.
538 vi Caroline[7], b. Jan. 8, 1806 ; m. George Chase.
539 vii Charlotte[7], b. Feb. 14, 1808.
540 viii Adeline[7], b. Sept 11, 1810; d. March 17, 1857.

219

EDWARD[6] BRADBURY (Wymond[5], Theophilus[4], Wymond[3], Wymond[2], Thomas[1]), married October 28, 1804, Abigail Hill. He died August 22, 1855.

Children:

541   i   Elbridge[7], b. Aug. 21, 1805; m. Mary J. Underhill.
542 ii   Abby[7], b. Sept. 25, 1806.
543 iii   Wymond[7], b. Nov. 20, 1811; d. unmarried Feb. 22, 1875.
544 iv   Mary Rogers[7], b. Nov. 18, 1816.

222

FRANCIS[6] BRADBURY (Theophilus[5], Theophilus[4], Wymond[3], Wymond[2], Thomas[1]), married October 6, 1803, Hannah Jones, daughter of John Jones and Nabby (Mears) Spooner of Dorchester, who died February 14, 1827. He died in 1837.

Children:

545   i   Frances[7], b. Aug. 4, 1808; m. 1st Samuel Woodbridge of
          Vergennes, Vt., 2d Otis Haven of Jamaica Plains.
546 ii   Francis[7], b. April 7, 1810; m. Sophia Tomlinson of Ver-
          gennes, Vt.
547 iii   Elizabeth Ann[7], b. ——; d. 1815.
548 iv   Sarah Elenora[7], b. Nov., 1816; m. George S. Curtis. She
          died March 28, 1872.
549   v   Elizabeth[7], b. 1818; d. 1820.
550 vi   John Jones Spooner[7], b. Jan. 10, 1822; m. June 14,
          1860, Devilia L. (Franklin) Cargill of Syracuse, N. Y.
          He died in 1874.

225

GEORGE[6] BRADBURY (Theophilus[5], Theophilus[4], Wymond[3], Wymond[2], Thomas[1]), married June 15, 1800,

Mary Kent of Falmouth, who died in 1819. He died November 17, 1823. He was a lawyer, lived in Portland; was senator in the legislature and served two terms in congress from the Cumberland district, 1813–17.

Children:

551   i   Mary Kent[7], b. Feb. 8, 1801 ; d. unmarried,

552   ii   John Kent[7], b. ——; died at sea.

553   iii   Caroline Keith[7], b. ——; m. June 12, 1837, Luther Daniel of Rutland, Vt.

554   iv   Frances[7], b. ——.

555   v   Francis[7], (?) b. ——, 1803 ; d. 1804.

227

CHARLES[6] BRADBURY (Theophilus[5], Theophilus[4], Wymond[3], Wymond[2], Thomas[1]), married June 17, 1810, Elenora Cumming, and died July 11, 1853. His wife was the only daughter of Thomas Cumming, who came to Falmouth from Scotland in 1773, and carried on business on India street.

Children :

556   i   Charles William[7], b. March 26, 1811 ; m. Eleanor F. Bradley.

557   ii   Mary Kent[7], b. ——; m. Nov. 20, 1845, Theodore Hart of Montreal.

558   iii   Elenora Cummings[7], b. ——; d. ——.

559   iv   Caroline Keith[7], b. ——; m. June 13, 1854, Francis O. Watts of Boston.

560   v   George[7], b. ——; d. 1845.

561   vi   Harriet Maria[7], b. ——; m. Charles L. J. Duchesnay.

562   vii   Thomas[7], b. ——; d. aged two years.

229

John[6] Bradbury (Rowland[5], John[4], William[3], William[2], Thomas[1]), married June 1, 1776, at Meridith, N. H., Susannah Hutchinson. He married second, Anna Emerson.

Children:

563   i   Polly[7], b. ——; m. Ebenezer Avery.
564   ii   John[7], b. Gilmanton, N. H., Sept. 27, 1779; m. Hannah Bubier.
565   iii   Susan[7], b. —— ; m. Royal Prescott.
566   iv   Stephen[7], b. ——; m. widow Locke.

By second wife:

567   v   Anna[7], b. ——; m. 1st —— Chute, 2d Stephen Gale.
568   vi   William[7], b. ——; m. Phebe Horr.
569   vii   Sally[7], b. ——; m. James Hunkins.
570   viii   Benjamin[7], b. ——; m. Lorinda Knowlton, or Joanna Weeks.
571   ix   Joseph[7], b. Oct. 16, 1793; m. Hannah Boyd.
572   x   Phebe[7], b. ——; m. at Guilford, Tufton Vittum, r. Sandwich, N. H.
573   xi   Jesse[7], b. ——; m. Susan Craig.
574   xii   Betsey[7], b. ——; m. at Gilmanton, John Hutchinson.
575   xiii   Jabez[7], b. ——; d. unmarried.

232

Paul[6] Bradbury (Rowland[5], John[4], William[3], William[2], Thomas[1]), married March 14, 1780, Ruth Weare, who was born in York, December 23, 1756. He moved from Salisbury to Tamworth, N. H., and died at Belgrade, Maine, December 21, 1832. His wife died in Industry, Maine, December 31, 1823.

Children :

576   i   John Stevens[7], b. Aug. 6, 1781 ; m. Lois Pinkham.
577   ii   Jane Choate[7], b. March 22, 1783 ; m. John Gould of Newton, N. H.
578   iii   Molly[7], b. Oct. 1, 1785 ; m. Daniel Townsend of Sidney.
579   iv   True[7], b. Jan. 31, 1788 ; m. Lydia Cushing Allen.
580   v   Hannah[7], b. ——, 1790 ; d. young.
581   vi   Abigail[7], b. ——, 1792 ; d. young.
582   vii   Sukey[7], b. Jan. 10, 1794 ; m. John Lord of Belgrade.
583   viii   Samuel Hidden[7], b. March 29, 1796 ; m. Bethiah H. Dinsmore.

234

EPHRAIM[6] BRADBURY (Rowland[5], John[4], William[3], William[2], Thomas[1]), married February 13, 1773, Molly Wier (or Weare). He died in Moultonboro, N. H.

Children :

584   i   Dolly Stevens[7], b. March 21, 1774 ; m. David Adams ; d. April 26, 1848, in Sandwich, N. H.
585   ii   Mehitable[7], b. Kensington, N. H.; m. Isaac Ryan of Plymouth, N. H.; d. in Plymouth, N. H., 1848.
586   iii   Eunice[7], b. Moultonboro ; m. Joseph Graves.
587   iv   Jane[7], b. March 11, 1782 ; m. Sept. 6, 1804, Ezekiel Merrill of Plymouth, N. H.; d. Dec. 22, 1817. He d. July 29, 1879.
588   v   Rebecca[7], b. —— ; m. Augustus Chandler of Moultonboro, N. H.
589   vi   Ephraim[7], b. —— ; d. aged 8 years.

235

WILLIAM[6] BRADBURY (Samuel[5], James[4], William[3], William[2], Thomas[1]), married in 1787, Polly Meacham.

Children :

591   i   Judith⁷, b. ——, 1789.
592   ii   Mary⁷, b. ——, 1791.
593   iii Sally⁷, b. ——, 1794.
594   iv   Samuel⁷, b. ——, 1796.
595   v   William⁷, b. ——. 1799.
596   vi   David⁷, b. ——, 1802.
598   vii Benjamin⁷, b. ——, 1803.
599   viii Betsey⁷, b. ——, 1806.
600   ix   Roswell⁷, b. ——, 1812.

236

JAMES⁶, BRADBURY (Samuel⁵, James⁴, William³, William², Thomas¹), married November 6, 1783, Sarah Coffin. She died October 6. 1828, and he died in January, 1847.

Children :

601   i   Ebenezer⁷, b. Dec. 11, 1784; m. Mary Thompson.
602   ii   Sarah⁷, b. Dec. 13. 1786; m. William H. Mitchell.
603   iii Nancy Coffin⁷, b. July 15, 1789; m. June 18, 1825, Moses Farrington.
604   iv   Polly⁷, b. ——; d. ——.
605   v   Mary⁷, b. Feb. 28, ——: m. Joseph Jones.
606   vi   James⁷, b. March 22, 1799.
607   vii John Coffin⁷, b. Sept. 11, 1801 ; m. Margaret Shaw Tilton.

239

SAMUEL⁶ BRADBURY (Samuel⁵, James⁴, William³, William², Thomas¹). married in 1806, Christiana Gates. He was a seaman with home in Baltimore. He was lost at sea in 1811.

Child :

608 i   John Talbot Morris⁷, b. ——, 1807; m. Mary Jane Robinson.

241

DAVID[6] BRADBURY (Samuel[5], James[4], William[3]. William[2]. Thomas[1]), married September 24, 1795, Abigail R. Simpson. He died April 30, 1845.

Children :

609   i   Samuel[7], b. Sept. 24, 1796; d. Jan. 24, 1817, unmarried.

610   ii   David B. S.[7], b. Nov. 6, 1797; d. Dec. 25, 1822, unmarried.

611   iii   Francis C.[7], b. Feb. 4, 1799; m. May 30, 1830, Orelia M. Pizaro, who was born in Italy; no issue.

612   iv   John[7], b. Sept. 18, 1800; d. Dec. 25, 1809.

613   v   Mary S.[7], b. March 27, 1802; d. March, 1875, unmarried.

614   vi   Sarah[7], b. Sept. 11, 1803; d. in Boston, Feb. 10, 1872.

615   vii   William Simpson[7], b. Feb. 8, 1805; m. Mary H. Oliver.

616   viii   George[7], b. Oct. 16, 1807; d. Dec. 9, 1835, unmarried.

617   ix   Abigail S.[7], b. March 3, 1810; m. 1853, Thomas A. Gross of Welfleet, Mass.

618   x   Belinda[7], b. June 17, 1812; m. Feb. 2, 1828, James Davis of New Sharon.

619   xi   Eliza S.[7], b. May 21, 1814; d. March 25, 1844.

620   xii   Pamelia C.[7], b. June 29, 1818; d. unmarried.

621   xiii   Harriet B.[7], b. July 3, 1820; m. 1845, William Billings of New Sharon; 2d, 1853, James E. Lewis of Providence, R. I. They both died in Providence.

244

DANIEL[6] BRADBURY* (Sanders[5], James[4], William[3], William[2], Thomas[1]), married September 15, 1791, Eliz-

*Daniel Bradbury was a native of Nottingham, N. H. When sixteen years of age he enlisted in a Salem, N. H., company and joined the patriot army at West Point. He served through the remainder of the war, and at its close received his discharge at the hands of Washington. After the war he spent some time in the service of Washington while he was president. He then settled in Haverhill.

abeth Lunt, who was born September 29, 1765, and died in 1853. He died September 21, 1852. Their children were born in Newbury and Haverhill, Mass.

Children :

622   i   Sally[7], b. April 19, 1792 ; m. James Bracy.

623   ii   Daniel[7], b. March 23, 1795 ; d. unmarried.

624   iii   Harriet[7], b. Feb. 2, 1797 ; m. Nov. 26, 1817, Benjamin Pettengill of Newbury, Mass.

625   iv   Mary[7], b. Sept. 23, 1800 ; m. Isaac Emerson of Methuen.

626   v   Betsey[7], b. Feb. 7, 1803 ; m. Benj. Smith of Haverhill.

627   vi   Hannah[7], b. July 10, 1805 ; m. William Kimball of North Andover.

628   vii   Nancy[7], b. Feb. 4, 1808 ; m. Joshua Witham.

247

JAMES[6] BRADBURY (Sanders[5], James[4], William[3], William[2], Thomas[1]), married April 5, 1795, Catherine Conant, who was born November 28. 1793, and died March 12, 1862, in Cambridge, Mass. He died October 14, 1811, in Hollis. N. H.

Children :

629   i   James[7], b. Jan. 4, 1796 ; m. Louisa Ayer.

630   ii   Catherine[7], b. March 25, 1798.

631   iii   William Sanders[7], b. Feb. 14, 1800 ; m. Elizabeth Emerson.

632   iv   Charles[7], b. July 4, 1802; m. Mary E. Worcester.

633   v   Elizabeth[7], b. Sept. 18, 1804 ; m. Nov. 7, 1841, Francis Caverly of Boston.

634   vi   Samuel Fox[7], b. Dec. 25, 1806 ; m. Mary Ann (Leathe) Brooks.

635   vii   Josiah Conant[7], b. Feb. 21, 1809 ; m. Almira Hemenway.

636   viii   Mary Ann[7], b. May 17, 1811.

251

Jacob[6] Bradbury (Sanders[5], James[4], William[3], William[2], Thomas[1]), married Mary Hutchinson, who was born in Windsor county, Vermont, in 1775, and died October 10, 1845. He died in Madison, Iowa, November 20, 1826. He moved from Hartford, Vermont, to Onondaga county, New York, and from thence to Manlius county, Ohio.

Children:

637   i   Cornelius Saunders[7], b. Dec. 11, 1799; m. Sallie Ann Spinney.

638   ii   Elizabeth[7], b. ——, 1804; d. South Carolina in 1825.

639   iii   Marcus Tullius Cicero[7], b. March 14, 1808; m. Catherine Thorne.

640   iv   Emily[7], b. July 16, 1810; m. —— Westgate.

641   v   Charlotte[7], b. Jan. 14, 1812; m. Enoch Doane.

642   vi   Mary[7], b. ——, 1814; m. 1851, Whiston Bristow.

643   vii   Charles William[7], b. July, 1816; m. ——, no issue.

644   viii   James[7], b March, 1820. He was residing in Ohio unmarried in 1858.

252

William[6] Bradbury (Sanders[5], James[4], William[3], William[2]. Thomas[1]), married in 1805. Sarah (Lunt) Mitchell, who was born September 9, 1779, and died in St. Louis, Mo., November 8, 1850. He died in Brattleboro, Vt., July 13, 1845.

Children:

645   i   William Lunt[7], b. Dec. 23, 1805; m. April 26, 1829, Sarah Martin. He died in New York, 1850.

646   ii   Elizabeth Chapman[7], b. Oct. 31, 1808; d. Milford, N. H., March 27, 1833.

647 iii   Joseph Sanders[7], b. July 22, 1811 ; m. Mary M. Lunt.
648 iv   Sarah[7], b. March 14, 1814 ; d. Milford, N. H., Oct. 15, 1814.

253

JOSEPH[6] BRADBURY (Sanders[5], James[4] William[3], William[2], Thomas[1]), married January 29, 1804, Hannah Putnam, who was born April 29, 1785, and died in South Boston, May 27, 1841. He died in Hillsboro, N. H., April 9, 1832. Their children, born in Woodstock, Vermont, were :

649   i   Alma Lorassi[7], b. Dec. 23, 1804 ; d. April 9, 1832.
650   ii   Laura de Sedolitz[7], b. Dec. 23, 1806 ; d. Jan. 4, 1833.
651   iii   Susan Amanda[7], b. Aug. 9, 1808 ; d. Aug. 8, 1834.
652   iv   Sarah Colby[7], b. March 18, 1810 ; m. Feb. 9, 1834, Sabins Travers.
653   v   Lefe Pierce[7], b. Jan. 13, 1812 ; m. April, 1840, James Percival. She died in Hillsboro, N. H., Aug. 17, 1848.
654   vi   Mary[7], b. Sept. 7, 1813 ; d. Sept. 25 following.
655   vii   Martha[7], b. Sept. 7, 1813 ; d. Sept. 30 following.
656   viii   Joseph[7], b. Aug. 27, 1814.
657   ix   George Washington[7], b. June 19, 1816 ; m. Ann Rebecca Wright.
658   x   James Putnam[7], b. March 19, 1818 ; d. Aug. 21, 1849.
659   xi   Charles[7], b. Dec. 24, 1819 ; d. July 17, 1821.
660   xii   William Henry[7], b. July 24, 1821 ; d. Nov. 13, 1840, in Boston.
661   xiii   Charles Augustus[7], b. April 8, 1823 ; d. Dec. 2, 1826.
662   xiv   Edward Mortimer[7], b. April 18, 1825 ; d. Oct. 25, 1844.
663   xv   Hannah Frances[7], b. April 17, 1827 ; d. 1867 at Woodstock, Vt.

257

JAMES[6] BRADBURY (James[5], Crisp[4], William[3], William[2], Thomas[1]), married January 20, 1805. Mary Scammon, who was born August 4, 1788. He died at sea in September, 1803.

Children:

664   i   Rufus[7], b. Nov. 27, 1805; d. Sept. 7, 1806.
665   ii   Octavia[7], b. Aug. 6, 1807; m. Oct. 9, 1828, Joseph Lane. She d. Jan. 12, 1841.
666   iii   Nathaniel[7], b. June 13, 1809; m. Lucy Sawyer.

260

CRISP[6] BRADBURY (James[5], Crisp[4], William[3], William[2], Thomas[1]), married June 13, 1824, Mary Rumery, and died in Biddeford, April 17, 1828. His widow married William Berry of Old Orchard, and again became a widow. She was the daughter of Edward, jr., and Rebecca (Scammon) Rumery.

Children:

667   i   James Paine[7], b. March 23, 1825; d. Aug. 23, 1826.
668   ii   Edward Rumery[7], b. June 17, 1827; m. Harriet Newell Noble.

267

JABEZ[6] BRADBURY (William[5], Benjamin[4], William[3], William[2], Thomas[1]), was by occupation a millwright. He married Priscilla Joselyn and moved to Hodgdon, Maine. His wife had deceased prior to 1850, and at that time he was living in the family of Christopher C. Bradbury in Hodgdon, whose wife was his wife's sister.

Children :

669　i　George W.⁷, b. ——, 1830.
670　ii　David⁷, b. ——, 1834,

280

JACOB⁶ BRADBURY (Jacob⁵, Thomas⁴, Jacob³, William². Thomas¹), married Jane Piper.

Children :

671　i　John⁷, b. March 22, 1805; d. Feb. 24, 1834.
672　ii　Benjamin⁷, b. ——; d. aged two years.
673　iii　Jane⁷, b. Jan. 9, 1809.
674　iv　Albion⁷, b. May 6, 1810; m. Elizabeth L. Wentworth.
675　v　Sally⁷, b. March 31, 1815.

282

THOMAS⁶ BRADBURY (Jacob⁵, Thomas⁴, Jacob³, William², Thomas¹), married Sally Webster, who died in 1840, perhaps at Bangor. He died in 1849 at Charlestown, Mass.

Children :

676　i　Amanda⁷, b. ——; m. Micajah Haskell.
677　ii　Charles Webster⁷, b. Oct. 30, 1807; m. Sarah Merrill.
678　iii　John Thomas⁷, b. ——; d. aged ten years.
679　iv　Horace James⁷, b. Dec. 7, 1811; m. Harriet Newell Ulrick.
680　v　Edwin⁷, b. ——; m. and lived in Georgetown, Cal., and died there.

283

JOSEPH⁶ BRADBURY* (Jacob⁵, Thomas⁴, Jacob³, William². Thomas¹), married at Andover, Mass., Elizabeth,

*Joseph Bradbury settled in Exeter, Me., and after a few years, in 1816, emigrated westward. Something over fifty years after he left Ex-

or Betsey Stevens, who was born April 21, 1776, and died October 4, 1838. He was one of the early settlers of Exeter, Maine. He died in Cheshire, Ohio, Sep-ter, in 1872, three of his sons, Caleb, Asa and Joseph, came from their distant homes to visit the place of their birth, on which occasion the late David Barker composed the following lines:—

THE BRADBURY BOYS.

I know how people talk and feel,
    About this noise and fuss,
This meeting here today between
    The Bradbury boys and us.

How time whirls on—in figuring up
    We find the fact appears,
Since last we met these Bradbury boys
    'Tis more than fifty years.

Perhaps you know these Bradbury boys,
    If not, you ought to know
This tall, gray fellow here is Cale,
    And then come Ase and Joe.

These other fellows lubbering round,
    Are all our boys you see—
Here's Noah and Nat and Dan and Mark,
    And also Lew and me.

These Bradbury boys, one left his law,
    And one his grapes and corn,
And traveled near a thousand miles
    To find where they were born.

Look:—here's where *old* Joe Bradbury lived—
    The place that Bradbury tilled,
And there's the chopping father cleared
    The year that he was killed.

And there's where Thomas Townsend dwelt,
    Where on his leathern seat,
He took those measures year by year
    Of our tired, pattering feet.

tember 1, 1828. His children were born in Limerick
and Exeter, Maine, and in Cheshire, Ohio, and were:

681   i   Caleb⁷, b. Jan. 10, 1801; m. Almira Elizabeth Brown.
682 ii Ammi R. C.⁷, b. ——; d. aged 16 months.

> Those feet have trod some slippery paths
>   Since death one day so grim,
> Took Townsend from his kit of tools
>   And then his breath from him.
>
> That broken clam-shell skimmer there,
>   This moment found by Joe,
> His mother used for skimming milk
>   Some sixty years ago.
>
> Poor Joe—but then my muse can wait
>   Until your cheeks are dry.
> Some think that nought but loss of fees,
>   Can make a lawyer cry.
>
> That wall—hold on—Nat's pigs are out—
>   Good gracious what a fuss
> Mid pigs and tears to rhyme about,
>   The Bradbury boys and us.
>
> Don't ask—that thought has bothered me:—
>   This *how* and *where* and *when*,
> We six shall meet and recognize
>   These Bradbury boys again.
>
> Friends of life's early youth accept
>   This humble gift of mine,
> A wreath wrought with a hurried hand
>   Around this pilgrim shrine.
>
> However faint a fickle faith
>   Some future bliss insures,
> Amid each agony of doubt
>   One present bliss is yours.
>
> If you will bear to western homes
>   Old memories frought with joy,
> As Æneas bore Anchises through
>   The burning gates of Troy.

683   iii   Mary Stevens⁷, b. Jan. 28, 1804; m. 1st Aug. 24, 1823, Thomas Russell, and 2d, Dec. 11, 1834, Jacob Boice.

684   iv   Asa⁷, b. Nov. 22, 1805; m. Electa Harding.

685   v   Joseph⁷, b. Sept. 12, 1807; m. Eliza Strong.

686   vi   Samuel⁷, b. Aug. 4, 1809; m. Clarissa Hackett.

687   vii   Phebe⁷, b. Sept. 18, 1811; m. Dec. 30, 1830, William Giles Sisson.

688   viii   Nancy⁷, b. July 13, 1813; m. Aug. 2, 1854, Nathan Edmundston.

689   ix   Sarah⁷, b. April 19, 1815; m. Nov. 15, 1847, Zachariah Rathgeb.

690   x   Moses Russell⁷, b. May 13, 1818; m. Mary Harding.

289

SAMUEL.⁶ BRADBURY (Moses⁵, Thomas⁴, Jacob³, William², Thomas¹), married Abigail Cleaves of Biddeford, and resided in that town.

Children :

691   i   True⁷, b. Jan. 27, 1785; m. Sally Nason.

692   ii   Ebenezer Cleaves⁷, b. June 2, 1788; m. Clara Adams.

694   iii   James⁷, b. ——.

695   iv   Abigail⁷, b. ——.

696   v   Mary⁷, b. ——; m. Benjamin Gilpatrick of Limerick.

697   vi   Samuel⁷, b. ——.

698   vii   Christopher Columbus⁷, b. June ——, 1794; m. Mary Joselyn.

296

JABEZ PAGE⁶ BRADBURY (Thomas⁵, Thomas⁴, Jacob³, William², Thomas¹), married at Limerick, May 27, 1786, Sarah Hilton Whitney.

Children :

699   i   Sarah⁷, bap. June 20, 1790 ; m. Isaac Fellows of Athens.
700   ii   Abner⁷, b. Dec. 29, 1787 ; m. Eunice Hall of Augusta.
701   iii   Josiah⁷, b. ——.
702   iv   Jabez⁷, b. ——.
703   v   Mary⁷, b. —— ; m. Caleb Linscott.
704   vi   Anna⁷, b. —— ; m. Jacob Grosheimer.
705   vii   Lucy⁷, b. —— ; Andrew Cloutman.
706   viii   Lucinda⁷, b. —— ; m. Rufus Jones of Parkman.

297

DANIEL⁶ BRADBURY (Thomas⁵, Thomas⁴, Jacob³, William², Thomas¹), married in Buxton, November 27, 1788, Mary Wingate, who was born in Saco, August 24, 1769. They lived in Limerick. Cornville and Athens, Maine. She died June 5, 1835, and he died at Athens, November 23, 1850.

Children :

707   i   Emery⁷, b. June 14, 1789.
708   ii   Thomas⁷, b. Feb. 18, 1791 ; m. Dolly Morse.
709   iii   Daniel⁷, b. April 7, 1793 ; m. Mary ——.
710   iv   Silas⁷, b. May 2, 1795.
711   v   William⁷, b. Dec. 31, 1797 ; m. Comfort Taylor.
712   vi   Ruth⁷, b. April 1, 1800; m. Lewis Turner.
713   vii   Simon⁷, b. Sept. 19, 1802 ; m. Hannah Wood.
714   viii   Wingate⁷, b. Feb. 9, 1805 ; m. Sarah Hodgdon.
715   ix   Margaret⁷, b. April 22, 1807 ; m. George Locke.
716   x   Benjamin⁷, b. Oct. 9, 1809.
717   xi   Leonard⁷, b. Feb. 20, 1813 ; m. Fanny Hight.

299

THOMAS⁶ BRADBURY (Thomas⁵, Thomas⁴, Jacob³, William². Thomas¹), married March 6, 1806, Abigail Boothby. He lived in Buxton, and died May 29, 1832.

Children:

718   i   Achsah[7], b. Jan. 20, 1807; m. Feb. 7, 1835, Parker Beede of Sandwich, N. H.

719   ii   Mary[7], b. Nov. 13, 1808; m. Dec. 2, 1837, Peter G. Mason of Tamworth, N. H.

720   iii   Cyrus[7], b. April 20, 1811; m. Elizabeth E. Cheney; no issue.

721   iv   Thomas[7], b. March 31, 1831; m. Emeline Edgerly.

722   v   Harriet[7], b. July 28, 1815; m. Nov. 4, 1850, Jonathan Boothby of Saco.

723   vi   Gratia Rand[7], b. Jan. 20, 1818; m. June 9, 1834, Elijah Tarbox of Buxton.

724   vii   Edward Warren[7], b. July 2, 1820.

725   viii   James[7], b. April 27, 1823.

309

JOHN[6] BRADBURY (William[5], Thomas[4], Jacob[3], William[2], Thomas[1]), married in 1815, Hannah Hanscom. He died April 19, 1858.

Children:

726   i   William Hanscom[7], b. Sept. 7, 1816.

727   ii   Jesse Lee[7], b. March 1, 1819.

728   iii   Eugene[7], b. Dec. 14, 1821.

729   iv   John Seavy[7], b. Jan. 3, 1831.

311

BENJAMIN[6] BRADBURY (Benjamin[5], Thomas[4], Jacob[3], William[2], Thomas[1]), married November 19, 1795, Betsey Eaton, who died November 23, 1814, and he married second, —— Bryant.

Children:

730   i   Ruth[7], b, Aug. 11, 1797; m. Samuel Hill.
731   ii   Mary[7], b. Jan. 5, 1801; m. Alonzo Cobb.
732   iii   John Eaton[7], b. April 23, 1803; m. ——.
733   iv   Sarah[7], b. Aug. 8, 1806.
734   v   Harriet[7], b. Sept. 9, 1808.
735   vi   Thomas[7], b. July 18, 1811.

By second marriage:

736   vii   Gibeon[7], b. ——.
737   viii   Benjamin Franklin[7], b. ——.
738   ix   Betsey[7], b.——; d. unmarried. (She may have been first wife's child.)

315

GIBEON[6] BRADBURY (Benjamin[5], Thomas[4], Jacob[3], William[2], Thomas[1]), married ——.

Children:

739   i   Ichabod[7], b. ——.
740   ii   Gideon Witham[7], b. ——; m. Eliza[7] Bradbury.
741   iii   Thomas[7], b. ——.
742   iv   Mary[7], b. ——; m. Nathaniel Temple.
743   v   Sarah[7], b. ——; m. Aaron Fagan.
744   vi   Huldah[7], b. ——; m. James Pollock.
745   vii   Rachel[7], b. ——; m. —— Williams.

316

MOSES[6] BRADBURY (Benjamin[5]. Moses[4], Jacob[3], William[2], Thomas[1]), married April 13, 1802, Agnes Hunt, who was born in Kentucky, October 4, 1785, and died September 17, 1840. He moved to Cincinnati about the year 1800, removed to Illinois and died August 10, 1849.

Children :

746   i   Phebe[7], b. Aug. 18, 1803 ; m. Nicholas Walker.

747   ii   Rachel[7], b. Nov. 14, 1804 ; m. N. H. Turner.

748   iii   Elden[7], b. Nov., 1806 ; d. April 16, 1818.

749   iv   Mary[7], b. 1808 ; m. Abel Chase, M.D.; d. Aug. 6, 1839.

750   v   Levi Hunt[7], b. July 6, 1810 ; m. Mary A. Turner.

751   vi   Sally G.[7], b. May 18, 1812 ; d. July following.

752   vii   Benjamin[7], b. May 30, 1813. He was a Baptist minister.

753   viii   William[7], b. Oct. 7, 1815 ; d. next day.

754   ix   Sarah[7], b. June 4, 1817 ; d. June 4, 1831.

755   x   Andrew Sherborn[7], b. June 6, 1819 ; m. Sarah Ann Brunson.

756   xi   Ruth[7], b. Sept. 8, 1821 ; d. Dec. following.

757   xii   Cynthia Ann[7], b. Jan. 26, 1823.

758   xiii   Thomas[7],   ⎞   He went to California.

                          ⎬ twins, b. March 8, 1826.

759   xiv   Elizabeth[7],   ⎠   m. May 5, 1844, A. H. Holman.

317

JACOB[6] BRADBURY (Benjamin[5], Thomas[4], Jacob[3], William[2], Thomas[1]), went to Ohio, where he married Patience (Rounds) Quinby, who was born November 1, 1782. She was the widow of Archibald Quinby of Saccarappa, who moved to Ohio and died a year after. She had by her first marriage one daughter, Polly (Quinby), born May 18, 1801. In 1827, Jacob Bradbury went down the Ohio in a flat-bottom boat, built by himself, to the Mississippi, up the Mississippi to the Illinois, then up the latter to Naples, Scott county, where he settled.*

*In June, 1848, a family gathering of the descendants of Jacob Bradbury was held at the residence of his son, Lemuel Bradbury, in Pike county, Illinois. A local paper, published at the time, has the following:

Children :

760	i	Thomas⁷, b. Jan. 23, 1804; m. Pamelia or "Milly" Copeland.
761	ii	Lemuel⁷, b. April 18, 1805; m. Lydia Troy.
762	iii	Sally⁷, b. Nov. 30, 1806; m. 1826, Vincent Gray.
763	iv	Ruth⁷, b. April 24, 1809; m. John C. Wadsworth.
764	v	Lucy⁷, b. Oct. 20, 1810; m. Cephas Simmons.
765	vi	Nathan Boulter⁷, b. Sept. 20, 1812; m. Dorcas Bogges.
766	vii	Betsey⁷, b. July 9, 1814; d. same month.
767	viii	Samuel⁷, b. Dec. 3, 1815; m. Julia A. Merris.
768	ix	Katy⁷, b. Sept. 19, 1817; m. Francis A. Kirkpatrick.
769	x	Eliza⁷, b. Sept. 10, 1819; m. 1837, Gideon Witham Bradbury (740).
770	xi	Jacob Gary⁷, b. Sept. 29, 1821; m. Susan Gould.
771	xii	Jotham Bragdon⁷, b. March 12, 1824; m. Mahala J. Hobbs.

318

THOMAS⁶ BRADBURY (Benjamin⁵, Thomas⁴, Jacob³, William², Thomas¹), married Katherine Hunt, who was born April 17, 1788, and died October 7, 1843. He

" Jacob Bradbury and wife, who now reside a mile and a half south of Perry, in this county, were natives of Maine. Mr. Bradbury was born Nov. 7, 1783, and Mrs. Bradbury was born Nov. 1, 1782. They came to Ohio in 1800, and afterward emigrated to this state, landing at Naples twenty-one years ago. Their numerous descendants, numbering ninety-one, inclusive of those united to members of the family by marriage, now all reside within six miles of their parents. Eighty-five of these (one being absent in Mexico, and five hindered by sickness), assembled recently by appointment at the house of Lemuel Bradbury, the second son. They were marshalled into a beautiful grove where they listened to an address by the Rev. B. B. Carpenter, and then repaired to a richly spread table one hundred and ten feet long where they feasted. And after spending awhile in social chat, they separated, feeling that their attachment for each other was strengthened by their social interview."

died August 19, 1845. His children were born in Wayne county, Indiana, and were:

772   i   Smith Hunt[7], b. Nov. 30, 1812; d. Feb. 1, 1837.
773   ii   Gideon Eldon[7], b. March 4, 1815; d. July 23, 1833.
774   iii   Mary[7], b. March 31, 1817; d. April 27, 1841.
775   iv   Charles Ellison[7], b. Feb. 2, 1819; m. Margaret Beard.
776   v   Rebecca[7], b. March 8, 1821; d. Feb. 25, 1840.
777   vi   Zenas George Washington[7], b. Jan. 31, 1823; m. Eveline Beard.
778   vii   Benjamin Franklin[7], b. Jan. 17, 1825; m. Maria J. Colvin.
779   viii   Sarah[7], b. Jan. 21, 1828; d. March 4, 1842.
780   ix   Thomas Perry[7], b. Aug. 31, 1830; d. Oct. 25, 1835.
781   x   Nathan Eldon[7], b. April 17, 1833; r. Knox county, Ill.

319

NATHAN[6] BRADBURY (Benjamin[5], Thomas[4], Jacob[3], William[2], Thomas[1]), married Mehitable Warren; and second, Mary Hobbs.

Children:

782   i   Nancy[7], b. ——, 1817; m. John Vertriece.
783   ii   Mahala[7], b. Nov. 24, 1818; m. Jacob Hobbs.
784   iii   Samuel[7], b. Sept. 8, 1821.
785   iv   Carthena[7], b. Oct. 26, 1823; m. Nathan Butler Bradbury.
786   v   John Warren[7], b. Jan. 1, 1826; m. Mary Jane Elliot.
787   vi   Cephas[7], b. Aug. 25, 1828; m. Emily Ann Ward.

320

SAMUEL[6] BRADBURY (Benjamin[5], Thomas[4], Jacob[3], William[2], Thomas[1]), married July 4, 1810, Mary Hanley, who was born November 11, 1790, and died August 22, 1827. He died August 30, 1835. He lived in Brown county, Ohio.

Children :

788   i   Elizabeth⁷, b. July 27, 1811; m. Feb. 8, 1831, Thomas Sheldon.

789   ii   Louisa⁷, b. Nov. 28, 1812; m. June, 1831, Allen B. Reynolds.

790   iii   Lydia⁷, b. Dec. 20, 1814; m. Charles Butler.

791   iv   Jacob⁷, b. Oct. 26, 1816; m. Ruth Bogges, r. St. Augustine, Ill.

792   v   Elden⁷, b. July 23, 1818; d. Aug., 1831.

793   vi   Rebecca⁷, b. June 23, 1820; m. 1839, John McDonald.

794   vii   Dorcas⁷, b. June 4, 1823; m. John Flemming.

795   viii   James Madison⁷, b. Aug. 4, 1826; m. Naomi Wilson. He resides in Pike county, Ill.

321

Moses⁶ Bradbury (Jacob⁵, Jacob⁴, Jacob³, William², Thomas¹), married September 18, 1791, Mercy Garland, and died January 12, 1816. She died January 8, 1840. He resided in Buxton, Me., in a house he purchased of Joshua Kimball.

Children :

796   i   Mary⁷, b. April 8, 1792; m. Sept. 2, 1814, Abraham L. Kimball.*

*Abraham L. Kimball, son of Joshua, jr., and Abigail (Earl) Kimball, and grandson of Joshua Kimball who came to Buxton, Me., from Marblehead, Mass., and married April 20, 1767, Martha, daughter of Captain John Elden, born in Buxton, Nov. 3, 1789, married Polly or Mary, daughter of Moses Bradbury, and had the following children: i Joshua, b. July 7, 1815, d. Dec. 29, 1816; ii Mary, b. Dec. 22, 1816, m. Alfred Crosby, d. in De Kalb county, Ill., April 25, 1842; iii Horace, b. June 8, 1818, m. Lois Crosby; iv Oren, b. Sept. 14, 1821, m. Agnes M. Brown, d. Aug. 25, 1852, at La Crosse, Wis.; v Richard, b. Jan. 15, 1825, served in the late war and died at La Crosse, Jan. 22, 1865; vi Harriet, b. July 19, 1827, d. at Buxton, Oct. 27 following; vii William, b. July 18, 1828, d. at Oshkosh, Wis., Feb. 13, 1851; viii Charles Bradbury, b. March 31, 1831, m. Mary

797 ii Jacob[7], b. May 1, 1793; m. Sally Bradbury.
798 iii Joanna[7], b. July 16, 1795; m. Nov. 19, 1817, Nathan Goodwin.*
799 iv Catherine[7], b. May 17, 1797; m. Elias Banks.
800 v Elizabeth[7], b. Aug. 28, 1799; m. Rufus Atkinson.
801 vi John Garland[7], b. Dec. 6, 1801; m. Mary Emery.
802 vii Sophronia[7], b. Dec. 31, 1803; m. Jan. 19, 1834, Arcadus E. Meserve.
803 viii Moses Garland[7], b. April 24, 1806; m. Eliza Hemphill.
804 ix Mercy[7], b. Feb. 14, 1810; m. Moses Emerson.
805 x Hannah[7], b. Dec. 1, 1811; m. Jonathan Purington.
806 xi Charles Coffin[7], b. Dec. 26, 1812; m. Mary M. Hall.

Ann Clough of Racine, Wis.; ix Martha, b. May 5, 1833, m. Penuel L. Clark, r. La Crosse; x Elizabeth, b. Dec. 23, 1835, d. Feb. 14, 1851. The first seven were born in Buxton and the last three in Howland.

*Nathan Goodwin was a descendant of Daniel Goodwin who had a grant of land in Kittery, in 1652, and several subsequent grants; married first, Margaret, daughter of Thomas Spencer, and second, Sarah, daughter of John Sanders and widow Peter Turbot. The descent is Daniel[1], William[2], m. Deliverance Taylor; John[3], and wife Patience Willoughby; Joseph[4], and Elizabeth Warren; Joseph[5], and Mary Heseltine, and Nathan[6], who married Joanna Bradbury. These last were the parents of William Frederic Goodwin, who was born in Buxton in 1823, graduated from Bowdoin College in 1848, taught academies a few years, studied law and received the degree of L.L. B. from Harvard College, and was about to enter into practice when the war broke out. He entered the service as first lieutenant in the regular army, was severely wounded and disabled at the battle of Chickamauga, was breveted captain and placed on recruiting service. He remained in the service to the close of the war, then settled in Concord, N. H., where he died from the effects of his wounds in 1872. He was an enthusiastic historical student, compiled the early records of Buxton, which were published; aided Dennett in restoring the old plan of Buxton, showing the location of the early settlers; and was a constant contributor to Dawson's Historical Magazine. He obtained through Miss Harriet Bainbridge much important information respecting his ancestry in England, both on the maternal and paternal side. His death was much lamented.

324

Edmund[6] Bradbury (Jacob[5], Jacob[4], Jacob[3], William[2], Thomas[1]), married December 24, 1797, Martha Whitney.

Children:

807   i   William[7], b. Aug. 5, 1798.
808   ii   Priscilla[7], b. Feb. 4, 1800.
809   iii   Ruth[7], b. July 14, 1802; m. July 10, 1834, William Whitten.
810   iv   Gibeon[7], b. Jan. 28, 1804.
811   v   Mary[7], b. June 20, 1806.
812   vi   Eliza[7], b. Feb. 6, 1810.
813   vii   Catherine[7], b. Sept. 16, 1812.
814   viii   Jacob[7], b. Aug. 6, 1815.
815   ix   Olive[7], b. Aug. 16, 1819.

326

Simeon Goodwin[6] Bradbury (Jacob[5], Jacob[4], Jacob[3], William[2], Thomas[1]), married April 28, 1805, Ruth Sands, who died April 18, 1807. He married second, Sally (Davis) Emery, November 13, 1808, who died August, 1830. He married third, Thankful Paine.

Children:

816   i   Albert Gallatin Goodwin[7], b. Jan. 12, 1806; m. Clarissa Warren
817   ii   Ruth Sands[7], b. April 2, 1807; m. April 6, 1831, James Whitten.

By second wife:

818   iii   Lorenzo[7], b. Aug. 24, 1809; m. Ann Shackford.
819   iv   Edwin[7], b. March 9, 1813.
820   v   Cyrus[7], b. March 9, 1813.
821   vi   John Adams[7], b. March 8, 1815; m. Aug., 1838, Amanda Dearborn of Clinton.

822 vii Adeline[7], b. May 19, 1816.
823 viii Simeon Goodwin[7], b. Nov. 5, 1817.
824 ix Sally Davis[7], b. Nov. 5, 1817.
825 x Mary Goodwin[7], b. June 14, 1819.
826 xi Lucinda Leavitt[7], b. Feb. 2, 1821.
827 xii Rebecca Harding[7], b. June 14, 1822.
828 xiii Andrew[7], b. March, 1825.
By third wife :
829 xiv Josiah Paine[7], b. April 27, 1833.

328

WILLIAM FLINT[6] BRADBURY (Jacob[5], Jacob[4], Jacob[3], William[2], Thomas[1]), married Mary ——, who died April 18, 1825.

Children :

830 i Benjamin Adams[7], b. Sept. 7, 1822; d. Feb. 9, 1825.
831 ii Harriet[7], b. Feb. 8, 1824.

329

JOSEPH[6] BRADBURY (Jabez[5], Jacob[4], Jacob[3], William[2], Thomas[1]), married Susan Crockett, who died October 31, 1811. He married second, May 27, 1812, Sally Steele, born May 10, 1788. He died December 2, 1839.

Children :

832 i Samuel Crockett[7], b. Oct. 31, 1798.
833 ii Jabez[7], b. Sept. 10, 1800.
834 iii Eliza Crockett[7], b. July 22, 1802; m. Aug. 23, 1829, James Murphy.
835 iv Sally[7], b. Aug. 25, 1804; m. Oct. 4, 1827, Nathaniel Babb.
836 v James Crockett[7], b. March 5, 1806; m. Eliza Smith. He was a physician, and died without issue.

837　vi　Silas[7], b. March 5, 1808; m. Lydia Hadley.
838　vii　Gardiner[7], b. Oct. 31, 1810; d. June 1, 1830.
　By second wife :
839　viii　Susan Crockett[7], b. April 1, 1813; d. Sept. 17, following.
840　ix　Jane Steele[7], b. July 3, 1815; m. Feb. 2, 1841, Andrew Woodman.
841　x　William Steele[7], b. July 31, 1817 ; m. Emeline Nason.
842　xi　Susan Crockett[7], b. Nov. 8, 1819; m. Sam'l Hopkinson.
843　xii　Nancy Page[7], b. Dec. 29, 1821 ; d. Jan. 2, 1859.
844　xiii　Abigail Flanders[7], b. Feb. 21, 1824.
845　xiv　Adelia[7], b. March 4, 1826; m. Feb. 25, 1858, Andrew Woodman.
846　xv　Charles Crockett[7], b. Nov. 6, 1828.
847　xvi　Gardiner[7], b. Feb. 23, 1831.

332

JABEZ[6] BRADBURY (Jabez[5], Jacob[4], Jacob[3], William[2], Thomas[1]), married Betsey or Elizabeth Page, who was born June 29, 1793, and died April 16, 1859. He died September 12, 1837.

Children :

848　i　Sarah Abigail[7], b. Dec. 9, 1819.
849　ii　Horatio Nelson[7], b. Feb. 10, 1822.
850　iii　Joseph Henry[7], b. Sept. 14, 1825 ; r. Minnesota.
851　iv　Albion Keith Parris[7], b. April 6, 1828.

337

ENOCH BILLINGS[6] BRADBURY (Jabez[5], Jacob[4], Jacob[3], William[2], Thomas[1]), married August 29, 1833, Mary Chase Huse, who was born June 20, 1803.

Children :

852　i　Caroline[7], b. June 14, 1834.
853　ii　Lydia E.[7], b. Nov. 24, 1836.

854 iii Susan⁷, b. Oct. 26, 1838; d. June 23, 1845.
855 iv   Julia Ann⁷, b. May 30, 1840; d. March 11, 1841.
856 v   James⁷, b. Aug. 13, 1842.
857 vi   Charles⁷, b. March 22, 1844.
858 vii Sarah⁷, b. March 24, 1846.

341

Elijah⁶ Bradbury* (Elijah⁵, Jacob⁴, Jacob³, Wil-

*When Elijah Bradbury moved to Brownfield that entire region was comparatively newly settled and wild beasts, more especially bears, were very numerous. The following adventure which Mr. Bradbury had with a trio of these animals is still related by his descendants. One day as he was with his team in his wood-lot some fourth of a mile from his house, he noticed a hole under the roots of a decayed tree which curiosity prompted him to examine. Appearances indicated that it might be the lair of some wild beast. After knocking about the entrance for some time, and neither being invited in nor ordered off, he introduced the brad-end of his goad stick, which coming in contact with the hide of some animal, caused it to utter a deep and angry growl, and to spring out of the hole with evident hostile intent. Mr. Bradbury sprang one side and the bear, for such it proved to be, immediately returned to the back part of the den. It soon became evident that bruin was not the sole occupant of these snug quarters, but that her family, consisting of two half-grown cubs, shared the place with her. Waiting at the entrance until all became quiet, Mr. Bradbury went and picked up his ax and returned to the house. After spending nearly four hours in fruitless efforts to obtain help, he returned to the woods and again introduced his goad-stick for the purpose of stirring the animals up, which he had no sooner done than all three rushed out upon him. He gave the foremost one, which was one of the cubs, a blow with the ax which put him out of the contest. The second cub he stunned with a blow upon the head, and the next blow broke the jaw of the dam. She then retired into the den, and after dispatching the one he had stunned, he attempted to force the dam from her retreat, but without avail. He then stopped the entrance to the den by means of blocks of wood, and then proceeded with his ax to make a new opening just over her. As soon as this opening was made the enraged beast sprang out, when she received the blade of the ax upon her head which broke through the skull and entered the brain. This was twice repeated before she succumbed and fell to the ground. Mr. Bradbury loaded his three bears upon his sled and returned home, well pleased with his achievement.

liam², Thomas¹), married February 1, 1810, Sallie Gleason, daughter of Joseph and Rebecca Howard of Brownfield, and sister of the late Judge Joseph Howard of Portland. She was born in Billerica, Mass., September 8, 1779, and died December 11, 1849. For second wife he married Ann Pray Hunt, who died June 26, 1885. He died in Buxton, February 7, 1869.

Children :

859   i   Susan Wilson⁷, b. Buxton, Dec. 17, 1810; m. Leonard A. Berry.*

860   ii   Elijah⁷, b. Brownfield, Jan. 19, 1813; m. Caroline Day. He died Nov. 4, 1888.

861   iii   Moses Howard⁷, b. April 12, 1814; m. Eliza Ann Colby.

862   iv   Sarah Ann⁷, b. Dec. 23, 1815; m. Daniel Kimball; d. July 27, 1854.

863   v   Rebecca Howard⁷, b. Oct. 23, 1817; m. James Wentworth; d. Jan. 10, 1890.

864   vi   George Washington⁷, b. Nov. 1, 1819.

865   vii   Joseph⁷, b. Dec. 25, 1822; d. May 3, 1825.

866   viii   Mary Jane⁷, b. Sept. 17, 1824; m. Thomas F. Parks.

*Leonard Alonzo Berry, son of Samuel and Dorcas (Shattuck) Berry, was born in Westbrook, Me., March 4, 1805. He was the grandson of George and Sarah (Stickney) Berry, great-grandson of George and Elizabeth (Frink) Berry, proprietor of Berry's shipyard at Back Cove, in Falmouth, and great-great-grandson of George and Deliverance (Haley) Berry, shipwright of Kittery, Me. Leonard A. Berry moved with his father's family from Westbrook to Denmark in 1808. He became a mechanic and carried on the manufacture of carriages at Denmark corner for many years. He was a quiet man, but a man of sterling integrity, of excellent judgment and one who enjoyed the fullest confidence of his town's-people during his entire business life. He married Susan W. Bradbury, Dec. 18, 1833. His children were: i Samuel⁸, b. Nov. 9, 1839, d. Nov. 30 following; ii Nellie Maria⁸, b. July 19, 1841, m. Sept. 21, 1876, George Washington Gray who was born in Sebago, March 4, 1833; and iii Henry Wallace⁸, b. Dec. 5, 1843, d. March 12, 1844. Mr. Berry died Feb. 25, 1876. His widow resides in Denmark.

867   ix   Eliza H.[7], b. Aug. 22, 1825; m. Albion Pierce Merrill; d. Oct. 7, 1884.

868   x   Joseph Howard[7], b. April 28, 1827; m. Susan B. Walton.

869   xi   Marion B.[7], b. Aug. 27, 1829; d. Dec. 8, 1845.

870   xii   Henry Alonzo[7], b. Aug. 2, 1831; m. Lizzie A. Hunt. He died Oct. 22, 1865.

343

ISAAC[6] BRADBURY (Elijah[5], Jacob[4], Jacob[3], William[2], Thomas[1]), married Abigail Small Lane, March 8, 1812. His children were born in Hiram, Me., but he moved to Haynesville, Aroostook county, Me.

Children :

871   i   William L.[7], b. Nov. 12, 1812.
872   ii   Elizabeth H.[7], b. Oct. 21, 1817.
873   iii   Sarah[7], b. Aug. 27, 1820.
874   iv   Mary Ann[7], b. March 22, 1823; d. July 21, 1841.
875   v   Joanna C.[7], b. May 2, 1825.
876   vi   Jabez[7], b. March 12, 1827; d. July 6 following.
877   vii   Alcia J.[7], b. Nov. 9, 1829; d. May 4, 1852.
878   viii   Jabez[7], b. March 2, 1831.
879   ix   Ann M.[7], b. March 19, 1833.
880   x   Louisa E.[7], b. April 9, 1835.
881   xi   Isaac H.[7], b. July 14, 1837.

345

JABEZ[6] BRADBURY (Elijah[5], Jacob[4], Jacob[3], William[2], Thomas[1]), born in Buxton, September 22, 1790, lumberman and farmer, married Ann Maria Knight of Calais. He settled in the town of Hollis, where he was a public spirited and active business man; he

10

served in the state legislature, and was also a member
of the executive council. He was often intrusted with
town office, the duties of which he always discharged
with integrity and distinguished ability. He was a
man of great influence in town and county. His
cousin, Thomas K. Lane, being violently sick, as was
supposed of fever, Mr. Bradbury took care of him;
but the disease proved to be small pox, and while
Mr. Lane recovered. Mr. Bradbury took the disease
and died in May, 1836, while in the prime and vigor
of life. His widow is still living at the old homestead
in Hollis, aged ninety-three years.

Children :

882   i   Mary Weston[7], b. Hollis, July 30, 1816; d. May 16, 1836.
882½   ii   Eliza Ann[7], b. Oct. 15, 1819; m. 1837, Sewall Water-
            house.
883   iii Albion Keith Parris[7]; b. Nov. 15, 1822; (Bowdoin Col-
            lege, 1844; M. D. Harvard, 1854); m. Helen E.
            Smith. He died in Santa Barbara, Cal., June 23,
            1875, leaving one child, Philip H.
884   iv   Henry Knight[7], b. Oct. 5, 1826; m. Emily C. White.
            He graduated at Bowdoin College in 1844, spent some
            time in the South as private tutor, studied law, was
            admitted to the bar, practiced in Wilton and Hollis,
            also in Southern California, Pennsylvania and West
            Virginia. He now resides at Hollis. He has been
            three times elected representative to the Maine legis-
            lature. His wife died in 1873, leaving one child,
            Bernhard Paul, b. May 19, 1869.
885   v   Thirza Maria[7], b. April 2, 1835.

347

JOHN⁶ BRADBURY (Joseph⁵, Jacob⁴, Jacob³, William², Thomas¹), married Alice Tyler, and second, Mary Locke.

Children:

886　i　James⁷, b. Oct. 21, 1800; m. Pamelia Woodman.
887　ii　Joseph⁷, b. Oct. 27, 1802; m. Eliza Goodwin.
By second wife:
887½ iii　Stephen Locke⁷, b, Dec. 8, 1808.
888　iv　Brice Boothby⁷, b. April 19, 1810.
889　v　Samuel Locke⁷, b. Nov. 7, 1811.
890　vi　Olive Piper⁷, b. Sept. 5, 1812.

348

JOSEPH⁶ BRADBURY (Joseph⁵, Jacob⁴, Jacob³, William², Thomas¹), married Sept. 8, 1812, Ruth Libby.

Children:

891　i　Ansel⁷, b. April 13, 1813,
892　ii　Gilbert Gerrish⁷, b. July 10, 1814.
893　iii　Cyrus King⁷, b. July 27, 1816.
894　iv　Levi Loring⁷, b. May 4, 1818; d. July 15, 1828; drowned.
895　v　Joseph Francis⁷, b. July 22, 1820; d. July 15, 1828; drowned.
896　vi　Oliver Harris⁷, b. Feb. 28, 1822.
897　vii　Arthur Gerrish⁷, b. Feb. 6, 1826.

349

WINTHROP⁶ BRADBURY (Joseph⁵, Jacob⁴, Jacob³, William², Thomas¹), married Lucy McKenney.

Child:

898　i　Betsey⁷, b. Oct. 27, 1806; d. Sept. 17, 1830.

353

BENJAMIN⁶ BRADBURY (Joseph⁵, Jacob⁴, Jacob³, William², Thomas¹), married June 6, 1813, Mehitable or Jane Plaisted, who was born March 29, 1791.

Children:

899   i   Isabella Mellen⁷, b. Sept. 12, 1813; m. Alvah Pennell.

900   ii   John Bacon⁷, b. July 22, 1818; m. Louisa Wentworth Hill.

901   iii   Granville Mellen⁷, b. Dec. 17, 1821; m. Louisa Partridge.

902   iv   Adelia Louisa⁷, b. Dec. 12, 1825; d. Jan. 21, 1833.

358

JOSEPH⁶ BRADBURY (Benjamin⁵, Moses⁴, Jacob³, William², Thomas¹) married Tabitha Cotton and moved to Norway, Maine, after having lived in New Gloucester and Poland.

Children:

903   i   Charles A.⁷, b. July 19, 1789; m. Feb. 28, 1812, Mary S. True.

904   ii   Sophia⁷, b. Nov. 6, 1790; m. Sept. 12, 1815, Amos Young; d. in Bethel.

905   iii   Ruth⁷, b. Aug. 29, 1792; m. Oct. 15, 1817, Joseph Stevens of Norway.

906   iv   Eleanor⁷, b. April 21, 1795; m. Nov. 18, 1820, Asa Packard of Greenwood.

907   v   Betsey⁷, b. April 11, 1797; d. June 23, 1798.

908   vi   Jacob⁷, b. June 25, 1799; m. Jan. 1, 1822, Sally King Ripley.

909   vii   Nathan A.⁷ (M. D.), b. June 20, 1801; m. Oct. 15, 1827, Eliza Millett; he lived in Woodstock and Sweden, Maine.

910   viii   Moses⁷, b. July 12, 1803; m. Dec. 11, 1825, Hannah Knight.

911   ix   Nathaniel M.⁷, b. Dec. 18, 1806; m. Oct. 27, 1831, Julia A. Foster.

360

Benjamin[6] Bradbury (Benjamin[5], Moses[4], Jacob[3], William[2], Thomas[1]), born May 8, 1775; died May 9, 1840. He married Anna Hersey who was born May 8, 1775, and died April 11, 1839. He resided in Minot.

Children:

911 1-5   i   Hersey[7], b. March 26, 1800; m. Mary Ann Harlow.

911 2-5   ii   Temperance[7], b. April 20, 1807; m. John C. Briggs; d. Jan. 20, 1882.

911 3-5   iii   Moses B.[7], b. Feb. 22, 1809; m. Sarah F. Briggs.

911 4-5   iv   Benjamin[7], b. April 9, 1812; m. Betsey D. Pettengill; d. Nov. 4, 1869.

361

Samuel[6] Bradbury (Benjamin[5], Moses[4], Jacob[3], William[2], Thomas[1]), born in New Gloucester, December 3, 1777, moved with his father's family when a child to Minot, the Bradbury's being among the quite early settlers of that part of Bakerstown which became the town of Minot. He married in March, 1802, Jane Gurney, who died in 1843.

Children:

912   i   Samuel Gurney[7], b. 1804; m. Hannah Pettengill.

913   ii   Olive Hersey[7], b. 1806; m. Josiah Blaisdell of Lewiston.

914   iii   Benjamin Thomas[7], b. 1808; m. Bathsheba Davis.

915   iv   Ammi Ruhamah[7], b. Dec. 3, 1810; m. Caroline Livermore Johnson of Farmington.

916   v   Joseph Fellows[7]; b. 1814; he was twice married and d. in Greene, June 30, 1889.

917   vi   Jennie Derby[7], b. 1818; d. 1831.

918   vii   Levi Loring[7], b. Feb. 1821; graduated from Bowdoin College, class of 1846. He taught school in Rhode Island two years, went South, studied law, was married there, and died at Montgomery, Texas, of disease of the heart in 1860.

364

DAVID[6] BRADBURY (Benjamin[5], Moses[4], Jacob[3], William[2], Thomas[1]), married first, Mary Robertson, and second, Sarah Vickery, who was born in Auburn, April 17, 1794. He lived in that part of Minot now Auburn. His father settled on Bradbury Hill in Minot as early as 1777, and with his brother Moses cleared up farms there.

919   i   David[7], b. March 1, 1817.
920   ii   Mathias Vickery[7], b. Jan. 13, 1819; m. Eunice Watson. He lives in Garland, had three children, all died unmarried.
921   iii   Sarah[7], b. Jan. 12, 1821.
922   iv   James[7], b. June 16, 1823.
923   v   Olive Jane[7], b. July 11, 1825.
924   vi   Eleanor[7], b. Sept. 28, 1827.
925   vii   Lucinda[7], b. Feb. 13, 1830.
One died in infancy.

366

JACOB[6] BRADBURY (Benjamin[5], Moses[4], Jacob[3], William[2], Thomas[1]), born in Poland, March 10, 1779, married first, October 16, 1810, Sally Chamberlain. He married second in 1820, at Auburn, Rachel Chamberlain. He died November 1, 1865.

Children :

926 i Silas C.⁷, b. Minot, Feb. 25, 1811, d. Oct. 3, 1838.
927 ii Royal J.⁷, b. May 25, 1813 ; m. Jane L. Parker.
928 iii Sally⁷, b. June 16, 1816 ; d. July 13 following.
  By second wife :
929 iv Adoniram J.⁷, b. Sept. 1, 1822 ; d. Oct. 3, 1853.
930 v Jacob S.⁷, b. Aug. 12, 1828 ; d. Sept. 26, 1841.
931 vi Sarah J.⁷, b. April 9, 1833.
932 vii Silas S.⁷, b. Aug. 17, 1839 ; d. Feb. 22, 1880.

368

CHARLES⁶ BRADBURY (Moses⁵, Moses⁴, Jacob³, William², Thomas¹), married Polly Chase, who was born September 23, 1787. He moved from Sumner to Anson, where he died November 1, 1843. His widow died February 9, 1864.

Children :

933 i Mary Jane⁷, b. Dec. 28, 1809.
934 ii Cyrus⁷, b. Sept. 26, 1812 ; m. Deborah Bunker, r. Mercer, Me.
935 iii Eliza⁷, b. July 20, 1814.
936 iv Moses⁷, b. March 3, 1816, r. Industry.
937 v Martin⁷, b. Dec. 10, 1817 ; d. Aug. 29, 1859.
938 vi Lucinda⁷, b. Dec. 18, 1819 ; d. Dec. 4, 1857.
939 vii Eunice⁷, b. Aug. 19, 1821.
940 viii Charles⁷, b. Feb. 23, 1824 ; d. April 23 following.
941 ix Sophronia⁷, b. April 7, 1825 ; d. Sept. 8, 1826.
942 x Julian⁷, b. July 22, 1827 ; d. June 19, 1829.
943 xi Enos⁷, b. June 9, 1829 ; d. Jan. 8, 1857.

370

JOHN⁶ BRADBURY (Moses⁵, Moses⁴, Jacob³, William², Thomas¹), married Alethea Hersey of Sumner, and died in Bangor, July 9, 1847.

Children :

944 i   Albion P.⁷, b. ——.
945 ii   Matilda A.⁷, b. July 27, 1821; m. Sept. 18, 1845, Jonathan W. Pottle of Foxcroft; r. Chelsea, Mass.

375

ENOS⁶ BRADBURY (Moses⁵, Moses⁴, Jacob³, William²,
Thomas¹), married May 30, 1833, Lucy, daughter of
John and Lucy (Chipman) Atkinson of Minot.   He
died in Minot December 3, 1848; his wife died January 19, 1840.

Children :

946 i   Mary Alice⁷, b. Aug. 31, 1835; m. Otis Sargent of Amesbury.
947 ii   Frances Amelia⁷, b. Sept. 3, 1837; m. Adelbert Greenwood of Hebron.

376

NATHANIEL⁶ BRADBURY (Moses⁵, Moses⁴, Jacob³, William², Thomas¹), married May 23, 1820, Nancy P.
Mitchell, and died in Foxcroft, March 16, 1827.

Children :

948 i   Nathaniel Millett⁷, b. March 29, 1821; m. Elizabeth Briggs.
950 ii   Lewis Leonard⁷, b. Nov. 6, 1823.   He went to California.
951 iii Minerva⁷, b. Jan. 9, 1826; m. Sept., 1849, Francis O. Millett.

378

HIRAM⁶ BRADBURY (Moses⁵, Moses⁴, Jacob³, William²,
Thomas¹), married May, 1830, Nancy, daughter of

Joseph and Mary (Waring) Washburn of Minot. He died February 18, 1841.

Children :

952   i   Henry William[7], b. March 24, 1831 ; d. April 3, 1831.
953   ii   Payson William[7], b. July 22, 1832.
954   iii   Clarendon Waters[7], b. May 10, 1834; d. Oct. 4 following.
955   iv   Mary Elizabeth[7], b. Sept. 20, 1836; m. William E. Wilson of Boston.
956   v   Eunice Joanna[7]; b. Feb. 10, 1839; d. May 11, 1841.
958   vi   John Clarendon[7], b. Sept. 21, 1840; d. March 8, 1841.

384

SAMUEL[6] BRADBURY (Samuel[5], Moses[4], Jacob[3], William[2], Thomas[1]), married February 14, 1828, Frances Mary Rochead. He died at West Troy, N. Y., February 24, 1847. His widow died at Wauhegan, Ill., December 25, 1847. Samuel Bradbury enlisted in the United States army in 1811, served through the war, then was placed on recruiting service, which occupation he followed for some twenty-five years.

Children :

959   i   Samuel I.[7], b. Nov. 8, 1828 ; m. Mary A. Spaulding.
960   ii   Frances M.[7], b. Jan. 21, 1830 ; d. Sept. 28, 1832.
961   iii   Margaret P.[7], b. Aug. 30, 1832 ; m. Charles M. Willey.
962   iv   Hannah N.[7], b. Jan. 27, 1834; m. Willard Scoville.
963   v   Sophia C.[7], b. April 25, 1836.
964   vi   Thomas P.[7], b. Nov. 6, 1837.
965   vii   Andrew R.[7], b. Aug. 22, 1839.
966   viii   William Worth[7], b. March 15, 1844.

EIGHTH GENERATION.

388

GEORGE LOWTHER[7] BRADBURY (John[6], Jacob[5], Wymond[4], Wymond[3], Wymond[2], Thomas[1]) married December 25, 1828, Elizabeth Condon, who was born January 28, 1802. He died September 21, 1850.

Children:

967	i	John Andrews[8], b. Oct. 7, 1829; d. April 15, 1831.
968	ii	George William[8], b. Nov. 4, 1831; d. April 21, 1835.
969	iii	Thomas Condon[8], b. Nov. 22, 1834; m. Sarah Sawyer.
970	iv	George Henry[8], b. May 22, 1837; d. May 14, 1838.
971	v	George Alexander[8], b. July 22. 1839; d. Sept. 8, 1840.
972	vi	Francis Henry[8], b. July 31, 1841; d. Aug. 28, 1843.
973	vii	Ann Elizabeth[8], b. Oct. 13, 1843.

401

EDWARD[7] BRADBURY (Reuben[6], Jacob[5], Wymond[4], Wymond[3], Wymond[2], Thomas[1]), married July 3, 1834, Mary Ann Crockett, who was born July 17, 1809. He died October 29, 1857. He married second, 1843, Ann Eager, who was born July, 1820.

Children:

974	i	Martha Abercrombie[8], b. July 23, 1835; m. May 16, 1867, Capt. Henry Coffin of Portland.
975	ii	Edward[8], b. Aug. 24, 1837; m. Ellen Corey Roberts.

By second wife:

976	iii	Frank Henry[8], b. Aug. 1, 1844; d. Sept. 20 following.
977	iv	Julia Theresa Sager[8], b. Jan. 18, 1846.
978	v	Virginia Howe[8], b. April 9, 1850; d. Sept. 6 following.
979	vi	Marion Lee[8], b. Jan. 31, 1852.
980	vii	James Walter[8], b. Feb. 11, 1855; d. Mar. 20, following.
981	viii	Susan Ingraham[8], b. Feb. 8, 1857; d. Sept. 29, following.

408

SAMUEL ANDREWS[7] BRADBURY (Wymond[6], Jacob[5], Wymond[4], Wymond[3], Wymond[2], Thomas[1]), married April 5, 1841, Lucy R. Butler. He died November 16, 1845.

Child:

982 i Charles Herbert[8], b. April 5, 1843; d. June 25, 1844.

411

CHARLES[7] BRADBURY (Wymond[6], Jacob[5], Wymond[4], Wymond[3], Wymond[2], Thomas[1]), married October 4, 1846. Nancy M. Butler.

Children:

983 i ' Charles B.[8], b. ——.
984 ii Ardelle[8], b. ——.
985 iii Almyn[8], b. ——.

413

HENRY PAINE[7] BRADBURY (Wymond[6], Jacob[5], Wymond[4], Wymond[3], Wymond[2], Thomas[1]), married May 22, 1852, Nancy C. Suckforth.

Child:

986 i Percy[8], b. ——; d. young.

414

GEORGE[7] BRADBURY (Wymond[6], Jacob[5], Wymond[4], Wymond[3], Wymond[2], Thomas[1]), married January 28, 1854, Irene Kalloch, who was born January 25, 1836.

Children:

987 i Augusta[8], b. ——.
988 ii Ida[8], b. ——.

419

THEODORE MUZZEY[7] BRADBURY (Andrew[6], Jacob[5], Wymond[4], Wymond[3], Wymond[2], Thomas[1]), married Lucy Chadborne.

Child:

989 i   Mary Frances[8], b. ——.

425

JOSEPH[7] BRADBURY (Daniel[6], Thomas[5], Wymond[4], Wymond[3], Wymond[2], Thomas[1]), married Mary Bryant. They were married in Elkton, Md.

Children:

990 i   Mary Eliza[8], b. ——.
991 ii   Joseph Henry[8], b. ——.
992 iii Francis Edward[8], b. ——.

431

CHARLES[7] BRADBURY (Thomas[6], Thomas[5], Wymond[4], Wymond[3], Wymond[2], Thomas[1]), married at Skowhegan, Me., Martha McPherson.

Children:

993 i   Alphonso[8], b. ——.
994 ii   Henry[8], b. ——.

438

JOHN HINCKLEY[7] BRADBURY (William[6], Thomas[5], Wymond[4], Wymond[3], Wymond[2], Thomas[1]), married June 27, 1852, at Portland, Mary E. (Treat) Park of Frankfort, Me. He lived at Eastport, and died April 21, 1861.

Child:

995 i Mary Hinckley⁸, b. Oct. 17, 1854; d. 1862.

441

WILLIAM HENRY⁷ BRADBURY (William⁶, Thomas⁵, Wymond⁴, Wymond³, Wymond², Thomas¹), married October 10, 1851, at Pittston, Maine, Lydia Ann Tobey. He lived at Eastport and Portland.

Children:

996 i ——, b. ——.
997 ii ——, b. ——.
998 iii Charles Wesley⁸, b. Feb. 15, 1857.
999 iv Frank⁸, b. ——.
1000 v —— ⎫ twins, b. ——.
1001 vi —— ⎭

442

GEORGE FREEMAN⁷ BRADBURY (William⁶, Thomas⁵, Wymond⁴, Wymond³, Wymond², Thomas¹), married October 5, 1865, at Perry, Me., Sarah Jane Griffin, who was born at Grand Menan, December 5, 1842.

Child:

1002 i Ernest Clinton⁸, b. Oct. 27, 1867.

443

COTTON⁷ BRADBURY (Edward⁶, Cotton⁵, John⁴, Wymond³, Wymond², Thomas¹), married Mary, daughter of Samuel Hobbs of Parsonsfield, who died June 3, 1853. He died May 16, 1854.

Children :

1003　i　John Cotton⁸, b. March 8, 1814; d. Feb. 5, 1815.
1004　ii　Sarah Maria⁸, b. Oct. 27, 1815; d. Aug. 26, 1817.
1005　iii　Mary Jane⁸, b. June 4, 1817.
1006　iv　John Cotton⁸,* b. Dec. 17, 1819; m. Sarah, daughter
　　　　　of Edmund Currier, r. Saco. No issue.
1007　v　Lydia Maria⁸, b. June 13, 1822; d. Dec. 25, 1837.
1008　vi　Edward⁸, b. Nov. 10, 1824; d. Aug. 17, 1832.
1009　vii　Harriet Elizabeth⁸, b. April 19, 1826; m. Dorrance
　　　　　Littlefield.
1010　viii　Eunice Melinda⁸, b. Jan. 10, 1830.

445

GEORGE⁷ BRADBURY (Daniel⁶, Cotton⁵, John⁴, Wymond³, Wymond², Thomas¹), married at York, Me., Maria Norton, and died in June, 1826. She died June 13, 1835.

Children :

1011　i　Josiah⁸, b. ——, 1816.
1012　ii　Daniel⁸, b. May 8, 1820.
1013　iii　Hannah Maria⁸, b. Oct , 1824; m. Oct., 1847, Albert
　　　　　Wallace of Beverly, Mass.

448

NATHANIEL HARMON⁷ BRADBURY (Joseph⁶, Cotton⁵, John⁴, Wymond³, Wymond², Thomas¹), married July 16, 1820, Sophia Moulton.

---

*John Cotton Bradbury has been a leading man in Saco for many years. He has held various positions of trust in the city, including that of treasurer and collector and alderman, trustee and treasurer of Thornton academy, a director of other institutions, and a valued bank official for more than a generation.

Children :

1014   i   Albion H.³, b. Sept. 16, 1822.
1015   ii   Sophia Anna³, b. Feb. 4, 1824; d. Sept. 17, 1826.
1016   iii   Caroline³, b. Nov. 2, 1825.
1017   iv   Martha Ann³, b. Dec. 27, 1827; m. 1851, James W.
             Frederick.

455

Hon. James Ware[7] Bradbury, ll. d. (James[6], Cotton[5], John[4]. Wymond[3], Wymond[2], Thomas[1]), son of Dr. James and Ann (Moulton) Bradbury, born in Parsonsfield, June 10, 1802, attended the public schools of his native town, then a term or two at the academies at Saco, Limerick and Effingham, N. H., and completed his preparatory course at Gorham academy, under the charge of Preceptor Nason. He entered the Sophomore class at Bowdoin college in 1822. and graduated from that institution with the famous class of 1825. Among his class-mates were Henry W. Longfellow, Josiah Stover Little. Jonathan Cilley, Nathaniel Hawthorne, John S. C. Abbott and George B. Cheever. Josiah S. Little took the first rank for scholarship in the class. At the commencement, three English orations were assigned to the class ; Little had the valedictory and Bradbury and Longfellow the remaining two.

After graduating Mr. Bradbury came to Hallowell and had charge of the academy for one year. At that time no town or city in Maine was more distinguished for culture and literary acquirements. Dr. Benjamin

Vaughan, formerly a member of the English Parliament, had taken up his residence in Hallowell, and he and his family gave a high tone to society there, while the good doctor was ever doing some kind act to improve the condition of all classes. At the expiration of his engagement at Hallowell, Mr. Bradbury entered upon the study of law in the office of Hon. Rufus McIntire of Parsonsfield, and after a year entered the office of Hon. Ether Shepley of Portland, subsequently the honored chief justice of the supreme judicial court of the state, and completed his studies there. The required term of study for admission to the bar was three years, and having a few months on his hands before a term of court would be held at which he could be admitted, he went to Effingham, N. H., and opened a school for the instruction of teachers. The notice of such an innovation in teaching, brought together a large class, some fifty or more, who were drilled and instructed in much the same manner as has since been practiced in our normal schools. Most of the pupils had been teachers in public schools, and those who had not were about to engage in teaching. They were all put into one class and drilled daily in the methods recommended to be employed in instructing in all the branches then taught in the common schools. The importance of such schools had been impressed upon Mr. Bradbury while visiting the schools of the period, and if a similar school had previously been taught in New England, he then had no knowledge of it.

In 1830, Mr. Bradbury removed to Augusta, the capitol of the state, and here has since been his home, a period of sixty years. Here he opened an office for the practice of law to which he had been admitted. The Kennebec county bar at this time was unsurpassed for ability and brilliancy by any in the state. Among the distinguished names of those then in practice here, were Peleg Sprague, George Evans, Reuel Williams, Frederic Allen, Henry W. Fuller, William Emmons, Timothy Boutelle, Samuel Wells and Hiram Belcher. To obtain a foothold in a field so ably occupied, required ability and untiring effort. Mr. Bradbury was in love with his profession and devoted his entire time to it. In the space of four years he had secured a large and lucrative practice, which continued and increased until he was elected to the United States senate in 1846. During these sixteen years he was one of the busiest men on Kennebec river. The business of his office was not surpassed by any in the state. He was constantly employed from early morning until late at night, on consultations and office business, and in the numerous trials before the jury and the court arising from his extensive practice. The extent of his business best shows in what estimation he was held. He was a sound and discriminating lawyer, a skillful and eloquent advocate, who never failed to do full justice to the cause of his client. In 1833, he formed a co-partnership with Mr. Horatio Bridge, which continued for one year, when Mr. Bridge left the legal pro-

fession to engage in other pursuits. In 1838. Richard
D. Rice. afterward associate justice of the supreme
court. entered Mr. Bradbury's office as a student. and
upon his admission to the bar was admitted into partnership. This became necessary on account of Mr.
Bradbury's largely increasing business. and the partnership continued until 1848. when Governor Dana
appointed Mr. Rice to the bench.

Mr. Bradbury then formed a partnership with the
late Lot M. Morrill. who had just come to Augusta from
Readfield. During this partnership Mr. Morrill was
elected state senator and three times governor of
Maine. Finally he was elected United States senator,
and the partnership was terminated. In 1856. Joseph
H. Meserve was admitted to the firm. of which he remained a valued member until his death in 1864. Mr.
Bradbury then associated with himself his son James
Ware Bradbury. jr.. and kept up the firm largely for the
purpose of establishing the son in business. He was a
young man of excellent character and marked ability,
and his death in 1876 was a great loss to the community. and a crushing blow to the family.

When he first came to Augusta Mr. Bradbury. for
one year. and for the purpose of becoming better acquainted with the people of the state. edited a democratic paper published in Augusta. called the "Maine
Patriot." This paper was democratic in sentiment. and
Mr. Bradbury commenced life and has always continued
a democrat from conviction and principle. He has
ever believed that a strict adherence to democratic

principles as expounded by the fathers, and as generally exemplified by the policy of democratic administrations, is best calculated to secure the rights of the people and the permanency of the union of the states. While openly and firmly maintaining his own views on political questions, he always considered the equal rights of others, and he never allowed his social relations to be disturbed on account of difference of political opinion. He never allowed politics to interfere with his business. In 1835, he was appointed county attorney by Governor Dunlap, and accepted it, this being in the line of his profession.

From the time of his coming to Augusta he took a leading part in the political movements of the day, and especially in organizing and harmonizing the political forces of his party in county and state, for which service he possessed uncommon tact. When the contest arose between the Jackson democrats who supported Martin Van Buren, and the friends of Mr. Calhoun, Mr. Bradbury took a decided stand in favor of the former. He was a delegate to the Baltimore convention of 1844, in which the supporters of Van Buren had a decided majority, but not the required two-thirds necessary to secure a nomination. They determined, however, that if Mr. Van Buren could not be nominated, they and not their opponents in the convention should make the selection. After a struggle of several days continuance, they presented the name of James K. Polk which was received with demonstrations of joy, and he was at once nominated and triumphantly elect-

ed. During this canvas Mr. Bradbury departed from
his usual custom and took the stump in favor of Mr.
Polk, speaking often and in various parts of the state.
He strongly urged the admission of Texas, which was
an issue in the campaign, to prevent that great section
of country from becoming subject to British influence.
The organization and success of the democratic party
in that campaign was largely due to Mr. Bradbury's
influence.

At the session of the Maine legislature in 1846, Mr.
Bradbury was chosen United States senator for the
term of six years from the fourth day of March following. At the commencement of the session in December, 1847, he took his seat. His first speech in
that body was an eulogy on the life and character of
his colleague, Hon. John Fairfield, who died fourteen
days from the opening of the session. It was a fitting
tribute to an able and patriotic son of Maine. Mr.
Bradbury's entrance into the United States senate happened at a very interesting period of our history,
whether with regard to the character and composition
of the senate, or the subjects presented for action.
Among the members of this branch of the government
were Daniel Webster, Henry Clay, John C. Calhoun,
Thomas H. Benton, Lewis Cass, Stephen A. Douglass,
William H. Seward and Salmon P. Chase, giants in in-
tellect, and others of scarcely less ability and distinc-
tion. When Mr. Bradbury took his seat the war with
Mexico was going on, and he gave his hearty support
to the national administration in all its measures to

sustain and strengthen our army then in the heart of Mexico, and surrounded by hostile forces vastly superior in numbers to themselves. There was strong opposition to the administration in the senate, and in the other branch there were those who refused to vote supplies for the armies in the field. The ratification of the treaty of peace with Mexico was bitterly opposed and came near being defeated.

Mr. Bradbury was made chairman of the committee on printing; also a member of the judiciary committee and of the committee on claims. He served on the judiciary committee, which was a very hard working one, until the close of his term. The question of slavery began more and more to excite the attention of Congress upon attempts to form governments for the territory acquired from Mexico. The South claimed that the territories were the common property of all the citizens of the United States, and that they should have the right to migrate there with their families, including their slaves, and that Congress had no right to deprive them of this privilege. This was met by the denial of the right of the citizens of any state to carry their local laws into the territories, and the assertion of the power of Congress to prohibit slavery therein. A bill introduced to establish territorial governments for Oregon, California and New Mexico, led to a long discussion. Mr. Bradbury opposed the bill because it avoided the question as to whether Congress had or had not the power to legislate upon the subject of slavery in the territories; also because it devolved

upon the court the determination of questions that
properly belonged to Congress to settle. This bill, he
claimed, would not finish the controversy but only
postpone it. He ever regarded the administration of
Mr. Polk as one of the most important in our history.

General Taylor was elected president in 1848, and
during the campaign he stated that in case of his election, he would remove no person from office on account
of politics. His pledges were not kept in this regard,
and Mr. Bradbury introduced a resolution which called
upon the president to cause to be laid before the senate a list of the removals from office since the preceding fourth of March, with a statement of charges filed
against them, his object being to vindicate the democratic party from the charge of proscription of their
political opponents, which was most triumphantly accomplished, the records going to show that his party
had been much less proscriptive than those of their
opponents.

In 1849, Mr. Clay introduced a compromise measure
covering the question of government for the territories,
including an adjustment of the boundaries of Texas.
This bill was assailed by extremists, both from the
North and South. A majority of the senate were in
favor of the general features of the bill, but its passage
was blocked upon the question of the amount of indem-
nity to be paid to Texas. Mr. Bradbury offered an
amendment providing for commissioners, both on the
part of Congress and Texas, to agree upon a boundary
and equivalents, which was adopted by a close vote.

But the section to which this amendment was added was subsequently stricken out, which again opened the whole question. Mr. Bradbury supported Mr. Clay's compromise bill because he was convinced its provisions were proper in themselves, and were a peaceable adjustment of matters in controversy.

In 1852, Mr. Bradbury was upon a special committee on French spoliations, and had charge in the senate of a bill looking to the adjustment of these long delayed claims. The bill was strenuously opposed, but Mr. Bradbury made an eloquent and exhaustive speech in its favor and the senate passed it by a large majority. With much labor and preparation, he secured the passage of a bill to indemnify Maine and Massachusetts for losses sustained in the settlement of the boundary between Maine and New Brunswick. It was also through his efforts that the first appropriation was made for improving the navigation of the Kennebec river. He was an active and hard-working member throughout his entire term, looking carefully after the public good, and especially looking out for the interests of his constituents. He was a ready debater, a fluent speaker, always presenting the strong points of a case in a clear and concise manner. He was also a most indefatigable worker in the committee-room. He declined a re-election, and at the close of his term retired to private life and at once resumed the practice of his profession. He has had no desire for office since; and a few years ago, having given up the practice of law, he has since given his time and attention to the management of his private affairs.

In the settlement of contested election cases in the Maine legislature Mr. Bradbury has had a larger experience than any other Maine citizen. For very many years he was on one side or the other of almost every contested case, and his clients were generally successful. He has also had large experience in drafting bills to be presented to the legislature, and some of the most valuable measures passed for the management and restriction of railway corporations have been proposed by him. His efforts have been directed to securing the rights of all parties, and especially the rights of small stockholders against the grasping policy of railway managers. In his law practice he was always faithful to his clients, and ever ready to advise and promote a settlement between parties when it could be fairly and equitably effected, and especially in family difficulties. He was opposed to litigation in trifling matters, and always refused all such business.

He has ever kept up his interest in Bowdoin College. He was for several years a member of the board of overseers, and for thirty years a member of the board of trustees. Since 1866 he has been chairman of the committee of finance. He attends all the commencements, and looks after the welfare of the college in all its interests. The college conferred upon him the honorary degree of doctor of laws in 1872. He has long been an active and efficient member of the Maine Historical Society, and was its president from 1873 to

1889. He obtained from the Maine legislature a grant
of land, the sale of which forms the bulk of the per-
manent fund of the society at the present time. He
has long been an active member of the Congregational
church in Augusta, and is much interested in the good
of the cause at large. He has charity and fellowship
for all denominations of Christians, and would have
them work harmoniously in the great work committed
to their charge.

As a citizen Mr. Bradbury has ever taken an active
part in all the public enterprises of the day, and has
ever been ready to contribute of his time and means
for the advancement of any measure calculated to ben-
efit the city of his adoption, and the state. He opposed
the construction of two parallel lines of railway through
the state, and still believes it would have been better
for the state had his views been carried out. He was
a director of the Somerset & Kennebec railroad, and
had much to do in effecting a union of this road with
the Portland & Kennebec. At the time of this writing
(March, 1890), Mr. Bradbury, though he has passed
the eighty-seventh mile-stone, is still remarkably vig-
orous, takes charge of a large private business, attends
to his duties as a bank president, is a constant atten-
dant at church on the Sabbath, and attends the meetings at Portland of the standing committee of the
Maine Historical Society, of which he is one. His
mind is still unimpaired, and his enjoyment of life and
its work is apparently as great as ever.

On the occasion of Mr. Bradbury's eighty-fifth birthday (June 10, 1887), the Maine Historical Society tendered him a complimentary dinner at the Falmouth Hotel. There were present beside the leading members of the Maine Historical Society, Hon Cyrus Woodman* of Cambridge, Abner C. Goodell, jr., president of the New England Historical and Genealogical Society, and Charles Deane, LL. D.,* of Cambridge. Letters were received from distinguished men from various parts of the country. Prof. Henry L. Chapman of Bowdoin College presided in a very able and acceptable manner. His opening speech was a model for such an occasion. On being presented Mr. Bradbury was received with cheers and made a very neat and appropriate speech. Speeches were also made by Hon. John A. Peters, chief-justice of the supreme court, Dr. Charles Deane, President Goodell, Hon. Hannibal Hamlin, Hon. Marshall Cram,* Rev. Dr. Fiske, Hon. George F. Talbot, and Hon. William Goold. The letters were read by the secretary, Hubbard W. Bryant. The occasion was one of unusual interest.

The following is an extract from Prof. Chapman's opening remarks:—

We are here today in grateful recognition of the debt we owe to the fidelity and wisdom of one who has been so many years our sachem—our esteemed and honored president. We all know, gentlemen, his unselfish devotion to the welfare of the society; his wise and watchful care over its varied interests; the kindly courtesy of his official and personal relations with us. It is a great pleasure to us to give some outward expression to the honor which our hearts have all along yielded to him. And in order to empha-

*Since deceased.

size the feeling that prompted this gathering we have been glad to invite and to welcome here the representatives of sister societies to unite with us in this tribute of esteem. We may thus confirm, by living contact and fellowship, the sympathies that run along the obscure lines of antiquarian research, and bind us together in the ties of common or similar pursuits.

Nor do we forget that the day is one that permits us to add to this token and assurance of our associated regard the kindly congratulations and good wishes which belong to a personal anniversary, an anniversary, it may be said, that recurs with startling frequency in all our lives. Whatever that was cherished and valuable the passing years may have taken away from our revered president, who today reaches another mile-stone on his journey, they have not taken away from him the continued power and privilege of serving his fellow-men in many noble ways. They cannot take away from him the record of that for which we honor him—a life distinguished by important duties worthily performed, by high trusts faithfully discharged, by great privileges blamelessly enjoyed. And, on the other hand, they have brought to him in their swift passage,—

> That which should accompany old age,
> As honor, love, obedience, troops of friends.

In his domestic relations Mr. Bradbury was signally fortunate. He married November 25, 1834, Eliza Ann, daughter of Thomas Westbrook and Abigail (Page) Smith of Augusta, who was born March 18, 1815. Mr. Smith, father of Mrs. Bradbury, was born in Dover, N. H., February 22, 1785, and in 1805 came to Augusta and engaged in trade, which he followed for many years and accumulated a large fortune for his day. The mother of Mrs. Bradbury was Abigail, daughter of Ezekiel and Betsey (Robie) Page, who came to Augusta from Haverhill, Mass., in 1762. Mrs. Bradbury

was a most womanly woman. Affectionate, cheerful,
full of energy and possessed of great executive ability,
qualities inherited from her parents, she was a model
wife, mother, friend and member of society. She lived
with her husband in happy union for over forty-four
years, and for the most part of that time enjoyed perfect
health. She died suddenly January 29, 1879, greatly
lamented by her surviving family, and deeply mourned
by the entire community. In her life-time she abound-
ed in deeds of charity and kindness. The Old Ladies'
Home in Augusta was one of her favorite charges, of
the management of which she was president at the
time of her death. She had been a member of the
Congregational church for many years, but for several
years before her death she attended the Episcopal
church. Her creed was much broader than that of any
denomination; she observed strictly the Golden Rule,
and hers were " the charities that soothe and heal and
bless." The epitaph engraved on her headstone is
truly expressive of her character :—

She loved to do good.

A local paper in a notice of the death of Mrs. Bradbury, said : "Her departure will be lamented by a wide
circle of friends who knew her sterling qualities of
mind and heart. She was a woman of large business
capacity, possessing uncommon executive abilities. She
was ever active and foremost in all benevolent and
charitable movements, and was engaged at the time of
her first attack of illness in preparing, through her own

labor and employed help, clothing for the poor and food to be distributed among needy families. In her the indigent and unfortunate ever found a sympathetic friend, ready with liberal hand to contribute to their necessities. They will mourn her death with unfeigned sorrow. She was a noble woman, possessing a kind heart and generous hand. Her life was filled with deeds of charity and of active benevolence, and her time and means were largely employed in supplying the wants and relieving the distresses of others." Another local paper, among other things, said: "Mrs. Bradbury inherited from her father great industry, sterling sense and correct judgment, softened in her by the womanly graces inherited from her mother. Her death casts a gloom over many a humble home, and her memory will be cherished by hundreds who have received bounty from her hand. The death of such a woman is a public loss."

The children of Hon. James Ware and Eliza Ann (Smith) Bradbury, all born in Augusta, were :—

1018 i Henry Westbrook[8], b. Feb. 10, 1836; m. Louisa H. Gregorie.

1019 ii James Ware, jr.[8], b. July 22, 1839; d. Sept. 21, 1876. He entered Bowdoin College in 1857, and graduated with honor in the class of 1861. He immediately entered upon the study of the law, in the office of Bradbury, Morrill & Meserve. Upon the completion of the regular course of studies and his admission to the bar, he entered upon the practice of his profession in partnership with his father. His industry and devotion to business were attended with success. In 1871, he passed the winter in Florida, where he formed the acquaintance and secured the attachment of many warm personal friends. Upon his return he resumed the labors of his office, and at the time of his decease the brightest prospects of professional success were opening before him. His conscientiousness, integrity and fidelity to the true interests of his clients secured their confidence and increased their number, and drew to him the best class of professional business. Always opposed to useless litigation and pettifogging in any form, he preferred equity to any advantage gained by stratagem and finesse. Hence it was that he often became a peacemaker when different advice would have led to expensive and often unavailing litigation. He was city solicitor of Augusta in 1868, filling the position to the satisfaction of the municipal authorities and the people. He was appointed U. S. commissioner in 1869, and held the office until his decease, discharging its duties with independence, ability and fidelity. Although not an ultra partizan, Mr. Bradbury ever took a deep interest in public affairs, and was strongly attached to the principles of the democratic party. They were with him a matter of conviction. He felt that the best interests of the country were to be secured by their maintenance, and he never wavered in their support throughout the long and hopeless minority of the party, though well knowing that it closed every avenue to political preferment. Prof. Packard said of him : " He left us with the impression that he possessed intellectual powers which promised much for his friends and for the public."

1020 iii Thomas Westbrook Smith[8], b. July 24, 1841 ; d. May 1, 1868. He was a young man of excellent character and habits, and his early death, the first in the family, was greatly lamented.

1021 iv Charles⁸, b. March 31, 1846; m. Nov. 9, 1870, Eva A. Lancaster of Augusta. He resides in Boston.

456

SAMUEL MOULTON⁷ BRADBURY (James⁶, Cotton⁵, John⁴, Wymond³, Wymond², Thomas¹), married first, 1831, Susan, daughter of James Brackett of Parsonsfield. She died, and in 1847 he married Elizabeth Brackett, a sister of his former wife. He studied medicine with his father and graduated from the Maine Medical school in 1831. He commenced practice in Parsonsfield and remained there until 1836. He then moved to Limington, where he continued in practice until his death.

Children :

By the first marriage :

1022 i John Brackett⁸, b. June 1, 1833. He graduated from Colby University, class of 1857. He died of consumption, April 27, 1858.

1023 ii daughter⁸, b. —— ; d. ——.

By second marriage :

1024 iii James Otis⁸, b. July 19, 1850; m. Aug. 5, 1877, Ella S. Butler. He is a lawyer in Hartland. They have Mary Alma, b. Sept. 26, 1862, and Eva.

1025 iv Eva Carrie⁸, b. Oct. 28, 1854; d. Aug. 24, 1862.

1026 v Frank M.⁸, b. Feb. 28, 1858; m. Feb. 13, 1886, Allie S. Cousins.

1027 vi Lizzie⁸, b. May 27, 1862.

458

COTTON M.⁷ BRADBURY (James⁶, Cotton⁵, John⁴, Wymond³, Wymond², Thomas¹), married February 3, 1861,

Susanna D. Hussey, who died in 1867, and second, Ella T. Harris.

Children :

1028 i James C.⁸, b. Oct. 11, 1864.
1029 ii Jennie⁸, b. July, 1866.
By second wife :
1030 iii Nellie⁸, b. Feb. 26, 1880.
1031 iv Frank⁸, b. Nov. 20, 1884.
1032 v Fred⁸, b. June 19, 1885.

464

JOHN ROGER WILLIAMS⁷ BRADBURY (John⁶, John⁵, John⁴, Wymond³, Wymond², Thomas¹), married January 3, 1822, Phebe R. Mayhew, who was born in 1801, and died June 16, 1844. He married second, Oct. 30, 1845, Lydia Chapman, who was born in Bethel, Me., in 1815. He was a house carpenter, resided at Bethel and other places.

Children :

1033 i Priscilla S.⁸, b. July 29, 1823; m. March 21, 1846, Reuben Penley.
1034 ii Sarah⁸, b. March 12, 1826; m. March 12, 1846, Joseph E. Goud, who settled and died in Caribou, Me.
1035 iii Andrew J.⁸, b. Jan., 1832; d. March following.
1036 iv Rachel J.⁸, b. April 27, 1834; m. George F. Ellingwood of Bethel.
1037 v Phebe Ellen⁸, b. April, 1844; d. Oct. following.
By second wife :
1038 vi John E.⁸, b. Nov. 5, 1847.
1039 vii Gilman Chapman⁸, b. Oct. 3, 1849.

465

BENJAMIN BURBANK[7] BRADBURY (John[6], John[5], John[4], Wymond[3], Wymond[2], Thomas[1]), married January 8, 1823, Betsey Lowell of Chesterville, who was born July 20, 1804. He was captain in the militia, moved from Chesterville to Newport, where he was in the apothecary business, and then to Bangor. He was also a musician. He died January, 1878.

Children :

1040   i   Hannah Elizabeth[8], b. March 16, 1827; m. July 17, 1859, George C. Goodwin of Charlestown, Mass.

1041   ii   Benjamin Franklin[8], b. Feb. 28, 1829; m. Annie Pierce, and second, Sarah Horton Woodman, r. Boston.

1042   iii   Julia Maria[8], b. May 8, 1835; m. Dec. 15, 1855, Robert F. Patterson of Bangor, now of Tennessee; she died in 1857.

1043   iv   Sarah Eliza[8], b. Feb. 23, 1837.

1044   v   Rachel Annie[8], b. July 3, 1838; m. Oct. 14, 1862, Rev. Charles F. Holbrook of West Boylston, Mass., now of Davenport, Mass.

468

JOTHAM[7] BRADBURY (William[6], John[5], John[4], Wymond[3], Wymond[2], Thomas[1]), married October 5, 1813, Nancy Merrick, who was born March 2, 1791, and died July 31, 1830. For second wife he married, January 9, 1831, Rachel (Hinckley) Merrick, who was born in 1798. He resided in Chesterville, Me. He was much interested in the undertaking of Mr. John M. Bradbury and collected material for this book. He was ensign and captain in the militia, member of the legisla-

12

ture, and in other official positions.   He died in 1889,
aged nearly ninety-eight years.

Children:

1045   i   Harriet Robbins[8], b. Sept. 5, 1814; m. May 23, 1847,
             Eleazer Elwell of Carthage, Me.
1046   ii   Jotham Dennis[8], b. Jan. 9, 1816; m. Sarah Hinckley
             Merrick.
1047   iii Naomi Jane[8], b. July 31, 1818; m. April 3, 1836, Al-
             exander Storer of Carthage, Me.
1048   iv   Meroe Ann[8], b. May 22, 1820; m. July 13, 1844, Hart-
             son Rice Brown of Mt. Vernon, Me.
1049   v   Abigail Bailey[8], b. April 18, 1822; m. Oct. 3, 1850,
             Francis B. Field of Farmington.
1050   vi   William[8], b. March 23, 1824; m. Lydia Ann Merritt.
1051   vii Mary Elizabeth[8], b. July 31, 1826; m. Oct., 1848, Em-
             met Toulmin of Rochester, N. Y.

By second wife:
1052   viii Ellen Julia[8], b. Feb. 27, 1837.

470

WILLIAM OTIS[7] BRADBURY (William[6], John[5], John[4],
Wymond[3], Wymond[2], Thomas[1]), married December 20,
1821, Lavinia Pierce, who was born March 28, 1800,
and died April 12, 1837.   He married second, November 20, 1837, Fanny Willard, who was born June 5,
1807.   He lived in Chesterville, where he was a re-
spectable and useful citizen, but became insane and
ended his days by suicide.

Children:

1053   i   Daniel Storer[8], b. Oct. 16, 1823; d. Oct. 5, 1826.
1054   ii   Otis Thurston[8], b. Aug. 28, 1827; m. Maria J. Daven-
             port, r. Minnesota.

1055　iii　Caroline Lavinia⁸, b. Aug. 8, 1829; m. Aug. 10, 1856
　　　　　　Ephraim Atwood of Buckfield.
1056　iv　Daniel Storer⁸, b. Sept. 3, 1832.
1057　v　George Boardman⁸, b. Oct. 19, 1834; m. Belinda Baker,
　By second wife:
1058　vi　Alfred William⁸, b. Aug. 2, 1846.
1059　vii　Vesta S.⁸, b. Oct. 19, 1849.

474

CHARLES LEIGHTON⁷ BRADBURY (Samuel⁶, John⁵, John⁴, Wymond³, Wymond², Thomas¹), married in Salem, January 14, 1838, Hannah Peavy Brassbridge, who was born at Alton, N. H., March 13, 1817. Their children were born in Salem and Boston.

Children:

1060　i　Sarah Maria⁸, b. Dec. 29, 1839.
1061　ii　Charles Samuel⁸, b. Oct. 5, 1841; d. Sept. 28, 1845.
1062　iii　Edward Emerson⁸, b. Nov. 24, 1843.
1063　iv　Anna Louisa⁸, b. May 14, 1847; d. Aug. 19, 1848.
1064　v　Alice Chamberlain⁸, b. May 30, 1849.

475

SAMUEL ADAMS⁷ BRADBURY (Samuel⁶, John⁵, John⁴, Wymond³, Wymond², Thomas¹), married in Boston, September 17, 1840, Louisa Maria Welch, who was born in Monmouth, Me., Feb. 1817. He died in Boston, May 3, 1852.

Children:

1065　i　Edward Valentine⁸, b. July 31, 1841; d. Aug. 8, 1842.
1066　ii　Charles Edward⁸, b. Nov. 9, 1842; d. Nov. 17, 1842.
1067　iii　Louisa Augusta⁸, b. June 27, 1844.
1068　iv　Sumner Theophilus⁸, b. Jan. 25, 1847.
1069　v　Edward Everett⁸, b. March 12, 1849; d. March 27, 1852.

477

Cotton Chase[7] Bradbury (Samuel[6], John[5], John[4], Wymond[3], Wymond[2], Thomas[1]), married May 28, 1844, Rebecca Beaver, who was born in Providence, R. I., January 10, 1819.

Children:

1070	i	Charles Chase[5], b. ——; d. March, 1848.
1071	ii	William Francis[8], b. ——; b. March, 1848.
1072	iii	William Chase[8], b. Feb. 1, 1849.
1073	iv	Charles Francis[8], b. July 11, 1851.
1074	v	George Edward[8], b. Sept. 13, 1853.
1075	vi	Francis Brewer[8], b. July 28, 1859.

478

John William[7] Bradbury (Samuel[6], John[5], John[4], Wymond[3], Wymond[2], Thomas[1]), married November 22, 1855, Annie Eliza Wells. He resides in Petersburg, Va. He had in his possession the diary of his grandfather, John Bradbury of York, and presented the same to the Maine Historical Society.

Children:

1076   i   Annie Leighton[8], b. Sept. 7, 1856 ; m. W. E. Peebles.
      Their children are :

     1   John Bradbury[9] (Peebles), b. Oct. 1, 1881.
     2   Leighton Hartwell[9] (Peebles), b. Aug. 22, 1883.
     3   Annie Bradbury[9] (Peebles), b. Sept. 17, 1886.
     4   Mary Blanche[9] (Peebles), b. June 29, 1889.

1076 *a*   ii   Mary Anderson[8], b. Nov. 7, 1859; d. in infancy.
1076 *b*   iii   Charles M.[8], b. Sept. 9, 1862, r. Sago, Japan.
1076 *c*   iv   Catherine Emma[8], b. May 9, 1865.
1076 *d*   v   Miriam Louisa[8], b. Dec. 30, 1868.
1076 *e*   vi   Elizabeth Walworth[8], b. Dec. 12, 1872.

481

DAVID[7] BRADBURY (Joseph[6], John[5], John[4], Wymond[3], Wymond[2], Thomas[1]), married November 5, 1839, at Lockport, Ill., Julia A. Livingston, who was born in New York. He died December 27, 1866, at Port Lavaca, Tex., and she died Aug. 9, 1858, at Galveston. Mr. Bradbury was by occupation a contractor.

Children:

1077   i   Henry Clay[8], b. at Springfield, Ill., 1842, r. Kerrville, Tex.

1078   ii   Josephine Livingston[8], b. 1846, at Galveston, Tex.

1079   iii   Edward Livingston[8], b. 1849.

1080   iv   Simon Augustus[8], b. 1851.

483

SIMON PIERCE[7] BRADBURY (Joseph[6], John[5], John[4], Wymond[3], Wymond[2], Thomas[1]), married October 10, 1838, Mary A. Gowen, who died January 24, 1887. Mr. Bradbury has long been connected with educational matters, and is now supervisor of the Bangor schools.

Children:

1081   i   Frederic Gowen[8], b. Nov. 23, 1839; d. ——.

1082   ii   Edgar Howard[8], b. July 5, 1843.

1083   iii   Luella L.[8], b. March 26, 1846; m. —— Clark.

1084   iv   John Joseph[8], b. June 30, 1854.

491

HON. BION[7] BRADBURY (Jeremiah[6], Joseph[5], John[4], Wymond[3], Wymond[2], Thomas[1]), born in Biddeford, December 6, 1811, fitted for college at South Berwick and Gorham academies, and graduated from Bowdoin

College in 1830. The next year he was preceptor of Alfred academy, and in 1832 commenced the study of law with Daniel Goodenow of that town. He completed his studies with Hon. William P. Preble of Portland, and was admitted to the York county bar in May, 1834. He opened an office in Calais, and soon after formed a partnership with Hon. Anson G. Chandler, which continued until the latter was appointed to the bench of the supreme court. In 1844, Mr. Bradbury was appointed collector of customs for Passamaquoddy district, and moved to Eastport; he was twice re-appointed. He served in the Maine legislature in 1849, 1850, and again in 1862. The last time he was elected by the unanimous vote of both parties. He was candate for congress in 1858 and 1874, and for governor in 1863, but his party being in the minority, he was defeated. He was also a member of the National Democratic conventions of 1856, 1860 and 1880. During all these years Mr. Bradbury continued in the practice of the law, and always with marked success. He was a good counselor and a brilliant advocate. In 1864, Mr. Bradbury removed to Portland, and in 1885 was appointed surveyor of the port of Portland, which office he was holding at the time of his death. He died July 1, 1887. A cotemporary of Mr. Bradbury thus spoke of him: "One of the most distinguished and best beloved sons of Maine, has, after a life conspicuous for honorable activity and achievement, gone to his rest. The intelligence of his death will be received with profound regret by men of all parties and sects, and will occasion a feeling of personal loss to more people in this state, unrelated to him by kinship or political ties, than the announcement of the death of almost any other of the citizens of Maine." Mr. Bradbury married October 25, 1837, Alice H., daughter of Col. Johnson Williams of Brooklyn, N. Y., afterward of Waterville, Me., who was the son of Dr. Obadiah Williams, a distinguished citizen of Waterville, who came there from New Hampshire.

Children:

1085   i   Mary Langdon Storer[9], b. Calais, Aug. 12, 1838; m. Aug. 17, 1868, Charles Carroll, son of Judge and Governor Samuel Wells. They had one son, Charles. Mr. Wells died May 31, 1869.

1086   ii   Albert Williams[9], b. Jan. 29, 1840. He graduated at Bowdoin College in 1860. He entered the military service soon after the breaking out of the war as first lieutenant in the First Maine battery of mounted artillery. He was afterward promoted to captain of the battery, and then to major of the regiment. He was a brave and gallant officer, as his promotions sufficiently indicate. He is now in the practice of law in Portland, and is unmarried.

1087   iii   William Dow[9], b. Oct. 2, 1842; d. at Eastport, Aug. 20, 1854.

1088   iv   Bion Lucius[9], b. Eastport, Aug. 20, 1847; d. Jan. 30, 1848.

1089   v   Alice Williams[9], b. Jan. 25, 1849; m. Dec. 9, 1869, Charles F. Libby, a talented and popular lawyer of the Cumberland bar; resides in Portland.

1090   vi   Bion[9], b. Oct. 16, 1852.

1091   vii   Marcia Dow[9], b. Feb. 6, 1855; m. Feb. 28, 1882, Edward C. Jordan. She is a contributor to the public press, and has written some gems of poetry. They reside in Portland.

495

Emily[7] Bradbury (Jeremiah[6], Joseph[5], John[4], Wymond[3], Wymond[2], Thomas[1]), born in Alfred, May 18, 1821; married September 16, 1843, Francis Keyes Swan* of Calais. They resided in Calais until the autumn of 1865, when they moved to Portland. Mr. Swan was senior member of the well-known banking firm of Swan & Barrett until he retired a few years ago, with a competency. Mrs. Swan was a confirmed invalid during the last years of her life, but it was borne with remarkable fortitude and patience, with a forgetfulness of self, and a thoughtful consideration for others, which had been conspicuous traits in her character throughout her life. She died in Portland, December 4, 1877.

*William Swan, born in Boston, 1746, was a descendant in the third generation from Dr. Thomas Swan, who graduated from Harvard College in 1689. He married Mercy Porter of Weymouth, 1776. Removed to Gardiner, Me., 1795; subsequently to Winslow, where he died, 1835.

Francis Swan, third son of William, born 1785. Married Hannah, daughter of James Child of Augusta, 1814. Settled in Winslow, removing thence to Calais, 1834. He died June, 1862. Mrs. Swan died May, 1869. Children:

1 Sarah Porter, b. Feb. 6, 1816; m. Richard H. Manning of New York, Nov. 7, 1840; d. Dec. 21, 1841.

2 James Child, b. Aug. 4, 1817; m. Helen Trask of Portland, Sept., 1845; d. Oct. 15, 1853. She died Feb. 13, 1887.

3 William Henry, b. Jan. 13, 1819. Unmarried.

4 Francis Keyes, b. Oct. 20, 1820; m. Emily Bradbury, Sept. 16,1843; removed from Calais to Portland, 1865, where she died Dec. 4, 1877.

5 Charles Edward, b. Sept. 5, 1822. Graduated at Bowdoin College in 1844; m. Mary D., daughter of George Downes of Calais, Sept. 26, 1849. She died July 9, 1851.

6 Eugene Swan, b. July 23, 1824. Unmarried.

Ebenr Bradbury

Children ;

1092 i   Henry Storer⁸ (Swan), b. Dec. 8, 1844; m. April 7,
          1877, Mrs. Annie C. C. Shaw, daughter of R. A. L.
          Codman of Portland. He is a physician of Bristol, R.I.
1093 ii Emily Manning⁸ (Swan), b. Oct. 24, 1846; m. Dec. 31,
          1879, Dr. Frederic Henry Gerrish of Portland.
1094 iii Marcia Bradbury⁸ (Swan), b. May 31, 1853.
1095 iv   Florence Wainwright⁸ (Swan), b. Aug. 20, 1857.

509

EBENEZER⁷ BRADBURY (Theophilus⁶, Jonathan⁵, Theophilus⁴, Wymond³, Wymond², Thomas¹), was a silver-
smith by trade, and resided in Newburyport. He was
a noble specimen of the self-made man. He had a
large family, but by industrious and economical habits
he brought up his children in comfort, and gave them
a good education. By steady and methodical habits of
study he acquired a large amount of useful information. His benevolence and genial disposition, united
with strict integrity, won for him the respect and good
will of his fellow-citizens, and gave him great influence
in his native town. He had great interest in educational matters, which continued unabated all through
his useful life. He was frequently elected to municipal offices, and for five years was a member of the
Massachusetts legislature. In 1847, he was chosen
speaker of the House. For two years he was a member of the executive council, and in 1849 was elected
treasurer of the commonwealth, a position which he held
two years — as long as the party to which he belonged
was then in power. In 1853, he resided in Newton,

and was a delegate from that town to the constitutional convention. The next year he represented that town in the general court. Later in life he was judge of the municipal court in Milford. He was upright in his dealings, modest and unassuming in his demeanor, kind and obliging to every one, he served his town and state most faithfully, and his death, which took place June 19, 1864, was greatly lamented by a large circle of friends. He married December 10, 1815, Nancy Merrill, who was born November 12, 1796, and died January 13, 1832. He married second, July 3, 1832, Mary Tappan, who was born November 25, 1798. He had eighteen children, the eight first born in Newburyport, and the others, part in Newburyport and part in Southampton, Franklin county, Penn.

Children:

1096	i	Ebenezer[8], b. Dec. 10, 1816; m. Mary Todd.
1097	ii	John Merrill[8], b. Oct. 29, 1818; m. Sarah Ann Hayes.
1098	iii	Theophilus[8], b. Oct. 24, 1820; d. July 12, 1821.
1099	iv	Theophilus[8], b. July 28, 1822; m. Emily Jane Gray.
1100	v	Jonathan[8], b. Oct. 5, 1824; d. same day.
1101	vi	Samuel[8], b. Oct. 8, 1825; d. same day.
1102	vii	Albert Fayette[8], b. July 16, 1827; m. Frances Ayer Morrill.
1103	viii	Ann Maria[8], b. Aug. 18, 1830; d. Sept. 30 following.

By second wife :

1104	ix	George[8], b. April 19, 1833; m. Elizabeth L. Taisey.
1105	x	Ephraim[8], b. May 13, 1835; d. same day.
1106	xi	Eunice[8], b. May 13, 1835; d. same day.
1107	xii	Charles Edwin[8], b. Jan. 8, 1837; m. Sarah M. Hastings.
1108	xiii	Edwin Charles[8], b. Jan. 8, 1837; m. Harriet Jane Williams.

1109 xiv Francis Augustine[6], b. Oct. 30, 1838.
1110 xv Frances Augusta[8], b. Oct. 30, 1838; d. Mar. 4, 1841.
1111 xvi William Henry Harrison[8], b. Feb. 24, 1840; m. Clara
    Clement Adams.
1112 xvii Anna Mary[8], b. Sept. 28, 1841.
1113 xviii Washington Irving[8], b. March 14, 1843; m. Mary
    Ella Rounds.

513

JOHN[7] BRADBURY (Theophilus[6], Jonathan[5], Theophilus[4], Wymond[3], Wymond[2], Thomas[1]), married at Newburyport, September 7, 1825, Rebecca Moody Boardman, who was born at Newburyport, May 19, 1805. She died August 21, 1834, and he married second, October 6, 1836, Augusta Hayes, who was born in Gloucestor, Mass., March 6, 1809. He died in San Francisco, October 3, 1851.

Children, born in Newburyport:
1114 i Harriet Louisa[8], b. July 25, 1826; d. Feb. 14, 1873, at
    Naples, Italy.
1115 ii John Henry[8], b. Dec. 9, 1827; m. Oct. 23, 1861, Emily
    Olcott Robertson.
1116 iii Charles William[8], b. Nov. 18, 1830; m. at Cambridge,
    Mass., June 4, 1864, Sophia Louise Appleton.
1117 iv Rebecca[8], b. May 22, 1833; d. Nov. 16, 1849.
1118 v Elizabeth Marshall[8], b. Aug. 15, 1834; m. Truman H.
    Safford.*

*Truman Henry Safford is Professor of Astronomy in Williams College. Their children are:
1 John Henry[10] (Safford), b. June 11, 1861.
2 Louisa Parker[10] (Safford), b. Dec. 19, 1862; d. Sept. 26, 1864.
3 Walter Bradbury[10] (Safford), b. Dec. 23, 1864.
4 Arthur Truman[10] (Safford), b. Feb. 9, 1867.
5 Charles Louis[10] (Safford), b. Nov. 19, 1870.
6 Alice Elizabeth[10] (Safford), b. April 30, 1876.
Three of the sons are graduates of the college, and the other is a sophomore.

By second wife:

1119 vi Walter Scott[8], b. May 16, 1840; d. at Newbern, N. C.,
Jan. 22, 1863. He was a soldier in 44th Mass. vols.

1120 vii Augusta[8], b. Jan. 14, 1845; d. Boston, May 2, 1865.

519

CHARLES[7] BRADBURY (Smith[6], Jonathan[5], Theophilus[4], Wymond[3], Wymond[2], Thomas[1]), married November 3, 1828, Juliet Walker, who was born May 10, 1809. Captain Charles Bradbury was a sailor, and made several voyages as master of a vessel. He abandoned the sea when about thirty years of age, and became a school teacher. He was for many years a leading man in Kennebunkport. He was moderator in the town meetings for many successive years, served six years as a member of the school board, was town agent for several years, was representative to the state legislature two terms, and was one of the board of county commissioners for York county from 1831 to 1838. He was a man of marked ability and a devoted student of local history. His history of Kennebunkport, formerly the ancient town of Arundel, is a work of great merit, and is now very scarce. He went to Michigan about the year 1844, and died at Albion, in that state, July 4, 1864.

Children :

1121 i Octavia[8], b. Oct. 7, 1829.

1122 ii Juliet[8], March 17, 1840.

1123 iii Charles[8], b. Dec. 20, 1841.

528

WYMAN[7] BRADBURY (Charles[6], Wymond[5], Theophilus[4], Wymond[3], Wymond[2], Thomas[1]), married May 13, 1838, Elizabeth Ann Starbuck. He lived in Nantucket, where his children were born. He was lost at sea in July. 1852.

Children:

1124   i   Lucy Starbuck[8], b. March 23, 1839.
1125   ii   Mary Elizabeth[8], b. Dec. 21, 1840; d. Sept. 11, 1841.
1126   iii   Mary Ann[8], b. Dec. 3, 1841; d. Sept. 11, 1842.
1127   iv   Charles Wyman[8], b. Feb. 21, 1848.

530

JONATHAN OAKES[7] BRADBURY (Charles[6], Wymond[5], Theophilus[4], Wymond[3], Wymond[2], Thomas[1]), married October 9, 1845, Rachel G., daughter of Lieutenant Jonas G. and Betsey Stetson (Cutter) Brooks, who was born April 20, 1819. He died October 28, 1872.

Children, born at Charlestown, Mass:

1128   i   Emily Frances[8], b. May 25, 1846.
1129   ii   Mary Brooks[8], b. Oct. 19, 1850; m. Sept. 26, 1877, Joseph L. Jefferson of Chelsea.
1130   iii   George Oakes[8], b. Aug. 19, 1858.

541

ELBRIDGE[7] BRADBURY (Edward[6], Wymond[5], Theophilus[4], Wymond[3], Wymond[2], Thomas[1]), married April 20, 1840, Mary J., daughter of Richard Underhill of New York.

Children:

1131   i   Augustus Underhill[8], b. Bedford, Pa., Feb. 4, 1841.
1132   ii   Henry Chase[8], b. Aug. 18, 1844, at Williamsport, Pa.

556

CHARLES WILLIAM[7] BRADBURY (Charles[6], Theophilus[5], Theophilus[4], Wymond[3], Wymond[2], Thomas[1]), married January 18, 1846, Eleanor Farrand Bradley.

Children :

1133 i William Cumming[8], b. March 7, 1847.
1134 ii Charles Augustus[8], b. March 1, 1849; midshipman U. S. navy.
1135 iii Elenora Cumming[8], b. Sept. 4, 1851; d. Oct. following.
1136 iv George Winslow[8], b. Nov. 6, 1852.
1137 v Elenora Cumming[8], b. Nov. 18, 1854.
1138 vi Fanny Winslow[8], b. Sept. 16, 1856.

564

JOHN[7] BRADBURY (John[6], Rowland[5], John[4], William[3], William[2], Thomas[1].), married at Marblehead, February 7, 1807, Hannah Bubier, who was born at Marblehead, September 17, 1789. He died October 3, 1827, and she married again.

Children, born in Guilford, N. H.:

1139 i Hannah Jarvis[8], b. April 23, 1808; m. Jacob Rowe of Guilford.
1140 ii Mary[8], b. 1810; d. young.
1141 iii Susan[8], b. 1812; d. young.
1142 iv John Bubier[8], b. Feb. 15, 1814; m. Feb. 12, 1844, Eliza Follansbee, who was born Aug. 29, 1814. He resides at Waterville, Me. No issue.

570

BENJAMIN[7] BRADBURY (John[6], Rowland[5], John[4], William[3], William[2], Thomas[1]), married August 19, 1812, Joanna Weeks (one account says Lorinda Knowlton).

Children :

1143　i　Nancy[8], b. Oct. 25, 1812; m. Oct. 5, 1835, Augustus
　　　　　Wilson of Kittery.
1144　ii　Isabella[8], b. ——; m. March 24, 1846, William R. Davis
　　　　　of Boston.

571

JOSEPH[7] BRADBURY (John[6], Rowland[5], John[4], William[3], William[2], Thomas[1]), married at Guilford, N. H.,
January 30, 1815, Hannah Boyd, who was born at
Guilford, February 19, 1797. He moved to Wentworth, N. H.

Children, born at Guilford, N. H.;

1145　i　Arthur[8], b.——; d. young.
1146　ii　Darius[8], b. May 5, 1817; m. Emily Hobbs.
1147　iii　Luther Milton[8], b. Aug. 30, 1819; m. Nancy Hobbs.
1148　iv　Abigail[8], b. May 31, 1821; m. Jan. 30, 1844, John Vit-
　　　　　tum, r. Sandwich, N. H.
1149　v　Mary Jane[8], b. Dec. 15, 1829; m. July 9, 1853, Daniel
　　　　　Kidder Cummings of Wentworth, N. H.
1150　vi　Edgar[8], b. Jan. 19, 1832, r. Wentworth.

573

JESSE[7] BRADBURY (John[6], Rowland[5], John[4], William[3],
William[2], Thomas[1]), married in 1822, Susan Craig. He
died in 1830, and his widow married again.

Child :

1151　i　Olive Ann[8], b. April 28, 1824.

576

JOHN STEVENS[7] BRADBURY (Paul[6], Rowland[5], John[4],
William[3], William[2], Thomas[1]), resided in Industry, Me.,

and died there.   He married at Madbury, N. H., July
3, 1807, Lois Pinkham, who died January 15, 1854.

Children:

1151 i   Alfred⁸, b. Sept. 19, 1807; d. unmarried, July 26, 1886.
1152 ii Mary⁸, b. May 14, 1810; d. unmarried, April 4, 1876.

579

TRUE⁷ BRADBURY (Paul⁶, Rowland⁵, John⁴, William³,
William², Thomas¹), married Lydia Cushing Allen.

Children:

1153 i   Wyer⁸, b. June 14, 1814; m. Eliza Webber.
1154 ii   Samuel Hidden⁸, b. Sept. 18, 1818; m. Dec. 24, 1846,
             Mary E. Small, r. West Lubec.
1155 iii Mary Jane⁸, b. ——; m. William Guptill of Lubec.
1156 iv   Stephen Decatur⁸, b. ——.
1157 v   Sarah Ann⁸, b. ——; m. William J. Balch of Machias.

583

SAMUEL HIDDEN⁷ BRADBURY (Paul⁶ Rowland⁵, John⁴,
William³, William², Thomas¹), married at Cherryfield,
Me., Bethiah H. Dinsmore.   He moved to Brewer, Me.

Children:

1158 i   Rowland⁸, b. Aug., 1826.
1159 ii   Wyman Collins⁸, b. July 31, 1829.
1160 iii Mary⁸, b. Aug., 1836; m. John Ryan.
1161 iv   Susannah⁸, b. July 3, 1840; d. Aug. 17, 1857.

601

EBENEZER⁷ BRADBURY (James⁶, Samuel⁵, James⁴, William³, William², Thomas¹), married June 9, 1805, Mary
Thompson, who died in Boston about 1830.   He was
lost at sea in January, 1811.

Children :

1162   i   Ebenezer[8], b. Sept. 14, 1806.
1163   ii   James Williams[8], b. May 27, 1808.
1164   iii   Frederic Titcomb[8], b. Nov. 6, 1810.

607

JOHN COFFIN[7] BRADBURY (James[6], Samuel[5], James[4], William[3], William[2], Thomas[1]), married at Hampton Falls, July, 1829, Margaret Shaw Tilton. He lived in Newburyport and Boston, and died in Boston, March 23, 1870. His wife died and he married second, December 30, 1859, Fannie Jeanette Dyke, who was born at New Lebanon Springs, N. Y., in 1825 or 1826.

Children :

1165   i   Margaret Ellen[8], b. Jan. 14, 1830; m. Jan. 10, 1856, Marshall H. Lyman.
1166   ii   John James[8], b. 1832 ; d. same year.
1167   iii   Sarah Caroline[8], b. Feb. 20, 1834.

608

JOHN TALBOT NORRIS[7] BRADBURY (Samuel[6], Samuel[5], James[4], William[3], William[2], Thomas[1]), married in 1832, Mary Jane Robinson. He died in 1838, in Baltimore, where his children were born.

Children :

1168   i   John Wesley[8], b. 1833, r. Washington D. C.
1169   ii   Robert Robinson[8], b. 1835, r. Baltimore, Md.
1170   iii   Samuel Benjamin[8], b. 1836, r. Baltimore.

13

615

WILLIAM SIMPSON[7] BRADBURY (David[6], Samuel[5], James[4]. William[3], William[2]. Thomas[1]), married January 28, 1826, Mary Hallowell Oliver. He died May 24, 1862, at Ship Island. She is living in New Sharon. He was a farmer in New Sharon.

Children :

1171 i Francis, b. New Sharon, July 24, 1827, r. California.
1172 ii David Oliver[8], b. Dec. 28, 1829; m. Mary Oliver Cushman.
1173 iii Benjamin F.[8], b. April 4, 1832; m. Aug. 1854, Hannah S. Hunt; d. Kentucky, 1863, s. p.
1174 iv Emily J.[8], b. Sept. 6, 1835, r. New Sharon, unmarried.
1175 v Mary Jane[8], b. Sept. 6, 1835; m. July 7, 1854, Alden B. Folsom of Newburyport.
1176 vi George W.[8], b. Feb. 4, 1838; m. Augusta Jane Bump, r. Farmington.
1177 vii Wyman O.[8], b. April 11, 1841; d. Nov. 1, 1868, unmarried.
1178 viii Lyman O.[8], b. April 11, 1841; d. Sept. 28, 1841.

629

JAMES[7] BRADBURY (James[6], Sanders[5], James[4], William[3], William[2], Thomas[1]). married January 14, 1835, Lois Ayer. He died December 5, 1837, in Quincy, Mass.

Child :

1179 i Ann Susan[8], b. Jan. 14, 1836.

631

WILLIAM SANDERS[7] BRADBURY (James[6], Sanders[5], James[4], William[3], William[2], Thomas[1]), born in Hollis,

N. H.; married October 18, 1824, Elizabeth Emerson, who was born in Hollis, N. H., July 29, 1800, and died in Lawrence, Mass., October 4, 1870. They lived in Westminster, Mass.

Children :

1179½ i Elizabeth Emerson⁸, b. Aug. 18, 1826; m. April 11, 1848, Amos D. Nourse.
1180 ii William Frothingham⁸, b. May 17, 1829; m. Margaret Jones.
1181 iii Edward Emerson⁸, b. Feb. 7, 1832 ; m. Sarah Jane Sykes.
1182 iv Charles Fletcher⁸, b. April 10, 1836 ; d. Dec. 9, 1854.
1183 v Esther Caroline⁸, b. June 24, 1839 ; r. San Francisco, Cal.
1184 vi Charlotte Ann⁸, b. March 24, 1844 ; m. Aug. 23, 1864, Edward A. Eaton, r. Vallejo, Cal.

632

CHARLES⁷, BRADBURY (James⁶, Sanders⁵, James⁴, William³, William², Thomas¹), married in 1827, Mary E. Worcester. He lived awhile in Nashua, N. H., and died in 1830, at Oxford, Conn.

Child :

1185 i Mary⁸, b. 1829 ; d. an infant in Nashua.

634

SAMUEL FOX⁷ BRADBURY (James⁶, Sanders⁵, James⁴, William³, William², Thomas¹), married at Boston, June 14, 1836, Mary Ann (Leathe) Brooks, who died January 20, 1855. He died in New York, February 9, 1842.

Children :

1186 i Charles Brooks⁸, b. April 5, 1837 ; m. Emily H. Sykes.
1187 ii Ellen⁸, b. July 6, 1839 ; d. at Cambridge, Mass., Feb. 23, 1864.

635

JOSIAH CONANT[7] BRADBURY (James[6], Sanders[5], James[4], William[3], William[2], Thomas[1]), married November 27, 1864, Almira Hemenway, who was born at Framingham, Mass., March 18, 1809. He resided at Charlestown, Mass.

Children:

1188　　i　Frances Almira[8], b. Sept. 27, 1835; m. Edwin A. Roulstone; d. Dec. 13, 1856.

1189　　ii　James Dexter[8], b. April 11, 1837; d. May 15, 1842.

1190　iii　Mary Catherine[8], b. Feb. 21, 1839; m. at Boston, July 16, 1859, John Weld.

1191　iv　James Fox[8], b. Oct. 21, 1842; m. Julia A. Frye.

1192　　v　Charles Conant[8], b. March 1, 1845.

1193　vi　Frank Dexter[8], b. May 14, 1847.

1194　vii　Lucy[8], b. Aug. 7, 1850; d. next day.

1195　viii　George Gardner[8], b. Jan. 27, 1852; d. young.

637

CORNELIUS SANDERS[7] BRADBURY (Jacob[6], Sanders[5], James[4], William[3], William[2], Thomas[1]), married November 21, 1821, Sallie Ann Spining, who was born in Newark, N. J., March 8, 1803. He lived in Cincinnati and East Walnut Hills, Ohio. His wife died at the latter place November 20, 1854, and he married second, July 18, 1856, Frances E. Marsh.

Children:

1196　　i　William Edgar[8], b. Dec. 11, 1822; m. Sarah Hogan.

1197　　ii　Julius Oscar[8], b. June 9, 1824; m. Lavina Rothamer Moore.

1198　iii　Eliza Cornelia[8], b. Dec. 8, 1825; m. Feb. 18, 1852, John Stuart of Harrison, Ohio.

1199 iv Edward Augustus[6], b. March 8, 1827 ; d. Portland, Oregon, Oct. 20, 1851.

By second wife :

1200 v Charles Marsh[8], b. May 24, 1858.

639

MARCUS TULLIUS CICERO[7] BRADBURY (Jacob[6], Sanders[5], James[4], William[3], William[2], Thomas[1]), married July, 1835, Catherine Thorne of Hartford, Vt. He settled in Jefferson county, Ia., and afterward moved to Rising Sun, Ia.

Children :

1201 i Cornelius Jasper[8], b. July 1, 1838.
1202 ii James[8], b. March 9, 1843.
1203 iii Sarah Cornelia[8], b. March 11, 1845.
1204 iv Kate[8], b. Nov. 11, 1848.
1205 v Dauphine[8], b. March, 1858.

645

WILLIAM LUNT[7] BRADBURY (William[6], Sanders[5], James[4], William[3], William[2], Thomas[1]), married April 26, 1829, Sarah Martin, who died; and he married second, 1835, Maria Shipley Perkins, who was born in Mount Vernon, N. H., February 15, 1814, and was the daughter of Mark Dodge and Mahala (Jones) Perkins. He died in New York, November 10, 1850.

Children :

By second marriage :

1206 i Irene Perkins[8], b. New York, Jan. 9, 1839.
1207 ii Mark Perkins[8], b. Boston, 1843.

1208 iii William Jones[8], b. June 21, 1845; m. Emma Page Boynton.

1209 iv Maria Louise[8], b. Oct. 22, 1847.

1210 v Sarah Caroline[8], b. Sept. 12, 1849; m. Justin Edwards Hill.

647

JOSEPH SANDERS[7] BRADBURY (William[6], Sanders[5], James[4], William[3], William[2], Thomas[1]), born in Milford, Mass., married May 27, 1838, at Newbury, Mass., Mary M. Lunt, who was born in Newbury, August 17, 1803,

Children:

1211 i Mary Elizabeth[8], b. New York, Feb. 24, 1839; d. July 25, following.

1212 ii Margaret Elizabeth[8], b. May 8, 1840; d. May 12, 1840.

1213 iii Charles William[8], b. Aug. 30, 1841.

1214 iv Octavia[8], b. Amherst, N. H., May 15, 1843.

1215 v Andrew Jackson[8], b. Newburyport, May 8, 1845.

1216 vi Joseph[8], b. Brooklyn, N. Y., April 30, 1847; d. Oct. 10, following.

1217 vii Sanders[8], b. Sept. 16, 1848; d. ——.

1218 viii Jenny Lind[8], b. Guyandotte, Va., Jan. 22, 1850.

1219 ix Joseph S.[8], b. Brimfield, Ill., April 22, 1852; d, Feb. 20, 1854.

1220 x Benjamin Franklin[8], b. July 7, 1853.

1221 xi Sarah Jane[8], b. March 24, 1855; d. Sept. 5, 1855.

1222 xii George Richard[8], b. July 23, 1856.

666

NATHANIEL[7] BRADBURY (James[6], James[5], Crisp[4], William[3], William[2], Thomas[1]), married March 10, 1833, Lucy Sawyer, who was born October 6, 1807. He died August 15, 1848.

Children :

1223   i   Gibeon Elden[8], b. July 30, 1833.
1224 ii   Walter Cutts[8], b. Nov. 27, 1834; d. 1854.
1225 iii Daniel Owen[8], b. May 26, 1836.

668

EDWARD RUMERY[7] BRADBURY (Crisp[6], James[5], Crisp[4], William[3], William[2], Thomas[1]), married in Boston, September 29, 1851, Harriet Newell, daughter of Andrew and Betsey (Blaisdell) Noble, who was born in Alfred, Me., April 29, 1832.

Children :

1226   i   Elizabeth Jane[8], b. June 11, 1854; d. Jan. 16, 1872.
1227 ii   Frank Edward[8], b. Dec. 25, 1860.
1228 iii Hattie Paine[8], b. March 21, 1863.

674

ALBION[7] BRADBURY (Jacob[6], Jacob[5], Thomas[4], Jacob[3], William[2], Thomas[1]), married January 10, 1856, Elizabeth Wentworth. He lived in Limerick.

Children :

1229   i   John Jacob[8], b. Jan. 18, 1857.
1230 ii   George Dana[8], b. Dec. 6, 1858.
1231 iii Henry Sawtelle[8], b. May, 1865; d, July 29, 1867.

677

CHARLES WEBSTER[7] BRADBURY (Thomas[6], Jacob[5], Thomas[4], Jacob[3], William[2], Thomas[1]) married January 16, 1838, Sarah Merrill, who was born at Sedgwick, Me., March 28, 1808. He resided at one time in Amesbury, Mass.

Children :

1232 i   Harriet Amanda⁶, b. Jan. 7, 1839.
1233 ii   Sarah Eliza⁶, b. Feb. 17, 1841.
1234 iii Susan Mary⁶, b. Dec. 27, 1842.
1235 iv   Hannah Joann⁶, b. June 4, 1844.
1236 v   John Thomas⁸, b. May 6, 1846; d. same day.
1237 vi   Emily Merrill⁶, b. March 3, 1848; m. 1868, Albert W.
           Todd, who was born at York, Me.

679

HORACE JAMES⁷ BRADBURY (Thomas⁶, Jacob⁵, Thomas⁴, Jacob³, William², Thomas¹), married June 30, 1834, Harriet Newell Ulrick, who was born in Portland, Me., November 19, 1815, and died at Castine, April 12, 1849. He married second, December 30, 1849, Winifred Chase Mayo, who was born in Hallowell, October 6, 1821, and died in Saccarappa, May 31, 1854. He married third, April 10, 1855, Lucy Fenderson Sands, who was born in Buxton, July 19, 1821. He was a Universalist minister lived in Westbrook, Hampden and elsewhere.

Children :

1238 i   Harriet Amanda⁸, b. Portland, Me., June 4, 1835; d.
           Aug. 22, 1836, in New York.
1239 ii   Louis Philippe⁸, b. Hermon, Me., Nov. 28, 1837; d.
           Sept. 25, 1840.
1240 iii Horace Webster⁸, b. Hampden, Dec. 26, 1839; d. Sept.
           23, 1840.
1241 iv   Horace Roscoe⁸, b. Aug. 2, 1841.
1242 v   Harriet Louisa⁸, b. Oct. 31, 1843; d. Nov. 7, 1845.
1243 vi   John Ulrick⁸, b. Dec. 18, 1845.
1244 vii Franklin Rogers⁸, b. Aug. 26, 1847.

By second wife :

1245 viii Charles Edwin⁸, b. Castine, June 2, 1850.

681

CALEB[7] BRADBURY (Joseph[6], Jacob[5], Thomas[4], Jacob[3], William[2], Thomas[1]), married at Cambridge, Mass., October 23, 1827, Almira E. Brown, who was born at Townshend, Vt., June 21, 1805. He was a glass-maker, and died in Cambridge, Mass., February 4, 1879. His wife died January 24, preceding.

Children, born in Cambridge:

1245½   i   Elizabeth Almira[8], b. Aug. 20, 1829; m. Jan. 3, 1850, Andrew Crane of Somerville, Mass.

1246   ii   Juliette[8], b. Oct. 19, 1831; d. Nov. 27, 1833.

1247   iii   Caleb Brown[8], b. April 9, 1835; m. Eliza Ann Fletcher.

1248   iv   Horace Denison[8], b. Oct. 9, 1837; m. Betsey Ann Dustin.

1249   v   Julia Maria[8], b. Oct. 21, 1840; m. Dr. William H. Carpenter.

1250   vi   Thomas Frederic[8], b. Nov. 19, 1848; m. Hattie J. White of Boston.

684

ASA[7] BRADBURY (Joseph[6], Jacob[5], Thomas[4], Jacob[3], William[2], Thomas[1]), married October 21, 1835, Electa Harding, who was born in New York, October 19, 1816. He lived at Kygerville, Gallia county, Ohio.

Children: .

1251   i   Sarah Samantha[8], b. Kygerville, O., April 26, 1836.

1252   ii   Joseph Perry[8], b. Feb. 22, 1838.

1253   iii   Augusta[8], b. Feb. 11, 1840; m. Sept. 16, 1857, Dr. James Johnson.

1254   iv   William[8], b. May 1, 1842.

1255   v   Frances Amanda[8], b. Sept. 26, 1844.

1256   vi   Horace Reed[8], b. Sept. 25, 1848.

1257   vii   Mary Alice[8], b. March 31, 1856.

685

JOSEPH[7] BRADBURY (Joseph[6], Jacob[5], Thomas[4], Jacob[3], William[2], Thomas[1]), married January 11, 1829, Eliza Strong, who was born at Salem, Meigs county, Ohio, September 26, 1813.

Children:

1258   i   Elizabeth[8], b. June 4, 1829 ; d. May 1, 1830.
1258½ ii Alonzo Russell[8], b. Dec. 14, 1830.
1259   iii Mary[8], b. Feb. 16, 1832 ; m. April 13, 1852, Sylvanus Powell.
1260   iv Amanda[8], b. Oct. 6, 1833 ; m. May 3, 1853, James M. Johnson.
1261   v Louisa[8], b. Feb. 24, 1835 ; d. Sept. 23, 1856.
1262   vi Nancy Lucinda[8], b. Feb. 28, 1837.
1263   vii Elijah Strong[8], b. April 9, 1840.
1264   viii Electa Pamelia[8], b. April 29, 1842.
1265   ix Oliver Lowell[8], b. Aug. 10, 1845.
1266   x Juliet Eliza[8], b. April 29, 1847.
1267   xi Joseph Stevens[8], b. March 14, 1849.

686

SAMUEL[7] BRADBURY (Joseph[6], Jacob[5], Thomas[4], Jacob[3], William[2], Thomas[1]), married May 23, 1837, Clarissa Hackett. He lived in Middleport, Meigs county, Ohio.

Children:

1268   i   Helen[8], b. Aug. 10, 1839.
1269   ii Jane Elizabeth[8], b. May 14, 1843.
1270 iii Caleb Willson[8], b. Aug. 31, 1846 ; d. Oct. 28, 1848.
1271 iv Charles Henry[8], b. June 5, 1850 ; d. March 1, 1851.

690

MOSES RUSSELL[7] BRADBURY (Joseph[6], Jacob[5], Thomas[4], Jacob[3], William[2], Thomas[1]), married Mary Harding. He died June 13, 1845.

Children :

1272 i Custis[8], b. Dec. 10, 1840.
1273 ii Emma[8], b. July 2, 1844.

691

TRUE[7] BRADBURY (Samuel[6], Moses[5], Thomas[4], Jacob[3], William[2], Thomas[1]), married August 28, 1808, Sally Nason, who was born March 20, 1790. They lived in Limerick and moved thence to New Limerick, Aroostook county, Me., where their last two children were born; she died June 17, 1844. He died January 7, 1856.

Children:

1274 i Aaron Nason[8], b. Aug. 31, 1809.
1275 ii Moses[8], b. Sept. 15, 1811 ; m. Olive Scammon Emery.
1276 iii Cyrus King[8], b. Sept. 11, 1813; m. Sally Shields.
1277 iv Samuel[8], b. June 24, 1816; m. Juliann B. True.
1278 v Thomas Merrill[8], b. May 30, 1840 ; m. Catherine Dow.
1279 vi True[8], b. Jan. 7, 1822 ; d. April 7, 1835.
1280 vii Benjamin Gilpatrick[8], b. March 11, 1825 ; d. Nov. 29, 1852.
1281 viii Joshua Putnam[8], b. May 25, 1827 ; d. May 25, 1856.
1282 ix John Quincy Adams[8], b. Nov. 29, 1829 ; d. Jan. 11, 1856.
1283 x Henry Clay[8], b. April 29, 1833.

692

EBENEZER CLEAVES[7] BRADBURY (Samuel[6], Moses[5], Thomas[4], Jacob[3], William[2], Thomas[1]), married December 7, 1813, Clara Adams, who was born January 27, 1791.

Children :

1284   i   Hall Jackson⁸, b. Oct. 13, 1815.
1285   ii   Tryphosa Cleaves⁸, b. June 3, 1817.
1286   iii   Clement Adams⁸, b. March 18, 1819.
1287   iv   Christopher Columbus⁸, b. April 18, 1821.
1288   v   Ebenezer⁸, b. Feb. 28, 1823 ; d. ——.
1289   vi   Stephen Little Adams⁸, b. March 27, 1827.
1290   vii   Simon Adams⁸, b. March 10, 1829.
1291   viii   Charles Freeman⁸, b. July 25, 1832.
1292   ix   Daniel Webster⁸, b. Aug. 18, 1835.

698

CHRISTOPHER COLUMBUS⁷ BRADBURY (Samuel⁶, Moses⁵, Thomas⁴, Jacob³, William², Thomas¹), married February 21, 1824, Mary Joselyn, who was born October 15, 1789. He went to West Virginia and died there. He was born in Limerick, afterward lived in New Brunswick, and in Hodgdon, Me.

Child :

1293 i   James Tyler⁸, b. in Prince William, N. B., Jan. 19, 1826 ; m. Ann Judson, daughter of Rev. Royal C. Spaulding. He fitted for college at Houlton academy, and entered Waterville, from which he graduated in the class of 1855. He was an exemplary student and a good scholar. After graduating he was Principal of Waterville, and also of Vassalboro academy, and in 1859, he moved to West Virginia and became a teacher and then principal in the academy at West Liberty. Here he died of diphtheria, June 14, 1863. His widow and two sons returned to Houlton, Me.

700

ABNER[7] BRADBURY (Jabez Page[6], Thomas[5], Thomas[4], Jacob[3], William[2], Thomas[1]), married Eunice Hall, who was born in Augusta, January 16, 1796. They lived in Athens, Me.

Children:

1294   i   William Harrison[8], b. April 30, 1815; m. Julia Ann Staples.

1295   ii   Sarah Hilton[8], b. April 29, 1817; m. Philander Pierce, s. Wisconsin.

1296   iii   Ziba Hall[8], b. Jan. 12, 1820; m. Lucy Lilly Blackman

1297   iv   Eunice Fletcher[8], b. April 18, 1822.

1298   v   Benjamin Franklin[8], b. Nov. 3, 1824; m. Clarissa Calphurnia Bowers.

1299   vi   Nancy Jane[8], b. Aug. 14, 1825.

1300   vii   Lucy Maria[8], b. Oct. 20, 1828.

1301   viii   Cyrus Stilson[8], b. Aug. 2, 1829; m. Mary Althea Willard.

1302   ix   Mary Eliza[8], b. July 29, 1832.

708

THOMAS[7] BRADBURY (Daniel[6], Thomas[5], Thomas[4], Jacob[3], William[2], Thomas[1]), married Dolly, daughter of Benjamin Morse of Rumford. His children were born in Byron and Canton, Me. Thomas Bradbury born February 18, 1791, moved from York county to Byron, and died in Canton, October 15, 1857. He was a farmer.

Children:

1303   i   Albion E.[8], b. March 8, 1822.

1304   ii   Cynthia[8], b. Sept. 2, 1825; d. April 29, 1857.

1305 iii Charles Dana⁸, b. Feb. 16, 1828; m. April 26, 1854, Me-
            lona Rosaltha, daughter of Hon. Thomas Chase of
            Buckfield. He is a physician and resides in Buckfield,
            Me.

1306 iv   Fannie⁸, b. Oct., 1830; m. March 19, 1850, Amos Child.

711

WILLIAM⁷ BRADBURY (Daniel⁶, Thomas⁵, Thomas⁴,
Jacob³, William². Thomas¹), married December 25,
1823, Comfort Taylor, who was born in Belfast, Me.,
October 25, 1801. They lived in Athens and Byron,
Me.

Children :

1307   i   Mary Wingate⁸, b. Sept. 7, 1824; m. Dec. 25, 1849,
            George Dana Austin.

1308   ii   Horatio Taylor⁸, b. Oct. 15, 1825; m. Ann Eliza Parlin.

1309   iii Climena Burley⁸, b. June 12, 1827; m. Dec. 25, 1849,
            Danforth L. Harlow.

1310   iv   Hazen⁸, b. July 25, 1828; m. Martha Thompson Ad-
            ams.

1311   v   William Grafton⁸, b. April 6, 1830.

1312   vi   Albert Leviston⁸, b. July 31, 1832.

1313   vii Abigail Piper Taylor⁸, b. May 25, 1834; m. Lucien M.
            Blanchard.

1314   viii Heman Lincoln⁸, b. July 12, 1836.

1315   ix   Comfort Olina⁸, b. April 20, 1839.

1316   x   John Quincy Adams⁸, b. July 18, 1841.

1317   xi   Margaret⁸, b. April 7, 1843.

713

SIMON⁷ BRADBURY (Daniel⁶, Thomas⁵, Thomas⁴, Jacob³, William², Thomas¹), married April 20, 1832, Hannah Wood. They lived at Athens, Me.

Children :

1318 i Mary⁸, b. April 24, 1833.
1319 ii Henry⁸, b. April 24, 1835.
1320 iii Hannah⁸, b. Oct. 4, 1838.
1321 iv Sarah⁸, b. Oct. 17, 1841.
1322 v Wingate⁸, b. Feb. 18, 1843.

717

LEONARD⁷ BRADBURY (Daniel⁶, Thomas⁵, Thomas⁴, Jacob³, William², Thomas¹), married July 12, 1836, Fanny Hight; he resided in Athens, Me.

Children:

1323 i John Fairfield⁸, b. June 1, 1841.
1324 ii Alsena⁸, b. Nov. 25, 1843.

721

THOMAS⁷ BRADBURY (Thomas⁶, Thomas⁵, Thomas⁴, Jacob³, William², Thomas¹), married June 13, 1836, Emeline, daughter of John Edgerly of Buxton. She died some years ago, and he survives and resides at West Buxton.

Children :

1325 i Thomas⁸, b. Buxton, March 31, 1844; m. Emma S. Fabyan.
1326 ii Charles Edwin⁸, b. May 31, 1847; unmarried.

732

JOHN EATON⁷ BRADBURY (Benjamin⁶, Benjamin⁵, Thomas⁴, Jacob³, William², Thomas¹), married ——.

Children:

1327 i William⁸, b. ——; m. ——; resides in Indiana.
1328 ii James⁸, b. ——; m. ——, and d. No issue.

740

GIDEON WITHAM[7] BRADBURY (Gibeon[6], Benjamin[5], Thomas[4], Jacob[3], William[2], Thomas[1]), married Eliza[7] Bradbury (769).

Children:

1329 i Gideon Aaron[8], b. March 12, 1839.
1330 ii Jacob Nathaniel[8], b. April 13, 1841.
1331 iii Emily Gray[8], b. ——, 1843.
1332 iv Morris[8], b. ——, 1845.
1333 v Theodore Fagan[8], b. July 5, 1847.

750

LEVI HUNT[7] BRADBURY (Moses[6], Benjamin[5], Moses[4], Jacob[3], William[2], Thomas[1]), married in Brown county, Ia., December 20, 1832, Mary A. Turner, who was born in Kentucky, October 25, 1813, and died March 21, 1488. He married second, November 16, 1848, Mary A. Kreider, who was born in Pennsylvania, July 8, 1823, and died June 12, 1857. He married third, March 24, 1858, Sarah A. Perry, who was born in Orleans county, New York, September 25, 1820.

Children, born at Utica, N. Y., and St. Augustine, Ill.

1334 i James Monroe[8], b. Feb. 28, 1836; m. Julia Ann Craybill.
1335 ii William Marshall[8], b. Jan. 1, 1839.
1336 iii Nathan Andrew[8], b. May 30, 1842.
1337 iv Benjamin Franklin[8], b. Nov. 4, 1844.
1338 v Jesse Turner[8], b. March 5, 1845.

By second marriage:

1339 vi Mary Elizabeth[8], b. Oct. 29, 1849.
1340 vii Elden Walker[8], b. April 30, 1851.
1341 viii Thomas Orion[8], b. May 14, 1853.
1342 ix Civilion[8], b. Oct. 12, 1855; d. May 8, 1856.

752

BENJAMIN[7] BRADBURY (Moses[6], Benjamin[5], Moses[4], Jacob[3], William[2], Thomas[1]), married March 12, 1840, in Knox county, Ill., Mary Frinley, who was born in Wayne county, Ill., March 31, 1817, and died April 27, 1841. He married second. November 1, 1846, Hannah Arnold Stevens, who was born in Harrison county, Ind., March 9, 1826.

Children :

By second wife :

1343   i   James Joshua[8], b. April 17, 1848, in Knox county, Ill.
1344   ii   Levi Anthony[8], b. April 7, 1850, in Fulton county, Ill.

760

THOMAS[7] BRADBURY (Jacob[6], Benjamin[5], Thomas[4], Jacob[3], William[2], Thomas[1]), married January 31, 1826, Pamelia or "Milly" Copeland, who was born October 27, 1806.

Children :

1345   i   William Kinney[8], b. Dec. 6, 1829 ; m. Melinda Jarritz.
1346   ii   Caroline Patience[8], b. Oct. 7, 1831 ; m. July 30, 1853, William Smith Ellsbery.
1347   iii   George Bragdon[8], b. Jan. 4, 1833 ; m. Mary Jane Goolman.
1348   iv   Eliza Jane[8], b. Jan. 23, 1835 ; m. Otto Jarritz.
1349   v   Thomas Copeland[8], b. May 31, 1837.
1350   vi   Ann Maria[8], b. April 18, 1839 ; m. May 10, 1870, Henry Rollins.
1351   vii   Lucinda Arvilla[8], b. Jan. 27, 1842 ; m. Sept. 3, 1867, Jesse D. Hitchcock, r. Carthage, Mo.
1352   viii   Horace Alphonzo[8], b. Oct. 12, 1844.

14

761

LEMUEL[7] BRADBURY (Jacob[6], Benjamin[5], Thomas[4], Jacob[3], William[2], Thomas[1]), born April 18, 1805, married Lydia Troy, *nee* Repsher. He moved from Ohio to Morgan county, Ill., and from thence to Pike county, Ill., and finally to Pike county, Mo., where he died February 20, 1877. His wife was born July 7, 1799, in New Jersey, and died August 14, 1875, in Missouri.

Children :

1353   i   Harriet[8], b. Nov. 14, 1828; m. 1843, James T. Lynthicum.

1354   ii   Eleanor[8], b. Nov. 25, 1830; m. 1854, Samuel Kaylor.

1355   iii   George[8], b. Nov. 23, 1832; m. Ann E. Mummey; d. in Missouri, 1882.

1356   iv   Nathan[8], b. Dec. 18, 1834; m. Frances Lindsey, r. Kansas.

1357   v   Anson[8], b. April 22, 1837; m. Feb. 15, 1865, Mary M. Tedrow. He lives in Pike county, Mo., and has four children.

1358   vi   Thomas[8], b. Aug. 10, 1839; m. Mary Derry. He was killed at the battle of Murfreesboro, Jan. 6, 1863.

1359   vii   Charles[8], b. Sept. 2, 1842; m. Jan., 1866, Elmira Balou. He resides in Kansas.

765

NATHAN BOULTER[7] BRADBURY (Jacob[6], Benjamin[5], Thomas[4], Jacob[3], William[2], Thomas[1]), married 1838, Dorcas Bogges, who died in 1843. He married second, 1853, Carthena[7] Bradbury, who was born October 26, 1823.

Children :

1360   i   Melissa[8], b. 1839 ; d. 1841.
1361 ii   Lucetta[8], b. 1840 ; d. 1842.
1362 iii   William Wallace[8], b. 1841.
1363 iv   Robert Bruce[8], b. 1842 ; d. 1843.
By second wife :
1364   v   Alice[8], b. 1854.
1365 vi   Edwin Ruthven[8], b. 1856.
1366 vii   Bruce[8], b. 1858.

767

SAMUEL[7] BRADBURY (Jacob[6], Benjamin[5]. Thomas[4], Jacob[3], William[2], Thomas[1]), married in 1836, Julia Ann Merris Oliver. He resides in Canon City, Col. He is a man of respectability and highly esteemed in the city of his adoption.

Children :

1367   i   Thomas[8], b. March 10, 1838 ; d. 1846.
1368 ii   James Marion[8], b. Nov. 27, 1839 ; m. Oct. 5, 1871, Annie E. Hill. He graduated at the St. Louis Medical College, March 18, 1869, and is in practice in Canon City. No issue.
1369 iii   Stanton Merris[8], b. April 20, 1843 ; m. Mary Williams. He is by profession a dentist.
1370 iv   Charles Monroe[8], b. Aug. 23, 1846 ; m. Rachel Wharton. He is by occupation a carpenter.
1371   v   Daniel Albert[8], b. May 2, 1849 ; m. Grace Okey. He is an architect and builder.

770

JACOB GARY[7] BRADBURY (Jacob[6], Benjamin[5], Thomas[4], Jacob[3], William[2], Thomas[1]), married in 1843, Susan Gould.

Children:

1372   i   James⁸, b. 1844; d. same year.
1373   ii   Vincent Gray⁸, b. Nov. 26, 1846.
1374   iii   Charles⁸, b. Jan. 10, 1848.
1375   iv   Marshall⁸, b. Feb. 12, 1862.
1376   v   Enola⁸, b. Aug. 8, 1865.
1377   vi   Nettie⁸, b. March 13, 1870.
1377 *a* vii Laura⁸, b. May 4, 1871.
1377 *b* viii Alta⁸, b. Feb. 11, 1873.
1377 *c* ix   Jennie⁸, b. May 24, 1875.
1377 *d* x   Jay⁸, b. Nov. 8, 1877.
1377 *e* xi   Connie⁸, b. Dec. 18, 1880.

771

JOTHAM BRAGDON⁷ BRADBURY (Jacob⁶, Benjamin⁵, Thomas⁴, Jacob³, William², Thomas¹), married in 1846, Mahala Jane Hobbs.

Children:

1378   i   Cornelia Elizabeth⁸, b. ——, 1847.
1379   ii   Sylvester Hoyt⁸, b. 1850; d. 1853.
1380   iii   Marion Henry⁸, b. ——, 1854.
1381   iv   Lillian⁸, b. ——, 1856.
1382   v   Ernest Carpenter⁸, b. ——, 1858.
1383   vi   Nicholas S.⁸, b. July 24, 1863.

775

CHARLES ELLISON⁷ BRADBURY (Thomas⁶, Benjamin⁵, Thomas⁴, Jacob³, William², Thomas¹), married March 9, 1842. Margaret Beard.   He resides in Richmond, Ind.

Child:

1384   i   Mary Katherine⁸, b. Feb. 10, 1844.

• 777

ZENAS GEORGE WASHINGTON[7] BRADBURY (Thomas[6], Benjamin[5], Thomas[4], Jacob[3], William[2], Thomas[1]), married March 9, 1844, Eveline Beard. He resides in Illinois.

Children :

1385 i   Emily Eliza[8], b. March 29, 1846.
1386 ii Missouri[8], b. April 21, 1848.
1387 iii William[8], b. Aug. 1, 1850.
1388 iv Virginia[8], b. March 2, 1853.

778

BENJAMIN FRANKLIN[7] BRADBURY (Thomas[6], Benjamin[5], Thomas[4], Jacob[3], William[2], Thomas[1]), married September 9, 1847, Maria Jane Colvin.

Children :

1389 i   Thomas Elden[8], b. Oct. 14, 1849.
1390 ii Rebecca Irene[8], b. Aug. 2, 1854.

786

JOHN WARREN[7] BRADBURY (Nathan[6], Benjamin[5], Thomas[4], Jacob[3], William[2], Thomas[1]), married Mary Jane Elliot.

Children :

1391 i   Heber[8], b. ——, 1854.
1392 ii Franklin[8], b. ——, 1856.

797

JACOB[7] BRADBURY (Moses[6], Jacob[5], Jacob[4], Jacob[3], William[2], Thomas[1]), married January 11, 1819, Sally[6] Bradbury, who was born December 17, 1791, and died

October 21, 1844. For second wife he married in June, 1845, Sally Merrill, who died November 22, 1856. He died in Buxton, June 2, 1865.

Children:

1393 i Moses William[8], b. April 8, 1820; m. Catherine Pomroy Wentworth.

1393½ ii Mary Crockett[8], b. April 26, 1822.

1394 iii Jacob[8], b. April 21, 1824; m. Sarah McCann.

1395 iv Julia Ann[8], b. April 21, 1827; d. Sept. 22 following.

1396 v Harriet[8], b. April 5, 1832; d. Jan. 20, 1849.

By second wife:

1397 vi James Henry[8], b. Oct. 12, 1849.

1398 vii Samuel Corydon[8], b. April 4, 1852; d. Sept. 26, 1854.

801

JOHN GARLAND[7] BRADBURY (Moses[6], Jacob[5], Jacob[4], Jacob[3], William[2], Thomas[1]), married September 18, 1823, Mary Emery, who was born December 11, 1805.

Children:

1399 i Almira[8], b. Jan. 27, 1824; m. June 4, 1845, John Nelson Shaw.

1400 ii Hiram Woodman[8], b. July 12, 1826.

1401 iii Thomas Emery, b. Aug. 30, 1830; m. Angelette Elwell.

1402 iv Charles B.[8], April 24, 1834; m. Caroline Eliza Peabody.

1403 v Mary[8], b. April 5, 1840.

803

MOSES GARLAND[7] BRADBURY (Moses[6], Jacob[5], Jacob[4], Jacob[3], William[2], Thomas[1]), married Eliza Hemphill of Rome, Ga., and second Mary Ann Cunningham.

Children:

1404 i William[8], b. ——.

1405 ii Isabel[8], b. ——.

806

CHARLES COFFIN[7] BRADBURY (Moses[6], Jacob[5], Jacob[4], Jacob[3], William[2], Thomas[1]), married Mary M. Hall. He died in Fairfield, Me., December 8, 1855.

Children:

1406   i   Martin[8], b. ——, 1846.
1407   ii   George[8], b. ——, 1848.
1408   iii   Charles[8], b. ——, 1850.
1409   iv   Charlotte[8], b. ——, 1852.

816

ALBERT GALLATIN GOODWIN[7] BRADBURY (Simeon Goodwin[6], Jacob[5], Jacob[4], Jacob[3], William[2], Thomas[1]), married Clarissa Warren.

Children:

1410   i   Adeline Knight[8], b. Jan. 2, 1830.
1411   ii   Sarah Jane Goodwin[8], b. July 16, 1831; m. Feb. 13, 1862, David W. Legallee.
1412   iii   Henry Augustus[8], b. Dec. 31, 1832; d. Aug. 28, 1833.
1413   iv   Charles Henry[8], b. Sept. 16, 1834.
1414   v   Georgiana[8], April 5, 1836; d. Dec. 13, 1836.
1415   vi   Franklin[8], b. April, 1838.
1416   vii   Mary Ellen[8], b. April, 1840.
1417   viii   Georgianna[8], b. May 2, 1841.
1418   ix   Frank Madison[8], b. Aug. 4, 1846.

818

LORENZO[7] BRADBURY (Simeon Goodwin[6], Jacob[5], Jacob[4], Jacob[3], William[2], Thomas[1]), married June 16, 1836, Anna Shackford, who was born April 22, 1816. He resides in Gorham, Me.

Children :

1419 i   Franklin⁶, b. June 25, 1837 ; d. Feb. 16, 1842.
1420 ii Isabella Sands⁸, b. June 12, 1839.
1421 iii Sarah⁸, b. June 12, 1839.

821

JOHN ADAMS⁷ BRADBURY (Simeon Goodwin⁶, Jacob⁵, Jacob⁴, Jacob³, William², Thomas¹), married in 1838, Amanda Dearborn, who was born in Clinton in 1816, and died in Fairfield, July 5, 1851. He still resides in Fairfield, and is a lumberman.

Children :

1422 i   Edwin⁸, b. May 21, 1839 ; m. Sept. 6, 1866, Phebe A.
        Emery, who died March 25, 1874, and he married
        second, Ida M. Gibson, March 12, 1876.
1423 ii Augustus⁸, b. Feb. 3, 1841 ; m. Jan. 9, 1866, Lizzie A.,
        daughter of Harrison and Mary Gifford, who died
        May 24, 1869. He married second, Dec. 9, 1875,
        E. Florence, daughter of John and Achsa J. Cragin
        of Embden. He resides at Fairfield. He served as
        sergeant in the Seventh Maine battery in the late war.
1425 iii Addie⁸, b. March 29, 1843 ; d. March 6, 1864.
1426 iv Russell S.⁸, b. Nov. 29, 1848 ; m. May 26, 1875, Clara
        M. Sturgis.

849

HORATIO NELSON⁷ BRADBURY (Jabez⁶, Jabez⁵, Jacob⁴, Jacob³, William², Thomas¹), married December 27, 1843, Lydia C. Hutchinson, who was born May 26, 1842.

Children :

1427 i   Robert Page⁸, b. April 27, 1845.
1428 ii Anna Elizabeth⁸, b. Dec. 28, 1846 ; d. Sept. 29, 1853.

1429 iii Joseph Henry[8], b. Oct. 11, 1848.
1430 iv Horatio Nelson[8], b. Feb. 14, 1851.
1431 v Lydia Helen[8], b. March 3, 1853.

860

ELIJAH[7] BRADBURY (Elijah[6], Elijah[5], Jacob[4], Jacob[3], William[2], Thomas[1]), married November 30, 1842, Caroline Day.

Children :

1432 i Helen L.[8], b. Clifton, Sept. 5, 1843; m. Edward J. Penney; d. June 18, 1882.
1433 ii George E.[8], b. July 6, 1845. Killed in the battle of Spottsylvania Court House, May 12, 1864.
1434 iii Marion[8], b. April 4, 1847.
1435 iv Mary A.[8], b. Nov. 29, 1848; m. Nov. 27, 1876, Horace A. Wilder.
1436 v Susan M.[8], b. Nov. 20, 1850; m. June 28, 1870, William E. Lawn.
1437 vi Elijah G.[8], b. Dec. 9, 1861.
1438 vii Georgianna[8], b. May 6, 1864; d. June 20, 1866.

861

MOSES HOWARD[7] BRADBURY (Elijah[6], Elijah[5], Jacob[4], Jacob[3], William[2], Thomas[1]), married October 1, 1840, Eliza Ann Colby, who was born October 27, 1821. He lived in Denmark, Me.

Children :

1439 i Ahban Frank[8], b. Denmark, June 8, 1842; m. first, Sarah Frances Jordan, and second, Linda Witham.
1440 ii Carrie Matilda[8], b. Feb. 15, 1845; m. Jones B. Holt.
1441 iii Leonard Alonzo[8], b. Jan. 2, 1849; m. Eliza Wentworth.
1442 iv Sarah Gleason[8], b. ——; m. Edgar Watson.
1443 v Ella[8], b. ——; m. Charles F. Howard.
1444 vi Flora Mabel[8], b. Feb. 18, 1863; m. Foster Pingree.

868

JOSEPH HOWARD[7] BRADBURY (Elijah[6], Elijah[5], Jacob[4], Jacob[3], William[2], Thomas[1]), married in 1850, Susan B. Walton.

Children:

1445 i   Charles[8], b. Denmark, Aug. 1, 1851.
1446 ii Emma E.[8], b. Oct. 16, 1854; d. Oct. 2, 1870.

878

JABEZ[7] BRADBURY (Isaac[6], Elijah[5], Jacob[4], Jacob[3], William[2], Thomas[1]), married ——.

Child:

1447 i   Clarissa E.[8], b. April 9, 1845.

886

JAMES[7] BRADBURY (John[6], Joseph[5], Jacob[4], Jacob[3], William[2], Thomas[1]), married June. 1820, Pamelia Woodman.

Child:

1448 i   Isaac W.[8], b. Sept. 14, 1821; m. Harriet Gray.

887

JOSEPH[7] BRADBURY (John[6], Joseph[5], Jacob[4], Jacob[3], William[2], Thomas[1]), married first, August 14, 1828, Eliza Goodwin, and there was no issue. He married second, September 9, 1837, Sally Pennell.

Children:

1449 i   John Francis[8], b. Sept. 20, 1842; d. young.
1450 ii Eliza[8], b. Aug. 22, 1844; d. June 17, 1851.
1451 iii Adelia[8], b. April 29, 1847; d. July 3, 1848.
1452 iv John Francis[8], b. Sept. 20, 1849.
1453 v Lydia Ellen[8], b. Feb. 23, 1853.

900

JOHN BACON[7] BRADBURY (Benjamin[6], Joseph[5], Jacob[4], Jacob[3], William[2], Thomas[1]), married August 11, 1842, Louisa Wentworth Hill, who was born January 29, 1820.

Children:

1454   i   Lewis Henry[8], b. June 2, 1843.
1455   ii   Benjamin Franklin[8], b. April 26, 1847.
1456 iii   George Edwin[8], b. Aug. 4, 1849.

901

GRANVILLE MELLEN[7] BRADBURY (Benjamin[6], Joseph[5], Jacob[4], Jacob[3], William[2], Thomas[1]), married Louisa Partridge, who was born May 16, 1834.

Child:

1457 i   Charles Henry[8], b. Nov. 10, 1857.

903

CHARLES ADAMS[7] BRADBURY (Joseph[6], Benjamin[5], Moses[4], Jacob[3], William[2], Thomas[1]), married February 28, 1812, Mary S. True. His children were born in Norway.

Children:

1458   i   Winthrop True[8], b. March 9, 1815; m. Sept. 15, 1836, Judith P. Haskell. He died Nov. 3, 1864.
1459   ii   Mary Oakes[8], b. Dec. 20, 1817; m. May 20, 1837, Israel True. She died Sept. 5, 1845.
1460 iii   Lydia Jane[8], b. Dec. 7, 1830; d. Sept. 3, 1838.

908

Jacob[7] Bradbury (Joseph[6], Benjamin[5], Moses[4], Jacob[3], William[2], Thomas[1]), married Sally King Ripley of Paris. He lived in Norway, Me., and died there August 2, 1880.

Children :

1461   i   Sabina F.[8], b. Dec. 15, 1822; m. Feb. 27, 1846, William P. Stevens.*

1461 *a*   ii   Matilda A.[8], b. Sept. 15, 1824; m. Nov. 25, 1847, William A. Marston.

1461 *b*   iii   Nathan Osgood[8], b. Oct. 4, 1826; d. Dec. 25, 1828.

1461 *c*   iv   Osgood Nathan[8], b. Oct. 28, 1828; m. Ellen R. Scribner. He is a physician at Norway.

1461 *d*   v   Henry Ambrose Merrill[8], b. Aug. 20, 1830; m. Feb. 8, 1855, Persis Ripley.

1461 *e*   vi   Harriet N.[8], b. July 12, 1832; m. March 4, 1853, William K. Ripley.

1461 *f*   vii   Sarah A.[8], b. Oct. 28, 1834; m. March 26, 1854, Alden Woodbury.

1461 *g*   viii   Euphena[8], b. March 10, 1837.

1461 *h*   ix   Jacob F.[8], b. June 10, 1839.

1461 *i*   x   Nellie F.[8], b. Aug. 20, 1841.

1461 *j*   xi   James Gordon Bennett[8], b. Jan. 22, 1846.

1462   xii   Ida E.[8], b. Sept. 12, 1846.

909

Nathan Adams[7] Bradbury (Joseph[6], Benjamin[5], Moses[4], Jacob[3], William[2], Thomas[1]), married October 15, 1827, Elizabeth Millett of Norway. He was the first settled physician in Woodstock, Me., and from there he moved to Sweden, Me., where he died April 18, 1878.

*They were the parents of W. H. Stevens, of the firm of Stevens & Jones, book-sellers of Portland.

Children :

1463 i Angerone Emeline⁸, b. Sweden, April 5, 1830 ; m. Dec.
9, 1847, George A. Holden of Sweden. She died
Feb. 16, 1881.

1464 ii Elizabeth Millett⁸, b. Aug. 10, 1831 ; m. June 19, Luther
P. Babb, M. D. They settled in Eastport. Mrs. Babb
also graduated in medicine, and engaged in practice.
They had children :

> 1 Cora Millett (Babb), b. June 3, 1856, graduated
> at Philadelphia Medical College, married
> Daniel W. Holden of Florida, and resides there.
> 2 Grace Lee (Babb), b. Feb. 23, 1860, graduated at
> the Philadelphia School of Pharmacy, married
> Griffith C. Abbot, M. D., of Philadelphia, and
> resides there.

1465 iii Nathan Clinton⁸, b. Feb. 23, 1834 ; d. of scarlet fever
results, Oct. 15, 1849.

910

Moses⁷ Bradbury (Joseph⁶, Benjamin⁵, Moses⁴, Jacob³, William², Thomas¹), married December 11, 1825,
Hannah Knight. He lived in Greenwood, Me.

Children :

1466 i Erastus Grosvenor⁸, b. June 23, 1826 ; d. April 30, 1881,
at Diamond Springs, Cal.

1467 ii Joseph Augustus⁸, b. May 28, 1829 ; m. Sarah J. Mixer.

1468 iii Daniel Osborne⁸, b. May 10, 1833 ; m. Mary Jane Mc-
Kellips, r. Watertown, Wis.

1469 iv Moses Warren⁸, b. March 2, 1834 ; m. Elizabeth Jane
Jordan, r. Hastings, Minn.

1470 v Roscoe Emery⁸, b. July 23, 1843 ; m. Clara Hortense
Bonney; no issue.

1471 vi Eugene Lafayette⁸, b. Oct. 25, 1845 ; m. Sadie E. Evans, r. Portage City, Wis.

1472 vii Agnes Francette⁸, b. Oct. 25, 1845 ; m. Andrew J.
Jackson, r. Ionia, Mich.

911

NATHANIEL M.[7] BRADBURY* (Joseph[6], Benjamin[5], Moses[4], Jacob[3], William[2], Thomas[1]), married October 27, 1831, Julia A. Foster, who was born in Livermore, February 7, 1811. He died May 8, 1859. His children were born in Livermore.

Children :

1473   i   Henry Newell[8], b. Dec. 3, 1832; m. Harriet Mann of Lowell, Mass.

1474   ii   Edwin Franklin[8], b. Feb. 17, 1834; m. at Mechanic Falls, 1860, Susanna H. Gilbert.

1475   iii Frances Emily[8], b. Aug. 17, 1835; m. Gancelo Cram.

1476   iv   Rowena Jane[8], b. May 24, 1837; m. May 31, 1856, George F. Raymond.

1477   v   Emery Weston[8], b. June 1, 1839; m. Mary Bolter; d. March 31, 1883.

1478   vi   George Oscar[8], b. March 21, 1841; d. unmarried, Oct. 4, 1867.

1479   vii Julia Estelle[8], b. Feb. 5, 1850; m. Sept. 5, 1867, Benjamin F. Keene; d. June 20, 1870.

911½

HERSEY[7] BRADBURY (Benjamin[6], Benjamin[5], Moses[4], Jacob[3], William[2], Thomas[1]). married December 2, 1830, Mary Ann Harlow. He died August 23, 1860.

Child :

1480   i   Julia Ann[8], b. May 12, 1833; d. Aug. 21, 1885.

*When a young man, while he was felling trees in Norway, a tree which he had cut fell upon another. He climbed up to dislodge it, when the tree came down and caught Millett by his head between this and another tree, and he was suspended in mid-air until relieved by his brother. He was senseless for sometime, and it was found that his skull was badly fractured. He lived many years and reared a family, but he never fully recovered, and finally died from the effects of the injury.

911¾

Moses B.[7] Bradbury (Benjamin[6], Benjamin[5], Moses[4], Jacob[3], William[2], Thomas[1]), married June 6, 1833, Sarah F. Briggs. He died August 8, 1888.

Children:

1481 i Amanda K.[8], b. Nov. 20, 1833; d. Dec. 2, 1854.
1482 ii Horace A.[8], b. Sept. 30, 1839.

911⅖

Benjamin[7] Bradbury (Benjamin[6], Benjamin[5], Moses[4], Jacob[3], William[2], Thomas[1]), married December 30, 1841, Betsey D. Pettengill, who died November 25, 1886. He died November 4, 1869.

Children:

1483 i Ann Susan[8], b. Oct. 12, 1842; m. Nov. 28, 1864, Royal M. Mason. They have: Everest Franklin (Mason), b. Aug. 25, 1865; Eugene (Mason), b. April 16, 1868; d. May 20 following; and Annie Evelyn (Mason), b. Feb. 20, 1873.

912

Samuel Gurney[7] Bradbury (Samuel[6], Benjamin[5], Moses[4], Jacob[3], William[2], Thomas[1]), resided in Minot, and was a farmer. He married November 17, 1825, Hannah Pettengill, who was born in Bridgewater, Mass., April 13, 1799. He died Sept 10, 1868, and his wife died December 21, 1863. For second wife he married Asenath ——.

Children:

1484   i   Heman P.[8], b. Sept. 5, 1826; m. Vesta A. Pratt; d. Nov. 11, 1880.

1485   ii   Elizabeth A.[8], b. Feb. 10, 1830. She resides in Auburn.

1486   iii   Josiah C.[8], b. Nov. 13, 1832; d. March 2, 1835.

1487   iv   Josiah C.[8], b. July 19, 1835; m. Sept. 5, 1858, Mary M. Dillingham. 'He died April 6, 1889.

1488   v   Mary W.[8], b. Aug. 15, 1837; m. Dec. 16, 1854, A. Sidney Phillips.

1489   vi   Samuel J.[8], b. Feb. 3, 1845; m. first, Nov. 27, 1867, Susan F. Stockman; second, 1884, Eva M. Noyes.

915

AMMI RUHAMAH[7] BRADBURY (Samuel[6], Benjamin[5], Moses[4], Jacob[3], William[2], Thomas[1]), graduated from Bowdoin College in the class of 1837. Among his classmates were the late Governor Andrew of Massachusetts, Dr. Fordyce Barker of New York, Rufus K. Sewall of Wiscasset, and Dr. Thomas F. Perley of Bridgton. After graduating he entered the Theological Seminary at Bangor, but did not complete his course. He was two years a teacher at the seminary in Parsonsfield, then went to Yale Theological school, where he graduated and remained a year after. He then went to Smithfield, R. I., and was associate principal of the seminary there for four years. In 1849 he preached at Springvale, Sanford and North Berwick, and then became pastor of the Freewill Baptist church at Portsmouth, N. H., where he remained four years. He then became principal of Strafford, N. H., seminary, and was subsequently pastor of a church in Biddeford.

He also preached in Bangor and elsewhere in Maine and in Massachusetts. In 1861 he was invited to accept the pastorate of a church in Providence, R. I., and soon after removed to that city where he has since lived. He has been a member of the Board of Missions and the Education Society, and being among the first of his denomination to receive a liberal education, he has held many prominent positions. He has published sermons, composed hymns for special occasions and for the press. He was corresponding editor of a denominational paper for seven years, and wrote a sermon and two hymns for each number, three hundred and fifty sermons and seven hundred hymns. He has also written odes and many short poems on scriptural subjects. He married February 20, 1844, Miss Caroline Livermore, daughter of Rev. Mr. Johnson of Farmington, and afterward at the head of the Smithfield, R. I., seminary. She was born March 16, 1814.

Children :

1490   i   William Ammi[8], b. Nov. 3, 1847 ; graduated from Brown University, 1870, and died two years after.

1491   ii   Abbie Jennie[8], b. North Berwick, Nov. 30, 1849.

1492   iii   Frederick Whitten[8], b. Oct. 8, 1851 ; he was three years in college, and is a physician in Auburn, R. I. He married first, Celeste Hopkins who died, and second, Clara M. Brown.

1493   iv   Sam Johnson[8], b. Portsmouth, N. H., Dec. 5, 1853. He was three years in Brown University, studied medicine and is in practice in New York City.

15

927

ROYAL J.[7] BRADBURY (Jacob[6], Benjamin[5], Moses[4], Jacob[3]. William[2], Thomas[1]), married July 13, 1837, Jane L. Parker, who was born in Greene, Me., May 25, 1816. He resides in Auburn, Me.

Child:

1495 i Louisa Maria[8], b. Oct. 9, 1838. She married first, Horace Randall, who died Oct. 28, 1861, and second, Alonzo F. Morrill. They have :

    1 Ida E. (Morrill), b. Jan. 27, 1864; m. Charles F. Curtis.

    2 Frank E. (Morrill), b. Feb. 23, 1866; m. Linda A. Morrill.

    3 Angie B. (Morrill), b. Aug. 2. 1869 ; m. P. C. Record.

934

CYRUS[7] BRADBURY (Charles[6], Moses[5], Moses[4], Jacob[3], William[2], Thomas[1]), married April 20, 1836, Deborah Bunker, who was born January 24, 1809.

Children, born in Anson, Me.:

1496 i Cyrus[8], b. April 21, 1839; d. Oct. 4, 1857.
1497 ii John[8], b. May 25, 1840.
1498 iii Charles[8], b. Sept. 23, 1841.
1499 iv Moses[8], b. May 14, 1846 ; d. Aug. 21, 1869.
1500 v Sylvia[8], b. July 31, 1847.
1501 vi Eben M.[8], b. Oct. 10, 1850; d. Aug. 8, 1871.

936

MOSES[7] BRADBURY (Charles[6], Moses[5], Moses[4], Jacob[3], William[2], Thomas[1]), married in 1841, Abigail, daughter of Capt. Benjamin and Deborah (Luce) Manter of Industry, Me. She died November 1, 1846, and he married second, Mrs. Anna West (Manter) Luce. They were divorced shortly before her death, which occurred December 19, 1860. He married third, November 11, 1862, Clementine O., daughter of Simeon and Anna (Hutchins) Fish of Stark. He died in Stark, Me., March 5, 1885. There was no issue by either marriage. Mr. Bradbury was a man of marked ability. He was a trader and farmer in Industry, and often held town office. He also resided at times in Cornville and Anson.

948

NATHANIEL MILLETT[7] BRADBURY (Nathaniel[6], Moses[5], Moses[4], Jacob[3], William[2], Thomas[1]), married November 2, 1843, Elizabeth Briggs. He died November 7, 1853. She was recently living in Garland, Me.

Children:

1502 i John Lewis[8], b. Aug. 6, 1844.
1503 ii Helen Louisa[8], b. Dec., 1851.

959

SAMUEL I.[7] BRADBURY (Samuel[6], Samuel[5], Moses[4], Jacob[3], William[2], Thomas[1]), married November 8, 1828, Mary A., daughter of Luther and Charlotte Spaulding, who was born at Marcy, Oneida county, New York.

Children:

1504 i Frances Mary[8], b. Sept. 24, 1852.
1505 ii Henry De Witt[8], b. Jan. 10, 1854.
1506 iii Samuel H.[8], b. May 3, 1858.

NINTH GENERATION.

969

THOMAS CONDON[8] BRADBURY (George Lowther[7], John[6], Jacob[5], Wymond[4], Wymond[3], Wymond[2], Thomas[1]), married June 3, 1854, Sarah Sawyer, who was born November, 1834.

Children :

1507 i   George Lowther[9], b. Aug. 4, 1856.
1508 ii   Charles Whitney[9], b. June 21, 1859

1018

HENRY WESTBROOK[8] BRADBURY (James Ware[7], James[6], Cotton[5], John[4], Wymond[3], Wymond[2], Thomas[1]), was long in business in Augusta, and was a very successful merchant. He was also engaged in business more or less in other places, both in Maine and in the South. He was a man of strict integrity and highly esteemed by his associates, and also in the community where he was born and reared. His death in middle life was greatly deplored. He died January 10, 1884. He married May 16, 1879, Louisa H., daughter of Dr. Thomas Hutson Gregorie of South Carolina, an accomplished lady who survives him, and resides at the Bradbury homestead in Augusta.

Children :

1509 i   Eliza Louisa[9], b. May 25, 1880.
1510 ii   Alice Gregorie[9], b. Dec. 16, 1883; d. April 2, 1885.

1040

HANNAH ELIZABETH[8] BRADBURY (Benjamin Burbank[7], John[6], John[5], John[4], Wymond[3], Wymond[2], Thomas[1]), born in Chesterville, Me., March 16, 1827, received her education in the common schools and at Farmington academy. She early developed a talent for composition, and has a well established reputation as an authoress in both prose and poetry. Her father, Benjamin B. Bradbury, moved from Chesterville to Newport, and thence to Bangor, and here under her initials Miss Bradbury wrote numerous short stories and poems, which were very popular and had a wide circulation. Her later productions, such as " Dr. Howell's Family," " One Among Many," " Our Party of Four," and " Christine's Fortune," have greatly widened her reputation. To the " Poets of Maine," published in 1888, she contributed " Lake Lucerne," " A Winter Sunset," " Only Ferns," and " A Child's Dream." These four short poems are gems, and among the best in the collection, but the author is best known to the literary world as a writer of fiction. She married July 17, 1859, Mr. George C. Goodwin of Charlestown, Mass. They now reside in Boston.

1041

BENJAMIN FRANKLIN[8] BRADBURY (Benjamin Burbank[7], John[6], John[5], John[4], Wymond[3], Wymond[2], Thomas[1]), married March 31, 1856, Anna M. Pierce, who died at Bangor, July 28, 1863. He married second, at Charlestown, Mass., Sarah Horton Woodman, in 1864. Mr.

Bradbury is a druggist at number 443 Washington street, Boston.

Children :

1511   i   Samuel Pierce[9], b. Bangor, Sept. 7, 1857; d. Sept. 10, 1858.

1512   ii   William Benjamin[9], b. Oct. 18, 1859; m. July 30, 1883, Bertha Jane Pittsinger, who was born at Keene, N. H., May 9, 1859. They have had: Edward Benjamin[10], b. Keene, N. H., July 18, 1884; d. same day; William Pittsinger[10], b. New York City, Nov. 19, 1885, and Annie Congdon[10], b. Mt. Vernon, N. Y., Jan. 9, 1887; d. Dec. 15, 1889.

1513   iii   Anna Pierce[9], b. May 15, 1863; d. at Barre, Mass., June 25, 1871.

By second wife :

1514   iv   Woodman[9], b. Bangor, April 9, 1866.

1515   v   George Goodwin[9], b. Jan. 7, 1868 ; d. 1886.

1516   vi   Marion Elizabeth[9], b. Sept. 5, 1871.

1517   vii   Grace Lovell[9], b. March 26, 1873.

1518   viii   Hannah Edith[9], b. Melrose, Mass., Aug. 1, 1877.

1046

JOTHAM DENNIS[8] BRADBURY (Jotham[7], William[6], John[5], John[4], Wymond[3], Wymond[2], Thomas[1]), married September 18, 1842, Sarah Hinckly Merrick, who was born in 1823, and died August 13, 1850. He married second, March 8, 1853, Ann Huntington.

Children :

1519   i   Edward Payson[9], b. July 11, 1843.

1520   ii   Emma Angeline[9], b. March 8, 1846.

By second wife :

1521   iii   George D[9], b. June 17, 1854.

1050

WILLIAM[8] BRADBURY (Jotham[7], William[6], John[5], John[4], Wymond[3], Wymond[2], Thomas[1]), married September 18, 1848, Lydia Ann Merritt, who was born in Bath, April 19, 1827. He died at Newton, Mass., July 27, 1874.

Children:

1522   i   William Merritt[9], b. Chelsea, Mass., Sept. 30, 1849.
1523   ii   Arthur Hallum[9], b. Chelsea, Mass., Oct. 5, 1851; d. 1875,
1524   iii   Anna Carrill[9], b. Chesterville, Me., Aug. 30, 1854; d. Aug. 8, 1855, at Bath.

1096

EBENEZER[8] BRADBURY Jr. (Ebenezer[7], Theophilus[6], Jonathan[5], Theophilus[4], Wymond[3], Wymond[2], Thomas[1], married at Newburyport, November 1, 1859, Mary Todd. He died in Newburyport, March 13, 1885.

Child:

1525   i   Ebenezer[9], b. Milford, Mass., June 6, 1861.

1097

JOHN MERRILL[8] BRADBURY (Ebenezer[7], Theophilus[6], Jonathan[5], Theophilus[4], Wymond[3], Wymond[2], Thomas[1]), born in Newburyport, October 29, 1818, spent his youth in his native town, where he received a good English and classical education, and also at Dummer academy, then in charge of Dr. Nehemiah Cleveland. In Newburyport he was at one time the pupil of Albert Pike, the poet. One of his early schoolmates, Rev. Dr. George D. Wildes, in his recollections of the youth of Mr. Bradbury, written for the family, said : "Of no one of the associates of my boyhood could I write more that would illustrate the value of useful example. Among personal influences tending to mold the purpose and direct the efforts of any of his early companions who have attained to station, whether of usefulness or honor, I am sure a large place will be conceded to their association more or less intimate with John M. Bradbury, the boy and the man. I cannot recall the time when I did not know him. The image of a bright, little chubby-faced boy, with bright eyes, a quick step and a laughing, morning face, coming to school from the North End in old Newburyport, almost always comes first in the retrospect of my own school days ; and I have an impression that when scarcely more than six or seven years of age, we were at our first man's school, under the instruction of the late George Titcomb."

Dr. Wildes states that they were in the same class and almost uniformly occupying neighboring desks in the Latin department of the high school, where Mr. Elias Nason afterward taught, but which was then under the charge of Rev. Roger S. Howard. He represents his school-mate as a good classical scholar, but excelling in mathematics. He also represents him as entering into the sports of boyhood, in which his good nature and buoyant spirits made him a universal favorite. He also represents him as a well-grounded historical scholar, and says he was no less indebted to him for guidance and help in what to him was distasteful, namely, mathematics, than for a common sympathy in historical studies and a taste for English classics.

In April, 1835, Mr. Bradbury entered Dickinson College at Carlisle, Penn., where he studied three years. He went to Philadelphia, intending to go into business there, but after a residence of six months he returned to his native town of Newburyport, where he became an assistant in his father's business, and held that position over two years. In 1841, he taught a district school in Newbury, and was subsequently appointed a teacher in a grammar school of Newburyport, which position he held for a year. After a year's interval he was appointed to a similar position which he held for six years. In May, 1849, he removed to Boston and was appointed to a clerkship in the state treasury, and in December, 1850, was advanced to chief clerk. He afterward engaged with a banking firm in Boston, and continued with them through various changes until 1868, when he retired with a competency. His business cares did not eradicate his literary tastes. His leisure hours were employed with books, his favorite reading being history and belles-letters. By this means he added constantly to his fund of information.

In September, 1868, Mr. Bradbury with his wife visited Europe and traveled through the British Isles and the principal countries on the continent. He spent some time in London, engaged in historical research in the British Museum and in the courts of probate. He also made frequent excursions into the country, especially to those places where his English ancestors had

lived. In a letter to Mr. John Ward Dean, from
whose obituary notice these facts concerning Mr. Bradbury are gleaned, he wrote: "My visit to Wicken-
Bonant was the pleasantest experience I have had in
England. The rector was away on a vacation, and I
did not therefore see the registers which would have
been a gratification, and I was indebted to the church-
warden's wife for admission to the church. You are
familiar with its appearance, both before and after res-
toration, from the photographs I have shown you. It
is a small church still, and the addition made to its
length by Mr. Sperling, the late rector, has not improved its proportions. Of course the surfaces, internal
and external are new, and there is nothing to remind
the visitor of its age, except a mural tablet in the
chancel, date of 1697, and a square font standing on
five square supports, which is a veritable piece of antiquity. Undoubtedly Thomas Bradbury, baptized
February 28, 1610-11, supposed to be the emigrant,
was baptized at this font. From the church our conductress guided us to the Brick House, where we were
most cordially received by its proprietor, Mr. John Pollitt. He took us through the old mansion, pointing
out the alterations and additions which had been made,
giving us its traditions and history. He also showed
us over the grounds which are well laid out and nicely
kept, and took us to points where we could get the
best views of the house and its surroundings, as well as
of the village generally."

Mr. Bradbury returned to Boston in July, 1871, and

resided there until the next spring, when he purchased a place in Ipswich where he lived to the time of his decease, which occurred on Tuesday morning, March 21. 1876. He left a widow. but no children. He became a member of the New England Historical Genealogical Society in 1853. and a life member in 1863. He served on the finance committee and also on the board of directors. He was also a member of the Prince Society of Boston. and of the Essex Institute at Salem. Mr. Bradbury made valuable collections for a genealogy of the Bradbury family, and had his health and life been spared, it was his purpose to publish a book on the subject. His manuscript is embodied in this volume, and while there were many hiatuses to be filled and some lives but little traced, it has been of great service to the compiler, and in fact constitutes the larger portion of the entire volume. Mr. Bradbury was married August 28, 1843, to Miss Sarah Ann, daughter of Daniel and Abigail (Sargent) Hayes of Gloucester, a lady of cultivated taste, who appreciated and encouraged the studies of her husband, and made his home pleasant and attractive. For a more extended account of Mr. Bradbury, the reader is referred to a notice in the Genealogical Register for October, 1877.

1099

THEOPHILUS[8] BRADBURY (Ebenezer[7], Theophilus[6], Jonathan[5], Theophilus[4], Wymond[3], Wymond[2], Thomas[1]), married May 1, 1846, Emily Jane Gray, who was born April 26, 1823. He resides at Newburyport, Mass.

Children:

1526   i   Albert Hale[9], b. Newburyport, Nov. 20, 1847; d. Aug. 12, 1848.

1527 ii   Anne Merrill[9], b. Newburyport, Nov. 29, 1853.

1528 iii   Emma Frances[9], b. Georgetown, Cal., Feb. 25, 1856.

1529 iv   Clara Louisa[9], b. June 8, 1858; m. March 9, 1885, Henry Hills Morse. They have had:
     1 Henry Hills[10], b. Jan. 12, 1886; d. Aug. 27 following.
     2 Annie Frances[10], b. Jan. 21, 1889.

1530 v   Lincoln Gray[9], b. July 24, 1860; m. Oct. 15, 1884, Robina Annie, daughter of Andrew and Sarah Crombie, who was born May 9, 1864. They have:
     1 Carrie Gray[10], b. Jan. 16, 1886.

1531 vi   Walter Ross[9], b. Sept. 21, 1862; m. Jan. 19, 1880, Lottie Hale, daughter of Charles Hale and Sarah Frances Collins of Newburyport, b. July 29, 1864. They have:
     1 Edith Ross[10], b. June 22, 1880.
     2 Frank Hale[10], b. April 30, 1883.
     3 Wilbert Stewart[10], b. Dec. 13, 1884; d. Sept. 3, 1886.

1102

ALBERT FAYETTE[6] BRADBURY (Ebenezer[7], Theophilus[6], Jonathan[5], Theophilus[4], Wymond[3], Wymond[2], Thomas[1]), born in Newburyport, July 16, 1827, resided there until 1834, when his father moved to Franklin county, Penn. In 1837, Albert Fayette returned to Newburyport where he entered the high school and remained until 1842. His father having returned to Newburyport in 1838, and engaged in the stove business, Albert Fayette on leaving school assisted for two years in the store. In 1844, he entered the employ as

~. F. Bradbury

clerk and bookkeeper of the Salisbury (woolen) Manu-
facturing Company at Amesbury, Mass., where he remained, with the exception of a single year, until 1863,
when he became associated with Dale & Robinson in
the ownership of the Dexter Woolen Mills. Mr. Bradbury moved with his family to Dexter in 1864, and has
since that time remained there as resident agent and
manager, which position he holds at the present time.
He took a leading part in the building of the Dexter
and Newport railroad, and has been a director since
the organization of the company. For the past two
years he has also held the position of treasurer. He
was one of the corporators of the Dexter Savings
Bank in 1867, and its president until 1888, when at
the earnest solicitation of the trustees he accepted the
position of treasurer, which position he still holds. He
also assisted in organizing the Dexter National Bank,
and has been a director from the first. He is also a
director of the Dexter Loan and Building Association.
His life has been an exceedingly busy one, and though
often urged to accept political or town office, he has
generally felt obliged to decline. He is a trustee of
the Dexter Town Library and of the School Fund. Originally a whig in politics, he aided in organizing the
republican party, and has since been one of its zealous
supporters. He is a member of the Protestant Episcopal church, and has been clerk of the Church of the
Messiah at Dexter since its formation in 1866. Mr.
Bradbury is genial, kind hearted and universally
respected. He married April 21, 1853, Frances Ayer,

daughter of Ichabod Barnard and Ethelinde (French) Morrill of Amesbury, Mass., an intelligent and accomplished lady, and his home at Dexter is a model one.

Children, all born at Amesbury, Mass.

1532   i   Alice May[9], b. May 14, 1854. She resides with her parents, and assists her father in the management of the Dexter savings bank.

1533   ii   Fanny Morrill[9], b. Jan. 10, 1856. She married at Dexter, Nov. 22, 1877, Levi Bridgham, who is a druggist at Dexter. They have:

      1 John Merrill[10], b. March 25, 1882.

      2 Ethelinde French[10], b. Jan. 23, 1885.

      3 Louisa Frances[10], b. July 18, 1887.

1534   iii   Albert Hale[9], b. Sept. 11, 1857, who is a clerk in the Dexter woolen mills.

1104

GEORGE[8] BRADBURY (Ebenezer[7], Theophilus[6], Jonathan[5], Theophilus[4], Wymond[3], Wymond[2], Thomas[1]), married November 17, 1859, at Madison, Wis., Elizabeth Lodama, daughter of Matthew and Jane (Johnson) Taisey of Almont, Mich.

Child, born at Cincinnati:

1535   i   George Wilson[9], b. July 9, 1865; d. March 6, 1867.

1107

CHARLES EDWIN[8] BRADBURY (Ebenezer[7], Theophilus[6], Jonathan[5], Theophilus[4], Wymond[3], Wymond[2], Thomas[1]), married at Charlestown, Mass., July 2, 1870, Sarah Martha Hastings, who was born at Newburyport, October 31, 1842, and died April 19, 1873. He resides at Newburyport, Mass.

Children:

1536 i Lillie Mary⁹, b. Brighton, Mass., June 25, 1871.
1537 ii Sarah Martha⁹, b. Newburyport, Dec. 4, 1872.

1108

EDWIN CHARLES⁸ BRADBURY (Ebenezer⁷, Theophilus⁶, Jonathan⁵, Theophilus⁴, Wymond³, Wymond², Thomas¹), married at Haverhill, Harriet Jane Williams. He resides at Lawrence, Mass.

Children:

1538 i Anna Jane⁹, b. Oct. 14, 1858.
1539 ii Louis W.⁹, b. April 12, 1868.

1109

FRANCIS AUGUSTINE⁸ BRADBURY (Ebenezer⁷, Theophilus⁶, Jonathan⁵, Theophilus⁴, Wymond³, Wymond², Thomas¹), married at Omaha, Neb., June 4, 1880, Fannie A. Lindstrom. He died at Springfield, Mass., November 13, 1887.

1111

WILLIAM HENRY HARRISON⁸ BRADBURY (Ebenezer⁷, Theophilus⁶, Jonathan⁵, Theophilus⁴, Wymond³, Wymond², Thomas¹), married at Newburyport, January 16, 1868, Clara Clement Adams, who was born at Kenduskeag, Me., February 27, 1847. He resides at Hammonton, N. J.

Children:

1540 i Georgie Anna⁹, b. Vineland, N. J., Aug. 28, 1868.
1541 ii Wymond Henry⁹, b. Elwood, N. J., Dec. 1, 1869.
1542 iii Clara Adeline⁹, b. Philadelphia, Aug. 22, 1871; d. Feb. 18, 1876.

1543 iv   Ella Adams⁹, b. Nov. 20, 1874; d. May 28, 1876.
1544   v   Charles Kimball⁹, b. April 28, 1877.
1545 vi   Howard Melville⁹, b. Nov. 7, 1881.
1546 vii   William Irving⁹, b. Hammonton, N. J., July 28, 1886.

1113

WASHINGTON IRVING⁸ BRADBURY (Ebenezer⁷, Theophilus⁶, Jonathan⁵, Theophilus⁴, Wymond³, Wymond², Thomas¹), married at Springfield, Mass., February 27, 1867, Mary Ella Rowndes, who was born at Upton, Mass., August 9, 1846. He resided at Milford, Mass., where he died May 8, 1883.

Children :

1547   i   Mary Bosworth⁹, b. Milford, Mass., Oct. 16, 1867.
1548 ii   Essie Irving⁹, b. Dec. 21, 1872; d. Dec. 28 following.
1549 iii   Fannie Eliza⁹, b. Sept. 23, 1877.

1115

JOHN HENRY⁹ BRADBURY (John⁷, Theophilus⁶, Jonathan⁵, Theophilus⁴, Wymond³, Wymond², Thomas¹), married October 23, 1861, Emily Olcott Robertson, who was born in Charlestown, N. H., February 14, 1839. He is a merchant and resides at New York City. He has taken special interest in the publication of this work, and has furnished material aid therefor.

Children :

1550   i   Harriet Rebekah⁹, b. Sept. 11, 1862; m. April 28, 1886, Charles Alonzo Rich, and has: Dorothy Severance¹⁰ (Rich), b. Nov. 11, 1887, and Margaret Bradbury¹⁰ (Rich), b. Nov. 26, 1888.
1551 ii   Mary Robertson⁹, b. Dec. 22, 1864.
1552 iii   John Henry⁹, b. March 26, 1866.
1553 iv   Richard Robertson⁹, b. Dec. 6, 1875.

1116

CHARLES WILLIAM[8] BRADBURY (John[7], Theophilus[6], Jonathan[5], Theophilus[4], Wymond[3], Wymond[2], Thomas[1]), was born in Newburyport, Mass. Forced by circumstances to abandon a college course of study, for which he had a strong inclination, he entered a store at a early age, and continued in mercantile pursuits during his life. He was a young man of excellent character, honest, faithful, upright in all his transactions; decidedly scholarly in his tastes, he made up in part his failure to secure a collegiate education, by dilligent study and reading. With the English classics he became thoroughly familiar, and he continued a systematic course of reading during his life. His course embraced Motley, Prescott, Froude, Bancroft, Macaulay and other noted historical works. In 1877, he and his wife visited England and the ancestral home at Wicken-Bonant, which was a source of great enjoyment. Mr. Bradbury had a love for the sea, amounting to a passion. His summer vacations were spent upon the New England coast, either in boating or yachting, always accompanied by his wife, who was equally fond of life upon the ocean wave. His ear for music was sensitive and correct, and he had an excellent bass voice. He greatly enjoyed singing old English ballads and songs of the sea. He was engaged in business for the most part in New York City, but he was much attached to his native New England and spent all his vacations here. He died at Winchester, Mass., December 5, 1881. Mr. Bradbury married at

16

Cambridge, Mass., June 4, 1864, Sophia Louise Appleton. She was the daughter of Charles John and Sophia (Haven) Appleton of Cambridge, Mass., and grand-
daughter of Hon. John Appleton, at one time charge
d'affairs at Calais, France. She is a lady of culture,
refinement and varied attainments. She greatly enjoyed her European trip and wrote very interesting
letters of the ancestral home of the Bradburys at
Wicken, extracts of which have been given in another
place. She survives her husband and resides a widow
at Winchester, Mass. They had no issue.

1146

DARIUS[3] BRADBURY (Joseph[7], John[6], Rowland[5], John[4],
William[3], William[2], Thomas[1]), married at Wentworth,
N. H., February 17, 1844, Emily Hobbs, who was born
May 17, 1813. He died in Ohio, August 27, 1853.

Children :

1554 i   Charles Darius[9], b. Feb. 22, 1845.
1555 ii Emma Augusta[9], b. Plymouth, N. H., Aug. 6, 1849.
1556 iii Alida[9], b. April 1, 1852, at North Gainesville, N. Y.

1147

LUTHER MILTON[8] BRADBURY (Joseph[7], John[6], Rowland[5], John[4], William[3], William[2], Thomas[1]), married at
Wentworth, N. H., December 17, 1843, Nancy Hobbs,
who was born at Wentworth, January 17, 1821. He
resides at Quincy, Mass.

Children:

1557   i   Nathan Taylor[9], b. Aug. 27, 1844.
1558   ii   Luther Milton[9], b. Aug. 28, 1846.
1559   iii   Flora Helen[9], b. Oct. 5, 1847.
1560   iv   Charles Francis[9], b. Sept. 11, 1848; d. Oct. 11, 1848.
1561   v   Florence Isabelle[9], b. Oct. 28, 1852 ; d. Dec. 24, 1856.
1562   vi   Hannah Aola[9], b. Sept. 26, 1854.
1563   vii   Ida May[9], b. Sept. 20, 1858.

1153

WYER[8] BRADBURY (True[7], Paul[6], Rowland[5]. John[4], William[3], William[2], Thomas[1]), born June 18, 1814; married at Lubec, Eliza Webber, who was born in Perry, Me., September 4, 1817. He lived at Machias, and died there March 7, 1882. His widow survives, and resides at Machias.

Children:

1564   i   Isaac Snow[9], b. Sept. 11, 1839; m. May 30, 1861, Caroline Hanscome. He was acting ensign U. S. navy, and with all on board was lost on the coast of Florida, Jan. 3, 1865. He had served in the navy through the war, and was once severely wounded.

1565   ii   James True[9], b. May 22, 1841. He was a member of Co. C, 6th Me. vols., and was killed at Rappahannock Station, Nov. 3, 1863. He was a brave and faithful soldier. Bradbury Post, G. A. R., of Machias, is named in honor of the above patriots.

1566   iii   William Wyer[9], b. Feb. 10, 1843; m. Aug. 8, 1872, Josephine A. Fisher. He is a merchant at Machias.

1567   iv   Benjamin Franklin[9], b. Aug. 1, 1849; unmarried.

1568   v   Lydia A.[9], b. Oct. 29, 1850; m. Nov. 4, 1884, William S. Lawrence.

1172

DAVID OLIVER[8] BRADBURY (William Simpson[7], David[6], Samuel[5], James[4], William[3], William[2], Thomas[1]), married January 18. 1857, at Woolwich, Me., Mary O. Cushman, who was born March 10, 1832. He lived a few years at Woolwich, moved to Augusta and died there, December 24, 1888. She died in Bath, June 10, 1868.

Children:

1568½ i   Lydia Viola[9], b. Woolwich, Nov. 4, 1857 ; m. Dec. 12, 1877, Oscar H. Groves, r. Augusta.

1569   ii   Emma Lanta[9], b. Dec. 2, 1859 ; d. Aug. 22, 1865.

1570   iii   Millie Mary[9], b. Aug. 10, 1862, r. Augusta.

1571   iv   Flora Cushman[9], b. Jan. 9, 1864, r. Augusta.

1572   v   Dora Frances[9], b. Bath, Feb. 14, 1867 ; m. Oct. 2, 1888, Walter C. Packard, r. Augusta.

1176

GEORGE WASHINGTON[8] BRADBURY (William Simpson[7], David[6], Samuel[5], James[4], William[3], William[2], Thomas[1]), married Augusta Jane Bump, who was born in New Vineyard. He lives in New Sharon and is a house-carpenter.

Children:

1573   i   Esther May[9], b. Aug. —, 1866 ; m. Frank W. Lawry, r. Farmington.

1574   ii   Mattie[9], b. ——; m. Verne Millett, r. Farmington.

1575   iii   Bertha Emma[9], b. ——.

1576   iv   William Francis[9], b. ——.

1577   v   Daisy[9], b. ——.

1578   vi   Augusta[9], b. ——.

1180

WILLIAM F⁁OTHINGHAM[8] BRADBURY (William Sanders[7], James[6], Sanders[5], James[4], William[3], William[2], Thomas[1]), married August 27, 1857, Margaret Jones of Templeton.

Children:

1579 i William Howard[9], b. July 28, 1858.
1580 ii Marion[9], b. Dec., 1863.

1181

EDWARD EMERSON[8] BRADBURY (William Sanders[7], James[6], Sanders[5], James[4], William[3], William[2], Thomas[1]), married November 26, 1856, Sarah Jane Sykes, who was born at Deerfield, Mass., February 25, 1831.

Children:

1581 i Hattie Bowker[9], b. Dec. 23, 1863, at Brooklyn, N. Y.
1582 ii Alice Emerson[9], b. Aug. 20, 1865.
1583 iii Edward Gatling[9], b. June 14, 1870.

1186

CHARLES BROOKS[8] BRADBURY (Samuel Fox[7], James[6], Sanders[5], James[4], William[3], William[2], Thomas[1]), married July 1, 1863, Emily Harriet Sykes.

Children:

1584 i Charles Fox[9], b. ——.
1585 ii Ellen[9], b. ——.

1196

WILLIAM EDGAR[8] BRADBURY (Cornelius Sanders[7], Jacob[6], Sanders[5], James[4], William[3], William[2], Thomas[1]), married September 9, 1852, Sarah Hogan.

Children, born at Pendleton and Cincinnati, Ohio.

1586 i   William Edward[9]; b. Aug. 27, 1853.
1587 ii   Frederick Wyman[9], b. Dec. 29, 1856.

1197

JULIUS OSCAR[8] BRADBURY (Cornelius Sanders[7], Jacob[6], Sanders[5], James[4], William[3], William[2], Thomas[1]), married November 18, 1848, Lavina Rothamer Moore, who died at Cincinnati, May 18, 1858. He died at same place, August 3, 1854.

Children :

1588 i   Cornelius Sanders[9], b. Dec. 12, 1849.
1589 ii   Laura Gano[9], b. Sept. 6, 1851.
1590 iii Julius Oscar[9], b. July 29, 1854.

1248

HORACE DENNISON[8] BRADBURY (Caleb[7], Joseph[6], Jacob[5], Thomas[4], Jacob[3], William[2], Thomas[1]), married February 24, 1859, Betsey Ann, daughter of Samuel and Betsey Ann (Bagley) Dustin of Stanstead, P. Q., who was born in Stanstead. He is a public accountant in Boston and resides in Cambridge.

Children :

1591 i   Harriet Louise[9], b. Cambridge, Oct. 8, 1863.
1592 ii   Anne Dustin[9], b. Nov. 3, 1868.

1275

MOSES[8] BRADBURY (True[7], Samuel[6], Moses[5], Thomas[4], Jacob[3], William[2], Thomas[1]), married December 29, 1835, Olive Scammon Emery who was born August 16, 1813.

Children :

1593   i   Frederick L.⁹, b. July 20, 1837 ; d. Nov. 27, 1858.
1594   ii   Sarah Elizabeth⁹, b. April 8, 1839 ; d. Oct. 3, 1852.
1595   iii   Edward⁹, b. June 7, 1841.
1596   iv   Augustus Freeman⁹, b. July 6, 1843.

1276

CYRUS KING⁸ BRADBURY (True⁷, Samuel⁶, Moses⁵, Thomas⁴, Jacob³, William², Thomas¹), married Sally Shields. His children were born at New Limerick, Aroostook county, Me.

Children :

1597   i   Martha Fairfield⁹, b. Nov. 12, 1838.
1598   ii   Rachel Day⁹, b. March 17, 1840.
1599   iii   Mary Frances⁹, b. Jan. 12, 1842.
1600   iv   Samuel James⁹, b. April 27, 1843.
1601   v   True⁹, b. Feb. 3, 1845.
1602   vi   Christiana⁹, b. June 22, 1846.
1603   vii   Cyrus King⁹, b. Feb. 19, 1848.
1604   viii   Abigail⁹, b. March 10, 1850.
1605   ix   John Quincy⁹, b. Aug. 11, 1851.
1606   x   Henry Putnam⁹, b. Nov. 23, 1855.
1607   xi   Major⁹, b. July 8, 1858.

1277

SAMUEL⁸ BRADBURY (True⁷, Samuel⁶, Moses⁵, Thomas⁴, Jacob³, William², Thomas¹), married Juliann B. True. Their children were born in New Limerick, Me.

Children :

1608   i   Sarah Abigail⁹, b. Jan. 2, 1839.
1609   ii   William True⁹, b. Jan. 15, 1842.
1610   iii   Mary Joselyn⁹, b. June 27, 1843.
1611   iv   Christopher Columbus⁹, b. July 1, 1846.

1612 v Thomas Merrill⁹, b. Jan. 25, 1850.
1613 vi Juliet⁹, b. Jan. 19, 1852.
1614 vii Kate Dow⁹, b. April 17, 1855.
1615 viii Eleanor Amelia⁹, b. Feb. 3, 1858.

1278

THOMAS MERRILL⁸ BRADBURY (True⁷, Samuel⁶, Moses⁵, Thomas⁴, Jacob³, William²,Thomas)¹, married Catherine Dow. He is a merchant in Houlton.

Children:
1616 i Francis Webster⁹, b. Feb. 24, 1854.
1617 ii Jefferson⁹, b. April 8, 1858.

1294

WILLIAM HARRISON⁸ BRADBURY (Abner⁷, Jabez Page⁶, Thomas⁵, Thomas⁴, Jacob³, William², Thomas¹), married July 4, 1850, Julia Ann Staples, who was born at Wellington, Me., August 10, 1822.

Children:
1618 i Sarah M.⁹, b. May, 1851.
1619 ii Almon⁹, b. March, 1853.
1620 iii Elura Ellen⁹, b. Aug., 1855.
1621 iv Leander Abbot⁹, b. Dayton, Wis., Aug. 7, 1858.

1296

ZIBA HALL⁸ BRADBURY (Abner⁷, Jabez Page⁶, Thomas⁵, Thomas⁴, Jacob³, William², Thomas¹), married February 19, 1852, Lucy Lilly Blackman, who was born in Massina, New York, April 26, 1831.

Children:
1622 i Lucien Leavitt⁹, b. May 2, 1854.
1623 ii Willie Leslie⁹, b. Nov. 7, 1858, at Ripon, Wis.

1298

BENJAMIN FRANKLIN[8] BRADBURY (Abner[7], Jabez[6], Thomas[5], Thomas[4], Jacob[3], William[2], Thomas[1]) married at Sharon, Penn., May 5, 1853, Clarissa Calphurnia Bowers.

Children:

1624 i Ada Jane[9], b. March 11, 1854.
1625 ii Charles Ira[9], b. Dec., 1855.

1299

CYRUS STILSON[8] BRADBURY (Abner[7], Jabez Page[6], Thomas[5], Thomas[4], Jacob[3], William[2], Thomas[1]), married February 7, 1854, Martha Althea Millard, who was born in Delhi, Delaware county, N. Y., June 12, 1828.

Children:

1626 i Agnes Eveline[8], } twins, b. Jan. 1, 1857.
1627 ii Abner Percival[9], }

1308

HORATIO TAYLOR[8] BRADBURY (William[7], Daniel[6], Thomas[5], Thomas[4], Jacob[3], William[2], Thomas[1]), married December 27, 1851, Ann Eliza, daughter of Robinson Parlin of Paris. He was born in Byron and after marriage lived in Paris.

Children:

1828 i William Robinson[9], b. Byron, Me., Nov. 13, 1852; m. Mary G. Chase.
1629 ii Charles Hannibal Brown[9], b. Paris, Me., Oct. 25, 1854; d. Jan. 25, 1859.
1630 iii Effie Annie[9], b. March 19, 1863; m. William Hammond.
1631 iv Mary Abbie[9], b. April 19, 1866.
1632 v Jennie Lura[9], b. July 21, 1868.

1345

WILLIAM KINNEY[8] BRADBUBY (Thomas[7], Jacob[6], Benjamin[5], Thomas[4], Jacob[3], William[2], Thomas[1]), married 1854, Melinda Jarritz.

Children :

1633 i Elmore Douglass[9], b. ——.
1634 ii Leonora Ann[9], b. ——.

1355

GEORGE[8] BRADBURY (Lemuel[7], Jacob[6], Benjamin[5], Thomas[4], Jacob[3], William[2], Thomas[1]), married April 23, 1855, Eliza Mummey. He died in Pike county, Mo., March 1, 1877. [Date incorrectly given on page 210.]

Children :

1634 a i Charlotte[9], b. Aug. 3, 1856; m. March 20, 1873, Morgan Bordman; d. March 1, 1877.
1634 b ii William Sylvester[9], b. Feb. 10, 1859.
1634 c iii Lemuel[9], b. July 22, 1861; m. Dec. 27, 1888, Evelyn Shepard; d. March 31. 1889.
1634 d iv Carrie[9], b. April 20, 1866.
1634 e v Amy[9], b. Feb. 6, 1869; m. Dec. 27, 1888, Lewis James.

1356

NATHAN[8] BRADBURY (Lemuel[7], Jacob[6], Benjamin[5], Thomas[4], Jacob[3], William[2], Thomas[1]), married Sept. 27, 1856, Frances Lindsey. He resides in Kansas.

Children :

1634 f i Cora Bell[9], b. July 25, 1860; m. Dec. 23, 1877, George Basye.
1634 g ii Walter Clarence[9], b. Sept. 4, 1862; d. July 4, 1888, at Chicago.
1634 h iii Charles Edwin[9], b. Feb. 19, 1865.

1357

Anson⁸ Bradbury (Lemuel⁷, Jacob⁶, Benjamin⁵, Thomas⁴, Jacob³, William², Thomas¹), married February 15, 1865, Miss Mary M. Tedrow. He resides in Bowling Green, Pike county, Mo.

Children :

1635 i Edward Ross⁹, b. Oct. 27, 1865; m. Delue F. Tinker, March 11, 1890.

1635½ ii Lydia Iva⁹, b. Jan. 1, 1868; m. March 12, 1889, James V. Davis.

1636 iii Lizzie⁹, b. Sept. 30, 1869.

1637 iv Ora M.⁹, b. Dec. 3, 1878.

1358

Thomas⁸ Bradbury (Lemuel⁷, Jacob⁶, Benjamin⁵, Thomas⁴, Jacob³, William², Thomas¹), married Mary Derry or Derrah. He was killed in battle at Murfreesboro, January 6, 1863.

Child :

1637 *a* i Thomas Preston⁹, b. Dec. 25, 1962.

1393

Moses Williams⁸ Bradbury (Jacob⁷, Moses⁶, Jacob⁵, Jacob⁴, Jacob³, William², Thomas¹), married January 11, 1848, Catherine Pomeroy Wentworth, who was born March 27, 1824.

Children : ,

1638 i Theodore Robert⁹, b. Nov. 22, 1848; d. March 6, 1852.

1639 ii Catherine⁹, b. Jan. 30, 1851; d. Jan. 31, 1851.

1640 iii Harriet Angusta⁹, b. Dec. 6, 1853; d. Sept. 29, 1854.

1641 iv Emma Kelley⁹, b. Oct. 28, 1855.

1642 v Clarence Sumner⁹, b. March 29, 1858.

1643 vi Samuel Kelley⁹, b. March 29, 1858.

1394

JACOB[8] BRADBURY (Jacob[7], Moses[6], Jacob[5], Jacob[4], Jacob[3], William[2], Thomas[1]), married January 21, 1855, Sarah McCann.

Child:

1644 i   George[9], b. March 1, 1856.

1401

THOMAS EMERY[8] BRADBURY (John Garland[7], Moses[6], Jacob[5], Jacob[4], Jacob[3], William[2], Thomas[1]), married June 20, 1858, Angelette Elwell, who was born 1834.

Child:

1645 i   Frederic[9], b. Dec. 11, 1858.

1402

CHARLES B.[8] BRADBURY (John Garland[7], Moses[6], Jacob[5], Jacob[4], Jacob[3], William[2], Thomas[1]), married October 14, 1857, Caroline Eliza Peabody, who was born March 4, 1839.

Child:

1646 i   Harriet Caroline[9], b. Feb. 10, 1858.

1439

AHBAN[8] BRADBURY (Moses[7], Elijah[6], Elijah[5], Jacob[4], Jacob[3], William[2], Thomas[1]), is a farmer and millman, and resides in Denmark, Me. He married first, December 12, 1866, Sarah Frances, daughter of Elder Larkin Jordan, who died December 26, 1887, and second, November 6, 1889, Melinda Witham.

Children:

1647   i   Minnie C.⁹, b. May 28, 1868; m. ——; she d. July 17, 1884.

1648   ii   Fred R.⁹, b. May 28, 1870.

1649   iii   Henry⁹, b. June 12, 1872; d. Sept. 10 following.

1650   iv   May L.⁹, b. July 25, 1878.

1651   v   Perley R. F.⁹, b. July 22, 1880.

1454

OSGOOD NATHAN⁸ BRADBURY (Jacob⁷, Joseph⁶, Benjamin⁵, Moses⁴, Jacob³, William², Thomas¹), graduated from the Maine Medical School in 1864. He had previously been in East Machias, from 1852 to 1855, and from that date to 1860, in the fruit trade in San Francisco, Cal. He moved to Springfield, Me., in 1860, and had his home there until 1873. He was acting assistant surgeon at Augusta from June, 1864, to December, 1865, and then was in charge of Cony Hospital until July, 1866, when it was discontinued. He served in the Maine legislature as representative from Springfield, and two terms in the Senate from Penobscot county. In 1873 he returned to his native town of Norway, where, with the exception of three years spent in the South and three years at Paris Hill, he has since lived and been in practice. He served as examining surgeon for invalid pensioners thirteen years. He married June 13, 1852, Ellen R. Scribner, who was born in Springfield, Me.

Children :

1652 i Bial Francisco[5], b. Springfield, Feb. 5, 1861; m. March 22, 1882, Mabel F., daughter of Dr. George P. Jones of Norway. He graduated at Atlanta, Ga., in Feb., 1882, and is a skillful and popular physician in Norway.

1653 ii Guy[9], b. Springfield, March 24, 1872; d. Norway, May 17, 1876.

1467

JOSEPH AUGUSTUS[8] BRADBURY (Moses[7], Joseph[6], Benjamin[5], Moses[4], Jacob[3], William[2], Thomas[1]), is a farmer and carpenter; residence, Norway, Me. He married August 14, 1862, Sarah Jane Mixer, who was born in Paris, Me., July 21, 1842.

Children:

1654 i Algenora[9], b. Paris, July, 1863.
1655 ii Elsie Flora[9], b. Feb. 11, 1865.
1656 iii Herbert[9], b. July 23, 1866.
1657 iv Ray[9], b. Dec. 24, 1871.
1658 v Inez May[9], b. June 12, 1878.

1473

HENRY NEWELL[8] BRADBURY (Nathaniel M.[7], Joseph[6], Benjamin[5]. Moses[4], Jacob[3], William[2], Thomas[1]), married at Lowell, Mass., Harriet Mann. He resides in Lewiston, Me.

Children :

1659 i Avery Belcher[9], b. April 26, 1855; m. Jan. 23, 1879, Mary Elliot.
1660 ii Arthur W. M.[9], b. Dec. 21, 1857; d. Feb. 25, 1870.
1661 iii Hattie Rosena[9], b. March 15, 1859.
1662 iv Elmer E.[9], b. Nov. 26, 1861; m. Ida Albee.

1474

EDWIN FRANKLIN[8] BRADBURY (Nathaniel M.[7], Joseph[6], Benjamin[5], Moses[4], Jacob[3], William[2], Thomas[1]), married at Mechanic Falls in 1860, Susanna H. Gilbert. He resides in Lewiston.

Children:

1663　i　Linus Edward[9], b. Nov. 7, 1861; m. Alice Springer.
1664　ii　George Oscar[9], b. Oct 30, 1868.
1665　iii　Emery Wallace[9], b. Feb. 7, 1871.
1666　iv　Rosa Isabella[9], b. March 24, 1876.
1667　v　Mildred Winnifred[9], b. July 20, 1882.

1487

JOSIAH C.[8] BRADBURY (Samuel Gurney[7], Samuel[6], Benjamin[5], Moses[4], Jacob[3], William[2], Thomas[1]), married Mary M. Dillingham, who was born June 30, 1838. He resided at Livermore and died there April 6, 1889.

Children:

1668　i　John E.[9], b. May 20, 1859; m. Hattie T. Joselyn of Farmington. He is a physician in Livermore.
1669　ii　Ada A.[9], b. May 30, 1860.
1670　iii　Albert C.[9], b. July 27, 1866.
1671　iv　M. Alice[9], b. April 18, 1870.
1672　v　Dana B.[9], b. May 25, 1871.
1673　vi　Alden G.[6], b. Oct. 16, 1880.

APPENDIX

APPENDIX.

WILL OF MARY BRADBURY.

In the name of god Amen the 17th day of February in the 8th year of his majestys reign, King William ye 3[d] of England &c. I Mary Bradbury, widow, of yt town of Salisbury in ye county of Essex in ye Province of Massachusetts Bay in New England being weak of body but of sound and perfect memory praise be given to god for ye same, and knowing ye uncertainty of this life on earth and being desirous to settle things in order do make this my last will and testament in manner and form following that is to say first and principally I commend my soul to God my Creator assuredly believing that I shall receive full pardon and free remission of all my sins and be saved by ye precious death and merits of my blessed saviour and Redeemer Jesus Christ and my body to ye earth from whence it was taken to be buried in such decent manner as to my executor hereafter named shall be thought meet and convenient, and now for the settling of my temporal estate and such goods, chattels and debts as it hath pleased God far above my deserts to bestow upon me, I do order, give and bestow and dispose the same in manner and form following, that is say.

First I will that all those debts and duties that I owe in right or conscience to any manner of person or persons whatever, shall be well and truly contented and paid or ordered to be paid within convenient time after my decease by my executor hereafter named.

Item I give and bequeath unto my beloved daughter Mary Stanyan of Hampton in the Province of New Hampshire and my daughter Jane True of Salisbury in the Province of Massachusetts Bay in New England all my estate and substance of what kind or nature soever to be equally divided betwixt my two well-beloved daughters as aforesaid as namely goods, chattels, leases, debts, ready money, plate, household stuff, apparel, brass, pewter, bedding and all others my substance whatsoever and I do constitute and make my well-beloved son-in-law Henry True to be my sole executor of this my last will and testament. In witness whereof, I have hereunto set my hand the day and year above-stated.

MARY BRADBURY
widow.

Witness
Elisᵃ Stanyan
Richard I. R. Long.

ABSTRACTS OF WILLS, DEEDS, &c.

ESSEX (MASS.) COUNTY RECORDS.

Jacob Bradbury's will, dated May 3, 1718, proved May 21, same year. To son Thomas one-half of homestead and lands in cow common, gravelly ridge, and one-half of meadow and marsh. To sons Jacob and Moses the other half. To daughters Anne, Elizabeth, Dorothy and Sarah £10 each. Reasonable allowance to his honored mother, Sarah Stockman. To wife Elizabeth his Stockman house, lot, orchard, &c. Wife Elizabeth administratrix. Witnesses, John Eaton, Jeremiah Wheeler and Sarah Bradbury. Inventory, real property, £402; personal, £48.4.

Thomas Bradbury appointed guardian of his brothers, Jacob and Moses, February 27, 1722

October 25, 1731, Jacob Bradbury of Salisbury (weaver), and Moses Bradbury of North Yarmouth (yeoman), deed their portions of their father's estate to their brother, Thomas Bradbury of Salisbury (yeoman).

Thomas³ Bradbury, will dated March 8, 1719, proved May 14, 1719. To wife Mary one-third of all lands, and one-half of lands during life. To daughter Jemima all lands and meadows which he had of his grandfather Bradbury, except the portion of her mother. Wife Mary appointed executrix. Inventory: real, £590; personal, £201.12.

William³ Bradbury's will, dated April 12, 1748, proved June 7, 1756. Sons John, Jacob, James, Crisp and Barnabas, and daughters Rebekah, Joanna, Mary and Sarah. To son Benjamin all his real estate.

William and Jemima (Bradbury) Chandler of Amsterdam farm, near Woodstock, Conn., March 21, 1726, for £650 good bills of public credit, sold certain lands is Salisbury, the estate having been the homestead of Capt. Thomas Bradbury, inherited by his grandson, Thomas Bradbury, who bequeathed it to his daughter Jemima, who became the wife of William Chandler.

DIARIES.

DIARY OF DEA. JOHN BRADBURY (66) OF YORK, GIVING AN ACCOUNT OF HIS SERVICES IN THE WAR FOR THE CONQUEST OF CANADA, IN THE YEAR 1760.

York February ye 20/1760.
then Received Beating orders from his
Excellency governor pownall.

April 5   went to Saco to inlist men.

ye 9   Returned to York.

18   Received orders to go to Biddeford to order the men to march to worcester.

20   Returned to York.

21   Received orders to Stop the men till further orders.

May 7   Received orders to march to worcester.

8   Received a Second Lieutenants Commission from governer pownall by the hand of Nathaniel Spawhake Esq. under Capt. Johnson moulton.

May ye 15   this Day Took my Departure from old york came as far
1760   as hampton Lodged at mr. Levets.

May 16 Came to Newbury Lodged at mr. Bradburys.

16 marched to Andover Lodged at mr. foster's 30 miles from Newbury.

Sabbath 18 marched 14 miles went to Brakefast at mr. Osgoods went to meeting Heard mr. Clark preach from John ye 11ᵉ & 11ᵛ Dined at mr. pollards. Marched to Concord heard mr. Bliss preach afternoon from Job 7 & 21. Lodged at Capt. meros (?)

19 marched from concord Drank punch at Sudbury Dined at malbury at Colonel Williams had for Dinner p t & g marched as far as Shrewsbury Lodged at a private house. Rained hard.

20 Brakefasted at mr Eagers arived at worster at 12 oclock Dined at Capt. Stevnses.

21 our men passed muster and we made up the Billiting Roll.

22 Carried it to the muster got the Billiting money.

23 paid the men their Billiting money.

24 marched from worcester at 5 oclock afternoon marched to Leicester Lodged at mr Serjants.

Sabbath E. marched 6 miles; heard mr. Eaten preach from Jeremiah the 16 & 12 forenoon. Dined at mr. Flags. marched as far as Brookfield put up at mr. Buckminsters.

26 marched to Westown. Dind at Kingstown at mr. Shaws; marched to palmer; put up to mr. Scoots had good entertainment.

27 Brakefasted at Brimfield to mr. graves Drank punch at mr Days at Springfield mountains. Dined at mr parsons Arrived at Springfield at 4 oclock afternoon; put up at Mr Whites Lodged and Brakefasted at the same place.

28 marched 4 miles Dined at mr Eles arived at westfield at 4 oclock afternoon put up at Capt. Claps.

May 29   marched to Brimfield. Dind at mr peases marched 2 miles into the green woods. had a good nights Lodging.

    30   marched 12 miles Dind at mr Shadreeks, half way through the woods; arived at mr Chadwicks through the woods at 4 oclock afternoon.

    31   marched 10 miles came to Sheffield put up at mr Burgets, an old honest Duchman.

June 1   marched 4 miles Drank punch at mr. Roberts; marched as far as Nobletown without any provision either from the King or taverns. Arived at Squire Ingersols at 7 oclock afternoon.

    2   marched 6 miles Drank wine at the Stone house at hoggabooms arived at Kenderhooch at 1 oclock put up at the Commisarys and Drew provision for the men.

    3   marched to green Bush arived hear at 4 oclock afternoon Extreme hot weather put up at a Duch house without victuals or Lodging or any convenience.

    4   went over to Albany Brakefasted at mr Sawyer's Returned Back the Same Day.

    5   went over to Albany Drew provision and tents marched a quarter of a mile above the city and encampt. Rained the afternoon had a good nights Lodging in a mud hole.

    6   Still very Rainy weather and tent Leake and we in an uncomfortable Situation and So Lik to continue as the weather is increasing.

    7   Heard of a little wind at N West.

Sabbath   this Day went Down to the Commisary with a party of men and Drew provisions—unsettled weather as yet.

    9   Capt. Jackson & Capt. wentworths Companies were ordered to march to Crown Point.

      ordered by the colonel to Draw 80 men out of 5 Companies for waggoners. Drew them out and marched them Down to the parade and made Return to general Amherst and Returned to the Tents and Dind.

June 10 at 8 oclock this morning one of Cap. Chadbournes men named John Johnson, a young man, Died.
4 oclock was Buried.

11 went down to the Commisaries with a party of men Took provision for 4 Days Received orders to Draft 180 men out of 5 Companies for Waggoners—taken with a pain in my head Went down in the city Lodged at mr Sawyers.

12 ordered to march still weak and poorly; imbarked on board the Battoes Received 3 Letters from old york. Set off from Albany at 9 oclock arived at Colonel Seilers at one oclock and Dined there; went 2 miles and incampd. Still weak and a bad pain in my head. Lodged at a Duch house on a Little wad of straw.

13 Set off for half moon; arrived their at 12 o'clock pushed up 2 miles and incampt.

14 Set out for the Refts (?) arived at the half way house at 12 oclock. Set out at 2 oclock arrived at the Rafts at 6 oclock. Landed our provision and Encampt.

Sabbath 15 Set off for fort Edward arived at Stillwater at 12 o'clock; took provision for 2 Days and Encampt and went to bed very sick.

16 felt a little Better in the morning Struck our Tents and set up for Saratoga; arived hear after Sun set. Rained and thundered very hard went on Shore and pitched our Tents on the wet ground; went to bed sick—had a good Nights Lodging.

17 Struck our tents came 3 miles and unloaded our provision—Set up a Little way and pitcht our tents— Rained all night and I grew worse.

18 arived at fort miller or the falls; unloaded our provision, halld Round the falls and Encampd—Still very poorly.

19 arrived at fort Edward at 1 o'clock unloaded our Battoes and Encampt.

June 20 the Companys marched off to Lake george and Left me at fort Edward in a very poor state of helth. Likewise Samuel Bradbury carried to the hospital having very badly cut himself. Also Joseph Main Left in the hospital Joseph Baker Left to Look after them.

21 Drew provisions for 4 men for 4 Days went over the River to see the Sick and Lame. Kept with Capt. Brown Commanding officer of the fort at present. Eat Drank and Lodgd with him and Lieut. Berry Both provincial officers.

Sabbath 22 this Day I should have set out for the Lake but being something worse was obliged to tarry Longer and was Bled; went over the River to see the Sick or lame.

23 Still very weak the weather cold & stormy & uncomfitable.

24 fair weather; wind at N West and I still sick went to the Doctor and got some phisick: took it and felt something Better.

25 Took provision for 4 men 4 Days felt Better than I have since I came here.

26 a french officer Came in from montreal and gone Down to the general.

27 Took a walk in a fine garden where I eat green pease pleasant weather in the forenoon Rainy Afternoon. Joshua McLaws arived hear at night with a packet for Lake george and is stationed hear ride post.

28 went over the River to see the Sick & Lame and find them Something Better. Took provision for 5 men 4 Days nothing Remarkable hapned till night.
at 10 o'clock at night was called out to another Barrack to see Mr. Henry otote a young Duch gentleman Commisary, that was taken in an uncommon fit where he Lay Just Expiring and with a great deal of Difficulty got him from where he was jamd Between the Bed and wall and after the Doctor had pricked him

5 times Drew Blood from him and before Day had 2 more of the Like.

Sabbath this morning he was better Rainy weather cleared off at noon. Colonel Willard arived hear at 10 oclock Samuel Marthews Esq. invited me to Dine with him I accepted had a fine Dinner.

June 30 marched from fort Edward arived at the half way brook at 12 oclock Dind with Col¹ Willard and major Burke and other gentlemen; arived at fort george at 5 oclock Went and viewed the Ruins of fort William henry Drank wine with Capt ingersol Drank Tea With Capt Stickney Lodged with Lieut March & Lieut. Freeman.

July 1 Brakefasted With Capt Stickney of Newbury Set off from Lake george at 9 oclock With Col¹ Willard & major Banks & Liet. Divil. arived at Ticonderoga Landing at 9 oclock at night. Lodged in a Little Hut.

   2 marched one mile & half to the mill went on Board the Battoes & arivd at ticonderoga fort at 12 oclock Set off at 2 arived at Crown point at 7 oclock; marched up to the Camps and Saw my friends, found all well except Lieut. Frost with Le¹ Richmon.

   3 Took a walk Round the fort and found it to bee a very Beautifull place invited out to Drink punch with a number of gentlemen that received their Commissions Drank Tea with Cap¹ Chadbourn Thundered & Raind very hard.

   4 orderd at 9 oclock to set on a cort martial immediately attended accordingly and finished at 11 oclock: went and Drank punch at a markee—a man carried from the camp sick with the small pox—this day 3 indians came in to major Rogers came with a french Scalp as they say Not Known where they Belong.

Crownpoint July ye 4 / 1760

this Day a Regimental Court Martial Set at the presedents tent by order of John Thomas Colonel to Try Peter Jones of Capt Martains Company confined by Capt Abial perce for Daming him and Denying his Duty when ordered by him and other insolent Language—the prisoner Pleads Ignorance of the Facts Aledgd against him by information of his officers the prisoner is very apt to be Deprived of his Reason by the Smallest Quantity of Spirits therefore it is the opinion of the Court that the prisoner peter Jones Shall Receive fifty Stripes on his Naked Back

Capt Samuel Jenks President

Members.
{
Lieut. Foster
" Small
" Sayward
" Bradbury
}

July 5 the sick man Died with the pox ; Likewise one of Capt Jacksons men Died very sudden. named William ferrentun (Farrington)

ordered on Duty took Command of 40 men went and Drew timber upon the Fort Dismist them at Sunset.

Sabbath 6 this day a sermon was to have Been preached at the head of ye 17 Regement But being very hot the priest chose Rather to drink wine under a shed ; one of the sutlers died with the small pox ; went down to the Commisary and took provision for 4 Days of Salt and 2 of fresh—one of the sutlers had 7 Barrels of spirits spilt for selling to the Regulars another ordered out of the incampment.

Samuel Bradbury Died with the Small pox at fort Edward the 7 of July.

Captain's Names as they Stand in Camp.

Capt. Chadbourne	Capt. Fellows
Capt. Heart	Capt. Jeffeds
Capt. Jenks	Capt. Pierce
Capt. Harris	Capt. West
Capt. Bailey	Capt. Barron
Capt. Butterfield	Capt. Small
Capt. Moulton	Capt. Dunbar
Capt. Martin	Capt. Wentworth
Capt. Jackson	Capt. Williams
Capt. Whitin	

July 8   this morning major Rogers had a Brush with the french indians; had one man Kild, 6 wounded and he pessued them and is not returned. ye 9 instant a soldier received 300 Lashes this Day.

9   Extreem hot weather.

Went in a swimming with a number of officers in the afternoon Returned Back and was ordered to take the pickquit gard. Took the gard after conferring with Capt Harris and Lieut. Spauldin.

10   peraded them at Revalle Beating; then Dismist them till further orders. Lieut. Sewall Took the quarter gard peraded them before the whipping post and one of Capt Jacksons men received 100 Lashes for Denying his Duty. Dismissed the pickquit after gun firing.

11   a Soldier Received 50 Lashes for insolent Language or-

12   dered on fatigue to work; another Received 500 for inlisting twice—took a party of 40 men and yoked them together and made oxen of them and Drew timber into the Fort.

13   Drew 4 Days Salt & 3 fresh provision. 2 Sutlers Died with the Small pox. a Regular Soldier put under our guard for impudent talk and before they had time to send him to their guard there came 20 of the Regulars with their Clubs and Took the prisoner and ran

away; our guard and picket all under arms and Surrounded the Block house took 2 of the mob and sent them to their own guard—2 or 3 guns fired at them and one or 2 of them wounded and the Camp all in Confusion; after a great Deal of Difficulty got Regulated. Lieutenant John Richmon confined to his tent soon after.

July 14   Crownpoint July ye 14 / 1760.

this day a Regemental Court martial set at the presidents Tent by order of Brigadier general Ruggles Esq. to Try James Carsey William Dillerue henry Boy & Jacob Hersey all of Capt Jenks Company Confined by S^d Jenks for writing of orders to the Sutlers and sining (signing) of them theirselves &c &c.

Capt Humphrey Chadbourn
President

Members {
    Lieut Bradbury
    Lieut Bayley
    Lieut Wicker
    Lieut Boyonton

this Day Ensign Frost came hear from putmans post 6 miles from here

the prisoner James Carsey apeared before the court & being examined plead guilty and Bed^d the mercy of the Court; it is therefore the opinion of the Court that James Carsey Receive 250 Stripes on his Naked Back.

William Dillerue being Brought before the Court plead guilty and Beg the mercy of the Court.

tis therefore the opinion of the Court that William Dillerue Receive 150 Stripes on his naked back.

Henry Boy being Brought before the Court pled Not guilty; and by evidence Received 'tis the opinion of the Court that he is not guilty he is therefore acquited.

Jacob hersey being Brought before the Court pled not guilty; by evidence given he is guilty 'tis the opinion of the Court that he shall receive 50 stripes on his Naked Back. Which was put into execution this morning. Relieving the guard.

July 15   one of the Regulars Whipt 75 Lashes for Strik one of Lt. fosters men. I ordered on fatigue.

Took 30 men and went into the garden Dismissed them after gun firing.

16   Mr. Sewall ordered on fatigue tomorrow.

17   Lieut. Frost took the quarter guards. Nothing Remarkable to Day.

18   Took a Walk into the Woods With 3 men; went round the head of the Bay; got some Elm rine to make a Bed; arrived home at 12 oclock a very Smart Shower afternoon; ordered to perade the men for prayer; the first prayers I have heard since I Left Concord.

Received a letter from Capt Brown at fort Edward Dated ye 10 instant With the Sorrowful News of the Death of Samuel Bradbury. ordered on fatigue tomorrow.

19   Took 100 men With Capt Harris Lieut Bennet & Ensign Richards went into the woods and Drew timber Returned in after sunset very tired. Went on the perade heard prayers and Singing psalms.

Sunday E.   took 4 Days provision.

Sent letters to york by mr. Bowler very hot weather. I ordord on a general cort martial tomorrow morning 8 oclock.

21   Cort martial adjourned till tomorrow; took a walk in the woods 3 miles from hear with some gentlemen to get Rasberries; Returned Back at 7 oclock. Drank punch at pasons. Went to the perade & heard prayers.

22   got myself in Rediness to attend on ye Court Martial; the Court Still adjournd till tomorrow 8 oclock. Went down to the Lake to see Capt Jones Returned at 10 oclock Went to the guard house Drank wine with

Lie' Farnum, the officer of the guard. Returned to my tent at 1 oclock.

Dined at 12 oclock.

attended on prayers after Sunset.

Crownpoint July ye 23 / 1760

this Day a general Court martial set at the presidents Tent or house to Try Lieutenant John Richmons For Disobeying Colonel Haverlings orders and other things aleged against him &c.

Whereof Briggader genl timothy Ruggles Was president.

Capt Preble of the Regulars Judge Advocate.

N. B. S⁴ L' Richmon was found guilty and rendered incapable of doing Duty in the Service this campain and so Dismissd from the Service.

Members of S⁴ Court Martial	Major Hawk
	Colonel Saltenstall Massachusetts
	Capt Rose Rodiland
	Capt Bradford
	Capt Harris
	Capt Fellows
	Capt. L' Humfris
	Lieut Speers Rodiland
	Lieut Trip Rodiland
	Lieut Bradbury
	Lieut Byrun
	Lieut McLaws

court martial sat at 8 oclock finished most of the Business and then adjourned till tomorrow 10 oclock.

24   a number of the members met to coppy off the Result.

25   this Day the Court Disolved. I went down to Ticon-deroga with 300 of Regulars Rangers & Rodilanders Loded each Batto with 20 Barrels of provision and arived at Crownpoint at 11 oclock at night and Landed 1800 Barrels of provision.

26   turned out at Revalle Beating and unloaded our Battos for weather still rainy most of the day.

July 27 this day as I am informed is Lords day and I have some
Reson to Believe it as there is the signal hoisted viz:—
the flag and not only this But the people have began
their Sabbath Day work viz:—Cursing and profane
swearing and taking the name of God in vain. Serjant Dillewa ordered to ticonderoga with 7 men on
express.

the wether cleard off pleasant.

ordered on the parade to attend on prayer & preaching—preach from Exodus 20^e/7^v. cold night.

28 took a walk into the Fort went on the perad & heard
prayers as usual. afternoon walk Down opposite the
New fort and heard a very fine sermon preached by a
Regular Soldier.

29 took the command of 60 men went down to the old fort
and hald provision to the New fort.

30 provintials taken to go to meet the hamshier forces & 30
Regulars instead of them Dismissd them at sunset ;
heard prayers as usual. Supt with Lieut foster.

30 Lt. Sewall took the guard—a Regular Received 1000
Lashes—one of Capt fellows men carried to the hospi-
tal with the small pox—one of Capt pierces men died
Last night. took a walk into the woods forenoon.
Rote letters afternoon.

31 Ensign Whiting relieved the guard. helped to prize the
cloaths of Levi hatch diseased of Capt Jeffards Company with Capt fellows & Ensign King; took walk
into the woods with a number of officers & pactisd ex-
ercising. John Bunker & Solomon goodlin & 2 more
Deserted from the Raddo.

800 of the hampshier got in this night almost starved.
Rained all night.

Aug. 1 Still Rainey weather tents Leak Cleared off a little at 9 oclock Showery all day ordered to take the picket this night. a Regular Soldier Received 1000 Lashes 2 more to Receive 1000 each tomorrow morning. 3 more forgiven. one provintial Received 50 Lashes. heard prayers as usual.

2 took the picket went into the woods & hald 2 Lods of timber for the hospital—one of the Drummers tried by a Court Martial for not whiping the prisoners hard enough. A Detachment out of 1000 men out of all the Regements Embarked on Board the vessels to go down the Lake Capt Bradford Lieut Lucus Lieut Bailey of the massachusetts ordered with them. went with the picket afternoon and covered Battoes Dismissd after gun firing. heard prayers as usual.

Drew 4 Days provision this Day. Nothing Remarkable to Day. ordered on a Regemental Court Martial tomorrow 8 oclock.

Aug. 4 atended at S^d time appointed. fowl weather.

(margin: heard a sermon preached from Matthew ye 3/14 very short. 3d Day of July. omitted through mistake.)

Crownpoint August ye 4/1760.

Agreable to the ordors of Brigadear general Timothy Ruggles Esq. the Regemental Court Martial sat to try all prisoners Brought before S^d Court.

Capt Nathaniel Bailey President.

Members.

Lieut Dummer Sewall Lieut John Bradbury Lieut John Frost Ensign Jere^h Chubbuk.

peter Linsey of Capt Martains Company Confined for mutinous Talk and Theft. the prisoner being Brought plead not guilty; by evidence given he is guilty of part.

therefore tis the opinion of the Court that the prisoner peter

18

Linsey Shall Receive 250 Stripes on his naked Back with a Cat of Nine tails.

Richard galleway of Capt Baileys Company Confined for mutinous Talk & Swearing. the prisoner being Brought plead not guilty; by Evidence Brought to the Court he is guilty.

therefore tis the opinion of the Court that the above S^d prisoner Shall Receive 40 Stripes on his Naked Back.

Patrick Collins of Capt Hearts Company Confined for Denying his Duty when ordered by a Corporal—by Evidence it appears to the Court he is guilty.

tis there opinion therefore that the S^d prisoner patrick Collins Shall Receive 20 Stripes on his naked Back.

the above said Court Martial finished at 3 oclock afternoon the Result Carried to the Brigadear and aprooved off by him.

Likewise put in execution this Evening after gun firing.

ordered to take the quarter tomorrow.

Aug. 5 took the guard, had a number of gentlemen to see me in the afternoon—a Regular Soldier taken by the indians Sometime after (not legible). badly wounded the guard Reduced to a Serjant. thundered & Rain first part of the night. Wet in the guard house.

6 Carried my report to the Brigadear this morning his Reply was "I thank you Sir." nothing Remarkable to Day had a good Dinner of Baked meat & peas. went in the woods & exercised—heard prayers as usual.

7 took 3 Days provision of all Species took a walk in the woods.

this day the Enemy was Discovered Near the Block house as was Reported—an Express arivd at 2 oclock with orders to go forward orders to get things in Rediness by Sunday. ordered on fatigue tomorrow.

heard prayers as usual.

Aug. 8 took a party of 60 men with Liet. Saward, helpd to Lode ye Raddo with artillery 250 of the hampshier forces Drafted out and joind major Rogers. Received Letter from Brother Jas. old York Dated 17 of June.

   9 no fatigue men Sent for to Day all the outposts ordord in immediaetly. the Camp making preparation to Embark at the Least warning.

      Liet Sewall ordord to take a party of men and Encamp Near the granedeers fort till further ordors.

10 200 or 300 of the New Recruiters got in this Day.

      Richard galleway of Capt mortons Company tried by Court martial for mutinous talk and Received 900 Lashes on his naked Back;—

      heard a sermon preachd from Joshua ye 14 & 6.

      ordors to Embark tomorrow morning.

11 Struck our tents at gun firing imbarkd on board at 11 oclock.

      Set off at 10 oclock under ye Command of Colonel Haverlin with 5433 men Rowd 8 miles Landed on a Sandy point Set out guards & Lodged on Board ye Battoes.

12 Set off at 7 o'clock; fair weather. But the wind against us Landed at Buttenmold Bay at 3 oclock.

      the Days very hot Nights cold.

      Lodgd very uncomfitable on ye oars; taken Bad with ye Camp Disorder.

13 Set off at 9 oclock the wind Still against us. Rowd 3 miles ordord Back with 6 Battoes to help tow ye Legganear. Kept her in tow till 10 o'clock at night then cast & joined ye Regement; Slept till Light in ye Battoes.

Aug. 14 & then set off the wind fair But fowl weather; at 8 oclock ye wind & Rain increased to a very great Degree the Seas Ran very high and we Narrowly escaped being Either floundered or Dashed to peases against ye Rocks. one of Capt Bradstreets men fel over & was Drowned. another shot through ye Body.

at 2 oclock we arived at Chyles island & Landed Safe, the Lake 8 or 10 miles wide one Canoe of ye Rangers ,Cast away & 7 men Lost. one more of ye provintials Drownd. Set out guards & peraded our selves on Board ye Battoes.

15 Set off with a fair wind & Showery ; arived at Lenote Island at 2 oclock ordord on picket with Capt Martain & Ensign gilson ; the picket consisted of 50 men Set out 16 sentries ; the Regulars movd their Battoes & took our ground, we ordord to Land ye first when we Struck ye Shoar at St Johns.

Aug. 16 Set off at 4 oclock arived within 2 miles of ye fort at 3 oclock and Landed without opposition.

ye vessels Began to fire on ye fort & continued till night very moderate. I still very Bad with ye purging; took Command of ye picket guard Set ye Sentries & Lay on our arms. But not Disturbd; the nights extreem cold—a few guns from our vessels this night but none from ye Enemy.

17 ordord to Carry our Battoes Down to an Island 3 miles off and Land our provision & take 3 Days alowance. this morning an unlucky afair hapned ; one of ye Small Raddoes was ordord to go very near the fort the 2d Shot they Received from ye fort one 12 pounder, come through ye fashens and Cut off Both Capt Cleg's feet by his ankles. carried away ye Calf of Christopher Langlys Leg Nathaniel marsh Both his Legs Broke off, Robert townsend the pan Bone of his Knee & Shin Carried away.

James union one Leg by his Knee; the Capt & Nathaniel Marsh Died after having their Legs cut off.
ordord up to ye Brestwork to join our Companies &
Dismissd ye picket Lodgd under a few Bushes in a
Swamp.

Aug. 18 the army went and Cleard a Rode & Built a Bridg
almost opposite ye fort—Rainey weather and nothing
to Shelter us. But a few bushes the water and mud
half Leg Deep and I very weak & poorly with the
Camp Disorder and can get nothing to help me; got
a tent this night and Lodgd Dry.

19 ordord to Strike our tents & march Down within half
mile of ye fort; marched through a Low Sunken
Swamp and went to Building a Brestwork; the french
Came Down on a Little point to Erect a Battry; a
a few Shots from our Battries Soon Drove them off.
2 of ye Rangers Kild Last night; Built a Brestwork
to Keep ye Enemy from ye woods, But Nothing to
Keep ye cannon Balls from ye fort Except the trees.
2 Shots from ye fort this Day which cut several trees
over our heads But Did no Damage; one of them we
got. Slept well tonight on a wad of hemlock on ye
ground tho weak & poorly.

20 this morning as our guard was Comeing in there came a
french Deserter & Deliverd himself to Capt Butterfield Who sent him Directly to ye generall.

unsettled weather & Rain 8 or 10 Shots from ye fort
which cut of ye trees near our Camp one or 2 men
wounded.

ordord on picket tonight with Capt Jackson & Ensn
King.

Set the sentries & Stood to our arms all night; had a
very uncomfitable Night as it rained very fast the
chief of ye time—one 6 pounder came from ye fort as
wee ware Setting on ye Brestwork within 6 feet of my
head which we got.

Aug. 21   this Day all ye officers in Camp ware obliged to turne
out to Build a Breastwork to Keep off the Cannon
Ball which came from ye fort as we are very Near ye
fort; one man wounded from ye fort to-Day; 3 or 4
more this afternoon—one of Capt fellows Serjants
Named frost had his arm Shot off—fired Briskly from
ye fort at our Batteries that ware not finished. Lay
Down this night in peace But had not Lain Long Before every man in Camp was ordord to stand to his
arms and Line ye Brest work from end to end as there
had been Enemy Discovered & so Expected.

But nothing Remarkable this time. Lay Down till
towards Day when one of the Sentries fired at Something he Knew not what. which alarmed ye whole
Camp from one end to the other & he was the Best
man that could fire first as they thought But through
the goodness of god no Dammage Done Neither from
ye enemy nor from us.

22   Very pleasant this morning and all firing Still as yet. But
very Little firing to Day till towards Night when it
Began Something Smart tho I have heard of no Dammage as yet.

major Rogers got 3 french prisoners Last night which
gave acount that general Amherst was near; made
all ye officers obliged to work very hard Building and
finishing ye Breastwork. I ordord on fatigue tomorrow—went to Bed in peace tho Not well—Rained
hard all night.

23   took a party of men & helpd to mend ye Bridg to Draw
ye cannon & make a Brestwork Near the Battery, &
workd not only in Sight of ye fort But within musket
Shot where I could see ye french walk on ye walls.
2 men Kild & Scalpd to Day by ye indians Near our
first Breastwork; one of ye Battoes 60 feet long & 16
wide is now fit to play on ye fort But waits till the
other one is finished; finished all ye Battoes at 12

oclock at 8, all ye musick in camp playd 10 minutes
and then opend ye Batteries and playd on ye fort &
plaid from all quarters which soon made the houses
fly to peases.

Received one shot from them which cut off a Regu-
.ar's thigh—continued firing till after sunset, and then
ceased till one o'clock at night when our men endeavored to cut away the Boom. The enemy fired with
small arms very smart which caused all our artillery
to play on them, which soon stilled them. We continued playing till day. A little cessation for the value
of an (h)our at a time. Know not as yet what damage is done. Boom partly cut off.

Aug. 24   This morning our artillery begun to play briskly on them
again—One Bun (?) burst in ye air last night and the
peaces came into camp but did no damage. Jonathan
Door went out with 8 of the light infantry and in 4
days brought in three persons for which Col. Haverlin
gave him 32 dollars, besides other things; those that
went out with him 8 dollars each. These prisoners say
General Amherst is within 50 miles of Moreal (Montreal). Rainy, cold and uncomfortable weather. An
unlucky shower of musket balls came from ye fort last
night when we were erecting a new battery, which
wounded one officer and 14 men. Engineer Warren
received a ball in his back which lodged near his backbone—but likely to recover. Sergeant Furbush his
right hand shot quite off, his left broke, by which
means he lost his life. Our artillery played on them
briskly last night.

25   A very fair, pleasant morning; firing ceases but little.
The enemy attempted (to) come out against us with
their grand (not legible), but the wind drove her toward our shore, the rangers kept up such a fire on them
after shooting the Captain's head off, the others were
glad to surrender on any terms. We pursued the

schooner and other vessels, and by night we had command of all the vessels—took a number of prisoners and some cannon, besides other plunder. All the picket guards in camp called for to go to their relief. 20 prisoners were taken this afternoon—three of them officers. A shot from ye fort cut the neck bone of a young man clean off which killed him instantly. I (was) ordered on ye Royal Battery Guard—took 34 men with ensign Taylor and marched down opposite ye fort through a prodigious swamp within musket shot of ye fort and ye sentries, and staid within ye batteries with Lieut. Blakery of ye Regulars all night and all day, and by next night they threw 300 shells in the fort. I was relieved at 12 oclock at night by Capt. March—fowl weather. Lt. Sewall went on board of one of the French prizes to stay.

Aug. 27　This morning the enemy opened a battery against one of ours, and at 6 o'clock began to play briskly—but our 24 pounder soon stilled them. They begun to play from all the batteries and continued very smart on both sides until 2 o'clock. An unlucky shot from the enemy set our magazine on fire which blew one provincial 40 feet in the air and burned his life out, killed one regular (and) wounded others. I (am) ordered on picket to-night with Capt. Jackson and Ensign Childs. At two o'clock this night, there came a French deserter which gave an account that the French had left the island; at four o'clock there came 15 or 20 more which gave the same account.

28　This morning the regulars and the rangers took possession of the island & fort, the picket relieved and reduced to a Sergeant and 12. The others ordered to go to draw ye cannon and put them on board ye shipping. A sergeant and 6 men of ye rangers followed ye French army overtook a Doctor, took him back and took from him to the (amount) of 15 dollars each, chiefly in cash, one silver watch. A man in the siege was going along to the suttler's with a dollar in his hand, a cannon ball came and struck the dollar away and cut his fingers off. I (am) ordered on duty tomorrow, but being taken with a pain in my head and eyes, I could not go.

Aug. 29 The artillery all embarking on board, the vesselsendeavored to proceed to St. John.

30 Ordered to strike our tents at 5 o'clock and embark on board the battoes. Fowl weather and everything in confusion. The weather cleared off at 4 o'clock and we set off—arrived at St. Johns at 5 o'clock. The enemy burned the fort and most of the houses and fled to moreal (Montreal). Ordered to pitch our tents —got them in readiness—ordered to lay on our arms till further orders. Ordered to move nearer ye right and pitch our tents. Lodged in peace though in an enemy's country and but a little distance from Moreal. Major Rogers had a small brush with the enemy. Lost 2 killed besides wounded. Took seven prisoners. One man on guard heard guns at Moreal.

31 By all that I can learn from my almanac it is the last day of ye month. Tis Sunday and I heard there was a prayer made this morning, though I had not a chance to hear it or any other since I left the point. Received two letters from home. As much difference between preaching here and what I used to hear, as between blessing and cursing. Ordered to throw up entrenchments, to defend ourselves as we expected a visit from ye enemy every day. Ordered not to entrench as we expect to move soon. Took a walk into the fort when it was all burning to ashes—10 or 12 chimneys standing—2 of ye houses 4 stories high : one vessel on ye stocks and one burned. The fort not very strongly fortified. The land round it clear and level, about 10 acres, but no improvement except one small garden

which was destroyed. The night extreme cold and frosty. Ordered to strike our tents tomorrow morning at Reveille beating.

Sept. 1   Struck our tents and got ready according to the time and waited for orders till 4 o'clock and then set off. Rowed half a mile and then stopt—advanced ye pickit and slept in ye battoes.

2   Our men discovered track of ye enemy—Set off at 8 oclock, came down the falls half a mile long; the water very shoal and very swift, and rocks plenty which makes it very difficult to go over; arrived at St Theresa's at 11 oclock, 8 miles below St. Johns. A considerable number of houses standing in pleasant places—good land for grass or grain. Half a mile back on the road, a very fine field of wheat, peas oats, and other fruit, though we are not allowed to take anything on pain of death. Jordan with a party of 40 men to go to the 17 regiment to receive orders. Ordered to go into the woods to cut brush and pickets to build breast-works dismissed them at sunset.

3   A very cold Storm of rain. Major Rogers went to Chamble and took three prisoners—one an officer—

4   Very pleasant morning. A detachment of 2 officers 6 subs. and 140 privates to go to Chamble. Took a walk this afternoon in the village and saw plenty of women & children: at night Major Scain arrived here from Chamble with 30 Frenchmen who refused to fight and desired liberty to enjoy their estates which was granted to them; also an account that the fort was given up.

5   Four french officers belonging to Chamble took a walk through our camps this evening. A large detachment from the Provincials and Light Infantry this day to go and take possession of Chamble. At two oclock, a party of rangers arrived here from General Murray

with 6 French Officers — Seden of Murray's Rangers with them ; a number of horses brought likewise.

Sept. 6 Ordered to take 6 days allowance of pork and flour and hold ourselves in readiness to move tomorrow and join General Murry—A very hot day.

7 The French inhabitants employed to draw our artillery, provisions and baggage with 200 horses & wagons— ordered to strike our tents at 12 o'clock and take 2 days allowance more, and march for Moreal. March from St. Theresas at 12 and arrived at Chamblee at 4 oclock. Made a little halt and then marched on through villages and woods, till 12 o'clock at night, and then ordered to halt and lay on our arms—fowl weather and rainy all night and nothing to cover us except the clothes we had on—the baggage wagon was not ordered but we passed the night somehow.

8 Ordered to march at sunrise—Moved on through villages and might have got sauce, but were not allowed time to eat or drink. But through Divine Goodness, at 1 o'clock we arrived opposite the famous city of Moreal (Montreal)—a very beautiful place—so much fatigued with my march that I am scarce able to stand. Just as we arrived, the news came that the city was given up to General Amherst ; ordered to move forward and encamp. Got a little milk of a French-woman which revived me a little.

9 A very pleasant morning and the city appears exceeding beautiful, but am not allowed to go over. Took a walk back in the woods. Ordered to strike our tents to-morrow at daylight, to march back to Crown Point.

10 March from Moreal at 10 oclock — Extremely hot weather. Marched very fast arrived at 3 o'clock on a plain where the French encamped when they left the Isle o nix—Paraded ourselves in their camps as our tents and baggage were bound to Chamblee by water. I (was) ordered on picket this night and nothing to

lodge on but the ground except a few bushes & nothing to cover me but the heavens except a large cloud ; there was rain in great plenty all night : passed the night though with little comfort.

Sept. 11 Ordered to swing;packs and march at daylight. Extreme bad marching—Rainy and slippery. Arrived at Chamblee at 12 o'clock ; halted and ordered to make bush camps and lodge to-night.

12 The battoes not arrived as yet and (we) are short on it for provisions. Spent the day in looking for the boats, but look in vain.

13 Not an officer in camp—Scarce anything to eat. I sent out and got one quart of milk and 2 /—York for 3 lbs of bread. The battoes arrived at last—the provisions, some stale and some spoiled—had not time to cook any. Marched off and arrived at St. Theresa's at Sunset and ordered to pitch our tents—Ordered to strike tents at day-light and embark on board the battoes.

14 Set off at 6 o'clock arrived at St. John at 12. Stopped till all the fleet arrived ; one of Capt. Morton's men badly burned by his horn ketching on fire in a French house. Set off at 2 o'clock ; arrived at the Isle o' Noix at 8, paraded on board the battoes, took our sick on board,

15 This morning, and set off at 8 o'clock—overcast weather and some rain all day—Rowed 20 miles and landed in a little harbor.

16 Set off at day-break with a fair wind—arrived at Crown Point at 12 o'clock at night ; paraded in ye canoes.

17 Carried our battoes around the Point and brought our things up and encamped. Received a letter from York and wrote two letters to York.

19 Nothing remarkable to-day.

20 Still unsettled weather, took a walk round the camps in the garden.

Sept. 21 This day the storm just set in. Nothing remarkable this day.

22 All the Rangers that have arrived are ordered to carry ye battoes back to the Isle o'noix. Lt. Sayward gone with them. A very sickly time in camp at present.

23 The weather pleasant & fair this morning.

24 4 Regimental Court Martials this day in camp. Capt. Moulton, President of one—Members Lieut. Magee, Lt. Boynton, Ensign Gilson, Ensign Wheelock. Rainy afternoon and night.

25 Still fowl weather. The 17th Reg't. and chief of ye vessels arrived here to-day. Nothing remarkable for this day, only I heard a prayer this night on parade, after that one of Capt. West's men received 500 lashes.

26 The weather cleared off warm—took a walk in the woods and find myself very weak. Roland Young died this morning. Ordered to draw 4 day's allowance of fresh beef to-day.

27 This day Jonathan Door arrived here and saith as he was coming over Moreal river with a Lieut and 3 privates of the regulars, the canoe was overset by which they all lost their lives except himself and he swam ashore but lost 25 guineas and 3 fine guns. I was chosen with Capt. Moulton, Lieut Foster and Lieut Leonard to prize the things of Rowland Young and Richard Maddox dead of Capt Jefferd's Company.

28 Foul weather and Rainey. 5 or 6 men carried out of camp with small pox—one from our company.

29 Wet and cold, uncomfortable weather.

30 Ordered on fatigue to-day. Stormy weather so that I was obliged to quit work. Dr. Williams died to-day of small pox.

Oct. 1 Still fowl weather and cold. Took a walk into the woods 3 or 4 miles to S. M. B. 24 men of the first and second batallion carried to ye hospital with the small pox since we came here.

Oct. 2   After 5 days of foul weather, we have this one day fair. Col. Haverling arrived here to-day from Moreal. Heard a short prayer this evening. One of Capt. Willard's men received 100 lashes for leaving his work. Lieut Sayward set off for Moreal with an express.

3   Joseph Allen died to-day. General Johnson arrived here this evening with some of his Indians.

4   Still pleasant weather. 2 Sergeants of ye 2d Battalion died last night.

5   Orders to move the sick near the hospital with their tents.

6   Ordered on fatigue this day. Took a party of 100 men with Capt. Howe and Ensign Whitney to carry Rocks for barracks.

7   James Springer died last night. Helped to prize (appraise) the clothes of 2 dead men of Capt. Brown's Company.

8   This morning at 4 o'clock Ensign Frost died, and this evening was decently buried. Lieut. Warren, Lieut. Foster, Lieut. Boynton, and Lieut. Goodenough, bearers.

9   Six men died in ye new Hospital last night. Called on this day to prize 2 dead men's clothes, of Capt Silas Brown's Company. Heard prayers this evening.

10   Major Hobble and Capt Fellows went off this day with a party of invalids to Albany.

11   This day the clothes and things of Ensign Frost were prized by order of Major Gerrish—Prizers, Capt. How, Lt. Humphrey and Lieut. Bancroft.

12   This day the guns and cartridge boxes of the sick and dead were ordered to be turned in. Heard a short sermon this afternoon preached by Doctor Felps, one of our Chaplains from second Kings 9—22. Ordered on fatigue to-morrow.

13   Took 40 men and went to the west side of the lake with 8 battoes, and loaded them with wood for the lime-kilns; returned at at 1 o'clock. This night the long expected storm set in.

Oct. 14 Rainy weather all day. One of Capt. Herrick's men carried out of Camp with the small pox, near on ye turn.

15 The weather cleared off cold. General Amherst arrived here this morning and ordered the sick to be sent off soon. This day received a letter from my father dated York ye 10th of September—paid one shilling—likewise two for Ensign Frost, deceased.

16 Orders for the men to turn out at 8 o'clock and work till 4 afternoon for the feetes. A regimental Court Martial held this day—Capt. Moulton, President Lt. Sewall, Lt. Humphrey, Lt. Willard and Ensign Woolcat, members.

17 Helped to prize the things of one of Capt. Whitney's men.

18 Nothing Remarkable.

19 Took a party of 100 men with Capt. West and went to raft timber for one of the redouts—a pleasant morning but a storm soon set in which caused us to quit work at 12 o'clock.

20 Lt. Sayward arrived here this day from Moreal.

21 Lt. Farnum of Capt. Baron's Company died this morning, and this evening was buried.

22 Cold weather and snow this day.

23 1 Field Officer, 3 Capts. and 6 Subs. went off this day with invalids through No 4 wood. Jordan on fatigue today very much unwell this past 2 days—took 30 men and drew timber into the fort.

24 This day a party of invalids went off by the way of Albany. This day a general court martial for the trial of all prisoners. One man of Capt. Moulton's Company died this day.

25 A very Smart storm last night. Cleared off this afternoon—3 men carried out of camp with small pox this day. Jordan on a court martial tomorrow.

Oct. 26 This day a Regimental Court Martial set by order of Brigadier Ruggles for the trial of all prisoners.

Capt. John Martin, President.

Members:

Lt. Spauldin

Lt. Robinson

Lt. Bradbury

Ens. Chubbuck.

Corporal Nathaniel Blackendon was tried for disobedience of orders denighing his duty—and was sentenced to be broken, and do duty in the ranks and shall receive 25 lashes on the bare back.

27 A party went this day to help the sick that went through number 4 which had got 15 miles and could go no farther. Gen. Amherst embarked for Albany.

28 Moderate weather.

29 Took 30 men down to the Granidear fort and assisted the Carpenters. Col. Thomas' Regiment arrived from Isle a'noix.

30 Pleasant weather.

31 Major Herrick set off for home.

Nov. 1 Cold, overcast weather.

2 Cleared off warm and pleasant.

3 Col. Willard and some others set off for New England to-day.

4 Took a party of men with Capt McFarlan and drew timber into the fort—finished by 1 o'clock.

5 & 6 Nothing remarkable.

7 I am ordered on a Court Martial.

Capt. Samuel How President.

Lt. Bradbury.

Lt. Washburn

Ens. How

Josiah Millbourn was tried for disturbance in camp and sentenced to receive 30 lashes. Sentence affirmed.

Nov. 8   overcast weather.

9   Stormy weather—Jordan on duty. Orders for the 1st and 2d Battalions to return in their arms this day.

10   Took a party and carried stones out of the trenches. Josiah Webber taken sick with the small pox.

11   Pleasant weather for ye season. Yesterday the guns of the fort were discharged in honor of the day.

12   Raw, cold weather and the mountains covered with snow. Capt. Chadbourne and Lt. Frost ordered off with the sick, through no. 4. A very cold storm set in.

13   Extremely cold and snow fell 6 inches deep. Jordan to take the guard this night.

14   Fair weather but extreme cold. Relieved this evening by Lt. Wheeler. Ordered on fatigue to-morrow.

15   No fatigue men called for to-day, it being so cold.

16   Ordered this morning to go to Ticonderoga for provisions. Extreme cold weather—the wind directly against us—arrived at the mills at sunset—loaded our battoes and set off with the wind against us still, and arrived at Crown Point at 12 o'clock at night. Still raw and cold.

17   Orders this evening to strike tents at day-break, and march to Ticonderoga and take provisions, and march to No. 4 and from thence to winter quarters.

18   Extreme cold this morning. Marched off at 10 o'clock, arrived at Ticonderoga at 3. Drew provisions and arrived at the landing at 6. Set off and rowed till 3 o'clock at night, and encamped near Sabbath Day Point. Paraded ourselves on the ground.

19   Set off at daylight, arrived at Fort George at 11 o'clock. Breakfasted and set off at 12 and arrived at Fort Edward at 8 o'clock, extremely fatigued, and some lodged in a little nest under ground with Lt. Stiles.

20   Set off at 9 o'clock; arrived at Saratoga at 2 o'clock and dined. Set off at 4, arrived at the "Greate fly" at 8. Lodged at Mr. Brown's.

19

Nov. 21 Set off at half after 6—breakfasted at Stillwater, arrived at "half moon" at 12 and dined at a Sutler's hut. Set off at 3 o'clock with one horse and 4 men; with difficulty got over the "four sprouts" at sunset. Arrived at widow Schuyler's at 8 much fatigued and with much difficulty got entertainment, viz: one bed for 4 of us.

NOTE. I got liberty of the Brigadier to go by way of Albany.

22. Set off at sunrise; arrived at Albany at 11 o'clock and breakfasted. Completed part of my business and arrived at Greenbush at 2 and dined at the widow Lumeses (Loomis). Set off at 4 and with much difficulty arrived within 13 miles of Kinderhook, being very lame, and through good Providence met with a house and lodged on a little straw.

23 Set off at day-break and arrived at Kinderhook at 10 o'clock, much fatigued. Breakfasted at Mr. Van Buren's—got our horses up at 4 o'clock and set off—arrived at the stone house at 8 and lodged there.

24 Set off at 7 o'clock, arrived at Lovejoy's at 8 and breakfasted. Very rainy weather and bad riding. Arrived at Sheffield at 12 o'clock and dined with Ensign King at his father's. Got our horses shod and rode 3 miles—arrived at Davises at 9 o'clock, lodged there.

25 Set off at 6 o'clock—rode 4 miles, breakfasted at Mr. Shaddrake's; the weather cold and bad riding. Arrived at Westfield at 8 o'clock—put up at a Mr. Ingersols.

26 Set off at 6 o'clock—arrived at Springfield at 8—put up at Mr. Churches & breakfasted. Rode 15 miles and dined at Scott's. Set off at 3 with much difficulty arrived at Brookfield at 8 o'clock. Put up at Mr. Nicolses.

27 Set off at 8 o'clock this morning with a very severe storm in our faces. Rode 23 miles, arrived at Worcester at 5 o'clock and put up at Mr. Sternses.

Nov. 28 Set off at sunrise—arrived at Concord at 4 o'clock—put up at Mr. Munrows.

29 Set out at 6 o'clock—dined at Cyrus Foster's at Andover—arrived at Boxford at 6 o'clock; tarried with Lt. Foster at his father's.

30 Fair weather but cold. Went to meeting.

Dec. 1 Rode from Boxford this morning at 7 o'clock, arrived at Haverhill at 11 o'clock: dined at Mr. B. (name not legible). Set out at 3, arrived at Hampton Falls at 6; put up at Mr. Levet's, the house full of countrymen and nothing but noise and confusion.

2 Set off this morning at 8 o'clock and arrived at Old York at 1 o'clock, found all things well and friends in good health.

Nothing happened more than common till the 12th of March at 2 o'clock at night, there was a considerable shock of an earthquake, followed soon by another.

Apr. 26 This day beating orders arrived to me by Capt. Moul-
1761 ton from Governor Bernard to enlist men for another campaign, but on considering and with much difficulty I refused them on the 28th.

Apr. 18 This day received a letter from Boston to give my an-
1762 swer whether I would go into the service this year— Sailed for Boston; arrived at the Capitol at 9 o'clock at night. Landed the soldiers at Castle William at 9 in the morning.

22 Sailed up to Boston. Went to church in the forenoon.

23 Gave in my answer and excepted.

24 Received beating orders and ordered with Ensign —— to return to York and recruit 75 men.

25 Sailed from the Long Wharf in Boston with Capt. David Bragdon at half after 12 and arrived at York Harbor at 8 o'clock.

29 Set out for the Eastward, arrived at Littlefield's at 2. Set out at 3 o'clock, arrived at Kimballs at 5.

Apr. 30 Rode to Cape Orpus (Porpoise) enlisted 4 men. Set off at 6 arrived at Wells at 9—enlisted 3 men.

May 1 Set off, arrived at York at 6.

2 Received a letter from Colonel Sparhawk to be ready by the first of ye week. Set out after meeting to see ye Colonel, not arrived home yet. Lodged at Kittery.

3 Arrived home at 1 o'clock; listed one man.

6 This day received news from Col. Sparhawk that he was sick in Salem and ordered to be in readiness when he arrived home.

9 The Colonel arrived home very much unwell, and ordered to bring the men down to his home and pass muster.

14 This day mustered the rest of the men and embarked on board at 12.

16 Set sail at 8 o'clock, the wind directly against us, and made Cape Ann.

18 Becalmed in Boston Bay: the wind sprang up and we arrived at the Castle at 5. Went to see the Governor.

19 Breakfasted with Capt. Phillips Captain of the Castle.

30 Went to Boston and drew 100 dollars. Likewise received beating orders from His Excellency for recruiting regulars for His Majesty's Service. Ordered to march our men to Springfield without loss of time. Set off from Boston at 4 o'clock afternoon; put up at Watertown. Fine shower to-day.

21 Marched 4 miles—breakfasted at Brown's. Set in for a storm—proves short. Marched 25 miles. Put up at a private house. Good entertainment.

22 Marched 4 miles—drank milk punch at Eames (?). Arrived at Webster at 12 o'clock. Dined at Mr. Brown's. Drew provisions for 4 days. No camp equipage and nothing to carry provisions in.

23 Hired a horse at Worcester to go to Springfield to get the billetting. Rode within 16 miles of Springfield, met Mr. Goldthwaite. Rode back 10 miles to a tavern—made up the billetting roll and received the

money: arrived at Springfield at 11 o'clock. Put up at Mr. Bliss. Dined with Col. Ingersol and Col. Goldthwaite and others.

May 25   This day the men arrived. Deny taking their billitting with difficulty—pursuaded some to take them. Drew camp Equipage and ordered to march off to Albany tomorrow. Lt. Woods was ordered to take command of the men and march them to Albany

   26   I set out from Springfield at 8 and rode within 6 miles of Worcester.

   27   Arrived at Worcester at 6 this morning. Breakfasted at Capt. Sternses. Set off at 9, arrived at Warren's at 8 o'clock. Patrick Digney, one of the party that joined us at the Castle, died here this evening. Thunder, lightning and rain.

   28   March 10 miles before breakfast. Marched to Cambridge by 12 o'clock. Dined at Mr. Bradishes. Arrived at Boston at 3 o'clock which makes 32 miles since 4 o'clock this morning

   31   Enlisted James Hambleton to-day, and got him down to the Castle.

June 1   Set out from Boston at 3 o'clock, arrived at Salem at 8: imbarked on board Capt. Winn. Set sail at 10, with a moderate breeze.

   3   Arrived at York harbor at 8 o'clock.

   4   Came ashore—rode down to Kittery Point. Set up my notification to enlist men.

   8   Did my Indeavor to recrute men but find them come slow.

   18   Rode to Portsmouth.

   20   Went down to Biddeford. Lodged at Mr. Bradbury's. Dined at Mr. Eaton's at Wells.

July 14   Received orders to be in Boston the 22d.

   20   Took departure from York; lodged at Newbury.

July 21 Breakfasted at Ipswich—arrived at Salem Ferry at 10. Arrived in Boston at half after four: put up at Capt. Ford's, much fatigued.

22 Waited on the Secretary of War at his office and received secret orders. Set out at Old York at 4 oclock.

23 Arrived at Newbury at 5 oclock—put up our horses at Mr. Greenleaf's, the tavern.

24 Set off at 7, arrived at York at 6.

26 Set out after a deserter—arrived at Berwick at 12—dined at Lord's. Set off from Berwick at 10 o'clock at night and arrived at Lebanon at 1. Laid by till 4. Waylaid the house where we thought the deserter was but found he was not there: went to the house where he was, but he going through the side of the house, made his escape into the woods.

27 Set out from Lebanon for home, arrived at Berwick and dined at Mr. Gowins: arrived at York at 5 oclock.

28 This day is by authority set apart as a day of prayer. Heard Mr. Lyman preach.

29 Set out to the Eastward to take deserters. Lodged at Biddeford.

30 Arrived at Falmouth at 4 o'clock. The deserters having got word of my coming got clear of me.

Aug. 4 Arrived home. A very dull time for news. No business going on, the earth drying up and everything looks with a gloomy aspect. And what seems to be worse still, the people stupid and senseless under the Judgment of Almighty God.

10 Rode to Cape Neddick but find no men.

11 This day was tried before a number of Justices of the peace James Davis, on suspicion of his having been the means of the death of John Semore, but finding no sufficient proof against him, he was set at liberty.

16 Set out after deserters. Rode to Kittery, Berwick, Somersworth, Cocheco and Mogester (?). But none to be enlisted or taken.

Aug. 17 Rode around Kittery but all in vain.

A few entries follow this one, of much the same tenor. He did not succeed in enlisting many men nor in arresting deserters. Peace was soon after firmly established, and there was no further call for troops for active service.

975

EDWARD[8] BRADBURY (Edward[7], Reuben[6], Jacob[5], Wy-mond[4], Wymond[3], Wymond[2], Thomas[1]), learned the printer's trade in the office of David Tucker of Portland, and worked at the business in Woburn, Cambridge, Barre and Worcester, Mass., and in Charleston, S. C. At the breaking out of the war of the rebellion, he enlisted and served for about a year in the department of the Gulf. He was at the seige and surrender of Port Hudson. He came home much broken down in health and did not re-enter the service. He married, April 26, 1864, Ellen Corey Roberts, who was born April 26, 1841. He carries on the job printing business at 242 Washington street, Boston.

Children:

1674   i   Mabelle Ward[9], b. May 7, 1865; d. June 9, 1885.
1675   ii   Nellie Roberts[9], b. Aug. 1, 1867.
1676   iii   Marion Elizabeth[9], b. Oct. 21, 1869; d. Dec. 16, 1870.
1677   iv   Ednah[9], b. July 11, 1872; d. Jan. 31, 1873.
1678   v   Ralph[9], b. July 21, 1874.
1679   vi   Jessie[9], b. Oct. 27, 1877; d. May 21, 1883.

INDEX

INDEX

OF THE DESCENDANTS OF THOMAS BRADBURY OF SALISBURY, MASS.,
CONTAINED IN THIS VOLUME.

A

B

C

1839	Horace R.	1241	1835	Harriet A.	1238		
1837	Horace D.	1248	1843	Harriet L.	1242		
1848	Horace R.	1256	1839	Helen	1268		
1833	Henry C.	1283	1838	Hannah	1320		
1815	Hall J.	1284	1828	Harriet	1353		
1825	Horatio T.	1308	1832	Harriet	1396		
1828	Hazen	1310	1843	Helen L.	1432		
1836	Heman L.	1314	1832	Harriet N.	1461e		
1835	Henry	1319	1851	Helen L.	1503		
1844	Horace A.	1352	1877	Hannah E.	1518		
1854	Heber	1391	1862	Harriet R.	1550		
1826	Hiram W.	1400	1854	Hannah A.	1562		
1832	Henry A.	1412	1863	Hattie B.	1581		
1851	Horatio N.	1430	1863	Harriet L.	1591		
1830	Henry A. M.	1461d	1853	Harriet A.	1640		
1839	Horace A.	1482	1858	Harriet C.	1646		
1826	Heman P.	1484	1859	Hattie R.	1661		
1854	Henry De W.	1505					
1881	Howard M.	1545		**I**			
1855	Henry P.	1606					
1872	Henry	1649	1787	Isaac	343		
1866	Herbert	1656	18—	Ichabod	739		
1750	Hannah	106	1837	Isaac H.	881		
1746	Hannah	136	1821	Isaac W.	1448		
1742	Hannah	146	1839	Isaac S.	1564		
1767	Hannah	170	1813	Isabel M.	899		
1773	Harriet	220	18—	Ida	988		
1781	Hannah	263	18—	Isabella	1144		
1773	Hannah	304	1839	Irene P.	1206		
1766	Hannah	357	18—	Isabel	1405		
1794	Hannah	374	1839	Isabella S.	1420		
1795	Hannah N.	386	1846	Ida E.	1462		
1805	Harriet	424	1858	Ida M.	1563		
1821	Harriet	436	1878	Inez M.	1658		
1786	Harriet	444					
1793	Hannah	469		**J**			
1793	Harriet	516	1647	Jacob	6		
18—	Harriet M.	561	1654	John	10		
1790	Hannah	580	1658	Jabez	12		
1820	Harriet	621	1667	Jacob	18		
1797	Harriet	624	1693	Jabez	19		
1805	Hannah	627	1697	John	21		
1827	Hannah F.	663	1704	Josiah	24		
1815	Harriet	722	1699	John	31		
1808	Harriet	734	1701	James	32		
18—	Huldah	744	1704	Jacob	34		
1811	Hannah	805	1710	Jacob	48		
1824	Harriet	831	1736	Jacob	55		
1834	Hannah N.	962	1736	John	66		
1826	Harriet E.	1009	1740	Joseph	67		
1824	Hannah M.	1013	1724	Jabez	69		
1827	Hannah E.	1040	1739	Josiah	79		
1814	Harriet R.	1045	1732	Jonathan	83		
1826	Harriet L.	1114	1727	James	91		
1808	Hannah J.	1139	1738	John	100		
1863	Hattie P.	1228	1749	James	105		
1839	Harriet A.	1232	1752	Jabez	108		
1844	Hannah J.	1235	1750	Jacob	113		

20

1826	James	922	1844	John L.	1502
1827	Julian	942	1866	John H.	1552
1840	John C.	958	1841	James T.	1565
1829	John A.	967	1854	Julius O.	1590
1855	James W.	980	1851	John Q.	1605
18—	Joseph H.	991	1858	Jefferson	1617
1814	John C.	1003	1859	John E.	1668
1819	John C.	1006	1638	Judith	3
1816	Josiah	1011	1645	Jane	5
1830	James W. jr.	1019	1711	Jerusha	27
1833	John B.	1022	1706	Joanna	35
1850	James O.	1025	1704	Jemima	41
1864	James C.	1028	1718	Jane	51
1847	John E.	1038	17—	Jemima	59
1816	Jotham D.	1046	17—	Jerusha	76
1854	John J.	1084	1735	Jemima	90
1818	John M.	1097	1768	Joanna	190
1824	Jonathan	1100	1771	Judith	215
1827	John H.	1115	1753	Jenny	230
1814	John B.	1142	1754	Janne	231
1808	James W.	1163	1769	Judith	240
1832	John J.	1166	1792	Joanna L.	346
1833	John W.	1168	1800	Joanna	377
1837	James D.	1189	1813	Jane	402
1842	James F.	1191	1810	Jerusha	453
1824	Julius O.	1197	1788	Jenny	467
1843	James	1202	1801	Judith	524
1847	Joseph	1216	1819	Jane M.	531
1852	Joseph S.	1219	1783	Jane C.	577
1857	John J.	1229	1780	Judith	591
1846	John T.	1236	1782	Jane	587
1845	John U.	1243	1809	Jane	673
1838	Joseph P.	1252	1795	Joanna	798
1849	Joseph S.	1267	1815	Jane S.	840
1827	Joshua P.	1281	1840	Julia	855
1829	John Q. A.	1282	1825	Joanna C.	875
1826	James T.	1293	1818	Jennie D.	917
1841	John Q. A.	1316	1846	Julia T. S.	977
1841	John F.	1323	1866	Jennie	1029
18—	James	1328	1855	Julia M.	1042
1841	Jacob N.	1330	1846	Josephine L.	1078
1836	James M.	1334	1840	Juliet	1122
1845	Jesse T.	1338	1850	Jenny L.	1218
1848	James J.	1343	1831	Juliette	1246
1839	James M.	1368	1840	Julia M.	1249
1844	James	1372	1847	Juliette E.	1266
1877	Jay	1377d	1843	Jane E.	1269
1824	Jacob	1394	1875	Jennie	1377c
1849	James H.	1397	1827	Julia A.	1395
1848	Joseph H.	1429	1850	Julia E.	1479
1842	John F.	1449	1833	Julia A.	1480
1849	John F.	1452	1852	Juliet	1613
1839	Jacob F.	1461h	1868	Jennie L.	1632
1846	James G. B.	1461j			
1829	Joseph A.	1467		**K**	
1832	Josiah C.	1486	1817	Katy	768
1835	Josiah C.	1487	1848	Kate	1204
1840	John	1497	1855	Kate D.	1614

Year	Name	No.	Year	Name	No.
1780	Mary	218	1810	Mercy	804
1760	Molly	233	1806	Mary	811
1771	Mary	249	1819	Mary G.	825
17—	Martha	255	1824	Mary J.	866
1772	Molly	281	1823	Mary A.	874
1708	Molly	294	1816	Mary W.	882
1784	Molly	307	1809	Mary J.	933
1708	Mary	310½	1821	Matilda A.	945
1782	Mary	327	1835	Mary A.	946
1769	Martha	322	1826	Minerva	951
1787	Mary	333	1836	Mary E.	955
1786	Martha	351	1832	Margaret P.	961
1788	Mary	352	1835	Martha A.	974
1798	Miriam	355	18—	Mary F.	989
1780	Mary	362	18—	Mary Eliza	990
1792	Mary	373	1817	Mary J.	1005
1808	Martha	398	1827	Martha A.	1017
1814	Mary	403	1820	Meroe A.	1048
18—	Maria	418	1826	Mary E.	1051
1801	Mary	421	1859	Mary A.	1076a
1811	Mary	434	1808	Miriam L.	1076d
1825	Mary	440	1838	Mary L. S.	1085
1796	Maria	462	1855	Marcia D.	1091
1819	Miriam S.	470	1840	Mary E.	1125
1819	Mary	484	1841	Mary A.	1126
1824	Matilda F.	485	1850	Mary B.	1129
1817	Mary L.	493	1810	Mary	1140
1825	Maria	497	1829	Mary J.	1149
1805	Mary A.	501	1810	Mary	1152
1803	Mary	514	18—	Mary J.	1155
1810	Mary L.	515	1830	Margaret E.	1165
1795	Mary	517	1835	Mary J.	1175
1817	Mary E.	529	1847	Maria L.	1209
1797	Mary	534	1839	Mary E.	1211
1816	Mary R.	544	1840	Margaret E.	1212
1801	Mary K.	551	1856	Mary A.	1257
18—	Mary K.	557	1852	Mary	1259
1785	Molly	578	1832	Mary E.	1302
17—	Mehitable	585	1824	Mary W.	1307
1791	Mary	592	1843	Margaret	1317
17—	Mary	605	1833	Mary	1318
1802	Mary	613	1849	Mary E.	1339
1800	Mary	625	1841	Melissa	1360
1811	Mary A.	636	1848	Missouri	1386
1814	Mary	642	1822	Mary C.	1393½
1813	Mary	654	1840	Mary	1403
1813	Martha	655	1849	Martia	1406
1804	Mary S.	683	1840	Mary E.	1410
17—	Mary	696	1848	Mary A.	1435
17—	Mary	703	1817	Mary O.	1459
1807	Margaret	715	1824	Matilda	1461a
1808	Mary	719	1837	Mary W.	1488
1801	Mary	731	1871	Marion E.	1516
18—	Mary	742	1867	Mary B.	1547
1808	Mary	749	1864	Mary R.	1551
1817	Mary	774	1862	Millie M.	1570
1818	Mahala	783	18—	Mattie	1574
1792	Mary	796	1863	Marion	1580

| 1807 | Temperance | 911 2-5 |
| 1817 | Tryphosa | 1285 |

V

1846	Vincent G.	1373
1850	Virginia H.	978
1849	Vesta S.	1059
1853	Virginia	1388

W

1637	Wymond	2
1649	William	8
1669	Wymond	15
1672	William	16
1695	Wymond	20
1699	William	30
17—	Wymond	77
1737	Wymond	86
1757	William	110
1744	William	112
1738	William	124
1763	Winthrop	141
17—	Wymond	154
17—	William	156
1783	Wymond	166
1781	William	175
1766	William	188
1769	William	214
17—	William	223
1759	William	235
1776	William	252
1783	William	264
1775	William	305
1791	William F.	328
1780	Winthrop	349
1816	William	395
1819	William	396
1810	Wymond	400
1819	William	406
1827	William H.	441
1793	William	447
1800	William O.	470
1816	William B.	489
1812	Wyman	528
1800	William M.	535
17—	William	568
1790	William	595
1805	William S.	615
1800	William S.	631
1805	William L.	645
1821	William H.	660
1797	William	711

1805	Wingate	714
1816	William H.	726
1815	William	753
1798	William	807
1817	William S.	841
1812	William	871
1844	William W.	966
1824	William	1050
1848	William F.	1071
1849	William C.	1072
1842	William D.	1087
1840	William H. H.	1111
1843	Washington I.	1113
1840	Walter S.	1119
1847	William C.	1133
1814	Wyer	1153
1829	Wyman C.	1159
1841	Wyman O.	1177
1829	William F.	1180
1822	William E.	1196
1845	William J.	1208
1834	Walter C.	1224
1842	William	1254
1815	William H.	1294
1830	William G.	1311
1843	Wingate	1322
18—	William	1327
1839	William M.	1335
1829	William K.	1345
1841	William W.	1362
1850	William	1387
18—	William	1405
1815	Winthrop T.	1458
1847	William A.	1490
1859	William B.	1512
1866	Woodman	1514
1849	William M.	1522
1862	Walter R.	1531
1869	Wymond H.	1541
1886	William I.	1546
1843	William W.	1566
18—	William F.	1576
1858	William H.	1579
1853	William E.	1586
1842	William T.	1609
1858	Willie L.	1623
1852	William R.	1628
1859	William S.	1634*b*
1862	Walter C.	1634*g*

Z

| 1823 | Zenas G. W. | 777 |
| 1820 | Ziba H. | 1296 |

INDEX.

———

*This name is incorrectly given as Stephen Mitchell on page 98.

INDEX.

www.ingramcontent.com/pod-product-compliance
Lightning Source LLC
Chambersburg PA
CBHW031340070726
47496CB00017B/1344